Finding Juliet

Finding Juliet

Dale Lisa Flint

Turtle Cove Press

Tallahassee and Ochlockonee Bay, FL
https://turtlecovepress.com

This is a work of fiction. Names, characters, events, and incidents are the products of the author's imagination or are used fictitiously. Any resemblance to actual persons, living or dead, or actual events is purely coincidental. Places mentioned are either fictitious or used fictitiously. Getting struck by lightning is not a recommended means of time travel.

ISBN 978-1947536203 (paperback)
ISBN 978-1947536210 (eBook)

Library of Congress Control Number: 2024941983

Printed in the United States of America
Cover Design by Babski Creative Studios
https://babskicreativestudios.com/

Turtle Cove Press

Tallahassee and Ochlockonee Bay, FL
https://turtlecovepress.com

For Lotte

Part 1: 2013

Chapter 1
Adversity's sweet milk

The drive to my new foster home was like traveling back in time.

Far from the city, the traffic faded to a double yellow stripe down a long country road. The landscape blurred with fallow fields and ancient tractors. A lone scarecrow looking lost. The smell was different, too. Gone was the city stink I'd known all my life—the bus exhaust, dank stairwells, sour streets—replaced by something more organic: cow poop, and the cloying sweetness of six winter melons bought from a farmer's flatbed. They rolled like bowling balls in two cardboard boxes in the backseat of Monica's SUV.

Seriously—how were two people going to eat this much fruit?

"I just love the country, don't you?" Monica asked, pulling into a gravel driveway and turning off the engine.

I nodded noncommittally.

Monica was Foster Mother #13. Lucky 13? By the time you're almost 18, foster kids like me don't believe in luck.

"Home, sweet home," she sang, tossing her keys into the center console. "Come on, I'll show you the view."

I slid out of my seat and leaned against the passenger side, scrutinizing Monica's single-story ranch house. Shuttered windows flanked the front door. I looked back down the road. No neighbors as far as the eye could see. It was as if the house had dropped from the sky into the middle of nowhere.

Totally not creepy.

I mean, with her autumn-themed sweater vest and crocheted purse, my new foster mom didn't *look* like a serial killer. But *if* she were, this would be the perfect crime scene: infinite places to hide the bodies and no one to hear you scream.

I followed Monica under a trellis of dormant vines, through an unlatched side gate. The pebbled walk led to an oasis of green grass and raised vegetable beds, lush against the golden hills. On the other side of a rusted barbed-wire fence, a cow stood scratching her face against the pointy spurs. A dozen more cows milled in the rolling pasture, a calf hopscotching amongst them.

"Do you like cows?" Monica asked. She tucked a strand of grey-streaked blond behind an ear. "Do you want to feed them? I'll get some alfalfa."

"Huh?"

"Stay right here." She disappeared into a shed, wedged between an overgrown rose bush and the fence. The sound of crashing metal tools preceded a muffled shout. "I'm okay!"

The cow and I stood like strangers at a party. "Come here often?" I asked.

She licked the rusty fence, then huffed, blasting my bangs with cud breath.

"Nice to meet you, too."

Now that the pleasantries were out of the way, she lifted her tail and released a geyser. The runoff ran a yellow current to my pink Converse high tops. "Hey, watch it!" I cried. In response, my friend (the Decidedly Well-Hydrated Cow) opened her mouth to her molars and *MOOOOOOOO'd*. I stumbled backward, catching my heel in a gopher hole. "What the—" I cried.

"Oooh, look who's hungry!" said Monica behind me, her arms full of hay. Sensing lunch, the rest of the cows charged the fence. "I see you've met Presley. She's a sweet girl."

"Presley?"

"Yep. Over there's Ringo and Joni. And that one's Joplin," she said, pointing to the screeching yellow calf. "She's a bottle baby."

"All the cows have names?"

"Just my favorites."

"How strong is that fence?" I asked, as a post lifted an inch out of the dry earth.

"It's been here at least a hundred years. Easy now, girls." Monica hoisted the hay over the top wire as the pandemonium on the other side approached stadium concert levels.

Monica shoved a tuft of alfalfa into my hands. "Go on," she encouraged.

"That's okay," I said, but Presley was quick. She lassoed the hay, her purple tongue like wet sandpaper on my thumb. I wiped the slobber on my skinny jeans. They were my only pair. Did cow spit stain?

"See, you did it!" cried Monica, pleased. "I'll make a country girl of you, yet!" She inhaled as the cows munched, the air scented with grassy gas. "It really is peaceful out here. Kind of like paradise."

Or a horror movie.

"Let's go inside," she said, brushing the hay from her sweater vest. "I'll show you your room. It's got a nice view of the pasture."

I fetched my backpack from the car and followed Monica to the front door. As we walked inside, an old Golden Retriever greeted us. "That's Bonnie," said Monica. "Clyde's around here somewhere. Do you like dogs? You're not allergic, are you?"

"No."

"No, you don't like dogs?"

"No, I'm not allergic. I like dogs." I held my hand out to Bonnie and let her sniff, her blond muzzle tinged with white. Maybe dogs really did resemble their owners. Or was it owners who resembled their dogs? Bonnie nudged my fingers towards her ear, which I obliged with a good scratch.

"She likes you already. Dogs can tell about people. Come on, I'll give you the grand tour."

Bonnie padded behind us, toenails clicking on the hardwood. The living room was simply furnished with a blue fabric sofa, woodstove, and small TV. A laptop sat on the coffee table. "The computer's normally in the kitchen," explained Monica. "I have dial up."

"Dial up?"

"For the internet. You plug the phone line into the computer. It's a little slow, but it works."

"Um. Okay," I said, still not understanding.

Midway down the hall, Monica opened a door and stood back so I could peek inside. "This is the bathroom. Hope you don't mind sharing."

One bathroom—that would be fun.

"This is my room," Monica said. It was tidy in a lived-in way, clean except for the dog hairs on the burgundy comforter. Nature posters in gold frames hung on the walls, the sort you'd see in a dentist's office: generic, pretty, and soothing, designed to take your mind off an impending root canal. On either side of the bed, books were stacked four high on matching nightstands.

"Do you know this one?" Monica asked, holding up a hardcover. "*Outlander*?"

I shook my head.

"It's a historical fiction, time-travel thing. I'm reading it for my book club. It's really good. Kind of like *A Connecticut Yankee in King Arthur's Court*, but with attractive Scottish Highlanders." She glanced at the cover—a picture of red plaid and a broken clock— then back at me, hesitating. "It might be a little mature, though," she said, placing the book back on top of *Parenting Teens with Love and Logic*.

I rolled my eyes.

"I'm sorry," she said. "I didn't mean to imply you weren't mature."

"I know. I was thinking of something else."

"I'm sure you could handle it. I was reading all kinds of stuff at your age. You can borrow it if you want. If you like to read. It's okay if you don't."

Was this love or logic?

Back into the hallway, we continued the tour. "This is the mud room," Monica said, showing me the laundry area in the back of the house, warm and fresh with the scent of fabric softener. "Your room is right next door. It used to be my office." She opened the door with a flourish, like a game show host. "I hope you like it."

I stepped into a Pinterest page. Pale yellow paint glowed in the afternoon light. The dresser was shabby chic, light green and artfully chipped. Ceramic figures sat on an antique vanity with a pillow-topped stool. Against the wall stood a wrought-iron trundle bed with a handmade pink-and-green quilt. White lace curtains fluttered in the breeze brought by the open picture window, blue sky sparkling beyond. On a corner bookshelf, a stuffed toy cow sat wearing a T-shirt that read "I'm Moody." I shuddered.

"Are you cold, Alexandra?"

"Alex." I gave her my best-effort smile. "No, I'm perfect."

Foster kids don't complain.

"I left the windows open this morning to help get rid of the new-paint smell. If you're cold, we can close them. I can even make a fire. I do that in the winter, when the mornings are cold, but this November's been unseasonably warm. Dry, too. We need the rain, but it's kind of nice to go around in shirtsleeves this time of year, don't you think? Do you want to take off your jacket?"

"I can't smell any paint." Just Pine Sol—buckets of it: bracing, but better than the industrial cleaner favored by the group home. Two weeks of breathing that stuff fried my nose hairs.

"Do you like your room?" Monica asked, eyes a little too wide, reminding me of Presley.

I bit my lip.

Monica was a First Time Foster Parent. After twelve homes in nine years, I knew the type. First Time Foster Parents wanted to save the world, one kid at a time, and that kid, a.k.a. *me*, better be grateful for it.

I pulled the string on my hoodie down to the bottom of my jacket. The other side bunched up at the neck. Six months. Half a year until I was eighteen. I could do this.

"It's a nice room," I said, still smiling. The back of my neck itched.

"I'm glad you like it," Monica gushed. "I'll leave you to get settled, then. I need to make a few phone calls." She didn't move.

Ah, the look. Was I going to steal the silverware? Run up the credit cards? Poison the dogs?

I dropped my backpack on the floor.

"Don't worry, Monica. I only kill people in their sleep."

She blanched. "Oh. Um, great."

"I'm joking."

She turned to the window. "KNOCK IT OFF!"

My stomach jettisoned like an ejector seat. "What?"

"Oh, sorry, not you. Presley likes to eat my winter roses." The cow had stuck her head through two rows of barbed wire, disregarding the jagged edges.

"Cows don't listen very well," I said, watching Presley munch the petals.

"No," she smiled. "They're kind of like kids."

"Yeah."

Monica flushed pink as her winter roses. "Oh, I didn't mean. Um." She latched the window and then sat on the edge of the bed. Still not leaving. "I got the house after the divorce. The dogs, too." Monica rested her hand on Bonnie's head. "Frank got the car. That Toyota was a piece of crap, anyways. Pardon my French."

Monica liked to talk. Driving here, she had filled the hour-long car ride with her life story. I learned she was a part-time librarian, forty-four years old with no children. Six years ago she divorced Frank, who didn't want kids and made her feel inadequate. That's when she stopped dyeing her hair: "Freedom from judgment is freedom from denial." She loved reading, hiking, gardening, animals, and the Ellen DeGeneres Show, which she watched every day at 4pm. She always wanted a girl.

And they say teenagers overshare.

"My book club meets next Friday." She was still talking. "I'm almost done with the novel. It's really great. You can borrow it if you want, and maybe come along—"

"Monica?"

"Yes?"

"Did you say you had some calls to make?"

"Oh, right." She stood, smoothing the quilt. "Well, I'll let you get settled then. Make yourself at home." She started to leave the room, and then turned. "Because you *are* home. Welcome."

I exhaled as she walked out the door. Bonnie stayed behind. "Monica's very *sincere*, isn't she?" I asked the dog, who thumped her tail in response.

I strolled a slow circuit around the room, then sat at the vanity. An audience of crudely-painted ceramic figurines—a jester with blue eyes and a green-and-red cap; a unicorn with a pink heart on its rear end; a girl with a blue dress—surrounded a music box ballerina. I picked up the jester. A hand-painted signature on the base read, "MONICA, AGE 8."

I opened the vanity drawer and shoved them all in.

"What's your problem?" I asked my reflection in the vanity mirror.

The girl in the mirror stared back, distant and defiant. Dark smudges formed crescent moons under her amber-brown eyes. She was thinner than I remembered, cheekbones sharp, skin pale as a ghost. Her long, brown hair hung greasy and gnarled.

"You need a shower," I said.

"Tell me something I don't know," my reflection answered.

The communal bathrooms at the Rainbow Canyon Home for Teen Girls were the only areas left unsupervised by the staff, a wild west of plate-metal mirrors, hidden cigs, and settled scores; ancient grudges leading to busted lips. Not a place to linger over a long shampoo.

I heard Monica's voice from the kitchen, talking on the phone. "So far, so good."

I got my hairbrush out of my backpack and ripped through the mass of tangles, wondering if I should just shave it all off. Freak out my new foster mom.

Monica knocked on the door, a light-knuckled *tap-tap, tap-tap-tap*.

"Come in."

Monica pushed open the door with the garbage bag of my clothes, setting it next to the princess bed. "I was thinking. If you're up for it, we could go shopping. It'll be a few hours before dinner, and I bet you need school stuff for Monday."

I shrugged.

"Or we could go to Walmart tomorrow after my garden club. I have Weed Whackers every Saturday," she said, repeating what she'd already told me on the drive home: garden club on Saturdays; Costco trips on Sundays; book club every first Friday. "On second thought, let's go now! If you're up for it. I could show you around town. You've never been to Jefferson County, right? There's not much to see, but you'll still want to see it." She laughed at her own joke. "Sorry. Babbling again. Do you want to go shopping, though?"

"Isn't the store closed until midnight?" I asked.

"What?"

"For Black Friday?"

"That's next week. But we don't have to wait for the sales. I can get you what you need now."

"Black Friday is tomorrow," I said.

"Tomorrow's Saturday."

"No, tomorrow's Friday."

"Then what's today?" she asked.

"Thanksgiving."

Monica opened and closed her mouth like a stunned guppy. "Dammit," she said. "Will you excuse me?"

"It's okay. I've heard cussing before."

"No, I mean—I need to use the restroom. I'll be right back."

I sat at the vanity, checking my hair for split ends. From down the hall, I heard the faucet running, then the toilet flushing, followed by the sink again. A moment later, Monica *tap-tap, tap-tap-tapped* on the open door. She'd put on a green corduroy jacket and a plastered grin.

"You don't have to knock if the door is open," I said.

"Okay." Her smile dimmed. "Alexandra?"

"Alex."

"Alex. I'm so sorry. I've been running around like crazy this whole week trying to get everything set up. When your case worker—I mean, Heather—called me on Monday, I went into overdrive. I'd like to celebrate Thanksgiving, though. Will you come with me to get a turkey?"

"It's 2 o'clock. Don't they take, like, forever to cook?"

"Well, how about a rotisserie chicken, then?" she asked, desperation creeping into her voice.

"I'm a vegetarian."

"You are? Oh, I knew that. Heather told me."

"It's okay."

"But we need to do something."

"It's fine," I assured her. "Really. Holidays are stupid."

"Yeah," she said, after a moment. "Frank didn't like them, either."

"I'm going to get unpacked, okay?"

Monica nodded. "Sounds good. I'll be in the living room if you need me."

***

That evening, Monica laid the Formica table with an old lace runner and purple candles from the bathroom. The scent of lavender mixed with garlic and tomato, as she presented "Stupid Holiday Spaghetti," a big pile of pasta in a wooden bowl, with shredded leaves of fresh basil, and mashed whole tomatoes from her garden.

"This is my first year canning tomatoes," she said, halfway through our meal. It was only five o'clock, but the sun had set. The kitchen's sliding glass door made a floor-to-ceiling window of the darkening sky, violet and orange streaks like oil pastels on a black canvas. Bonnie and Clyde lay with their heads at my feet, their noses lifting whenever I crunched a bite of garlic bread.

"I pressure-cooked the tomatoes first," Monica said, over-explaining as usual. She cited her sources better than Wikipedia. "That was one of the tips at the *Canning Our Summer Harvest Symposium*. I think I got it right," she added. "I hope we don't die of botulism."

"Now you mention it," I said, twirling pasta around my fork. I'd already gone back for seconds.

"One of the first signs of nerve paralysis is difficulty swallowing. Does your throat feel tight?"

I stopped chewing.

"I'm joking," she laughed. "I don't think we'll die."

"Well, that's a relief." I stabbed a tomato. "You have sauce on your cheek."

Monica dipped her napkin in her water glass and dabbed her cheek.

"No, the other side," I said.

"Well, I'm a mess."

"Nah. It'll help the coroner when he rules the cause of death."

"A double suicide?" she teased, motioning to my white shirt under the black hoodie, where a small red stain bloomed on my chest.

"Darn it." I reached for my own napkin. "A tragic ending. Like *Romeo and Juliet*, but with organic produce."

Monica laughed. "Well, you may be Juliet, but I'm no Romeo. I'm just your—" She caught the warning in my eyes, and finished the sentence. "Friend."

I nodded. "Friends don't let friends get botulism."

"Let's toast to that." Monica jumped up, retrieving two dusty champagne flutes from a top cupboard. After a quick rinse in the sink, she filled them with orange juice. "These were from my...never mind. Cheers."

We clinked our glasses together, knocking a couple drops of orange juice onto the white lace. She took a sip and lifted one side of her mouth. "Can I tell you what I'm thankful for?"

"That I'm going to wash the dishes?" I took my plate and untouched glass to the sink, which didn't have a disposal. "Where do you want me to scrape this?"

"Green waste goes in the compost bin. There's a stainless steel pail with food scraps under the sink."

I wrinkled my nose. "I just put the spaghetti in here?" I asked. The container had coffee grounds and orange peels.

"Yep. Composting is good for the garden. Good for the planet, too. Tomorrow we'll take it outside, and I'll show you how the worms do their work. They don't waste anything."

"Great." First cows and now worms.

Monica brought her own dish to the sink, then grabbed a trash can from the pantry, dragging it to the fridge. She opened the door and sat on the floor, using one of the produce drawers to prop it open. The motor kicked on as the cold air escaped. "I was a vegetarian once," she said, tossing a package of turkey burgers into the garbage. "When I first met Frank. Do you eat eggs?" she asked, holding up a carton.

"Yep. I'm not vegan. I like cheese too much."

"Me, too," she smiled. She took items out one by one, a jar of mayonnaise, Go-Gurts, a box of Lunchables, examining labels with reading glasses she pulled from her front pocket. "Any other dietary restrictions?"

"I don't think so."

"Peanut allergies?"

"Nope." I dried the last of the dishes, leaving them in the rack. I didn't know where anything went.

"Ooh, what about gluten? Gluten is big now."

"I'm fine," I said. "I can eat anything. Just no meat." The weight of the day grabbed my temples like a vise. I was so tired. All I wanted was a hot shower and a long sleep in a dark room. And quiet.

"Lactose intolerant?"

My muscles felt rubbery, like the sinews no longer connected to the bones. "I like cheese, remember?"

"Right," said Monica, standing up, pushing in the produce drawer with her foot. Clyde had his face in the garbage, making a case for the Lunchables. Monica nudged him aside, shutting the refrigerator door with a slam. "Let's get some ice cream, then."

Chapter 2
Supper is done

It was seven o'clock when we drove the seven miles into town, the city limit sign reflecting green and gold in the headlights: Jefferson, Population 2,053.

My last high school had a student body of 3,000.

We passed a bowling alley and a Kmart. Not just a Kmart. A Super Kmart.

I grew up in the Tenderloin of San Francisco, spent my teen years in Oakland, Berkeley, and Stockton. I rode city busses by myself from age eight, went to school with Russian, Filipino, and Hmong students. I knew the difference between chow mein and pad thai; malt liquor and beer; when to avoid eye contact and how to say "thank you" in Cantonese. I lived in apartments where burglar bars blocked fire escapes. I was sent to buy Kool-Aid and cartons of milk at the corner store, two aisles crammed with tampons next to motor oil. Before today, I'd never seen a cow or a compost bin. I didn't know Super Kmarts existed, much less in California.

Where was I? Kansas?

We stopped at a red light, no traffic behind or in front, the one-lane highway deserted and dark. "You think the ice cream shop's open?" I asked.

"Only one way to find out."

"We could look on your phone," I said.

"I don't have a cell."

"Really?"

"Yep. Amazing, huh? I got rid of my old one last year. There's no reception at the house. The signal starts down the road at the oak tree.

We should get you a phone, though. For emergencies. You might get stuck somewhere, no way to call home."

"Green light."

Monica looked both ways before crossing the empty intersection.

We pulled into a strip mall with a grocery store, discount hair salon, and ice cream shop. All closed. The car idled as we sat in silence, parking lot lights casting shadows on Monica's face as she gripped the steering wheel. After a moment, she said, "Well, cheese and crackers."

"What?"

"This is a bummer."

"It's okay."

"No. I have a better idea. Let's go to the movies. They're always open on Thanksgiving. After all, it's not a school night." She leaned over and winked, like we were outlaws. "I always wanted to say that."

"Great."

She drove to Jefferson's Main Street, a four-block row of antique shops, western wear clothing stores, and a kitschy cafe called Planet of the Crepes. Sitting in the center of the second block was an old-fashioned movie theatre. I blinked alert when I read the marquis.

"They're playing *Hunger Games*," I said. "I wanted to see this." It was the second of the series, *Catching Fire*, although the sign read *Catching Fir*. They must have run out of *e*'s.

Monica slid into a vacant spot, right in front of the ticket window. "Oh yeah, me, too. This'll be cool."

"Cool? You've read *The Hunger Games*?" I asked, stepping onto the high curb.

"I'm a librarian. I read everything. I need to stay hip with the kids." She beeped the lock of the Subaru. "What time does it start?"

"7:35."

"Perfect."

We got in line behind a teenage couple, the guy paying while the girl took selfies on a glitter-pink phone.

"Monica?" I said, as we stepped forward.

"Yeah?"

"First rule of staying hip?"

"Yeah?"

"Don't say 'staying hip.'"

"Got it. Fo Schnitzel."

The guy turned around, flicking his Hurley ball cap. "Come on, Aiden," said his girlfriend, hooking his arm toward the entrance. "Get me in front of the poster." She struck a duck-lipped pose in front of Jennifer Lawrence.

"It's Fo Shizzle," I muttered.

"Fo Shizzle? Well then, what's 'Fo Schnitzel'?" she asked, paying for our tickets.

"I don't know."

"Sounds like a brand of hot dogs."

I laughed. "Don't quit your day job, okay?"

"I better not," said Monica, as we entered the butter-scented blast of the lobby. "Look at the price of popcorn. $8.50 for a medium?"

"Oh, I don't need any—"

"Don't be silly. Go find our seats."

In an auditorium of six Thanksgiving refugees, seats were easy to find. I selected an empty row midway down the aisle, far from Hurley and Duckface, who sat in the back row snapping more selfies.

I sank into the plush, red velvet cushion of the movie seat, comfortable except for the coiled spring that popped against my left butt cheek. Disconcerting, but I was too tired to move. Tired and wired.

This morning, I'd woken up in the Rainbow Canyon Home for Teen Girls. Now I sat in a hundred-year-old movie theatre waiting for Glinda the Good Foster Mom of the North to bring me a bucket of $8.50 popcorn that I didn't want.

I felt disconnected from my body, limbs numb, eyes dry and itchy, brain like a giant pink soap bubble hovering over the land of Oz. *Somewhere over the rainbow...*

Yep, I was delirious.

But I was excited for *The Hunger Games*.

I loved the books, read the whole series in the eighth grade, but I hadn't seen the movies. Wasn't allowed. Too violent, said my previous foster mom. I guess she never read Shakespeare.

"Good seats," Monica said, as she scooted down the row, arms full of sodas and popcorn, two boxes of candy wedged under her chin. "Nothing has lard. I checked." She kept the bucket of popcorn on her lap, putting extra napkins in the cup-holder we shared. My Coke was too big to fit. I held it between my legs, the condensation seeping through my jeans.

"I saw previews for this on the Ellen Show," she said. "It should be good."

I bit off the end of a licorice twist and shoved it into my Coke like a straw. "I think it'll be awesome."

And it was: one of those rare times when the movie matched the pictures in my head. Jennifer Lawrence killed it. She was everything I imagined Katniss Everdeen to be. Victim. Survivor. Warrior. Monica and I stayed through the closing credits, the lights coming up on her red-rimmed eyes.

"Allergies," said Monica, shaking her head. She took a tissue from her purse and dabbed her nose. "They're really bad in the country. Great movie, huh?"

"Yeah." My sneakers made suction noises on the soda-sticky floor when I stood up. I stretched my hands over my head and yawned wide enough to pop my jaw.

"You want to see if the Starbucks drive-through is open?" Monica asked, putting the empty soda and candy containers in the popcorn bucket. Hurley and Duckface were making out in the last row. "Dystopian nightmares," Monica murmured. "A potent aphrodisiac."

I snorted, disrupting the happy couple.

Monica and I sped into the lobby.

"You're in trouble," I teased.

"It was *you* they heard."

"I'm surprised they heard anything with that Hoovering."

"Ha!" she laughed, chucking the popcorn bucket into the garbage can. "Starbucks, then?"

"I don't know. I'm—"

"Pumpkin Spice lattés are back," she tempted, swaying her upper body like a snake charmer. "We could get decaf."

"Sure."

I'd never tried Pumpkin Spice.

***

The Starbucks drive-through was closed. Despite my protestations that, no, I really did not need anything on top of candy, Coke, and popcorn with non-lard butter, Monica pulled into a 24-hour mini-mart. She left me in the Subaru with the engine on, heat blasting, and some country girl on the radio singing about Jesus driving her car.

Sort of strange, I thought. I mean, did Jesus even have a license? Did He have to take Driver's Ed? Would I be condemned to eternal damnation for thinking about this?

Monica returned with a white plastic spoon and a tub of Dippin' Dots.

"Voila," she said, handing me the tub. "I hope you like Cotton Candy flavored."

"What is it?" I asked, scooping a spoonful of tiny pastel balls.

"I think it's freeze-dried ice cream."

"Weird."

"Do you not want it? They also had ice cream bars, but I thought this looked interesting. I can get you something else." She unbuckled her seat belt.

"No!" I said with a mouthful of freeze-dried Dots. The texture was a bit like styrofoam. Definitely a unique taste sensation. "These are great."

Four hours and four thousand calories later, *Mission Impossible: Ice Cream* was Mission Accomplished. Monica pulled out of the gas station parking lot, humming to the radio, something about saving us from the road we were on.

***

After a long, hot shower with vanilla body wash, I shuffled into the kitchen, smelling like a Christmas cookie. Monica sat sipping hot tea from an oversized mug.

"Would you like a cup?" she asked.

"No, I'm great." I pulled out the chair in front of her laptop. "Stuffed, actually."

"Oh, good. Oh. Um. Did we overdo it?"

"No. Thank you for the movie. And everything."

"Of course. You know, I was reading in *Chicken Soup for the Teenage—*"

"Monica?"

"Yes?"

"Do you mind if I go on your computer?"

"Oh. No. Of course not," she said. She paused for a moment, seeming to want to say more, then grabbed a catalog from the top of her mail.

"What's your password?" I asked.

"Password."

"For your computer?"

"Password."

"Yeah. I need it to log on. Or, you could just type it in if you don't want me to know. I can look away."

"You can know. It's 'password.'"

"Your password is 'password'?"

"Yep."

•18•

"Um. Okay."

I logged in and clicked the desktop shortcut, but the internet showed no connection. "How do I go online again?"

"Like this," said Monica. She pulled a blue cable from the base of the kitchen cordless and plugged it into the laptop. I heard a dial tone, then an unearthly *screeeeeeeeeeeee-eeeeeee-eeee-EEEEEEEEEEEEEEEEEEE*.

Bonnie howled in harmony with the laptop, which continued in apparent self-destruct mode. *EEEEEEEEEEEEEEEEEEEEEEEEEEEEEEEE, PingPingPing, BehBurp, BehBurp, whiiiiiiiiiiiiiiiiiiiiiiiiiishhhhh.*

Silence.

I wiggled an index finger in my ear. "So that's dial-up?"

"Yep."

"Good thing you don't have neighbors."

"Just Mr. Albright," she said.

"Who?"

"He owns the ranch next door. The one with the cows?"

"Gotcha." The AOL homepage began loading a millimeter at a time. "You don't go on the internet much, do you?"

"Oh, I wouldn't say that. I check my email at least once a week." She drank her tea, thumbing her catalog. Her eyes twitched every time I clicked the mouse. So much for privacy. What did she think I was looking up? Naked cows?

"Is that the girl from the movie?" she asked, abandoning the pretense of not spying. "The one who played Katniss? What's her name?"

"Jennifer Lawrence. Yeah, it's her profile."

"Is this the Tweeter?"

"Twitter," I said, resting my arm on the table between us.

"That's different, isn't it?"

"Twitter?"

"No, the actress. She looks really different from her character." Jennifer Lawrence's profile showed her with a spiky, blond crew cut, nothing like the dark, back-length braid worn by her character, Katniss Everdeen. Monica scooted closer. "Pretty brave," she said.

"You think so?"

"Sure. To shave it off like that? I bet it's freeing."

I raked my fingers through my long dark hair, knotted and damp from the shower. I couldn't do it. Could I? It would be madness. "You think I'd look good with short hair?"

"Like her?" Monica motioned to the screen.

"No way. I'm not that pretty."

"Are you kidding? You're beautiful."

"Come on," I said, hunching my shoulders.

"I mean it."

"Whatever." I tried to imagine what it would be like to cut off seventeen years' worth of hair growth. I'd be a completely different person.

I could never do such a thing. Could I?

"You really think I could pull it off?"

"I think you could do anything you wanted."

Chapter 3
A hair more, or a hair less

The hair salon opened at nine the next morning. We arrived at quarter past, a copy of the latest *People* magazine under my arm. We'd picked it up at the grocery store next door, a visual aid for the hairdresser. Jennifer Lawrence was on the cover, dressed for an awards show, laughing at some unknown joke. Surrounding her in little picture bubbles were Nelson Mandela and Princess Kate, the headline, "25 Most Intriguing People!" scrawled above her off-white strapless.

The door chimed as we walked into the hair salon, an electronic *ding-dong, ding-dong.* "Look," said Monica, pointing to the sign next to the cash register. "Two-for-one haircuts. Maybe I should get mine chopped off, too. Like Ellen DeGeneres. What do you think? Okay, okay. Maybe not. Don't look so horrified. I'll just get a trim."

A girl in a black apron shuffled to the register, a broom in her hand. She looked early twenties, with purple ombre hair, dark roots fading to lilac. Her name tag read, 'Destynee.' She raised an eyebrow ring in greeting. "Hi guys, welcome to Jefferson Snips," she said, leaning her broom against the counter. "Are you here for the special?"

I rolled up the magazine with Jennifer Lawrence's face in my sweaty hands.

"Yep," said Monica.

Destynee click-clacked on her computer with long, manicured nails, silver-sparkled at the tips. "Okay, well, who wants to go first, you or your daughter?"

Monica glanced at me. I shook my head. Correcting would only lead to more questions, and did I really need to share my life story with a purple-haired, press-on nailed stranger named *Destynee*?

"I'll go," said Monica. "Mine'll be quick."

"Okay." I sat in a yellow plastic chair near the door. The legs were uneven heights, rocking when I shifted my weight. I cracked my neck, and unrolled the magazine. On the cover, Jennifer Lawrence's laugh now seemed to be directed at me. I studied the ad on the back, mascara that promised 200% more volume and zero clumps.

A man in a crew cut walked in, followed by his young son, brown mop flopping. They set off the door chime twice, which entertained the boy. The father sat across from me, next to the hair care display, while the boy went out and in the door. Again. And again.

Ding-dong. Ding-dong.

Ding-dong. Ding-dong.

Ding-dong-ding-dong-ding-dong-ding—

"Mikey, get in here and sit down," the father commanded, taking out his phone.

Ding-dong.

"It'll be about 20 minutes," Destynee called from her station, where she had piled Monica's hair on her head with a butterfly clip. "I'm by myself, and there's two ahead of you."

Ding-dong.

"Help yourself to a sucker!" Destynee yelled. Mikey bounded to the register in two-foot hops. He found the can of lollipops and pulled out a red one.

"Ooh! Cherry!" said Mikey, as he tore off the wrapper.

"Suck, don't chew," said his father.

"So, just a little, then?" Destynee asked Monica.

"Yep. My... Alex is the brave one, getting it all chopped off!"

What was I doing here? I'd never cut more than a couple inches, occasional trims with school scissors. I swallowed, a lollipop-sized lump in my throat.

I heard her voice. *"Fairy princesses don't have short hair."*

My mom—my *real* mom—understood that much, her own hair bleached to straw. I was her Rapunzel. *"Come on, baby. Leave it alone. For me?"* she pleaded, eyes glassy. I sat on the stained couch, tangles uncombed. *Dora the Explorer* was on TV. Dora had short hair. Dora swung from vines and followed the map. She'd never be trapped in a tower. She'd grab her backpack and go. *Vámonos!*

"Are you ready?" Destynee asked. Monica got up from the salon chair looking exactly the same as when she sat down.

I threw back my shoulders. "Vámonos."

"Ha ha. I took Spanish. Habla Español?" Destynee wrapped the little paper collar around my neck before lowering the black smock. Her purple hair glowed with green undertones in the fluorescent light. She studied the cover of the *People* magazine, tilting her head to one side. "Are you sure? I mean... you're sure?"

"Eh. Yeah. It'll grow back, right? Let's do it."

She undid my hairclip and took a small-toothed comb from her apron pocket. "So, are you doing anything over the long holiday weekend?"

"No, nothing much."

"Gonna do any Black Friday shopping?"

"Don't think so," I grunted, a knot catching.

"Wal-Mart's got some good door-busters. My boyfriend camped out overnight to get the XBOX 360."

"Cool."

"Yeah, they also have Call of Duty for $20 off. He's super stoked. I told him, 'Don't come out of that store without something for me.' I'm the one who has to work on a national holiday. But he's super sweet."

"Yeah."

"Nice weather for November, don't you think?" She put my hair in a low ponytail and took out a pair of six-inch steel scissors. "I think it's supposed to change next week, though. We might even get snow! I'm super stoked."

"Uh-huh." I breathed deep, in through the nose, out through the mouth, my approaching Zen interrupted by a piercing cry.

"I DROPPED MY SUCKER!"

"It's okay, sweetie!" Destynee called, her scissors hovering near my cheek.

"BUT I WASN'T DONE YET!"

"Go ahead and take another." She waved the pointy end of the scissors in the direction of the register, narrowly missing my eye.

"BUT THERE'S NO RED LEFT! I WANT RED!"

"Mikey, don't complain," his father said, glancing up from his phone. "You get what you get, and you don't throw a fit."

"I WANT A RED ONE!"

"There's orange," said Destynee. "That's super close to red, don't you think?"

"NOOOOO! ORANGE IS DIFFERENT FROM RED!!!" The boy collapsed into a puddle on the black-and-white checked tile. Monica picked up the can of lollipops and set them on the floor next to his head. "I've always liked green," she said, holding up a sucker.

"Put your chin down a little," said Destynee, pushing my nose to my chest. I closed my eyes as she hacked, my head jerking to the rhythm of the scissors.

"Breathe, honey," Monica said to the little boy. "You're turning purple, sweetie."

"Just ignore him," said his father.

"I think he fainted."

"He'll wake up."

By some miracle—or the self-asphyxiation of a small child—the salon quieted. Destynee made the final cut, reeling me in, hooked and released. I felt like a buoy in the middle of the ocean, untethered, bald, and bobbing.

Destynee laughed. She *laughed.* "Wow! I bet your head's light now."

"Uh."

She handed me my hair, eighteen inches bound in a black rubber band. "Do you want to donate it to Locks of Love?"

My nose tingled, my throat tight. "I'm sorry?"

"It's a cancer charity. They make wigs for sick kids. You could donate it. There are a lot of super unfortunate people in the world."

"Yeah," I said, voice neutral. My hair looked like a dead animal in my lap.

Oh God. What did I do?

"So, you want to donate it?"

I wanted to bury it. "Sure."

"Great," she smiled, a smudge of hot pink lipstick on her teeth. "I'll take that then, and we'll finish you up." She tossed my hair next to a can of disinfectant, then pulled an electric clipper from a drawer beneath the mirror. "I can't wait to try this style," she said, catching the cord on the chair. "Oops. There we go."

Blades buzzed. Warm metal vibrated against my scalp. This wasn't a haircut. It was lawn maintenance. Sheep-shearing at the county fair. Destynee consulted the picture of Jennifer Lawrence while continuing to mow my head. "You want a bit of length in the front, right?"

Length? What length? There was no more length. No more fairy princess. No Dora, either. I was Dora's cousin, Diego. Scratch that. Diego had longer hair. I gripped the armrests of the salon chair, tamping down hysteria, the skin on my face stretched tight against my skull.

"Are you okay?" Destynee asked. "I'm not hurting you, am I? I can use a higher setting. Whoops. No, I guess I can't."

"Oh. Ah. Ah-Ha." I forgot how to form consonants. There was airflow where none had been before, but none of it was reaching my lungs.

At last, the buzzing stopped.

A part of my brain registered the crying of a small child, sniffles and hiccups, Monica offering quiet reassurances. "There you go, Mikey," she comforted. "Are you feeling better now?"

Destynee handed me a pink plastic-framed mirror. "Take a look." She swung me around so I could see from behind. The back of my head was shaped like a flattened light bulb, oval and narrowing at the neck. On the upper left-hand side, a little nick marked the ridge of a small bump.

I HAVE A LUMPY HEAD!

"Almost done," Destynee said, putting away the clippers. "I just need to finish the front. It's coming out really nice. You don't really look like Jennifer Lawrence, though."

"I know," I said miserably.

"I mean, you're not blond, silly. You look like Anne Hathaway. Or Emma Watson."

Or Justin Bieber.

"You look great. Let's show your mom. Hey Mom! Come over here!" Destynee called. "She's all done. Mucho gusto!" She whipped off my smock. I rubbed my neck, still feeling the tightness of the paper collar. Then, I realized, I could *feel* my neck. No hair in the way. No hair. Where was my hair? What had I done?

"Wow, incredible," Monica marveled. I couldn't tell if she was serious or overcompensating. Maybe both.

Destynee bumped my shoulder with her hip, leaving tiny hairs on my hoodie. "Told you."

"I look okay?" I whispered.

"You look grrrrreat!" beamed Mikey, who sprang up behind Monica like a sticky-lipped Jack-in-the-Box, holding the entire can of lollipops.

"You think so?"

"Oh yeah! So cool!"

"Thanks, little guy," I sniffed.

"You're welcome! Are you a boy or a girl?"

Chapter 4
How now, who calls?

Thursday morning. My first day of school.

I would've gone Monday, but my transcripts were delayed, which was okay by me. At six days post Hair Trauma, I was still in Recovery Mode.

Inching forward in the drop-off line, Monica thumped her thumb on the steering wheel. "You have your iPhone, right? In case something happens?"

I sighed.

Jefferson Union High sat kitty-corner to a hay field. What did she think was going to happen? A tractor explosion? Runaway bales?

"Your iPhone?" she asked again, thinking I hadn't heard.

"It's a Cingular," I corrected.

"A singular what?"

"It's not an iPhone," I explained. "It's a Cingular."

Monica had salvaged the ancient flip phone from the electronics recycling drive put on by her Saturday garden club. I stayed home that afternoon to stare at the walls, bounce tennis balls for Bonnie and Clyde, and read the first few chapters of Monica's book club novel, which, disappointingly, didn't seem all that mature.

The rest of the week was spent hanging out with Monica at her part-time job at the library, helping her re-shelve books, reading through the entire *Hunger Games* series *again*, and waiting for my transcripts to arrive. Once the craziness of Black Friday and weekend returns had passed, Monica took me shopping in the next town over, where I scored a couple more hoodies, a new pair of jeans, and a cool new backpack. For dinner, we went to the Olive Garden. The pasta wasn't as good as

Monica's homemade spaghetti, but I ate enough unlimited breadsticks to make a food baby.

"It is singular, though, isn't it?" she asked.

"What?"

"An iPhone is a singular type of phone, right? Only Apple makes them."

"It's *Cingular*, not singul— Never mind. Yes. I have my iPhone." I unzipped the front pocket of my new backpack to show her the cracked outer screen. The guy at the AT&T store said we should sell the phone on eBay. He'd never seen such an old model. I, in turn, had never seen such a ginormous, blistering cold sore on a retail representative. Monica listened politely to his sales pitch, but declined the upgrade, as well as the plan with unlimited minutes. I didn't care. Who was I going to call? The Farmer in the Dell?

"It's working?"

"Yeah, we tested it yesterday, remember?"

Monica's house was in a dead zone, so I walked a half mile down the road to the old oak tree, where the signal picked up. While I was waiting for her to call, I played with the camera function and took a couple of selfies. The phone was so outdated, I had to flip the camera around to take the photo, which is how I ended up with three pictures of my forehead.

"It's charged?" she asked.

"Yep, see?" I showed her the battery power on the inside screen, which displayed a picture of an apartment complex, probably the old owner's. "It's still got half a life."

The old phone drained fast. Probably leaked radiation, too. Fabulous.

I powered it down.

"You could text me," Monica said, inching forward in the drop-off line. "At lunch maybe. Only if you wanted to." She picked at the sleeve of her faded Sacramento State sweatshirt, snapping a thread.

"You don't have a cell, Monica. I can't text a landline."

"Oh, right."

A school bus pulled behind Monica's Subaru, filling the side mirror with yellow and black. The double doors opened with a whoosh of compressed air, and a stream of kids flowed out. Other than a higher ratio of cowboy boots to sneakers, they looked like the teenagers from my old school, typical jocks and preps. My outfit wouldn't draw attention: blue jeans, fitted white T-shirt, new grey fleece hoodie. My only nod to color were my pink Converse high tops, worn more for sentimental reasons than a desire to stick out.

"Everyone's going to love you."

"Sure," I said, reaching for a split end. My hand hung suspended in midair, two seconds behind my brain in realizing I needed a new nervous habit.

"Did you have a question?" asked Monica.

"No, why?"

"You're, um, raising your hand."

"Just stretching," I said.

Why is this drop-off line so slow?

Anxiety cramped my stomach. I twisted my fingers in my lap, cracking a knuckle. I missed my long hair, comforting as an old scarf. I took a shallow breath and practiced the positive self-talk my case worker Heather was always suggesting.

My hair looked fine.

Sort of.

I had woken up at 5:15 a.m., reasonably confident of having a good day. Then, I saw my reflection in the bathroom mirror. Somehow in the night, my Not-Jennifer-Lawrence-But-Maybe-Okay haircut had morphed into Demented Rooster.

So, I washed it, combed it, dried it, and, in a fit of panic, curled it with Monica's mini-roller, found under the sink next to a bag of cotton balls.

Bad mistake. I looked like Napoleon Dynamite. Or Little Orphan Annie, which, paradoxically, is not a good look for an actual orphan.

I stuck my head under the sink and tried again with some half-dried mousse, surely a relic from Monica's pre-divorce days. Even worse. With my flat chest, I looked like the least popular member of a boy band, smelling like a hospital gift shop.

A brief time check put me at 7 a.m. I heard Monica bustling in the kitchen, probably needing to pee, but too polite to ask why I was heading for my second shower of the morning. After blow-drying my bangs straight, I threw in the towel—literally and figuratively—and emerged from the bathroom, arms aching, emotionally drained.

I thought short hair was supposed to be *easy*.

Monica pulled into the drop-off zone. "You look great, you know."

"Eh, I don't care."

Three girls stood outside my door, a gauntlet of wedge heels and spaghetti straps. Their breath fogged the November air, voices seeping through the vents like carbon monoxide.

"No way, you didn't!"

"She deserved it!"

"You should have seen her face."

"Those girls need sweaters," said Monica. "It's 40 degrees out."

"Mm-hmm." I zipped my backpack and pulled down the sun visor for one last check in the mirror.

"That haircut really suits you," said Monica. "It highlights your cheekbones and brings out your eyes."

"I don't think there's much to bring out." I flipped up the visor, raised my hood, and reached for the door handle.

"Do you want me to walk you in?" Monica asked.

"To the office?" Did she think I was in the third grade? "Nah, don't worry. I got this. I'm a professional New Girl," I joked, stepping onto the curb.

"Wait!" she called. "Let me take your picture!"

The spaghetti strap girls snickered.

"It's your first day at a new school!"

"*Monica,*" I hissed.

"Come on, it'll be great for the scrapbook."

"What scrapbook?"

A second school bus pulled behind the first, unloading a new flood of students. Mercifully, the sweaterless coven moved on.

"Oh, there's a scrapbooking group that meets bi-monthly at the library! That's every two months, not twice a month."

"We don't have a camera," I said, my teeth clenched.

"We've got your phone!" she bubbled. "The AT&T guy said it would take pictures."

"Yeah, I know," I said, sidestepping a girl with a tuba. "They all do that now."

"I know, how cool is that? Pretty soon these phones will be able to do everything. I bet someday you won't even need to ask for directions. The phone will just tell you where to go!"

"Okay, okay." I estimated picture-taking would be the fastest way of getting her to leave. "Can we make it quick, though? The bell's going to ring." I unzipped my backpack and tossed the phone through the open car window.

"You wanna take off your hood?" Monica asked.

I narrowed my eyes.

"All right, forget it. Your hood looks good. Hey, that rhymes."

"Monica."

"How do I take a picture?"

"Hand it to me." I jammed the buttons. "You have to turn it on first. Press here," I said, thrusting it back.

"This is so cool!"

"I know," I replied, grinding the heel of my palm into my right eye.

"Say 'fromage!'"

"What?"

"It's French for cheese!" She stuck her tongue to the side and crossed her eyes.

I shook my head and mashed my lips.

"Cheeeeeeeese," I said, trying not to smile.

It was stupid. And embarrassing.

But nice.

In a stupid, embarrassing way.

When she handed me back the phone, some force possessed me to say, "Okay, it's your turn."

"What, no! I'm not—"

I held up the phone. "Fair's fair. Say 'fritter'!"

"Cheese!"

I checked the pictures: Monica grinning; me in a grey hood, looking gaseous. Some random dude had made bunny ears behind my head. With a sigh, I flipped the phone closed.

Monica leaned into the passenger seat. "You're a great girl, Alex. I mean, sorry, *young woman*. I don't know how you do it: change schools so much—"

"Monica." I shut her down quicker than the phone. "It's cool. I've got this," I repeated. "Easy-peasy, lemon squeezy."

I froze. The world spun.

I closed my eyes to center myself, and

I was six-years old. The power was out. She hadn't paid the bill. After a cold SpaghettiOs dinner, we lay on the mattress in the corner of the living room, her arms achingly thin, like twigs. As the sunlight faded, we made shadow puppets on the wall. Her hands trembled, but mine were steady, still chubby with baby fat.

"Can you do me?" I asked.

"Yep, easy-peasy, lemon-squeezy."

The 'Allie-gator' marched across the ceiling, chomp, chomp, chomp.

"Do a unicorn!"

"Okay, but you have to help."

My pinkie became the horn, her fingers the hooves. We galloped across the ceiling, the neon lights from the bar across the street creating a kaleidoscope of color on my fingertips. "See, Allie, the unicorn has her rainbow."

"It's magic!" I cried.

"No, Allie-gator. It's us."

The case workers told me she wasn't a bad mom, just sick.

She died on a Wednesday. I was in the third grade, living in my second foster home. It was my day to be the teacher's special helper, to carry the attendance to the office, pass back papers, and circle the date on the calendar: February 11. I'd just stood up to walk to the front of the room when the secretary pulled me from class. They said my mom died of a drug overdose, but I knew the truth. She died because I wasn't there.

The school bus honked behind Monica's car. She wasn't supposed to sit so long in the drop-off. "Are you okay, Alex?"

"Yep. Allergies. They're really bad in the country."

Chapter 5
Toward school with heavy looks

"Jefferson Union, can you hold, please?" The attendance secretary handed me a copy of my schedule while juggling the phones, writing tardy slips, and yelling at an oblivious office TA. Glittering Hello Kitty stickers bedazzled her Jefferson Union nameplate, reading *Bob*. She had silver-white hair under a large headset, and, surrounded by blinking lights, resembled nothing so much as air traffic control. "What a ditz," she muttered. "Oh, not you, Mrs. Jorgenson. Pardon me for a moment while I put you on hold." She pressed a button, then finally looked at me. "Yes?" she grumbled.

"Um. Miss... Bob?"

"Just Bob. Jefferson Union, can you hold please?" She punched a button on her phone and clicked her headset. "Yes?"

"Me?" I asked.

"Who else is standing here?"

"Sorry," I said. "I think there's been—"

"I'll get someone to show you around. Shayna! I need you to take—I'm sorry, what was your name again?"

Feeling flustered, I checked my schedule for my own name. "Alex Riddle."

"Are you sure?"

"Yes." I cleared my throat. "Short for Alexandra."

"Right. SHAYNA!"

Shayna sat in a folding chair beside the office mini-fridge. Her long, blond hair hung like a perfect curtain, shielding her silver iPhone. She uncrossed her knee-high boots. "Yeah, Bob?" she replied.

"Shayna, even office TAs need to keep their phones off during school."

"Sorry. I was looking at the time. I'll put it away now."

The school phone began beeping again. Bob rolled her eyes and adjusted her headset, showing us her palm in the universal signal to wait.

Shayna observed me with pretty blue-grey eyes outlined in black, heavy on the mascara.

"Are you new?" She blinked. A corner top and lower lash stuck together.

"Yep. First day."

"Hmm. Not from around here?" she asked.

"No."

"Lucky." She blew air out her nose. "Nice haircut."

Bob covered the mouthpiece of her headset. "Shayna, show Alex where her classes are. She's got the print-out."

"Okay, but I'm getting picked up soon. Ortho appointment."

"You got your braces off last year."

"Checkup."

"Fine. Don't be long then."

A girl in green shorts limped through the door, asking for an icepack. "Again?" Bob asked. "What are you doing to yourself in P.E.?"

"I was *walking* to P.E."

"Excuse me," I interrupted. "There's a mistake on my schedule. I was assigned the wrong math class. I've already taken Trig. Also, I should have Art, not Drama." Behind on units, I planned a heavy course load: AP English 12, Chemistry, Economics, Psychology, AP Geography, Calculus, and Art. No study hall. With the chaos of the past year, I needed the extra classes to catch up for graduation.

"Did you meet with your counselor?"

"I met with Ms. Carmichael yesterday."

"I can't do schedule changes," Bob said. "You'll have to see your counselor. She's at the District Office all day. Just go to your classes, and we'll sort it out tomorrow. Follow Shayna. She'll give you a tour and take you to your first period."

Shayna was already outside, standing next to a statue of the school mascot. "What is that?" I asked. It looked like a boar with a hernia.

"We're the Jefferson Jackals."

"Oh."

"Machine shop project."

"Right."

"So, umm, your first period is over there." She pointed to a line of portables. "I'll walk you over, and then I think you'll be able to find the rest of your classes okay. You've got a map, don't you?" She pulled her phone from the waistband of her leggings, texting as we walked.

***

The morning passed uneventfully until 3rd period Econ, when my backpack started mooing.

"Someone has their phone on," said the teacher, a five-foot-tall man with slick black hair combed to cover his three-quarter balding head. "Someone has their phone on," he droned, walking the aisles of the classroom. "Who has their phone on?" As the entire class pointed and laughed, I unzipped my backpack, yanked out the phone (which I thought I'd turned off, but apparently the button was sticky) and mashed the power button.

"Who's calling? Old Macdonald?" hooted the acne-faced guy next to me.

"It must be an alarm," I said, my answer lost in the first-round chorus of E-I-E-I-O.

Needless to say, lunchtime was a relief.

The quad was small and open, with old pines and picnic tables. I sat in the shade of a wooden gazebo and thought about my last school, its concrete buildings, chain-link fences, and metal detectors. Out of 3,000 students, I had one friend. Well, acquaintance, really.

Delany and I shared 4th period Art. We weren't close, never talked much, but I missed sitting next to her, our friendly silence as we sketched. I wasn't even that good at art. I just liked the peacefulness of me and the canvas.

Delany seemed to feel the same, only she had real talent. Her specialty was body parts: a cleft lip, an ear gauge, a mole with three hairs. Before I withdrew last month, she opened her notebook and tore out a sheet. There was my left eye, brown with flecks of gold; beneath it, the teardrop scar I'd had since age three, the result of a botched crib escape.

Had Delany made a new friend since I left? Could I find a way to contact her? We'd never exchanged phone numbers, but maybe my old foster mom could help.

Yeah, right. Good one.

My last FP and I didn't exactly see eye-to-eye. For instance, I thought I was seventeen years old. She thought I was a toddler, incapable of making my own food choices. According to her, vegetarians were hippy radical socialists (whatever that meant), and besides, baloney was cheap.

Yes, she worked two jobs—I'll give her that—but the morning she called me "an ungrateful brat," I threw my lunch at her face. The Wonder Bread fell to the floor, leaving a smear of yellow mustard on her nose.

I laughed.

I shouldn't have done that.

She slapped me.

I reeled from the shock, more than the pain.

Heather, my case worker, picked me up from school that day, and brought me to the Rainbow Canyon Home for Teen Girls. I never said goodbye to Robert, my ten-year-old foster brother. He played Minecraft and wrote short stories. He hated baloney, too.

I opened my lunch sack: orange soda, sour cream & onion potato chips, a cheddar-and-dill-pickle sandwich with extra Dijon, and a

Ziploc of perfectly ripe honeydew melon cut into cubes. Unbelievably yummy.

I'd been a vegetarian for two years, ever since Debbie and Rick, my two favorite foster parents. Rick, short for "Erica," was vegan, but Debbie drank milk and sometimes ate shrimp. They were lesbians, married, living in Berkeley, where Debbie was a Women's Studies professor and Rick managed a coffee shop. I'd hang out there after school, drinking caramel lattés, listening to piped-in Joni Mitchell (Rick's favorite. She had it on perpetual repeat), and joking with the assistant manager Greg, a dorky guy with a small chin.

One night, the words "adoption" and "family" wafted under my bedroom door with the incense Debbie always burned. I clutched my blanket and breathed in the sweet, earthy smell that reminded me of fake Christmas trees. I was fourteen-going-on-fifteen, a freshman, and I had a forever home.

The next afternoon, I jogged into the coffee shop. Debbie and Rick waited for me at a corner table, nervous grins on their faces. Over double mochas, soy for Rick, decaf for Debbie and me, they told me their secret. *"Becoming parents is something we've always dreamed of. You're such a great kid, Alex. It's because of you, we've decided to go for it. We just know that, with a new baby, we couldn't give you the attention you deserve."* The coffee turned to acid in my stomach, but I smiled and said how happy I was for them.

My parting gifts (thanks for playing) were a Joni Mitchell CD, a copy of *Our Bodies, Ourselves*, and Debbie's pink Converse. We were the same size, and she knew I liked them.

Chapter 6
You kiss by the book

Drama class was after lunch. A rowdy group of students blocked the entrance to the theatre, pelting each other with Flamin' Hot Cheetos. I edged around the crowd, hoping to find the teacher before the bell rang.

As my eyes adjusted to the darkened auditorium, I spotted her in the back row, searching through a stack of papers. She took a pencil from her mouth and twisted her wild, black curls into a sloppy bun. As I edged down the row, stumbling over a water bottle, the students from outside streamed piggy-back down the aisle, singing *"Don't Stop Be-leeeeeving!"*

"Let's get going, everyone!" shouted the teacher. "We don't have much time. Hey, Connor, have you seen the prop list? Someone needs to lead warm-ups while I get the stage set up. JEREMY!"

"Yeah?" A tall, stocky, red-haired boy sauntered up, giving me a wink. His T-shirt read *National Sarcasm Society: Like We Need Your Support.*

"Get everyone on stage please. We've got a lot to do. The one-act is less than two weeks away. We need to run the first half of the show. DYLAN AND CHRIS! GRAB THE BLACK BOXES."

"Where are they?" asked either Dylan or Chris.

"Behind the wings!"

"What are the wings?"

"The long curtain things that hang down on the side of the stage!"

"Oh. Cool. Why are they called 'wings'?"

"Now!"

"Where do you want us to do warm-ups?" Jeremy asked.

"On the stage."

"While they're setting up?"

"No. Take the cast outside, but don't be too loud or Mr. Murphy will get upset."

He muttered something under his breath.

"Jeremy..." warned the teacher.

"What? I said 'hick.' All the teachers at this school are hicks."

"Mm-hmm."

"Except you, Ms. Lanyer. You're not a hick."

"You're a senior, Jeremy. Can you please set an example?"

"Yes, Ms. L. Very sorry." He turned to the class. "Okay, you lazy good-for-nothings, get outside! Time for warm-ups! Chaaarrrge!"

The students barreled back out the door. Ms. Lanyer saw me standing halfway down the row. "Just another day in Drama," she laughed, raising her eyes to the ceiling. "Thank God for tenure. Hi. Can I help you?"

I stepped forward. "I'm a new student. Alex Riddle. I'm not supposed to be in this class, though."

"That's too bad. Do you need to go up to the office?" she asked.

"No. They said to come back tomorrow, and they'd fix it."

"Okay, well. Why don't you sit in the audience then, and watch the rehearsal. We're doing a 40-minute version of *Romeo and Juliet* for the Riverbend Theatre Festival. Kind of a modern take on it, you'll see."

"Okay. Um. What's going on outside?" It sounded like a ritual sacrifice. *HAH HEY HEE HO HU! HAH HEY HEE HO HU! BUDDAGUDDA, BUDDAGUDDA, BUDDAGUDDA! GETTTA-BUDDA, GETTTABUDDA, GETTTABUDDA!*

"Vocal warm-ups," she explained.

A deep, male voice shouted something indecipherable, quieting the group.

"That's Mr. Murphy. He's such a hick." Ms. Lanyer smiled. "Now, if I could only find my prop list. And my camera for the publicity shots. And my mind. You're sure you don't want to stay in this class? I could use an assistant."

"I don't know. I'm supposed to be in Art."

"I need a poster for the show. You could design that. What do you think?"

Before I could answer, the cast returned, arms linked, everyone laughing. Six or seven surrounded me, chirping rapid-fire questions.

"Are you in this class now?"

"Where are you from?"

"Ms. Lanyer, did you know we have a new student!"

"What part is she going to play?"

"Hey, I like your haircut. Very Anne Hathaway."

"So, are you in Drama?"

The tall red-headed boy pushed his way to the front of the small crowd. "Hey, give the lady some space. Don't crowd, don't crowd. Allow me to introduce myself. I'm Jeremy, a.k.a., Benvolio, the most tragic figure in this play. Totally ignored. Does anyone care if I get the girl? No. It's always, *What's wrong with Romeo? Benvolio, tell us what Romeo said.* Does anyone ever ask how *I'm* doing?"

"Jeremy..." Ms. Lanyer said.

"Nope," he continued. "I tell you, Benvolio's depressed, and no one cares. The Zoloft isn't working. It's just making him fat." He shook a couple of meaty love handles for emphasis.

"Jeremy."

"Everyone talks behind his back. *Look, there goes Benvolio, Romeo's fat friend.*"

"Jeremy!"

"Sorry, Ms. L. It's just unfair, that's all I got to say. Some get the girl, while others sweep the stage. Hey nice shoes," he said, pointing to my pink Converse. He wore a pair of classic tie-dyed high-tops.

I grinned. "You, too."

A girl with a chin-length bob and large round glasses tapped me on the shoulder. She looked like Marcie from Peanuts, Peppermint Patty's best friend. "So are you in this class or not?"

"Yeah, I guess so," I said.

"Cool!"

Ms. Lanyer yelled, "Places, please!"

The kids bounded onto the stage, some taking the stairs, most doing box jumps over the front edge, landing hard.

"How about we wait until after the show to break legs?" called Ms. Lanyer. "Let's go from the top. Wait, never mind. Ronnie's not here. Dammit, where is he? Anyways, don't answer, no time, we can't do the opening fight. Let's take it from the party scene, everyone. Chris! I need you to reset the boxes for 1.5."

Chris poked his head out from behind the newly closed curtain and gave the teacher a blank look.

"That's *act one, scene five*," specified Ms. Lanyer. "Only in our script it's the third scene, page six. Remember, everyone, there's a music cue!"

"What's the cue?" shouted a disembodied voice.

"Track 3! My iPod's hooked up to the speaker. Can someone press it please!"

"Got it!"

A pulse-pounding beat shook the walls of the auditorium. I expected Renaissance music, not *Royals* by Lourde. The curtains parted to a party scene, but not with proper Elizabethan dancing. Strobe lights flashed. Kids grinded like they were at an under 18 club.

"Well, that's different," I said.

"You don't like it?" asked Ms. Lanyer.

"No, that's not it. It's just. Different."

"I'll take different."

The rave continued. Two characters fought in a whisper at the side of the stage. I remembered the play from freshman English. Juliet's dad and her cousin. Paris? No, her cousin was Tybalt. He pulled out a prop gun, tip orange in the neon strobe.

"No swords?" I asked.

"No. We're keeping it modern," replied Ms. Lanyer.

"Edgy."

"Let's hope," she smiled.

"You don't think Shakespeare will mind?" I teased.

"Shakespeare's dead."

At the end of the second chorus, the actors froze in position as Romeo entered, spotlight engaged.

He must've been backstage at the start of class, because he wasn't among the earlier group of students. He held a script in one hand while the other raked his dark, wavy hair. A square jaw offset a perfectly shaped mouth, lips full, almost girly. The dimple on his right cheek flashed as he squinted into the audience.

"Juliet's not here, Ms. Lanyer."

The teacher gave an audible sigh. "Why didn't someone tell me? Fine. Let's skip ahead." She checked her script. "No, we can't. We need to run this for the scene change. What's your name, again?"

Seconds passed before I realized she was addressing me.

"Um. Alex."

"Great. Alex, would you go onstage please? Ryan, give her your script. You're supposed to be off-book anyways."

Pickles and cheddar crept up my throat. "I'm sorry. I can't act. I'm not even supposed to be here."

"Well, you're in the class now, right? Don't worry about it." She softened, seeing my deer-in-the-headlights look. "You don't have to *act*. Just read. I need to run this for the timing. If you could stand there and say the words, it would really help us out."

The girl who looked like Marcie from *Peanuts* ran down and grabbed my hand. "It's all good. Come on. We need someone." She pulled me up the aisle.

Ms. Lanyer called to reset the music.

"What's your name?" asked Marcie, pushing her glasses up the bridge of her nose.

"Alex. What's yours?"

"Jamie. Nice to meet you. Ryan!" she bellowed. "We need your script!" She ran offstage and returned, handing me the pages. "Stand here. You don't have to do the dance. Ryan will come up to you. Just say the lines. You'll be great." She squeezed my shoulder and took her place as I waited for the music to start.

Drumbeat. Finger snap.

Pause. Finger snap.

Drumbeat. Finger snap.

Pause. Finger snap.

Like a heart pounding, skipping a beat.

Then the lyrics, sung like a secret: a jewel in the flesh.

The stage lights blinded me in their intensity. I closed my eyes. Red, blue, and green swirls swam beneath my lids. Dizzy, I opened my eyes. Ghost-like afterimages traveled towards the light, somersaulting, leaving prismatic traces in their wake. I blinked, and there was Romeo, a foot away. He took my hand and kissed it, lips as soft as breath.

"It's your line now." He pointed to my script.

"Sorry."

His eyes were an emerald green, more substantial than the light.

"Good pilgrim, you do wrong your hand too much..."

My hand began to sweat and stick to his. There was a second dimple on his chin, just above a razor cut.

"Then move not, while my prayer's effect I take."

The kiss was sudden, but, in retrospect, not surprising. I knew this scene. I just didn't think he'd actually *do it*. I floated above, watching myself in a dream. *This isn't me,* I thought, tasting the cinnamon Altoid on his breath. My hands were around his neck, then the back of his head. Lip, teeth, tongue. I lost where I ended and he began.

The music stopped. Someone cleared their throat. I thought maybe it was Ms. Lanyer saying "cut," until I heard her voice. She stood in the back of the auditorium, her blond hair lit red by the exit sign.

"Good thing I rushed back from my ortho appointment. Nice to see I wasn't missed."

Chapter 7
A troubled mind drave me to walk abroad

Shayna stormed out, Ryan right behind.

"She's his girlfriend," Jamie whispered.

"I kinda figured."

Jeremy put an arm around me. "Don't worry, kid," he said. "He's not worth it. Hey, what are you doing after rehearsal?"

"Jeremy...," warned Ms. Lanyer.

"Is Benvolio never allowed to get lucky?"

"We're moving ahead. Places for the Mercutio-Tybalt fight scene. Don't push me. I'm bringing out the weapons."

I retreated to the last row of the auditorium. Ryan came back with Shayna a few minutes later, his hand just below her waistband, leading her to the stage. Ms. Lanyer sat beside me in the darkness.

"Sorry for the added drama. A little goes a long way in this class. You were really good up there. Are you sure you've never acted before?"

"Positive."

"Well, you could have fooled me. You and Ryan had nice chemistry."

"Tell that to Shayna. Tomorrow you can identify my body."

"Don't worry about her. It's just acting. She'll get over it."

I made a noise in the bottom of my throat.

She continued, "Anyway, we could still use help backstage. I hope you'll stay."

"Thanks. Everyone seems nice, but I can't be in this class. It'd be too uncomfortable."

"I understand. *To thine own self be true*," she winked. "Okay, guys," she called to the actors onstage. "Let's take it from the party scene!"

I studied my nails and waited for the bell to ring.

***

After school, I went to the office to see if the counselor had returned, but no one was there, not even the attendance secretary. The campus supervisor, a heavyset woman wearing a Bermuda shirt and khaki shorts, sat in Bob's seat. She propped her Birkenstocks on the desk. "Can I help you?" she barked.

"No thank you. I'll come back tomorrow."

"No skin off my nose."

I found Monica waiting in the long line of cars outside. I hopped in and rolled down the window, then immediately rolled it back up. The events of the afternoon had left me without a sense of my own body temperature. *How did I end up kissing a guy in front of thirty people, including his own girlfriend?*

Monica pulled away from the curb, eyeing me from the side. "I was hoping you'd call at lunch," she said, her voice light. "I'm not trying to check up on you, I just was kind of waiting around for it." She paused. "I'm sorry. I'm doing this all wrong. You don't have to call me if you don't want to." She smiled apologetically. "Can we just start all over? Hello dear, how did your day go? Ha, ha."

"Fine." I wanted to hide under a blanket. I tried and failed to keep the tension out of my voice. "Can we just go home?"

Her shoulders tightened.

You wanted a teenager, I thought. *Look this up in your books and smoke it.*

"If you don't want to talk, that's okay. I respect that. But please don't tell me it's 'fine' if it's not. Just tell me you don't want to talk about it. Okay?"

"Okay. I don't want to talk about it."

The silence continued for the ten torturous miles to Monica's house. I stepped out of the car, gravel crunching under my feet. A dog barked in the distance. Birds twittered. There was no other sound. No cars drove along the pockmarked, country road. No phones rang. No people shouted to their neighbors.

I missed the hum of the city. Traffic shushing, buses rattling, sirens wailing, babies crying. The white noise lulled me numb, anesthetized my thoughts.

Here, the quiet left no room for anything *but* my thoughts. It compressed my chest, blazed my brain. *I can't believe I kissed him.* Dark brown hair, electric green eyes, *two* dimples—which shouldn't even be legal. The way his hand touched my cheek before his lips met mine. I felt heat rise up my neck, my *bare* neck. I held onto the car door and watched as Monica walked up the drive, giving me space. After years of crappy and/or average-to-indifferent homes, I finally had a foster mom who was nice and considerate—to whom I was a total jerk because she asked me how my day went.

I slammed the car door.

Monica turned at the sound, her house key halfway in the lock.

"Sorry," I said. "The handle slipped." I kicked a pebble and followed Monica into the house. She was already in the kitchen, cracking open her daily can of Diet Coke. Bonnie met me at the door, tail wagging. "Hey, girl," I said. "Where's your partner in crime?"

"Clyde's gone," said Monica, stifling a burp.

"Oh no. Again?"

"It's my fault. I thought I latched the sliding glass door. I swear, that dog has opposable thumbs."

"I think he nudges it with his nose."

"An opposable nose, then."

I smiled for the first time since the awkward picture in front of the school. "I'll get him this time," I said, setting my backpack next to the couch. Clyde had a romantic thing for the neighbor's cattle dog. When Monica fetched him yesterday, he was slobbering and covered in sticky foxtails, which, I discovered, have nothing to do with either foxes or tails.

"Are you sure?" asked Monica. "You've never been over there. Mr. Albright can be kind of crotchety."

"I'll be fine. I'd like to take a walk. Clear my head." I let out a breath. "And I'm sorry if I was grumpy in the car."

"No, I'm sorry, I— "

"Enjoy your *Ellen Show*," I said. "If you hear a shotgun blast, call 911."

***

According to Monica, Mr. Albright's ranch took up over 600 acres. I plodded down the road, over a hill and a bend to the left, the curve marked by an ancient oak. The trunk lay severed, one part upright, the other part, thick with mistletoe, leaning over the barbed-wire fence into the pasture. A hundred yards beyond, I reached Mr. Albright's gate, edging across an iron cattle guard. I passed an ominous-looking barn, two stories high, made of weathered grey wood and tin roofing, built in the last century. As I pondered how many corpses might be hidden inside, the ground started to shake.

A large cloud of dust followed what appeared to be hundreds of cows thundering in my direction. My mind raced. Should I make noise? Wave my arms? Run away? Were cows like bears? Would they chase? Did they smell fear? I settled for screaming, "STOP IT! STOP IT! STOP IT! STOP IT!"

They kept coming. I closed my eyes. Prayed for a quick death. The rush of one-ton bodies brushed past, bumping me with bristled hair, a lingering scent of mud and manure in their wake.

"Well, young lady. I see you ain't got the sense God gave a squirrel." An old man with a face like a desiccated pear stepped out of the barn, dusting the hay off his coveralls. He puckered and spat. "If you want to try the Running of the Bulls, may I suggest a trip to Pamplona? In the meantime, perhaps you shouldn't stand between a cow and her dinner."

"Sorry," I said, willing my heart to slow to its normal rate. "I grew up in the city."

"I never would have guessed. You look right at home on the range. Want a job as my next cowhand? You'd be about as useful as my grandson, and that's setting the bar high." I followed Mr. Albright's gaze to my pink Converse, sunk in a two-foot diameter cow pie. He snickered and slammed the barn door, locking it with a rusty spike.

"Your name's Alex, right?" Mr. Albright asked. "Monica called and told me you'd be coming. Clyde's up at the house, pestering my bitch in heat. Come on and get him. My grandson can drive you home. Wipe your feet before you go in the house, though."

Seeing as nothing could be done for my shoes without a high-pressure hose, I waited in front of Mr. Albright's wrap-around porch while he fetched Clyde from a backyard kennel. The Golden Retriever greeted me, tail wagging, oblivious to the trouble he'd caused. "You dirty old man," I said, waggling his ears. "Going after that young cow dog. Don't you know when a lady is above your stars?"

"Can't blame a guy for trying, though."

I looked up, straight into the eyes of Romeo. Mr. Albright was right behind him.

"Alex, meet my grandson, Ryan. He'll take you home."

Chapter 8
We must talk in secret

Ryan hoisted the arthritic Golden Retriever into the back of his truck. Front paws on the wheel well, doggy head dangling, Clyde barked happily. If this escapade was meant to discourage him from wandering, I'm not sure it worked. I climbed into the cab, thankful it had rubber mats. The bigger chunks of manure had flaked off, but the treads in my soles were still caked. I pondered the proper etiquette in a situation like this.

"Sorry about the mess," I said. "I didn't mean to step in it."

"It's not your fault. I kissed you back."

"What?"

"What?" Ryan repeated.

"I was talking about my shoe. What are you talking...? Oh my God. Okay."

"Well, this is awkward."

"What did you think I meant?" I asked.

"Nothing. Never mind." He jammed the gear shift into third, and the truck jumped, lifting me out of my seat. "Sorry. I'm still getting used to a stick."

"It's okay," I said, rubbing the top of my head.

Ryan turned the key and eased off the clutch. At the end of the driveway, he turned right towards Monica's. Just past the old oak, he pulled off, the truck sticking three feet into the road. He silenced the engine and flipped the hazards. The warning lights flashed, keeping tempo like a heartbeat.

He turned to me. "Hi, I'm Ryan," he said, wrist balanced on the steering wheel.

"Alex," I said.

"Alex?"

"Yeah. Short for Alexandra."

"Nice to meet you, Alexandra."

"Alex."

"Nice to meet you, Alex."

"You, too."

"You're the first person I ever kissed without introducing myself first," he joked.

"You're the first person I ever kissed."

Did I really just tell him that?

I fiddled with my ear lobe and waited four clicks of the hazards before looking up from the interesting view that was my lap. "You can stop staring at me like I have two heads," I said. "You should be watching the road."

I am a freak. Who gets to seventeen without being kissed? I had waited so long I was beginning to think it would never actually happen.

And then it did. Today. Without warning or thought. Kissing Ryan had been as natural as breathing, heads tilted to the left, eyes closed, bodies one.

"You never kissed anyone?" he asked. "Truth?"

"Yes, it's the truth," I huffed, cheeks on fire. "You think I'd lie about something so embarrassing?"

I dared him to laugh. To his credit, he didn't.

"Could have fooled me." The hint of a five o'clock shadow framed his jawline. His bottom lip was slightly larger than his top, seashell pink and smooth. Puffy. Pouty. Like lip pillows. *Stop looking at his lips.*

"Oh yeah, Mr. Expert," I said. "How many girls have *you* kissed?"

"On stage or in real life?"

Was there no limit to my embarrassment?

"More than one and less than a hundred," he said.

HONNNNNNNNNNNNNNNNNNNNNNNNNNNNNNNNKK.

A semi-truck loaded with cattle thundered by in the opposite direction, blasting its horn. Wind shear rocked the cab. I gripped the passenger door handle and waited for Ryan to start the truck—move us somewhere less life-threatening—but he was lost in thought.

"Four girls that mattered," he said. "The rest don't count. Any more questions?"

Tons. *What on earth are we doing here? Why don't you move this truck out of the passing lane of the next freight train?* More importantly. *Do you like me? Do you like your girlfriend? Is it serious? Did our kiss count? Is that an actual gun rack?*

I chewed the nail on my pinkie. "Yeah, I have a question," I said, looking out the passenger window. Beyond my reflection, Mr. Albright's property stretched to the horizon, rolling like a golden quilt. The cattle gathered under solitary oaks, peaceful and still in the twilight. Tired, I supposed, from trying to kill me. "How are people not afraid of cows? They're, like, a billion pounds."

"You remind me of my half-sister Kara."

Great. At least I knew the answer to a few questions.

"She's terrified of cows, too," Ryan continued. "You should have seen her the last time she visited. She wouldn't walk outside. She'd just stand on the porch taking selfies with the cows in the background, hashtag 'HelpMe.' Cows aren't anything to be afraid of, you know. They have dinosaur-sized brains."

"Comforting. Ever seen a T-Rex?" I asked.

"No, and I've never seen a cow with foot-long teeth. I know what you mean, though. They can be intimidating when you're not used to them."

"And when they're stampeding towards you."

"That, too. You know how to stop a bull from charging?"

"You take away his credit card. Got anything more original?" I asked.

"Not really. I do best when someone else writes the lines."

"Ha," I said, not a laugh or an affirmation, just a small noise.

"Have you done a lot of acting?" he asked.

"No way. I'm terrified of being onstage." The thought of it sent adrenaline rushing like a river through my veins, the retract of blood pooling in my heart.

"Could have fooled me."

"Twice in one day."

The cab grew dim, backlit by the setting sun. Dusk settled, the early dark of almost-winter. I'd been gone for almost two hours. Monica would be worried.

"You should take me home," I said.

"Yeah." He flipped off the hazards and fiddled with the gearshift, but kept the engine off. Would he kiss me? Here, in this truck? Not because it was written in a script, but because he wanted to?

"I know what we should do," he said. He leaned closer. Dried sweat and aftershave mixed with the mustiness of the old truck, mildewed hay, and dust on the dashboard. Plus a whiff of cow manure from my shoes.

"Yeah?" I asked, almost a whisper. I crossed my legs, tucking my hands under my knees. The vinyl of the truck seat squeaked.

"Meet me at midnight tonight at the old oak," Ryan said. The gleam in his eye was more Mercutio than Romeo.

"What? Why?" I asked.

"A little aversion therapy. I saw it on Doctor Phil."

That broke the tension. "You watch Dr. Phil?" I asked in mock horror.

"Don't change the subject," he said, jabbing me in the ribs, a sensation I would have found otherwise unpleasant had the jabber's fingers not been connected to a rock-solid ridge of forearm muscle, smooth and tan. Bulging biceps peaked from out of a white—

"I'm going to help you get over your fear," he said.

"What, about kissing?"

Oh. My. *God.*

"You're afraid of kissing?" he asked, and this time he laughed, loud and long.

I sighed.

"No, *cows*," Ryan said, as if it were obvious. "Really, you shouldn't be afraid of something lower than you on the food chain."

"Yeah, well. I'm a vegetarian."

"Whatever. You're not listening. Meet me at midnight tonight at the old oak. You know, the one we just passed." I turned around. The split tree looked like the grim reaper in the fading light, the lowered branches a sickle scraping the ground.

"How am I supposed to meet you?" I asked.

"You sneak out."

"I can't *do* that," I said, bewildered.

"Why not?" he asked.

"Monica would be upset."

"Not if she doesn't know."

"*You have a girlfriend*." Duh.

"She doesn't have to know either. Listen, I'm taking you cow tipping, not to a motel, *Alexandra*," he grinned, both dimples on full display.

Erase mental picture. Breathe. Focus on the most logical follow-up question. "Cow *what*?"

"Cow tipping. You wait for a cow to fall asleep, then sneak up and knock it over. It doesn't hurt them. It's just funny. What do you say? If it makes you feel better, I won't hold your hand. Then it can't be a date. You chicken?" Ryan teased.

"No, just a bit cowed."

"Ha, ha. Great. Midnight it is."

Chapter 9

Perchance she cannot meet him

The plan was set. Once Monica was asleep, I'd climb out my window, duck around the opposite side of the house, go out the side gate, and walk the half mile to the old oak to meet Ryan. I told him it was crazy; it would never work. He said he had tons of experience in this sort of thing, and that "nothing could be easier."

Easy-peasy, lemon squeezy.

I showered at ten-thirty. In a bathroom drawer, I found a Ziploc baggie of old Mary Kay cosmetics, which I stashed in the pocket of Monica's terrycloth robe. I wrapped a peach towel around my head, and found my foster mom sitting in the living room, a novel on her lap. "Bathroom's yours," I said, grabbing my backpack.

"More homework?" she asked.

I'd spent all evening at the kitchen table doing homework: chapter eight in *Employment, Labor, and Wages* for Econ; a test-prep packet on European rivers for AP Geography; a PowerPoint on Adolescent Development for Psych. While I waited an hour and fifteen minutes for the presentation to download, I skimmed the first six chapters of *Brave New World* for AP English. I still had a three-page problem set for Chemistry.

"Yeah. It's *my* first day, not everyone else's. I'll keep my door closed when you go to sleep, so the light won't bother you." Monica normally went to bed at eleven, taking Bonnie and Clyde with her. Plenty of time to make it to the oak tree to meet Ryan at midnight.

"Well, don't work too hard. You need your sleep." She adjusted her book light. "Let me know if the TV gets too loud."

"TV?" I asked. Monica read in the evenings. The only TV she watched was her afternoon talk show.

"Ellen's on *The Tonight Show*. I thought I'd stay up. She's so funny."

"Oh," I said, turning back to my room.

"Alex?"

"Yeah?"

"That's a dog towel. I keep them in the lower cupboard. Ours are in the top. I'm sorry I didn't tell you."

"That's okay." I shut my bedroom door and ripped the towel from my head, raking my scalp for good measure. My hair was already drying in random cowlicks. Fleas, dog dander, rooster peaks, what did it matter? Monica would be up past midnight watching that stupid show. I couldn't sneak out before she went to bed, and I had no way of telling Ryan plans had changed.

It was a dumb idea anyway. What kind of idiot sneaks out in the middle of the night—a *school* night—to go cow-tipping with a guy who has a girlfriend?

Right.

I plopped my Chemistry book on the vanity. I could finish the problem set tomorrow during lunch, but I was too keyed up to sleep. Might as well get it over with.

An hour later, I had the first page done. Only two more sheets to go.

From the reaction: $B_2H_6 + O_2 \rightarrow HBO_2 + H_2O$

My head pounded. The writing callus on my middle finger throbbed. I flexed my hand, frozen in the shape of a claw. The remainder of the problem set stared back at me like an animate thing.

What mass of O_2 will be needed to burn 36.1 g of B_2H_6?

It was all so pointless. When was I going to need this?

Defiance rose like hydrogen bubbles in a test tube, just before the gas ignites. Forget Aldous Huxley, this was *my* Brave New World. I crushed all three pages into a ball, strode to the window, flipped the metal latch, and lifted the frame. A rush of cold December air billowed the lace curtains. A warning or an invitation?

I chucked my homework, a comet across the sky. It disappeared just beyond the fence, breakfast for Presley.

Sorry, Teach, the cow ate my homework.

I stood for a moment, shivering, and not just because of the cold.

That felt good.

Yep.

Really good.

Now what?

I flopped on my bed. The ceiling fan spun on its lowest setting, a slow-motion tilt-a-whirl of shadow and light. I swaddled myself in the pink and green comforter. After a couple minutes breathing my own carbon dioxide, I jumped up, claustrophobic, mind unable to focus on anything except the magnitude of what I'd just done.

I returned to the vanity, chemistry book open, binder unsnapped, homework missing. My first zero in a grade book. No big deal, right?

Just one step closer to my mother, who never graduated from high school.

Pregnant at seventeen, the reason she dropped out. The reason she died.

My life for hers.

I'd get the worksheet back. Finish the problem set. Flatten out the creases between *World Geography* and *Employment, Labor, and Wages.* My bedroom door creaked as I poked my head out, listening for Monica.

"Need anything?" she asked, standing in the hallway next to the bathroom.

I jumped. "No, I'm good."

"Good. I'm just letting the dogs out. Ellen was really funny."

"Cool."

"You need to get to sleep."

"I know. Goodnight." I ducked back into my room.

The LED display on my alarm clock flashed 12:34. I'd wait for Monica to go to bed, climb out the window, and get my homework.

In the dark.

Past the barbed wire.

In a field full of cow pies.

I snapped my binder shut. Out in the yard, Bonnie began to bark. A someone-is-here sort of bark. I flew to the window, scanning the pale, empty shadows.

Three seconds later, a putrid smell hit me full in the face. The stench was a solid thing, heavier than air, with a thickness that coated the back of my throat, like rotten eggs, but worse. My eyes watered as I gagged.

Bonnie continued to howl, while Clyde joined the frenzy, snarling and snapping at the fence line. Monica appeared, running in her fuzzy slippers. "What on earth are you doing, dogs? CHEESE AND CRACKERS! Get inside! Now! Clyde, come! Bonnie, NOW!" She grabbed both dogs by the scruff of their necks and dragged them towards the sliding glass door.

"What's going on?" I pulled the terrycloth collar of my robe high above my nose. "What is that *smell*?"

"A skunk," called Monica.

"You're kidding!"

"Nope. Nothing like fresh skunk spray. It'll put hair on your chest."

"I'll keep that in mind." I fanned my hand. "The smell's all in my room."

"The breeze will take care of it. At least it didn't get the dogs. I'm fresh out of baking soda."

"What?"

"Baking soda, dish soap, and hydrogen peroxide. Secret recipe for getting rid of skunk spray on dogs. People use tomato juice, but it doesn't kill the smell. You just end up with a skunk-dog pizza."

"Nice."

Monica laughed. "I'll turn the heater up. Cycle the air. Maybe close the window in a couple minutes. It's already below freezing. Poor skunk is probably a popsicle."

"A skunk-dog popsicle pizza, huh? If I have strange dreams tonight, I'll know who to blame."

She smiled. "Good night."

"Good night."

I waited at the window, watching her go.

Well, waiting and watching to see if anyone else showed up.

Nope.

Stupid, stupid.

Who did I think I was? Juliet?

The truth is, I didn't know *who* I was anymore. I was so used to *things* changing—cities, schools, family—but not *me*. The person who chucked her homework was someone different, a chemical transformation wrought by what? Ryan? Monica? Memories of my mother? My mind reeled with problem sets, skunks, and comets.

Maybe I was just tired.

I slipped off my robe and stood in the moonlight, icy air bracing my skin. It felt good. Clean. Cold, but in an invigorating way, like the first shock of jumping into a swimming pool.

I pulled on my flannel pajama bottoms and white tank. Packed my binder and chemistry book into my backpack. Hung up my robe. I'd forgotten about the makeup bag tucked into one of the pockets.

I retrieved the dusty Ziploc and scrutinized the ancient blue eye shadow, dried concealer and baby-pink blush. The lipstick was a vampy red, a shade I couldn't imagine on Monica. Perhaps she led a secret life, slipped in between book club and Costco. The thought cheered me in a way I couldn't name. An alternate reality.

I applied the lipstick and kissed my hand, lingering over the sensation, soft lips on skin. The imprint was dark as blood, a token of my disembodied self.

"Red's not really your color, you know." The smell of skunk was stronger as Ryan stuck his head through the open window.

Chapter 10
O, wilt thou leave me so unsatisfied?

"What are you doing here?" I mouthed.

"Oh, you know. Trespassing in the dark. Attacked by a dog, sprayed by a skunk. The usual…What do you think I'm doing here? Why didn't you meet me? Cold feet? Cow got your tongue?"

"No. I couldn't sneak out. Monica's still *awake*," I emphasized.

"You said she goes to bed at eleven. What, does she have Spidey sense or something?"

"Probably. Did you know you're not wearing a shirt?"

He pushed up the window, allowing for an unobstructed view of his torso. Gooseflesh dimpled his bare chest, smooth but for a few dark, curling hairs circling each nipple, frozen to attention. I gulped and met his eyes, wondering if pupils could blush.

"I always walk around naked when it's 28 degrees," he said. "Yes, I know I'm not wearing a shirt. Do you mind if I come inside?"

"Yes!"

"It's below freezing out here."

"Where's your shirt?"

"Buried in the bushes with my jacket. It got most of the spray. My favorite Hollister, too. Luckily the skunk didn't get my face. How bad do I smell?"

I leaned forward and took a whiff: skunk, wood smoke, and grass. Male. He smelled very, very male.

Tap-tap, tap-tap-tap.

My heart cartwheeled to my throat at the knock on my bedroom door.

"Alex, did you need something?" Monica asked through the door. "I thought I heard you talking."

I flew across the room and wedged my foot against the bottom of the door. "I'm fine. I was practicing a monologue for Drama class."

"I thought you were going to bed. You need your sleep."

"I am. I just thought I'd practice one more time."

"Wait. You're taking Drama?" she asked, surprised. "I thought you had Art."

"There was a mix-up on my schedule. I'm getting it fixed tomorrow."

"Then why are you doing homework for a class you don't have?"

"In case I can't get it changed."

"Can I come in?" Ryan whispered from the window.

"No!" I hissed.

His teeth chattered. "I can't f-feel my hands."

"Stick them in your armpits."

"I can't f-feel my armpits!"

The door opened an inch. I jammed my foot harder, slamming it shut. "Sorry, Monica. I'm just changing into my pajamas." Another lie.

"Okay, well, all kidding aside, you need to get to bed. I read that kids nowadays are getting an hour less sleep than they did 30 years ago, which is linked to all kinds of problems, like obesity and ADHD—"

"Thanks, Monica," I called. "I get it. I'm going to bed now."

"Sorry."

"No problem."

"Hey," she said. "Do you mind if I come in for a second?"

Ryan had one leg through the window, straddling the frame.

"No!" I cried.

"Good," said Monica. The doorknob turned.

"Yes!" I shouted. "I do mind!"

Ryan smiled and put his finger to his lips. *Cheese and crackers, I'm having a conversation with my foster mother while there's a half-naked guy in my room.* I blinked. Yep, there he was.

"Monica," I said, voice calm as silk. "I'm sorry. I'm really tired. It's been a big day, and I just want to go to bed. Can we talk in the morning?"

"Sure, no problem," she said. "If you don't want to talk."

"Monica."

"It's no big deal if you don't want to."

"*Monica.*"

"Right. Goodnight, Alex." Monica padded down the hall, closing her bedroom door.

Ryan grinned.

"Are you crazy or just plain stupid?" I demanded. Quietly, of course.

"Neither. Maybe both."

"She could've caught us. You. What were you thinking?"

"I was thinking frostbite was about to claim one of my extremities."

"Well, you can afford to lose a few."

"All but one."

Speechless.

I blew through my lips. "Why are you here?" I asked lamely.

"To tell you, 'Never mind.'"

"What?"

"To forget about the cow-tipping."

I was right. The whole thing was a mistake. And probably animal cruelty.

Ryan ducked his head, having the decency to look ashamed. "And then, I saw you in the window. It was obvious you weren't planning on coming, and I wanted to know why. I don't get stood up often." He kept his tone light, but there was the ring of truth. "So, did you change your mind or something?"

"What does it matter?" I asked. "You obviously changed *yours*."

"I never said that."

"What are you talking about? Why else are you here?"

"I didn't want you to get in trouble over nothing."

Nothing. It was nothing, and I'm an idiot.

"Let me get this straight," I said. "You were out there in the field, just... spying?" A horrifying thought occurred to me. "How long were you out there?" Overwhelmed by almost being caught by my foster mother, I'd failed to comprehend the vast, potential humiliations this scenario implied, including, but not limited to, Ryan observing me naked in front of an open window, making out with my own hand.

"You need to leave," I said.

"Wherefore?" he smiled.

Freaking *Romeo and Juliet.* The galactic mortification of kissing him in Drama that afternoon.

"Just stop it," I fumed. "Number one: you shouldn't be here. Number two: you have a girlfriend. And number three: I get that I'm one big joke to you, but it's not funny."

"Are you always this dense?" Ryan asked.

"What?"

"You're right. It's *not* funny. Yes, Shayna is my 'girlfriend.' We hooked up because of the play. Not that I objected. She may be shallow, but she *is* kind of hot."

"Nice."

"I'm an idiot, okay? I mean, how cliché can you get? It doesn't matter that I can't stand her. I'm Romeo, she's Juliet, and if I dump her, the play's ruined. In two weeks' time, she can hate my guts, but for now, I'm stuck." He got quieter. The tip of his nose was red to match his lips, blistered from the cold. "I like *you,* okay? Don't let it get around."

I chewed the cuticle on my thumb. "You don't know anything about me."

"I know plenty. You just moved to town. You bite your nails when you're nervous. You like cheese and pickles."

I rubbed the bridge of my nose.

"And you're beautiful."

A nerve in my right cheek twitched. "Yeah, right. Where's the hidden camera?"

"I'm not kidding."

"Shayna's the one who's *hot*." I thought I imitated him pretty well.

"Would you stop that? Shayna's pretty, but she's phony. Don't be jealous."

"Who said I was jealous?"

I was, though, just not in the obvious way. Shayna possessed something indefinable, a confidence I'd never have. She was Juliet. I was no one.

I sat on the far edge of my bed, and looked at Ryan, studied him like he was a painting. He was so handsome, it was unreal. And he liked *me*? That, too, did not fall under the scope of things that happened in my reality. Who was I? What was this? Love?

"What was I saying?" I asked.

"I don't know."

"I don't either."

"I'll stay till you remember." He sat next to me. On the bed.

To say I had butterflies would be imprecise. These were fireflies, sparks swarming, arterial conduits glowing, stomach, heart, lungs. It burned to breathe. "I don't know what I'm supposed to say."

He nudged my shoulder. "You don't like compliments, do you?"

"What do you mean?"

"When I said you were beautiful—"

"I'm not," I said. "I'm plain, I'm awkward, and tonight I dried my hair with a dog towel." I held up the peach towel as Exhibit A.

"You're real. Everyone else I know is fake. You're also an amazing actress, even if you don't believe that."

I rolled my eyes. "Okay, now I know you're lying."

"I'm not. Didn't you *feel* that onstage today?"

"Yes," I said. The lights. The kiss. The losing myself. "But I wasn't acting."

"Neither was I. That was real. It's why I'm here." He slid closer. The iron rosettes of the bedpost dug into my back. Was this happening? I needed time to think.

"The skunk," I said, putting my hand on his chest. His bare chest. I felt the ridge of muscle under my hand, cool granite, but warming to the touch. This did not have the intended effect.

"What about it?" He pushed the bangs out of my eyes, let his hand slide to my cheek. Leaned in. "Do I stink that bad?"

"No. Maybe a little." The fireflies disappeared, replaced by pure electric current. I was a live wire, severed by a storm. Too fast, too fast, not fast enough. Stop. "I know how to get rid of the smell."

"Tomato juice, right?" His breath tickled my cheek.

"No," I said. "Baking soda, hydrogen peroxide, and dish soap. What kind of a country boy are you?"

"I'm from L.A. I moved here four months ago."

"Alex!" Monica was outside my door again. I bolted from the bed. "Yes?"

"Your light's still on."

"Sorry. I'm turning it off now. Goodnight, Monica." I flipped the switch, casting the room in shadow. I waited for the cataclysm in my heart to still, then crossed to the window. Trees and fence posts stood like sentries washed with silver. The moon dominated the starless sky with a brilliance I'd never seen in the city. There, street lamps and neon signs dimmed the reflected light of the sun, an artificial eclipse.

Ryan moved behind me. I felt his presence like a lunar tide.

"You need to go," I said.

"What's the matter?"

"We have school tomorrow."

"Today."

"You have a girlfriend."

"A pretend one."

I turned to face him. "Does she think so?"

•65•

He said nothing. His eyes were a luminescent green, like jewels in a pirate's chest.

"Good night," I whispered.

"Parting is such sweet sorrow?"

I punched him in the shoulder. Hard. We both laughed.

And then we stopped laughing.

"Don't you like me?" he asked.

"Go," I pleaded.

He hesitated a fraction of a second, then climbed out the open window.

"Wait," I said. "It's freezing." I tore the green-and-pink coverlet off my bed, stuck my head out the window, and wrapped the blanket around his shoulders. "I did have one question."

"To be or not to be?"

"If you quote Shakespeare one more time, I'll scream."

"Then Monica would hear, and we'd have to get married."

I ignored this. "You said earlier you didn't want to meet."

"To go *cow-tipping*. I'd never done it before, so I googled it. Turns out, it's an urban legend. Cows don't actually tip. That only happens in the movies."

Chapter 11
Dreamers often lie

Four hours of sleep.

I dressed in non-descript New Girl Outfit #2, black jeans, white T, and a grey sweater. Monica was already awake, sitting at the kitchen table with a cup of coffee.

"You're up early," I said, pouring Cheerios in a bowl.

"No rest for the wicked."

"Ha," I said, my fake laugh shortened by an attack of conscience. Monica trusted me. I'd violated that trust by lying and sneaking around with Ryan.

Not that anything happened. Right. Nothing happened.

Monica smiled. "Plus, I can't leave a good romance unfinished."

"What?"

"I think you spilled some of your Cheerios."

"Oh, yeah." I dumped the excess back into the box, and brushed the ones on the counter into the compost.

"I stayed up last night finishing my book club book."

"Oh," I breathed. I opened the fridge for some milk. "You know, lack of sleep can lead to obesity and ADHD," I teased.

"You're right," she yawned. "We're both guilty."

I nodded.

"Oh, and your sneakers are still damp."

We'd used the spray hose on my Converse last night, to get the cow manure out of the treads. "You want to throw them in the drier?"

"Nah. I don't want to wreck the rubber." The decade-old soles had begun to crack. "Do you have a pair of shoes I could borrow?"

"Um, sure. Check the hall closet. You're an eight?"

"Seven and a half."

"Go for my Doc Martens. They're a little tight on me. They should fit you fine."

Under a pile of shoes, I found them, dog hair and sawdust in the laces. "Are these steel-toe?" I asked, holding up the heavy, black leather boots. The rubber sole was an inch thick. "Tuff."

"Tough?"

I put the boots down and went back to the kitchen. "It means, you know, 'cool.'"

"Oh, like 'groovy.' You can wear them when you help me cut firewood."

"With an axe?" I asked, pouring the milk into my cereal. "Are you kidding me?"

"No," she smiled. "We'll use a chainsaw."

"A *chainsaw*?"

"Yep. Axes are for splitting. Chainsaws are for cutting. I'll teach you to do both."

I laughed.

"What's so funny?" she asked.

Monica was definitely a First Time Foster Parent. I assumed my case worker Heather had gone over the rules with her: water temperature set to safe levels, laundry detergent secured, knives locked up. Perhaps she forgot to cover chainsaws.

"Never mind," I said, crunching Cheerios. "Groovy."

***

I got to school ten minutes before the first bell, my boots making satisfying clunks on the office linoleum. The blinds were drawn in Ms. Carmichael's window.

I approached the attendance secretary's desk. "Is the counselor in?" I asked Bob.

She nodded while talking on the phone. "Yes, Mrs. Robertson," Bob said, anchoring her headpiece with her shoulder. "Jonah was not in 3rd period yesterday... I spoke with his teacher. She confirmed he was absent." She took a nail file from a cup holder

FINDING JULIET

and scratched under her arm. "I don't know where he was. That's why I'm calling... Right now, it's recorded as a 'cut.' The counselor is with him now... No, I'd rather not interrupt..."

Bob motioned me to a row of cubbies facing the wall. I sat between a boy in a death metal T-shirt and a girl doodling lightning bolts on her jeans with a black sharpie. Motivational signs plastered the cubby walls: *'It's never too late to be what you might have been.' 'You can't have a better tomorrow if you're still thinking about yesterday.'* And the classic kitten-dangling-from-a-tree-branch poster, reminding everyone to *'Hang in There.'* I set my backpack on the sticky desk, where someone had graffitied "Shcool SUX." Their illiteracy etched for the eyes of all posterity, as Ms. Lanyer might say.

The four hours' sleep had taken its toll. I rested my head on my backpack, the mechanical pencils in the front pocket poking my temple. I closed my eyes, dozing to the tinny sound of screamo coming from metal boy's earbuds.

"Long night, huh? Whatcha in for?"

I jerked awake.

Jamie, the girl from Drama, stood clutching a pink office call slip.

"What?" I asked.

"Yesterday was your first day, right? How'd you end up in In-House?" she asked, peering at me through her glasses. The large, round frames gave her eyes the appearance of looking the wrong way through a set of binoculars.

"I'm not suspended," I said, avoiding the stares of my neighbors. "Just waiting to see the counselor. I need a schedule change," I added.

"You're still going to be in Drama, though, right?"

"No, I don't think so," I said.

Sometime between Cheerios and chainsaws, I'd decided what I already knew.

Last night was a mistake. Ryan had a girlfriend. I was seven months from graduation, six months from my 18th birthday, the same age my

•69•

mother was when she had me. I would not jeopardize my future for a fake Romeo who wasn't even all that good looking.

Really. He wasn't. His lips weren't symmetrical. The lower one was much poutier. And he had a girlfriend. Must keep reminding myself of this fact.

"Is it because of Shayna?" asked Jamie. "You don't have to worry about her. She was upset at first about the kiss, but that's just because she's totally insecure about Ryan. She understands you were acting. It's no big deal."

I scratched my eyebrow. "I know. I got the wrong math class, though. My whole schedule is jacked up."

"Bummer. Well, maybe you can see the play. You wouldn't want to miss me as the apothecary. I have three whole lines." She cleared her throat. "*Such mortal drugs I have; but Mantua's law is death to any he that utters them.* It's pretty awesome."

"Sounds great."

"Where are you from anyways? Did you transfer from Shelton?"

"Shelton?"

"Shelton High? Next county over? Guess not. Where you from, then?"

Before I could answer—what would I have answered?—Bob took off her headset, smoothed her hair, and called to Jamie. "Whatcha got for me?"

Jamie handed her the slip.

"Driving test today, huh? Better clear the sidewalks."

"Very funny, Bob."

The door to Ms. Carmichael's office opened. A tall, sullen boy walked out, shoulders slumped.

Ms. Carmichael stood in the doorway. "Have a good day, Jonah."

He mumbled something unintelligible.

"Alex!" Ms. Carmichael called. "Fabulous! You're just the girl I wanted to see. Come on in." I gathered my stuff and went inside.

Her office smelled of citrus air freshener, candy sweet. I sat in a rolling armchair, the cushion still warm from its previous occupant.

"So, how was your first day?" Ms. Carmichael asked, clicking my profile on her computer. Family pictures covered her desk: two girls on a fishing boat; a senior portrait; Ms. Carmichael, her husband, and their daughters standing in front of the Grand Canyon. I played with the zipper on my backpack.

"Fine, I guess."

"Things going okay with your teachers?" She clicked her mouse, closing the window, then leaned forward, hands clasped.

"Yeah," I said. "Everyone's been real nice."

The phone beeped. Ms. Carmichael picked up the receiver. "I'm in with a student. Tell her I'll call back." She pressed a red button. "That's good," she said to me. "I'm sorry about the mix-up with your schedule."

"That's okay. I just need to get it fixed."

"I know. I'm sorry I didn't get a chance to warn you, but I was in meetings all day yesterday. Your schedule is set. I can't change it."

I pulled the sleeve of my grey sweater. "I don't understand. I'm supposed to be in Calculus. And I signed up for Art. I'm not a Drama person. I can't be in that class."

"I'm really sorry, Alex. Your transcripts came in Wednesday, after we'd already spoken. You need a full year of Pre-Calc."

"I had a semester and a half. I've been moved around a lot. I can keep up, though, if you give me the chance."

"It's not my decision. The math teachers have final approval over prerequisites, and Mr. Cantor wants you in Trig. After he has a chance to evaluate you, we can look into a double math load for Spring."

"Fine," I said, a little too abruptly. "I need out of Drama, though."

"About that. The schedule shift forced you out of 6th period Art. There isn't another 5th period elective besides Spanish I, which you've already had. I'm sorry. I'm sure Ms. Lanyer can find something for you to do that doesn't involve acting. Maybe you could design the poster for the show. She's doing *Romeo and Juliet*, right? I hear the leads are amazing."

There was a light knock on the door. Bob poked her head into the office. "I'm sorry, Ms. Carmichael. Jonah's mom is quite insistent. She needs to speak with you before she leaves for work. It's *vital*," she mimicked.

"Thank you, Bob. We're almost done. Keep her on hold, and I'll pick up in a second."

"Righty-O," said Bob as the door clicked behind her.

The final bell for first period rang. After a screech of feedback over the loudspeakers, a girl with a nasally voice recited the Pledge of Allegiance, then began the morning's other announcements: "It's Playoff season! The Jefferson Jackals take on the Roosevelt Roosters! ARE YOU READY FOR SOME FOOTBALL?!?!"

No, I thought, communicating telepathically to the senior portrait on Ms. Carmichael's desk.

"That's Megan," said Ms. Carmichael. "My baby." Megan looked like her mother, blond hair, brown eyes, the same stubby nose. She wore the standard black V-neck drape all senior girls wear and a single strand of pearls. "She's off to U.C. Santa Barbara. Seems like just yesterday she was five years old, watching Saturday morning cartoons and torturing her sister. It's hard when they grow up."

"Uh-huh."

Ms. Carmichael picked up the portrait, setting it on the shelf behind her desk. She rocked back in her chair. "I'm sorry about your schedule, Alex. I'll see what I can do to get it straightened out for next semester. If you ever want to talk, I'm here. I know you've been through a lot."

I shuffled my boots on the low-pile carpet. For all the sympathetic looks adults gave, the "special concern" masking condescension, I might as well tattoo "Foster Kid" on my forehead. I couldn't be a normal student. No. I was a charity case, to be pitied, helped along. I scratched at the side of my neck, grasping phantom pearls.

"Thank you," I said. The red light on Ms. Carmichael's phone blinked angrily. "I guess I'll let you get that phone call." I pushed myself up by the metal armrests, a shock zapping my fingers. "Ouch!"

"Are you okay?" asked Ms. Carmichael.

"Yeah," I said, shaking my hand. "Just a little static electricity. Must be these boots." I reached for the handle of the office door as it burst open, pinning me behind. Through the flapping blinds, I saw Shayna leaning over Ms. Carmichael's desk.

"Ms. Carmichael!" she cried, eyes puffed shut, cheeks streaked with mascara. "I need a schedule change!"

Chapter 12

That runaways eyes may wink

The chaos of the morning continued as Bob barged in after Shayna, yelling at her to wait outside, while the football team, cheerleading squad, and marching band paraded through the office to the sound of a bass drum. In the confusion, I slipped out, forgoing the late pass in favor of a quick exit.

Jogging towards class, I passed Mr. Albright's truck in the bus lane, motor running. Ryan reached over from behind the steering wheel and cranked down the passenger-side window. "Let's get out of here," he said.

I didn't pause. I yanked the door handle and jumped in, flinging my backpack beside the blanket he'd borrowed last night.

This was bad. I was supposed to be in first period Econ going over chapter eight in *Employment, Labor, and Wages*, not ditching school with a non-symmetrically lipped boy. I also had no idea where we were going.

"Have you ever been to the river?" Ryan asked, answering my unspoken question.

"No," I said, rolling up my window.

"Then I'll be the first to take you."

The windshield defroster blew muggy, warm air. The temperature outside was mild, maybe low 50s, but the air was thick with humidity. I clicked my seatbelt and folded my arms around my sweater, hands damp and sticky against grey wool. We drove through town, past the Quickie-Mart and the Shell station, into an open countryside of grass and old stone fences.

Fifteen minutes outside the city limits, Ryan turned left onto a narrow, unmarked gravel road. The truck lurched from pothole to pothole as a steep drop-off appeared on the passenger side. Far below the edge of the cliff, a river flowed, whitewater churning. Ryan drove slowly for another couple of miles, finally descending to a small parking area. A sign warned against swimming in the current. Beer cans and cigarette butts littered the ground. Ryan got out of the truck without a word, stopping only to pick up the garbage in the spot next to us. Tucking the cigarette butts inside the cans, he tossed everything in the back of his truck, crushed aluminum bouncing off the sides. "What's wrong with people?" he asked, not expecting an answer.

I threw an empty soda bottle in with the rest. It hit hard, but didn't shatter. "I know," I said.

I left my backpack but grabbed Monica's green-and-pink quilt and walked with him down the short, rocky slope. Near the bottom, I caught the toe of my boot on an upturned root. Before I face-planted, Ryan had me by the elbow, holding me steady. "Watch your step. We're almost there."

"There" was a secluded beach sheltered by cottonwood and pine. The river cascaded downstream, rippling waves of copper-green and white foam. Near the shore, the water turned jade, pooling in a calm inlet, suitable for wading. A knotted rope swing hung from a questionable branch (*Hang in There*, I thought). As boulders gave way to sand, I untied my laces and yanked off my boots, giving my socks a discrete sniff before tucking them into a ball.

I wiggled my toes, nails painted a glossy orange-red. Monica had taken me for a forty-dollar pedicure after the bargain-basement haircut. Too little, too late, but at least my feet were pretty.

"Nasty," Ryan said, pointing to a developing blister on my big toe.

"They're not my boots." I rolled my jeans and walked to the shore, the sand cool.

Ryan settled on the blanket, shoes on, resting his head on a bent knee, looking like a moody male model.

I dipped an orange-tipped toe in the freezing river.

"Cold, huh?" he asked.

"Glacial."

"Well, we'll save the skinny-dipping for another day," he joked, his face grim.

I held my breath.

"I dumped her," he said, after a moment.

"I guessed." I didn't mention I'd seen Shayna, eyes swollen from crying.

"She doesn't know about you," Ryan said. "Not that there's anything to tell."

I couldn't argue with that.

"I'm sorry," I said. I meant it.

"I'm not."

"No?"

"I feel bad I hurt her. But mostly, I'm just relieved," he confessed.

"What about the play?" I asked.

"I don't know."

I sat next to him, careful to keep my sandy feet off the quilt.

"I can't stay here anymore," Ryan sighed. He stood, leaned down to pick up a rock, and flung it into the river. Ripples radiated from the center, disappearing into the greater flow. The rope swing danced in the breeze like a hangman's noose.

"We can go back to school," I said, hiding the disappointment in my voice. I knew skipping was wrong. I knew I could be caught, but I'd come too far. Blood flowed through my veins like the river, and I felt more alive than I'd ever been. Something had compelled me to jump into Ryan's truck, and I wanted to find out what that was before returning to my regular life. Was it Ryan? Or was it something else?

"Not here. *Here.* This town."

"Why are you living with your grandfather?" I asked.

"It's a long story."

"I have time. Even if I didn't, you're my ride," I teased.

"I forgot. I'm sorry I got you into this mess. You should be at school."

"Eh. It's only my education," I said, leaning back, hands under my head in a show of exaggerated defiance.

Ryan smiled, like sunlight through the clouds. Above, a red-tailed hawk soared, black against the sky. Held aloft by unseen currents, it climbed and dipped, wings unmoving.

"I got in trouble at home," he confided.

"I figured as much."

"Girl trouble. Her name was Rosa. Our cook's daughter."

"You had a cook? Like, a servant?"

"She wasn't a *slave*. She just took care of our meals. My stepdad's kind of a big deal in L.A. He's an agent. Has some famous clients and stuff."

"Like who?"

"Not important," he said, agitated. "You see? That's why I never talk about it. All anyone wants to know is about *him*. Do you know what that's like? For people to never see *you*, just some sign on your forehead? *'Hi. I'm Jimmy Rutherford's stepson.'*"

"Yeah," I said. "I do."

"Anyways. Rosa helped her mom in the afternoons. She wasn't allowed to talk to me, except to translate. Anita couldn't speak English, so Rosa'd mess around, saying weird stuff like, *'My mom wants to know where you keep your anaconda.'*"

"Nice."

"It was just a joke," he said, defensive. "One day, in the basement laundry, I told her I loved her, in Spanish."

"What did she say?"

"She laughed and called me 'gringo,' because I said *me amo* instead of *te amo*. Three years of Spanish, and I still can't conjugate a verb." Ryan sat up, restless. "We lasted a month. She broke up with me. For a week after, I wanted to kill myself. Then Anita quit. I didn't think anything of it, but my mom was upset. God forbid she'd have to cook a meal in between her charity benefits. She hounded Anita until she got the whole story. Rosa told her mom about us."

He hurled another stone into the river. This one skipped, one, two, three times, then sank to the bottom.

The hawk screeched.

"My stepdad *freaked*," Ryan said, waving his hands in parodied anger. "He imagined a Schwarzenegger-style scandal. You remember when Arnold had an affair with the maid? Fifteen years later or whenever, some kid shows up looking like the Terminator. *I'll be back.*"

A sparrow joined the hawk in a hostile dance, perhaps protecting a nest. The smaller bird dive-bombed the predator, rising and circling, tossed in the turbulent air. "So my mom sent me to my grandpa," Ryan finished. "To *'provide the discipline I lacked.'* She has two kids with Jimmy. I get in the way of their perfect family."

Torn between feelings of rejection and plain-old morbid curiosity, I had to ask. "So, was Rosa...?"

"I don't know." Ryan sounded ill. "She never told me. I don't know where she is or how to reach her. She might be in Mexico. I don't know *anything*."

"How old was she?"

"Fourteen."

"Isn't that kind of young?"

"Juliet was fourteen when she got married."

"Thirteen," I corrected. "But we're not in the Stone Ages anymore."

"Elizabethan."

"Same difference," I countered.

"Not really."

"And it's a *play*."

Ryan stood up, annoyed. "I shouldn't be telling you this. There's no way you could understand something you haven't experienced."

"Isn't that what actors do?" I taunted, deflecting the low blow.

"This isn't a joke."

"I know. It's a tragedy." I went to him, still as marble at the water's edge, square jaw set in misery. "I'm sorry. Really, no, I am."

He met my gaze, unblinking.

"Do you still love her?" I asked.

His eyes were like the river, green and swirling.

"No. I don't know if I *ever* loved her," he said, voice tinged with regret. "It was just one of those things. Life or death while you're in the middle of it, but gone in the time it takes to say *'te amo.'*" Ryan filled his lungs. "She's a good person. I just hope she's okay." He returned to the blanket, flopping on his stomach, head pressed against his hands.

I sat beside him, bumping his arm with my hip. "So, what do you want to do?"

"I don't know," he said, flipping on his back. "I can't stay in this town much longer. It's like purgatory. Did you ever feel like there was so much inside you, you might explode?"

"All the time."

Ryan continued, lost in thought. "Part of me wishes I could live with my dad. My *real* dad. I don't think that's going to happen, though. Besides, he *really* lives in the middle of nowhere. You think this place is bad, try freaking Podunk, Canada."

"Canada?"

"Yep. He hated me so much he moved to another country. Oh, sorry. What I mean is he relocated for his *job*. Whatever." Ryan sat up. "No, I need to get back to L.A. If I grovel enough, my stepdad will let me come home. I want to be a professional actor. He could help me. I'd like to think he owes me *something* for the past fourteen years."

"You'd make a great actor," I said.

"I think so, too," he said, unabashed. "I know that sounds conceited, but I honestly believe I could do it. Go big time, you know?"

"I know." It was nice to have the old Ryan back, cheeky and grinning. "So, what's your stage name going to be?"

He ducked his head.

"Come on, I know you've thought of it. Would you use 'Ryan Rutherford' or 'Ryan Albright'?" I swiped my hand against the sky, picturing the marquee.

"Those aren't my last names," he said.

"Oops. I guess I should have asked."

"That's okay. I don't know *your* last name."

"Riddle," I said.

"Okay."

"Okay, what?"

"*Riddle me this, Batman,*" he said, impersonating Heath Ledger. I fake-cowered as he laughed.

"That's my name," I said. "Alex Riddle."

"No, seriously? Like 'He-Who-Must-Not-Be-Named'?" asked Ryan. If I had a nickel. *Harry Potter* was huge in my sixth-grade year. When it was discovered that the Dark Lord and I shared a surname, middle school hilarity ensued for everyone but me.

"Yes, but I am pretty sure I am *not* the love-child of Lord Voldemort."

"Positive?"

"Yeah. I don't even know who my dad is." The sudden admission brought me up short, left me feeling ashamed, like I'd admitted to a history of bedwetting. I quickly recovered, adding, "But it wasn't Voldemort."

"Well, Alex Riddle," said Ryan.

"Well, Ryan Somebody."

"Edwards. My last name is Edwards. After my dad. My *real* dad."

"Well, that should be your stage name, then. 'Ryan Edwards.' It suits you."

"You think so?" he asked. "I was going to use my middle name, but maybe you're right. I could just be myself. I'll have to change my Twitter handle." The twin dimples deepened.

"You're on Twitter?"

"Yeah. It's stupid. You?"

"Yeah, but just so I can follow Jennifer Lawrence. Which is even more stupid."

"Why?"

"I don't know. I just kind of like her."

"She's the one in the *Hunger Games* movies, right? I think my stepdad might have represented her at one point."

"*Really?*"

"Yeah. Aren't you glad you know me now?"

"No," I said.

"No?"

"I was glad I knew you before."

A single drop of rain landed on my cheek. The birds were gone. We were alone, not even a chattering squirrel.

"So what's *your* story?" Ryan asked, brushing the raindrop from my cheek. "I already told you all my deep, dark secrets. *Quid pro quo, Clarice.* Are you related to Monica?"

"No, and I don't like fava beans, either."

"Way to rock 90s movie trivia."

"One of my foster moms was a professor. She used *Silence of the Lambs* in her women's studies class. *I* probably wouldn't have let me see a movie about a sadistic serial killer at 14, but Debbie was pretty laid-back."

"You're kidding."

"No, I had nightmares for weeks."

"No, I mean, you're a foster kid? Like *Oliver Twist* or something? *Please sir, can I have some more?*" Ryan's English accent was almost as bad as mine.

"They don't do orphanages anymore, you doof. Well, they have group homes. Kinda like camp for juvies. I'll tell you about it sometime over a bowl of green Jell-O. On second thought, maybe not."

Ryan rubbed his nose with his thumb. "Well, I'm a jerk. Here I am feeling sorry for myself. I never stopped to think you might have it worse."

"That's funny. I thought the same about you," I grinned.

A dark lock fell across his forehead. "I'm sorry if I came on strong last night."

"It's okay."

"No, it's not. I just... I don't know what it is about you. When we were onstage yesterday, I felt something I hadn't in a long time. And then I made a fool out of myself—"

"You didn't," I insisted.

"You kept asking me to leave."

"Only because I was afraid of what I might do."

A second raindrop landed on my knee.

"Are you afraid now?" he asked.

"Yes."

His eyes smiled. "Good."

The word was a pebble tossed in the space between us, a ripple in the air. The breeze picked up, lifting a corner of the quilt. More drops of rain.

"I guess we should head out," Ryan said.

I nodded.

"I'm starving. How about you?"

I nodded again.

"We'll hit a drive-through on the way back to school. Don't worry. We'll make up some excuse. Bob loves me."

"What about you?" I asked.

"I love me, too." He dodged my imaginary punch. "Just kidding. I'm eighteen. I can sign myself out." Ryan folded the quilt as I dusted sand from my feet and wedged them back in my boots, wincing from the blister on my big toe.

Ryan took my hand without asking. The little hairs on the back of his hand tickled my fingertips, his palm soft. "Thanks for coming with me this morning." He smiled as he tucked the blanket under his other arm. "I like talking to you."

"I like talking to you, too."

We rounded the curve at the top of the hill, the quiet of nature giving way to the sounds of laughter and rap music blasting. A rusted camper van sat next to Ryan's truck, its rear doors swung open to reveal a party bus crammed with teenagers drinking beer and wine coolers.

"Hey, Ryan!" called one of the boys. His haystack hair reminded me of Shaggy from Scooby Doo. "Nice weather we're having, huh?"

"Yep," said Ryan, picking up an empty beer can and throwing it into the back of his truck. "Will you guys please clean up after yourselves? You're trashin' the place."

Shaggy responded with an enormous belch.

"Stay classy, Renfroe," Ryan said.

"Always. Who's your lady-friend? She know you got a girl?"

"MYOB dude."

"Got it. Keep it on the down low." He reached for another beer between the legs of two squealing girls.

Ryan shook his head and muttered, "Good time to leave. These idiots can get pretty stupid."

"You don't say."

Ryan opened the passenger-side door of the truck. "Your carriage awaits," he bowed.

"Why thank you, sir," I said, as a police cruiser pulled into the parking lot.

Chapter 13
What the law should end

Officer Jacobson sat across from me drinking burnt coffee. He was a burly man in his forties, with a standard buzz cut and a uniform half a size too small. He made periodic attempts at small talk as we waited for my case worker Heather to return one of the three voicemails I left on her cell. He wouldn't let me call Monica, although he let her know where I was. Apparently, she'd phoned hours earlier, frantic when the school reported my absence.

"Rain's picking up," he said, handing me a cup of cold tap water. The middle button of his shirt strained against the fabric.

"Uh-huh."

"Might even snow."

I sipped my water, teeth scraping against the Styrofoam.

"We need it. It's been a bad year for the drought."

"Huh." The clock on the lime-green wall was stuck at 4:08.

"So, tell me again what happened."

"We skipped school. It was a bad idea, but we weren't drinking."

Officer Jacobson leaned back in his chair, cradling his coffee cup. "I see," he said. "You weren't drinking, but you were with a group of kids who *were*, correct?"

"We weren't with them."

"You were just parked next to them?"

"Yes."

"And neither you nor your boyfriend had any idea who they were?"

"Ryan knows them, but he's not—"

"And those weren't beer cans in the back of your truck?" He set his coffee cup down on the table. It had a cartoon picture of a policeman cuffing a criminal, the tag line reading, *I can't fix stupid, but I can arrest it.*

"They were, but they weren't ours."

"Whose were they, then, the Tooth Fairy's?"

"I don't know."

"Well, what were they doing in the back of your truck?"

"We put them there. We were picking up garbage."

"Uh huh. Listen, kid, you think I don't remember being a teenager?" He flipped open a leather notebook, while I tore my Styrofoam cup into one long spiral. "Your boyfriend's eighteen, you know," he said. "He could be charged with contributing to the delinquency of a minor."

"He's not my boyfriend."

A young female officer poked her head into the windowless room. "Excuse me, sir. Alexandra's case worker is on the line."

"About time," Officer Jacobson said. "Will you take Miss Alexandra to the waiting room?"

The policewoman brought me to the front of the station, where Ryan slumped in a corner chair. He sat alert when saw me. "Are you okay?" he asked.

"Yeah." I attempted a smile, but my nerves got the better of me. Did this sort of thing go on your permanent record? The waiting room reeked of disinfectant, just like the Rainbow Canyon Home for Teen Girls. I pictured the rest of my life in places like this: cold, impersonal, institutional. I sat next to him, clasping my hands in my lap as if they were bound by invisible cuffs.

"Listen," Ryan said. "It's going to be fine. They're playing tough, but they'll let us off with a warning. My grandpa's furious." He leaned in, conspiratorial. "It's perfect."

"Why? How?"

"Don't you see? This is my ticket home. I can go back to L.A."

"What do you mean?"

"When I moved in with my grandpa, he said the first time I screwed up, he'd send me back to my mom. You should've heard him on the phone. I'm banished. He's ready to ship me off tonight."

"Tonight?"

Ryan was leaving?

I'd lied to Monica, cut school, been picked up by the police, maybe arrested. All for a boy who was leaving *tonight*?

He grabbed my hand. "You could come with me."

I stared, gape-mouthed.

"Okay, I know this sounds crazy, but hear me out."

A receptionist sat behind a window ten feet away, ignoring us as she typed, but Ryan lowered his voice anyway. "When are you 18?"

"Soon, but—"

"So, what's stopping you? By the time the police or whoever find you, you'll be an adult. I bet they don't even try."

The horrible, wonderful thing is that he was probably right. Who would look for a seventeen-and-a-half-year-old runaway foster kid? I'd be home free. Literally. No more foster homes. No one telling me what to do, where to go, who to call "mom."

Monica.

Ryan's eyes searched my face, tempting me to say 'yes.'

I tasted the word on my tongue.

The door to the station blew open with a gust of wind. Ryan's grandfather strode into the waiting room, rain dripping from his cowboy hat and full-length duster. He gave us a disgusted look, then marched to the receptionist. "I'm Mr. Albright. Here to pick up my grandson."

"Yes, sir," said the woman behind the glass. "I believe you've already spoken to the officer on the phone. I just need you to sign these forms."

"What do you think?" whispered Ryan. "Come with me."

"No. I'm sorry, no." I willed my voice to sound firm. "I can't do that to Monica. I don't even know if they're going to arrest me."

"You were just cutting class. Kids do that all the time. Listen, call me tonight."

"I don't have your number."

"No? That's right. Here." He grabbed a pen from a clipboard on a side table and wrote his number on my wrist. The area code wasn't familiar to me.

"613?" I asked.

"My dad gave me the cell. It's his area code. He has a new phone, new family. They got my dad, and I got a hand-me-down phone. Isn't it nice to feel loved?" He looked at me. "Maybe we're not so different after all."

Mr. Albright handed the forms back to the receptionist then walked out the door. Ryan stood to follow. "Call me," he said. "Everything's going to be okay."

But it wasn't okay. Not for me.

Heather burst into the station at a quarter to five, wearing a plus-size pencil skirt and running shoes that squeaked on the station tiles. Her look hadn't changed in the past nine years, ever since she held my hand walking into my first foster home, armed with a brand-new Barbie and raspberry Pop-Tarts. "Yeah, I'm here," she said into her Bluetooth earpiece.

She looked at me. "Oh my god, Alex! *What did you do to your hair?* You're not allowed to cut it without talking to me!" She shook her head and went back to her Bluetooth. "Yes, Monica, I see her. Come on down, and we'll talk. About a lot of things."

Monica arrived twenty minutes later, looking ash-grey, avoiding eye contact. She held my jacket, which she handed to me without a word.

Officer Jacobson escorted us to a private conference room, this one painted vomit yellow. Heather offered me a granola bar from her bag.

I hadn't eaten anything since the Cheerios this morning, but I shook my head.

"Let's cut to the chase, Alex," said Heather, plopping her portfolio binder on the table. She shoved her hair into a purple scrunchie, and ripped the wrapper off the granola bar with her teeth. "Your case will go to juvenile court on Monday. Until then, you'll be released to Monica on home probation."

"Juvenile court?" Monica asked. "She just played hooky. It's not like she robbed a bank."

"Truancy is a big deal for foster kids. So is underage drinking."

"But I didn't—"

Heather held up a hand to silence me. "Not to mention, Alex left her last home due to a physical altercation."

Yeah. Assault with a deadly condiment. I dug my thumbs into my temples.

"That's the bad news," Heather said, through a mouthful of granola. "The good news is that Alex doesn't have any priors, so I doubt they'd send her to juvenile hall. Just to an elevated level of care."

That was code for the group home. Fluorescent lights and lockdowns. Supervised walks and communal showers. Instant potatoes and plastic trays.

"Of course, Monica could petition the court for consideration."

My foster mom tied her purse strap into a knot.

Heather stood up. "We'll just have to see what the judge says. Excuse me, I have to talk with Officer Jacobson. You're free to go."

We walked out of the police station into the driving rain.

I couldn't think. I couldn't breathe. My heart felt lodged somewhere beneath my clavicle.

I opened the rear door to Monica's Subaru, and rode in the back seat just like in the squad car, cradling my comforter.

Monica lifted her eyes to the rearview mirror, then adjusted her sight to the road. At the first intersection, she signaled left.

Home was to the right.

"Where are we going?" I asked, fighting a not-so irrational panic. She wouldn't take me back to the group home now, would she?

"Book club."

"What?"

"My book club party is tonight."

"And we're *going*?"

"I think a distraction might be in order. What do you think?"

I nodded, numb. Anything would be better than sitting silently in her house, wondering if I should start packing. It wouldn't take long. Half my stuff was still in the black garbage bag.

Monica turned onto a quiet cul-de-sac, minivans stacked outside cookie-cutter houses. "I'm sorry," she said, turning off the ignition.

"For what?" I asked. "I'm the one who screwed up. Big time."

"I just. I don't know." She looked out the window, her breath fogging the glass. "I guess I've been in over my head. I don't know how to raise a teenager." She turned to me. "You had a boy over, didn't you? And I didn't even know."

My heart froze.

"I found Clyde rolling on a T-shirt in the backyard this morning," she said. "I don't suppose you wear a men's J.Crew, size large, smelling of skunk and cologne? Is that who you were with today?"

I bit my lip. Words wouldn't come.

"You had it all planned."

"No, I didn't, I—"

"Your quilt, Alex. Why else would you take it to school? I'm impressed it fit in your backpack with all that homework. Or was that a lie, too? Your chemistry assignment was under the bush with the T-shirt." She held up a hand. "It's okay. You don't have to answer. I'd rather not hear any more lies."

I focused on my lap, refusing to cry.

Monica got out of the car, taking a covered Tupperware bowl with her. Probably filled with cut-up honeydew melon to share with her friends. I sat in the backseat as the rain pounded on the roof of the car, water cascading down the windshield. I took out my phone. Thought about calling Ryan. What would I say? *Come get me?* And then what? Run away?

No, I wouldn't call. I'd sit in the car until Monica finished her party.

I sat for ten minutes.

Fifteen.

Twenty.

It was dark and cold and I hadn't eaten anything since breakfast. I grabbed my jacket, flipped up the hood, and tucked my phone into the pocket. If necessary, I could sit in a corner and pretend to text. I dashed through the driving rain, across the lawn to the front door.

An ancient man answered my knock. His hair was silver, his teeth unnaturally white. The left side of his lip sagged, like melted wax, the sclera of his eyes clouded yellow. "Who are you?" he demanded.

I knew this was the right house, but I uselessly checked the street number, as if I had any idea what address I was supposed to be at. "Umm..."

"Wait," he slurred, only one half of his mouth working. "I know you."

"I don't think so." I stood outside the eaves, fat raindrops pelting my hood.

"Dad, let her in before she drowns." A woman with curly black hair joined us at the door.

"Ms. Lanyer?"

Chapter 14

Perhaps you have learned it without book

"Welcome, Alex," said my drama teacher. "Dad, this is one of my students."

"Pardon?"

"Students," she said louder.

"Prudence?" he asked me. "Is that your name?" He peered close enough for me to smell his old-man breath.

"No Dad," said Ms. Lanyer. "This is one of my students from school. Her mother is a friend of mine. Her name is Alex."

"Alex is a boy's name. Prudence is a girl's name." He eyed me appraisingly. "Perhaps you should consider it."

"Okay," I said.

"Dad, you're supposed to be watching your movie in your room," said Ms. Lanyer. "This is ladies' night, remember?"

"Oh, yes. Next thing you'll be sending me out on the heath."

"All right, King Lear."

"You are my favorite daughter," he said.

"I'm your only daughter. Now shoo."

"Yes, yes. Goodnight, Prudence. It was nice of you to finally stop by." He winked at me with his non-drooping eye, then retreated up the open staircase.

"Please excuse my dad. He hasn't been the same since his stroke."

"I can still hear you!" called her father. "I'm old, not deaf!" He shuffled across the second-floor landing.

A geodesic chandelier illuminated the eclectically decorated foyer. A gold-framed mirror hung over an antique bench, sandwiched between tropical plants in African-looking urns. I stood dripping water on a red-and-gold Oriental rug and side-eyed my reflection in the mirror: a drowned rat in a soaked hoodie, like a street urchin Ms. Lanyer might have picked up on one of her world travels.

"I'm glad you're here, Alex." She put an arm around my shoulder. "Goodness, you're wet. Let's get you out of that jacket." I handed Ms. Lanyer my hoodie as the pocket began mooing. Not again.

"Do you hear something?" she asked.

"Yes," I sighed. "It's my phone." I pulled out the cell and flipped it open to the home screen, trying to silence the alarm.

"Hey, that's *my* phone!" Ms. Lanyer exclaimed. She held out her hand for a closer look.

"Hi, Alex," said Monica, coming down the hall. "I'm glad you decided to join us."

"What are you doing with my phone?" asked Ms. Lanyer.

Great. We could now add petty theft to the charges of truancy and underage drinking.

"It's yours, Pippa?" asked Monica. "Why is it mooing?"

"It's an alarm I set," said Ms. Lanyer.

"But why is it mooing?"

My thoughts exactly.

"I thought it was funny," said Ms. Lanyer. She looked at me. "How did you get my phone?"

"It was me," said Monica. "I rescued it from the e-waste drive last weekend. I probably shouldn't have taken it, but I needed a phone for Alex."

That's Monica, for you. The worst thing she's ever done is improperly recycle.

"And you got it to work?" asked Ms. Lanyer. There was no way I was going to think of her as *Pippa*.

"The AT&T guy performed his magic."

"Huh. All the places I tried couldn't do anything. Mind if I see?"

I handed it to her. "It's your phone."

She checked the home screen, a picture of some random apartment complex. Ms. Lanyer gasped. "Yep, it's mine. I can't believe it!"

"You can have it back," I said.

"Oh no. I have a new phone. That thing's been dead since I went through the full body scan at Heathrow—when was it? 2007, I think."

"Heathrow?" I asked.

"An airport in London," Ms. Lanyer said. "I'm itching to go back."

"I'm itching to go, period," said Monica. "All that history."

"Speaking of which," said a forty-something blonde, who materialized at Monica's shoulder. "Marjorie's ready with her book club questions, and we're out of Chardonnay. Oh, hi!" she said to me. "You must be Alex! Monica has told us all about you."

Really?

"Oh, Jane. I haven't told you hardly anything."

"Yeah, right," said Jane. "Only that 'Alex is an amazing artist, and an incredible student, and so mature for her age, with a unique sense of style, and she is *so* independent.'"

"Don't forget the Nobel Prize," I said. "Youngest recipient ever."

"You're kidding me!" Jane said.

"Let's get dinner started, then," Ms. Lanyer said.

"Great," Jane said. "Should we open the red?"

***

The ladies stood around a kitchen island, hitting me with rapid-fire introductions. Besides Ms. Lanyer, Monica, and Jane, there was a pregnant woman named Evie (making a study of the spinach dip in a bread bowl), another middle-aged librarian-type (Marjorie with the Book Club Notes), and a twenty-something dead-ringer for our hostess.

"This is my daughter, Natalie," said Ms. Lanyer. "Home for the weekend."

"Not that I don't love dorm food," said Natalie, holding a beer. "But I couldn't miss a book club meal."

"I didn't think you were that old," I said to Ms. Lanyer. The ladies laughed. "I mean, well, that's not what I mean. You don't look that old. Never mind. I don't know what I'm saying—"

"Oh, go on," said Natalie. "Mom loves it. And her ID certainly came in handy during high school."

"I did not hear that," said Ms. Lanyer.

"Oh, you love it, don't lie," said Natalie.

"Well, maybe a little. Let's just say, I had a wild and crazy youth. Natalie was my last and best mistake."

"I could argue that premise on a number of fronts," said her daughter. "But first, I think we are going to need another chair."

The table was set for six, my appearance calling for one more place-setting than anticipated. "I've got a folding chair in the garage," said Ms. Lanyer, opening a door off the kitchen.

Natalie dunked a slice of baguette in the spinach dip. "So, you're in my mom's class, huh? What's she doing this year, *Julius Caesar on Ice*?"

"She likes Shakespeare, huh?"

"Yeah, but doublets and hose are a bit too pedestrian for her. Here, have some." She slid the dip over to me. "For my mom, it's not art if it's not living and breathing, and preferably wearing some form of spandex."

"I only did that once!" exclaimed Ms. Lanyer, returning with the extra chair.

"Yeah, in my freshman year!" said Natalie. "Do you know how hard it is to play a character named 'Hymen' in high school? Much less, wearing hot pants?"

"Setting *As You Like It* in the 1970s was a perfectly valid artistic choice. You're now a Shakespearean scholar. I'd like to think your Berkeley professors would admire my vision."

"My therapist has an appreciation for it."

"Ha, ha," said Ms. Lanyer. "My genius daughter doth protest too much."

"I love you, Mom. Even if you put Hamlet in outer space."

"*Hamlet* is an existential piece. It lends itself to time travel."

"But you changed the most famous line. '*To be or not to be. That is the continuum.* Really?"

"Who says I can't change any of the words?"

"Shakespeare is rolling in his grave," said Natalie.

"Shakespeare's not *in* his grave."

"Oh God, not this again."

"Time to eat!" said Monica.

***

Ms. Lanyer offered me a regular seat instead of the folding chair, but I felt awkward enough without taking someone's spot. Wedged between Ms. Lanyer at the head of the table and Monica on the side, I sat six inches below everyone else, like a three-year-old without a booster, but Natalie was right about the food.

Ms. Lanyer placed the main dish, a fragrant stew, between two centerpieces of purple and green thistle. The ladies passed their bowls to Monica, who ladled chunks of beef, potatoes, carrots, and garlic, garnished with sprigs of rosemary. I accepted a small bowl, minus the beef, rationalizing that a starving vegetarian could sip a bit of bone broth. Fried corn dodgers, buttered leeks, grilled vegetables, and a large helping of sweet onion tart rounded out the meal.

"Oops, ladies," said Ms. Lanyer. "I forgot to pull the bay leaf from the stew. Good luck to whoever finds it."

"What's a bay leaf?" I whispered to Monica.

"It's an herb used for flavor. You don't want to eat it, though."

"Poison?"

"No," Monica laughed. "Just makes things taste good." She looked in my bowl. "Hey, it looks like you've got it." With her unused spoon, she scooped out a small, hard leaf. I picked up the stem and crunched the pointed tip. A bitter taste flooded my mouth. Monica smiled and passed me a glass of water.

"I should have listened to you," I said.

DALE LISA FLINT

"Some things you need to experience for yourself."

I set the leaf on the side of my bread plate. For luck. "I think I'll stick with the stew." And the fried corn dodgers. And the onion tart.

I ate everything on my plate, then had seconds, then thirds. Then Ms. Lanyer brought out something called a "cheese course," which I didn't even know was a *thing.* Toast points and miniature wine grapes accompanied a platter of gourmet cheeses labeled with handmade toothpick signs: smoked gouda, triple-cream brie, Point Reyes blue, and Humboldt Fog. I'd never seen so many non-orange cheeses. I sampled them all.

Throughout, Marjorie adjusted her red reading glasses and interrupted the ladies' gossiping with a list of pre-printed questions. She checked off each one as it was discussed, two red pens sitting next to her copy of the book.

"In the novel, how does Claire–" Marjorie began.

"Can you pass the veggie thing?"

"The succotash?"

"Well, that just sounds naughty."

"In the book, how does Claire–"

"That reminds me of what Richard said the other night."

Marjorie clinked her empty wine glass with her spoon.

"Pass the red to Marjorie," said Jane. "She's dry."

"Give her the succotash," said Natalie.

"You have a question for us, Marjorie?" asked Monica, looking flushed.

"Yes, this is a good one," said Marjorie, turning to a Post-It flagged page in her book. "In the novel, how does Claire adjust to her new life in 18th century Scotland?"

"Well," said Jane, stifling a belch. "One way was boinking a Highlander."

"Jane!" said Monica, but she was grinning. This was the most relaxed I'd seen my foster mom. "Give us another question, please."

"Dessert first," said Ms. Lanyer. Natalie cleared the table as my teacher set out plates of blackberry shortbread, cinnamon scones, and chocolate pudding with homemade whipped cream.

"Here you go, Evie," said Ms. Lanyer, handing her a slice of caramel cheesecake. "I made it just for you. Anyone want coffee?"

"I'll take some," said Monica. "Decaf, please."

Evie nodded and mouthed a "me, too."

"Is that red empty?" asked Jane.

"Yep, I'll open another one," said Natalie, going to the wine rack.

"Okay, here's a good one," said Marjorie, flipping to page three of her notes. "If you could, would you travel back in time?"

"Definitely," said Monica.

"Would there be a man in a kilt waiting for me?" asked Jane.

"Oh, I'd go even without the man in the kilt... although that *would* be a perk," said Monica, pouring cream in her decaf.

"That's why they wear those kilts. Nothing between you and the perks," said Jane.

"I'd settle for a foot rub," moaned Evie. She leaned back, her chair creaking dangerously. "Can someone pass the scones?"

Monica handed her a plate. "I'd love to go back in time. See history as it happened: the Renaissance, dashing knights in shining armor—"

"The Age of Enlightenment—"

"Exploring the New World, Shakespeare—"

"The bubonic plague," Natalie broke in, pouring wine for Jane. "Religious persecution, medieval torture chambers, witches burning at the stake—"

"Witches?" I asked.

"Women," said Natalie. "I meant women. Go back in time, less than a century, and women weren't allowed to vote. In *America*. What do you think life was like for them back in Shakespeare's time?"

"They couldn't appear on stage," said Ms. Lanyer. "No female actors or directors."

I remembered that bit from my English class, everyone snickering at the thought of a guy playing Juliet.

"Forget that," said Natalie. "How about real rights? Real power? The systemic oppression of women is embedded in our DNA."

Ms. Lanyer ever-so-slightly rolled her eyes, but Monica murmured agreement. She still had a "Hillary in '08" bumper sticker on her Subaru. "I get that," Monica said. "It's just, sometimes I've felt I was born in the wrong decade, you know?"

"I don't," said Natalie. "I'm grateful for everything we have nowadays. Hot showers, toilet paper—"

"Oh God, toilet paper," said Jane. "How could you live without toilet paper?"

"Deodorant!"

"Toothpaste!"

"Botox!"

"Panera Bread!"

"Marjorie, there won't be a quiz," said Jane.

Marjorie put down her pen. "Ballpoints?" she offered.

"Right," said Natalie. "No ballpoint pens, no cell phones—"

"I could live without cell phones," said Monica. Two Androids and three iPhones rested on the table, but the ladies murmured agreement.

"A 'simpler time,' I know," said Natalie. "But what I've learned in my upper division seminars—and Mom, you can stop giving me that look. You created me, sorry. One thing I've learned is that the ideal past doesn't exist. And you can't find yourself by becoming someone else."

"But you *can* boink a Highlander," said Jane, lifting her glass for a toast. "Got any Scotch?"

***

"I liked what you said in there," I told Natalie. "That stuff about systematic—"

"*Systemic.*"

FINDING JULIET

"Systemic oppression, and, like, women's legacy. It reminded me of someone." The rain had eased to a fine, frozen drizzle. Wrapped in blankets, Natalie and I sat in wicker chairs on the covered back patio. Monica was in the kitchen, helping Ms. Lanyer do the dishes. The other ladies had left a half hour earlier, Jane hitching a ride with Evie.

"I can't take all the credit. That's my ex-Women's Studies professor talking."

"You go to U.C. Berkeley," I said, making the connection. "Did you have Debbie? I mean Professor, umm, Wright?"

"Yeah, how do you know Professor Wright?"

"She was one of my foster moms."

"You're kidding me! What a coincidence."

"I know. I loved her. Well, not *loved*," I clarified, pulling the wool blanket to my chin. It was scratchy, but warm. "She's the reason I became a vegetarian."

"But you ate the stew."

"Not the meat, just the broth."

"So you're a relativistic vegetarian," Natalie smiled.

"No, just hungry. And Debbie ate shrimp."

Natalie lit a brown cigarette, blowing a puff of perfumed smoke. A golden light from the kitchen window bled onto the concrete slab. I checked, but Monica and Ms. Lanyer were engaged in serious conversation over the soap suds, ignoring us.

"It's okay," said Natalie. "I'm an adult now. And Mom doesn't consider cloves actually smoking. I won't argue with her."

"They're just as bad?"

"Totally," she inhaled. "But, I figured I'm allowed to make a few mistakes. So you're a foster kid?"

"Yeah. You study Shakespeare? From the way you talked, it seemed like you hated Shakespeare. I mean, your mom—"

"Yeah, she's kind of a kook, isn't she? But, what can I say? It's in my blood." Smoke from Natalie's cigarette curled skyward, deepening

•99•

the mist. "You really want to get my mom going, ask her about the 'Dark Lady' of Shakespeare's sonnets."

"The 'Dark Lady'?"

"Emilia Lanyer. Google it. A female Elizabethan poet, also assumed to be Shakespeare's *paramour*. Mom believes we're descended."

"From Shakespeare's girlfriend?"

"No, from Shakespeare."

"Wait... what?"

"Shakespeare. My mom believes Emilia *was* Shakespeare."

"H-how?" I stuttered.

"It's complicated. Mom thinks 'Shakespeare' was a pen name."

"A pen what?" I asked.

"A name an author uses to remain anonymous."

"Okay. And she thinks 'Shakespeare' did that?"

"She thinks whoever wrote as Shakespeare did that, including our great, great, great, etc., grandmother."

"Don't you think that's kind of impossible?"

"Practically, no," said Natalie, shifting her weight as she tucked a foot underneath her. "None of Shakespeare's plays survive in his own handwriting. There's no mention of any plays *at all* in his will. From all outward evidence, he was an illiterate country bumpkin."

"So you think your mom's right?"

"No, I think she's cuckoo. My master's thesis will prove that Shakespeare—bar the barn doors—actually *was* Shakespeare. I love my mom, but between her and my grandpa, I've heard enough conspiracy theories to last a lifetime."

"And your mom knows what you're doing?"

"Sure. She's my greatest fan. She thinks I'm wrong, but she doesn't stop me from *thinking*."

"So, if you could go back in time...?"

"I'd strap Shakespeare to a polygraph, and hand-deliver the results to Maury Povich. But, since I can't do that, I'll go with demonstrable facts."

"But what if you discover your mom's right? That Shakespeare was your grandmother?"

"There's faith, there's family, and there's something in between. The answer is one of two things." Natalie stubbed out her cigarette. "I'm either the product of the greatest cover-up in the history of Western Civilization, or I'm one in a long line of strong women. Either way, I'm okay. The past is there. I can't change it."

"But, you're still trying to prove your mother wrong?"

"Well, that's what a daughter *does*, right?"

***

Monica carried her Tupperware bowl, now full of grilled vegetables and leftover onion tart. I held a paper plate with half a caramel cheesecake secured with plastic wrap. Natalie retreated upstairs, while Ms. Lanyer led us to the door. We paused in the hallway, wall sconces lighting the burgundy wallpaper, a fleur-de-lis pattern on the baseboards. There was a row of silver-framed, black-and-white photographs, typical family portraits, all except one: a Polaroid snapshot in a simple wood frame. It was a man sitting in a dirt pit, grinning at the camera. He held a pipe between his teeth, his eyes twinkling, his smile straight.

I pointed at the photo. "Is that your dad?"

"That's right. It was taken in London. My dad was part of the archeological dig at the site of the Old Globe, Shakespeare's theatre. That was before the stroke, of course," she added sadly. "Here, give me your phone." She zoomed in on the image of the apartment complex and handed me back the phone. "The Globe burned in 1613. The thatch roof lit during a performance of *Henry VIII*. All that's left is that plaque right there."

"They paved paradise," said Monica.

"Put up a parking lot," I finished. Monica looked at me curiously. "My foster mom Rick loved Joni Mitchell," I said. "She played it all the time at her coffee shop."

"She sounds cool," said Monica, eyes bright.

"She was," I nodded. "*Totally* into vinyl."

"And now it's all iPads and Kindlings," said Monica. "If I ever get one those things, you'll know I've crossed over to the dark side."

"You'll get there, Monica," said Ms. Lanyer. "It's only a matter of time."

Monica smiled and took my plate of cheesecake, balancing it on top of the Tupperware. "Go, grab your jacket," she said. "I'll get the car warmed up. Thank you again, Pippa. It was legendary, as always." She kissed Ms. Lanyer on the cheek, and opened the front door.

Ms. Lanyer lifted my hoodie from a ceramic hook. "We missed you in class today," she said.

"I know. I'm sorry. I shouldn't have cut."

"It happens. You missed a lot of drama in Drama." She shook her head.

"I heard. What's going to happen now?"

"We'll cancel the show."

"Really?"

"Yeah. It stinks, but I don't have understudies. It's awfully hard to do *Romeo and Juliet* without a Romeo *or* a Juliet, despite Jeremy's bid to rename the production *Benvolio Superstar*."

"I'm sorry it didn't work out."

"Yeah, well. It's only a play."

Chapter 15
A lightning before death

The break in the weather was only temporary. On the way back to Monica's, the sky opened up. She drove, nose to the wheel, wipers failing to keep pace with the downpour. Past the shadow of the old oak, water ran in runnels down the sides of the road, creating the illusion that the car was suspended, idling in place.

I heard a rumbling in the distance, not a crack, but a deep, echoing growl. "Was that thunder?"

"Yep."

"I've never seen weather like this."

"Welcome to winter in the foothills," Monica said with a smile, her eyes tight in concentration. "Seventy degrees one day, a biblical torrent the next. Temperature's dropping, too."

Sheets of rain on the windshield mixed with slush, then back to rain. We crested the drive to her house, both of us breathing a sigh of relief at the golden glow of the porch light.

"Bonnie, Clyde! We're home! Oops," Monica said, opening the front door to a suspicious puddle. "I think one of them had an accident. The thunder scares them. I'll clean it up, but they need to go out. Do you mind? They'll be under my bed. Grab one of my raincoats."

"Sure."

"Oh, and the leashes, too," she said, heading to the kitchen to deposit the leftovers and grab paper towels and spray cleaner. "If it thunders again, I don't want them taking off."

"Got it." I headed to Monica's room. Bonnie came scooting out from under the bed skirt, but Clyde refused to budge. I lay on the hardwood, reaching for his leather collar.

"Come on out, doggie," I said. My hand landed on a pile of wet canvas cloth.

"CLYDE!" I shouted.

He exploded from under the bed, tail between his legs, leaving me holding the remains of my pink Converse. I threw my destroyed sneaker across the room, narrowly missing Monica's head as she peeked around the door.

"What's going on?" she asked. She picked up the Converse, slimy with dog drool, the rubber sole shredded. "Oh, Alex. I'm so sorry. He hasn't done that in ages. The storm must have really freaked him out."

"It's okay," I said, bottom lip trembling.

"No, it's not," Monica said. "I'll get you a new pair. We'll go Mon—" she stopped. Juvenile court was on Monday, the hearing where a judge would decide whether or not I should be placed back in the group home. "We'll go shopping tomorrow. Come sit with me," she said, holding out her hand. "It's a nice night for a fire."

I trailed her to the living room. Monica cleaned up the dog mess, then took them both out in the rain, while I sulked on the blue couch. I unlaced my borrowed boots and chucked them towards a basket near the front door. The steel toes landed with a satisfying *THUMP THUMP*.

"If they ever make shoe throwing an Olympic sport..." said Monica, coming back in with the dogs. She toweled them off while they jumped and bumped her nose. Released, Bonnie bounded back to Monica's room, trailing Eau de Wet Dog. Clyde slunk to the couch.

"Get off, dog," I said, kneeing the damp muzzle in my lap. He shoved his nose deeper into my thigh. "Fine," I said, patting his wet head. Satisfied, Clyde curled at my feet with the peace of the righteously forgiven.

Monica put kindling into the stove and lit a match. The room filled with the sweet scent of cedar. I pulled a plaid flannel blanket from the back of the couch and tucked it around my thighs, waiting for the warmth of the fire to reach me.

"I never made a fire when I was married," Monica said, adding logs to the kindling. "That was Frank's job. I never held an axe. Never touched a chainsaw. Then, he left. I knew if I didn't learn, I'd go cold. The furnace in this house is too old to be dependable." She adjusted the vent, then sat on the other end of the couch. Flames danced through the soot-covered window of the wood-burning stove. "I felt so helpless, so out of control. So... I did the me-thing, which was to read a book."

Monica eyed me sheepishly from the corner of her glasses. "Okay, I read a few books. One talked about 'manifesting life goals.' What you do is write them down. So, I started small. My first goal was to learn how to chop wood. I wrote it down on a receipt from Kmart. Then, I bought a journal. You could do the same, you know. Write down what you want—"

"Those e-readers are called Kindles, not Kindlings," I said.

"I know. I was trying to be funny. Fo Schnitzel?"

"Don't quit your day job," I said.

The wind whistled through the eaves. Rain battered the windows. Clyde gave a deep, rumbling sigh.

"They say it might snow," said Monica. "On the weather report. We don't get a lot of that here. Only maybe once a year. Not like the mountains. Just random. Isolated."

"I want to stay," I said.

The words floated above our heads like a small flurry.

Random. Isolated.

In the woodstove, a log shifted as it burned, shooting red-hot embers up the flue.

"I want you to stay, too," she said finally, eyes heavy. She wiped her glasses on her shirt, then pushed them higher onto her nose. "But maybe you need more than I can give you."

Humiliation rose in my throat, like stomach bile when there's nothing left to vomit. This was my fault. After nine years in foster care, against every piece of evidence I'd collected that people just don't care, I allowed myself to think, maybe—

Whatever.

I didn't need anybody. I could fill out my own college applications. Pick out my own prom dress. I gulped, choking on a sob.

"Can I go on the internet?" It was a question, but I was already up.

"Are you okay, Alex?" Monica asked, following me into the kitchen.

"Peachy."

"We can talk some more if you want." She stood at the counter.

I kept my eyes on the screen as I booted up her laptop. "Nah. I'd rather just surf if that's okay."

"Check your MySpace?"

Really?

"Yeah, that's it." I yanked the cord out of the phone, plugging it into the computer as the dial-up screamed.

"Can I make you some cocoa?" she asked, opening a cabinet.

Don't cry. Never cry.

"Could you please stop being so *pathetic*?" I shot.

She paused, a Hershey's tin in her hand. I tensed my shoulders, waiting for her to yell, to tell me what an ungrateful brat I was, to call Heather to pick me up. She bit her lip, setting the can on the counter. "Goodnight," she whispered, before calling Clyde to the bedroom. Her door closed with a click.

Yeah. Parting is such sweet sorrow.

I sat for a few minutes, frozen. The rain turned to hail, firing a machine gun splatter against the roof.

Think.

I was almost eighteen.

I googled "age out foster care," followed links to "emancipated minor," then got a chart of statistics: 1 in 5 homeless; 3% with a college degree; half of females pregnant by age 19. My future already written, laid out in gold-and-teal government graphics.

I'd rather die.

What would Katniss Everdeen do?

I cleared my browsing history and clicked on Twitter, counting to fifty as the page loaded with the speed of a glacier melting.

Jennifer Lawrence's page was unchanged. No new tweets. She must have better things to do than provide a storyline for my useless existence. *Who's pathetic now?*

My mouse hovered over the log-off, when I noticed I had a follower, my first, @actorjedwards. Beneath an ad for Amazon, three messages waited.

Ryan Edwards@actorjedwards ·Dec 6
@Imalexriddle leaving now
10:16 PM - 6 Dec 2013 · Details

Ryan Edwards@actorjedwards ·Dec 6
@Imalexriddle plane at midnight, wait 4 u?
9:24 PM - 6 Dec 2013 · Details

Ryan Edwards@actorjedwards ·Dec 6
@Imalexriddle leaving tonight, banished, r u there
7:14 PM - 6 Dec 2013 · Details

The oven clock blinked 10:38, but Monica set it ten minutes fast. My mind fumbled the simple calculation. Was it really 10:28 or 10:48?

10:28.

Ryan left twelve minutes ago. I could catch him. His cell number was on my wrist, faint, but legible. I reattached the phone line, and mashed the buttons of the cordless. Ryan picked up after the first ring, the reception crackling. "Alex?" he said, as thunder shook the walls, plunging the house into darkness. Electricity out. The phone was dead.

I crammed my swollen feet back into Monica's boots. I didn't even try my cell. I knew the signal didn't start until the old oak, half a mile away. I grabbed my jacket and backpack, and tore out the front door. By the time Monica realized I was gone, she'd have no way to find me.

I half-jogged, half-hobbled down the slick double yellow of the road, leaning into the wind. A flash of lightning burst on a nearby hilltop, branches of purple-white light fanning the sky, marking pathways on a celestial map. As my eyes adjusted to the dark, I saw the oak tree, snarled boughs outlined against a bruised sky. I sprinted the last two-hundred yards.

Under the shelter of the oak tree's heavy limbs, I opened the front pocket of my backpack to get my cell. It wasn't there. Not in the main pocket either. I dumped my books, binder, and all the other contents of my backpack on the muddy ground. Chapstick. A hairbrush. A ballpoint pen. A wallet with seven dollars and fifty-two cents. A pack of spearmint gum. My backpack sagged, empty. No phone. I crammed everything back in the backpack.

I checked the pockets of my jacket. Nothing.

This was crazy. I had my phone at Ms. Lanyer's house. She showed me the picture of Shakespeare's theatre. Or what was left of it.

The realization hit like a punch to the gut. She had my phone.

I sank to the ground, raking my back against the bark of the old oak. The wind blew sideways into my face, cold rain mixing with hot tears. I buried my forehead in my knees, nose dripping snot onto Monica's steel-toed boots. After nine years, this was the sum of my inheritance: a pair of old shoes. I had nothing else. Not Ryan. Not Monica. Not anyone.

I dug my fingernails into the mud, desperate for traction as the world spun off its axis. My consciousness drifted above, and I saw myself from the vantage of the sky: a part of nature, a bit of spongy moss clinging to the foot of the oak.

A radiant tunnel of light appeared at the outer edge of my vision.

Am I delirious? Or am I dead? I'd have believed either one.

But then the light grew.

It grew and it grew, until it divided. Two lights. Moving closer. It was a car. The freezing rain masked the noise of the engine, fast approaching.

Ryan!

I scrambled to the side of the road, waving my arms.

It wasn't Ryan's truck, though.

Was his grandpa driving him, or someone else from school? Maybe he took a cab. The car stopped. The passenger's side window rolled down. I heard a woman's voice. Monica?

"Did you need this?" A hand reached across the seat, holding my cell.

I blinked and refocused my eyes. "Ms. Lanyer? How did you—"

"My Dad said you needed your phone," she said. "That you had to have it—tonight. I wouldn't have come, but he was insistent." She unlocked the car door. "Alex, it's sleeting. You need to get out of this weather."

"I will." I had so many questions, but I brushed them aside. Could I still reach Ryan? "Thank you, Ms. Lanyer."

"You're soaked. Let me give you a lift back home."

"I'm fine. The phone is dead at Monica's house. She knows I'm out here."

"Why don't you get in the car and call?" asked Ms. Lanyer.

"It's personal," I said firmly. "Really, I'm fine. I'll go home right after I make the call. Thank you for bringing me the phone," I added.

"Okay, Alex." She started to say something, but shook her head, dismissing the thought. "Stay safe, okay?"

When I nodded, she pulled away, heading in the direction of Monica's house. Soon, they'd both be out here.

I picked up my backpack and flipped open the phone, hands trembling with cold. Three quarters of battery life, one bar. 10:46pm. I checked Ryan's number using the light from the screen.

Would he answer his phone or would a text be better?

The sleet turned back to hail, tiny white missiles almost like snow. For a second, I was entranced. The hail was so perfect, so little and round, like white Dippin' Dots.

I shook my head. I was out of time. Thunder boomed, echoing in my ribcage. My fingers slipped across the buttons as I keyed in 1-613—

before the lightning flashed and all went black.

Part 2: 1613

Chapter 16
The world is broad and wide

Dead.

For real this time.

No tunnel of light.

Just

                                        nothing.

***

I lay on the ground, hard beneath my back. Something had my leg, dragging me deeper into darkness. "Oof," I grunted, as my boot popped off. A boy brought his face to mine. He was my age or thereabouts, a hovering shadow, the world upturned.

He raised his arm, the boot clutched in his hand. I mouthed the word *help*, as the steel toe came down.

***

I woke to a strange dog licking my cheek. Not Bonnie. Not Clyde.

Mr. Albright's cattle dog? Its rancid breath fogged my face, hazing the night.

How much time had passed since the boy stole my boots? Three hours or three minutes?

The dog's yellow eyes gleamed like double harvest moons, its jagged brown teeth flattened by age.

"Nice doggie," I entreated, voice an octave high, heart beating triple-time.

The hound sat, head tilted, a hyena grin.

It was night. I was outside. That much was familiar. Yet the oak tree had vanished, replaced by the thin edge of a roof high above my head. Mr. Albright's barn? The building's towering dark outline stood in relief to the moonless sky, brilliant with stars. The ambient light picked up the pale orange polish of my toenails. I wiggled them, ten little piggies, wondering why anyone would steal my socks.

I shivered. My jacket was missing, too. Did some kid seriously thump me in the head?

Cold mud seeped through my sweater to my T-shirt, now sodden and sticking to my skin. Something else: a new scent overlaying the background note of ozone. Rank. Fetid. Foul.

I rolled back and forth for traction, then heaved myself into a sitting position with my back against the barn, head spinning. Yellow-Eyes whined in concern, circled a few feet away, then returned, plopping the tail-end of a dead rat in my lap. I closed my eyes and tipped my head, vomiting the onion tart from Ms. Lanyer's book club party.

Book club.

Ms. Lanyer.

Shakespeare.

Monica.

Fire. Rain. Tree.

A flash—Lightning!

I'd been hit by lightning.

I didn't remember it exactly. A bright light. A crack like wood splitting. Kindling for Monica's fire. No pain, just oblivion.

I'd been knocked unconscious once before, in elementary school. Eddie Juarez, the Kickball King, punted a spectacular line drive through first and second base while I guarded third, too busy yelling at the outfielders to see him barreling down the lane. I woke on black asphalt surrounded by twenty pairs of eyes. A playground aide hoisted me by the armpits and walked me to the office. I dialed my old number by mistake. By the tenth ring, I realized what I'd done, but kept my ear to the receiver anyways, willing my mother to answer.

She'd been dead for over a year.

Maybe I was dead now.

Nah. Not unless the afterlife had a very strong odor of poop.

Why would it smell like poop? Not cow poop, but *poop*-poop.

And why wasn't I at the tree? (I ignored the mystery of the boot-napper. There was a limit to what my brain could handle.) Perhaps I'd wandered, delirious, seeking shelter from the storm. Did Mr. Albright have an outhouse? I pictured his weathered face spitting, "Girl, what'd you do, *fall in?*"

And what about that cranky old man's grandson?

The emptiness in my stomach felt like the first long drop on a roller coaster. Ryan must be halfway to Los Angeles by now, soaring miles above the earth. Perhaps he leaned a cheek in one hand, forehead cool against the glass: green eyes over the abyss, and me in a field looking up.

Wherefore art thou?

Only "wherefore" didn't mean "where," but "why."

Forget it.

Ryan was gone.

Where was Monica? I had to find her, like *now*. If my foster mom called the cops looking for me after I'd already spent the day at the police station, I wouldn't need a dagger. My life would be over.

I patted the ground, searching for my phone. No luck. My back pocket was empty, too. I wiped my hands on the front of my jeans and brushed the bangs out of my eyes. The phone had to be at the tree. How far away was that? In which direction? The world had turned inside-out.

Mr. Albright's house. That's where I needed to go. He'd be mad, but he'd drive me back to Monica's. I didn't care what kind of drama I'd be walking into. It'd be worth it for fifteen minutes of pulsating shower massage and a bucket of vanilla body wash.

Pressed against the barn for support, I stood, fighting for balance like a newborn calf. Yellow-Eyes wagged his tail in encouragement. "Thank you, thank you," I said to the dog. "Now for my next trick." A lurching step turned my ankle. Mid-pirouette, I gripped the wall while white spots danced before my eyes and my knees turned to marshmallows.

Yellow Eyes took a step back as I arabesqued into the muck.

"Hello? HELLO! Mr. Albright? Monica?" I cried, voice cracking. "I'M OUT HERE!!! Hello!… Somebody, please…"

Yellow Eyes growled once, low and long, then took off.

I'd never felt more alone.

The dog was gone.

Ryan was gone.

Soon, I'd be gone, too, back to the Rainbow Canyon Home for Teen Girls, left to serve the six-month sentence until I turned eighteen. And then what? I'd already missed the fall deadlines for college. I had no money, no skills. No home. Where would I go?

My head throbbed. My body reeked. I didn't care. The stars told me how insignificant I was. They were so bright. The brightest I'd ever seen. I could reach out and touch them.

Wait a minute.

Where was the moon?

It was full last night. Tonight it was gone. Vanished like my phone. And my boots. And my socks. And my jacket. And, oh yes. My backpack, too. Great.

A full moon doesn't just disappear.

I couldn't puzzle it out. Too tired. I leaned against the barn, my eyelids heavy. A meteor flashed across the sky, and I made a wish, giving into sleep.

***

I dreamt of my mother. She sat on the edge of a wrought-iron daybed, wearing a Sacramento State sweatshirt. Her blonde hair was clean and swept low. *"See ya later, Allie-gator!"*

"Good morrow to thee!"

I sputtered awake to the sight of a very large woman, who was definitely *not* my mother, blocking the rising sun. She grinned, three missing teeth in a round face, like a friendly jack-o'-lantern.

"What?" I blinked. In the cold light of dawn, I saw plainly that I was not in Mr. Albright's pasture, but in the shelter of a large structure adjacent to a dirt road. Interspersed between rows of wood-planked buildings lay flat grassy plains, bearing little resemblance to the ranch's golden rolling hills. How far had I walked after the thunderstorm?

I sat up, not without difficulty. "What?" I asked again.

"What's 'what'? *That's* what." she replied, knocking me on the head with the flat of her palm. She shook a nest of bright red hair. "Rabbie told me you'd stolen away. Serve you right if I let the master find you, face down here, mouthing with Lady Mud."

"Lady Mud?" I asked, fingers to my crusty forehead, shielding my eyes.

"You look like a pig in a sty, Thomas."

I nodded once, synapses shooting blanks. My brain spun like a rocket on a hamster wheel. Who was Thomas? Was that the name of her pig? Did Mr. Albright even keep pigs? Or just cows?

Before I could reply, she twisted the neck of my sweater and heaved me into the frigid water of a nearby trough. I scrambled for purchase on the slimy bottom, clawing her giant arm, which dunked, twisted, and shook me like a bit of laundry on agitate.

"Better," she said, yanking me out. "At least now I can tell you're human."

"Who are you?!" I sputtered.

"Mistress Taylor, of course," she replied. "Your landlady? You look a wee bit worse for wear this morning. Are you that drunk?"

"Um."

"I think someone cut your hair. Pity. Master Burbage won't like that."

"Master Burbage?"

"Your *employer*. And lucky you have one, too, sneaking off and getting sauced. You're a might young to be this drunk, you know."

"I'm not drunk!" I exclaimed, throwing my hands in the air. Unfortunately, my equilibrium, although improved from last night, had not benefited by being put in the spin cycle of a horse trough.

"Tippled and reeling ripe," sighed Mistress Taylor. "Come on now, chuck. Let's get you dry and fed, so you can be back here when the other actors arrive."

That's it! I was on a movie set! I made it to Los Angeles with Ryan. Yes! Ryan brought me to the movie set and I was hanging out in his cool super-deluxe trailer but it was a long flight and I overslept and I accidentally stumbled out in the middle of a take and pretty soon Ryan would come along and kiss me and I'd be on TMZ with the headline *Mystery Girl Steals Heartthrob's Heart*!

Probably not.

For one thing, I didn't see a camera crew anywhere.

For another, I didn't smell very good: wet wool, mildewed straw, and a lingering hint of raw sewage. I couldn't believe the materialization of my wildest romantic dreams would involve me smelling like a wastewater treatment plant.

And, for a third (if we're counting): the woman. She wasn't an actor. Or if she was, she had really good makeup and costume. Like, professional quality. I mean, between the for-real missing teeth and the laced-up bodice, she looked straight out of a... whatchamacallit?

A Renaissance Faire!

In the seventh grade, my history teacher organized a Ren Faire at school, complete with Nerf Ball archery and jousting broomstick horses. I wore a peasant skirt, bought at the local thrift store, and a pointy hat made of pink construction paper. My booth sold Little

Debbies masquerading as meat pies, two for a dollar. Boys who were jerks in Nikes became gentlemen in paper bag tunics, crooking a knee to ask, *"How do you do, milady?"*

Did Jefferson Union have a similar event? If so, where were all the students? And was Ashton Kutcher hiding somewhere in the bushes, because I was beginning to feel punked.

"Well, come on then, Thomas," said Mistress Taylor. "Rabbie's waiting for you. He's been worried sick, he has. Me, I've got the porridge to stir, so let's get. You can thank me for saving your livelihood later." She took a few steps down the dirt road, then patted her thigh. "Here, boy," she whistled.

I plucked a bit of damp hay from my nose. One tentative step told me all limbs were again in working order, albeit shaky, like a marionette with the strings newly cut.

"Thomas! Are you coming, or do I need to drag you by your pillicock?"

I emerged from the shadow of the building, squinting against the light-saber sun.

"Your performance is tonight! Just think: *Romeo and Juliet* with the King's Men!" She turned me around to face the three-story tower, round like a globe, lit with the full glory of the dawn.

What could I say? Sometimes a cliché is the only proper response.

"I don't think I'm in Kansas, anymore."

"Marry, sweeting. This is London!"

Chapter 17
By the break of day disguised from hence

Mistress Taylor led me along a rutted dirt road, her wide hips swaying like the barges on the big, muddy river to our left. What was it called? I was studying for a quiz on European rivers two nights ago.

London River?

No.

London Bridge. The span up ahead. We'd sing the song in elementary school, taking turns walking under upstretched arms, waiting for the world to crash.

London Bridge is falling down,
Falling down, falling down.
London Bridge is falling down,
My fair la-dy.

Very weird.

Oarsmen bobbed on the gentle waves, hollering to passersby, offering rides. Gulls screeched. Across the way, a grey metropolis loomed, buildings jammed together, clouded by chimney smoke.

The Seine? Was that what the river was called?

No, that was in France.

The River Thames!

Ha! Yes! Score one for AP Geography!

Not that it mattered, but I found the recall of this bit of topographical trivia absurdly gratifying, an anchor on which to tether my sanity.

"Nice River Thames, huh?" I said to my companion.

"Are you daft?" asked Mistress Taylor. "Or just soft in the head?"

We passed pubs and shops, closed in the early morning hours. Creative signage adorned the doors of the taverns that faced the piers: *Hearty Pig and Thistle*; *Carpenter's Arms*; *Blue Boor*; and, my personal favorite, *The Dogged Duck*. Outside of a Harry Potter movie, I'd never seen such a scene.

"What time period is this?" I asked Mistress Taylor, still not sure I was awake.

"Half past six, or thereabouts," she replied. "Late or betimes, depending on your point of view."

Up ahead, the foot traffic increased. One lane joined two others. Fruit carts were met by horses and mules pulling wagons of eggplant and cabbages; people balanced baskets of fish on their heads, hauled wicker cages of white-feathered chickens. Children dashed between legs and horses' hooves. All headed in the same direction, to a gated tower that marked the entrance to—

"London Bridge?" I asked.

"Aye, lad," Mistress Taylor sighed.

I didn't know what I expected to see—something more like a *bridge*, I suppose, with cable spans or arches. But London Bridge looked more like a city block, with multiple-story buildings supported by groaning stone pillars, its narrow thoroughfare crowded with people. No wonder it came falling down.

My fair… la-dy.

"Are we crossing the bridge?" I asked Mistress Taylor.

"What for? No lad, we're headed back to your room. Blessed fig's end, those poor pates have more brains than you."

I followed Mistress Taylor's gaze to the top of the tower entrance.

"What the—?"

I shook my head in disbelief, then stopped, feeling both horror and sympathy at the sight above me. "Are those real?" I asked. They couldn't be. But they were. Impaled on tall metal spikes were heads— real human heads. I counted eight of them in various grotesque stages of decomposition. Flesh pocked, stripped, and melted with tar. I laughed nervously as a macabre nursery rhyme, lyrics inspired by the scene, danced through my head.

A grey and white gull
Sat on a skull
Pecking an empty eye socket.
Was this hysteria?

"Best not to stare," said Mistress Taylor. She grabbed my elbow and turned us right, far from the buzz of flies.

Past the bridge, the main avenue was slick cobblestone and mud, some parts compact and clay, others boggy, sucking my feet to the ankle. An occasional board lined the nastier bits, from heaps of vegetable scraps to animal dung, fish bones to *what-the-heck-was-that*.

Absorbed in the status of my blackening feet, I startled as Mistress Taylor clotheslined me against the wall of a brick building.

"What?" I choked.

"GARDYLOO!" shouted a lady at the third-story window. She dumped the contents of a ceramic pot into the street, a brown waterfall that crested our heads and splashed the cuffs of my jeans.

Appalled, I looked to my tour guide for an explanation, but Mistress Taylor was already rounding the corner. I chased her through a doorway under a painted sign: a fat sheep and a hand-lettered welcome to *The Shoulder of Mutton*.

A large hearth warmed the darkened restaurant. Tables and benches sat mostly empty, only a couple of men sipping from mugs. "Who's that you got there?" one asked Mistress Taylor. He had more gums than teeth.

"A runaway runt," she replied.

"Stick him on the spit," his friend laughed. "We'll have bacon tonight!"

"Nah, this one's a player," said Mistress Taylor, dropping her basket on the back bar. "A different kind of ham." She motioned me up a flight of steep, narrow steps. "This way, lad."

FINDING JULIET

The second floor was a narrow hallway, dimly lit, with heavy tan curtains draped across four door frames. She pushed aside one of the curtains to reveal a small bedroom, maybe twelve-foot square, with a stool, a table, a pitcher and bowl, a covered pot, and two mattresses. One bed was vacant; the other had a thin, patch-worked blanket covering a person-sized lump, which Mistress Taylor nudged with her foot.

"Rise and shine, Rabbie," she sing-songed.

"Leave off," the lump grumbled.

Sunlight drifted through the cracks of the shutters, which Mistress Taylor flung open with a *wham*, unleashing a burst of dust mites and muttered curses from beneath the blanket.

She gave the occupant's rear a firmer kick. "I found Thomas, I did, no thanks to you. Master Burbage does not pay nearly enough for me to spend my mornings traipsing after you boys. I'm an innkeeper, not a nursemaid. From now on, keep your friend on a tighter leash."

"Thomas, the pissant younker, is *not* my responsibility," grumbled the boy, cocooning himself tighter.

"Well, then, next time *you* tell Burbage his Juliet is gone. Meanwhile, if you would like to continue your lodging here, Thomas *is* your responsibility." Mistress Taylor yanked the cover from the boy, who remained curled like a shrimp. He wore a long linen shirt and nothing else. The light, curly hairs on his thighs glinted in the morning sun.

"Thomas, huh?" He peeped at me through a fringe of dirty blond bangs. A purplish mark ringed a grey eye. "Where'd you find him?"

"Where d'ya think? Outside the Globe Theatre, where you lads are due to meet Master Burbage in an hour."

"Seven hours, but close."

"Ooh, I love *Romeo and Juliet*," said Mistress Taylor, forgetting Rabbie for a moment. She beamed a gap-toothed smile. "I saw it in, what, '85? That was back at Rose Theatre, played by the old Chamberlain's Men. I was just a girl, then, mind you." Mistress Taylor fluttered her eyelashes. "But I fell in love with that boy playing Juliet."

She considered me for a moment. "Y'are not a bad looking lad, you know, but that boy from '85, now *he* was a beautiful girl."

"So, Thomas is an actor?" I asked, catching on at slothful speed.

"Yes, 'Thomas' *is* an actor," said Mistress Taylor, addressing me as if I were a feeble-minded toddler. "And 'Mistress Taylor' thinks Mistress Taylor needs to go downstairs before the porridge is burnt." She sighed at the boy in the bed who was now sitting up, regarding me with an uncomfortably close eye. "Mistress Taylor bids Masters Thomas and Rabbie to recover their wits before coming downstairs for breakfast."

She brushed past me through the open drape. Rabbie broke the silence by reaching for the pot between the two mattresses. Eyes wide, I stepped to the other side of the threshold before the boy could begin doing the business of what most people did when they first got up in the morning. I stood there while a toad-shaped man with copious amounts of white ear-hair exited one of the other rooms.

"Good morrow to you," he coughed, starting down the stairs.

I nodded.

"GARDYLOO!" Rabbie called, followed by the sound of a small splash out the window.

This was indoor plumbing?

I heard the ceramic scrape of a lid being placed on the pot.

"Are you still there?" Rabbie asked from the other side of the curtain.

"Yes." Where *would* I be? *River Thames, Jefferson County, Diagon Alley, a video simulation, some weird anxiety dream?*

"I'm here," I said. I re-entered the room, avoiding direct eye-contact with the chamber pot. Rabbie had put on pants. Well, shorts. Knee-length short pants. Whatever. At least I felt I could now let my eyes drift somewhere other than his hairline.

"You're not Thomas," he said.

"Duh," I said. It wasn't polite, but my brain had forwarded all reserve power to basic processing. I'd nothing left in the tank for artful deception.

"Da? Are you Russian, then?" he asked, a look of understanding on his face. "Govorish po russki?"

I shook my head in a vague way, mouth halfway open in an attempted response.

"MEEEE, Raaaabbie," he said loudly, affecting a vaguely Boris-and-Natasha accent. "WHO...ARE... YOU?"

"I speak English," I said.

"Well, then. Who are you?" he asked again.

"*Another* Thomas?" I offered. "Maybe?"

"Try again. I'm Rabbie," he said.

"Rabbie," I repeated.

"Robert James Dorchester, but that's only to me ma. And only when she's angry. And you are...?" he asked again.

"Mistress Taylor seems to think I'm Thomas," I said weakly.

"Mistress Taylor's eyesight rivals her ability to chew hard biscuit. She calls *me* Thomas half the time."

"Oh, well, then," I said.

"And if you had half the wits as she has teeth, you would not pretend to be someone whom you most clearly are not."

I sighed. "My name is Alex."

"*Alexander died, Alexander was buried, Alexander returned to dust,*" Rabbie said.

"Is that a threat?" I asked, side-eyeing the boy. He weighed less than I did, but seemed sturdy enough. Decent calf muscles.

"It's a line. From *Hamlet*. I'm a player," he said, running a hand casually through his side part.

One look at his dove-grey eyes told me this was probably the case. The black eye he sported added another layer to the bad-boy mystique.

"Actor, right? *To be or not to be,*" I ventured, remembering Natalie's recitation at the book club party. "*That is the continuum.*"

"I haven't heard that version," said Rabbie.

"Oh. I um— "

"Did you play *Hamlet* on the continent? Prussia? That would explain your accent. Is that how you know Thomas? Did he send for you?"

"Sure," I said, feeling that was as safe an answer as any.

Rabbie's eyes narrowed. "You stand surety for him, then? Does Burbage know?"

Burbage. Burbage. Burbage. The name burbled like a gaseous emission. Mistress Taylor mentioned a Burbage. Burbage was the Boss. Our Boss. Mine and this boy's. The Big Guy. Big Guy Big Boss Boy Burbage. I was tired. I felt like I was going crazy, which I probably was. I needed to sit.

I sank to the empty mattress, the one belonging to the missing Thomas. It was hard as a bale of hay, probably because it *was* a bale of hay. Little bits of twig poked my rear. Rabbie continued expounding on Thomas, Burbage, and continental players, and it all sounded like gibberish, so instead of trying to puzzle it out, I did the next most useful thing, which was to contemplate the continuing deterioration of my feet.

In addition to the popped blister on my big toe, I had several small scratches, one half torn nail, and a full-fledged cut on my left pinky-toe knuckle. How many diseases had I exposed myself to running through the streets? When was my last round of vaccines? Did toes even *have* knuckles?

"So, this has all been arranged with Burbage?" the boy finished. "When Thomas left... He didn't even tell me about you, the...," he trailed off.

"The pissant younker?"

"That would be him. But he's not. Sorry... I am not myself," the boy exhaled, belly-flopping dangerously on his own mattress. There was no reverberating bounce, just a soft but definite thud.

"What?" I asked, unclear where this was headed. I pushed aside the blanket, which looked and smelled as if it hadn't been washed in, like, ever.

"Thomas was my friend. Was. He was everything. Me? I am nothing." Rabbie pulled his own blanket over his head.

"You're a player…"

"I am a player," Rabbie confirmed, voice muffled. "But a bit one."

OMG, another insecure actor.

"You've done *Hamlet*, though, right? Your last play," I prompted. In, like, Shakespeare's own theatre. Sheesh. I flicked a tiny black bug off my knee.

"Yes."

"So… that's, well, amazing!" I said truthfully.

"It was," he said, flopping on his back. He balled up the blanket like a pillow, and rested his head, staring dreamily at the ceiling. "Burbage and the King's Men: simply the finest company in all London."

"See? You must be incredible." Between Ryan and Rabbie, I think my quota for encouraging moody male artists was satisfied. Just for curiosity's sake, I asked, "So, what did you play in *Hamlet*?"

Rabbie sat up. "The Second Spear Carrier."

Laughter floated from the floor beneath.

"Oh. Well. Um," I said unhelpfully. "That sounds cool."

"Cool?"

"You, know, spears and all." Sounds of the restaurant below were growing louder, mugs clinking, raised chatter. Homey smells wafted through the floorboards. My stomach rumbled. It had been doing a lot of that lately. "Do you want to get some breakfast?"

"What roles have *you* played?" asked Rabbie, sitting up, elbows on his knees. "Viola? Celia? Cordelia? Ophelia?"

"Ophelia! I know that one!" Among Monica's nightstand collection of self-help books was *Reviving Ophelia: Saving the Selves of Adolescent Girls*. I wasn't sure who Ophelia was or why she needed reviving, but at least the name was familiar.

"So, you've played her?

"Well—"

"That was Thomas's part, as well."

"Oh." I flicked another speck off my arm.

"He was glorious," said Rabbie. "A vision in wilted wildflowers." Restless, Rabbie stood and crossed to the open window. He braced both hands on the shutters. "I didn't think he'd actually leave. *My bounty is as boundless as the sea.*"

"What?" I asked.

"Juliet's lines," said Rabbie. He turned from the window. "Now it is to be you."

"Wait a minute," I said, standing up. "Me what?"

"You who..."

"You-hoo?"

"You keep repeating me. Are you certain you speak English?" he asked, one eyebrow arched. "I've known parrots with a greater facility for language. *You* who plays Juliet. Tonight." He picked up a cloth satchel from the floor, and pulled out a roll of parchment. "Here is Thomas's cue-script," he said, tossing it rather hard at my chest.

"What am I supposed to do with this?" The roll was an inch thick, attached to twin dowels, bound with twine. Hand-inked, with cues marked, the first line was, **Madam, I am here. What is your will?**

"You *read* it," said Rabbie. "Can you not read?"

"Of course I can read."

"What did they teach you in your old company? Speak the speech. Act the part."

"I'm not acting anything," I insisted. I thrust the scroll back at Rabbie, but he recoiled.

"You stand surety for Thomas. That is what you said, is it not?" He yanked open the brown curtain that signaled the room's threshold. "Otherwise, take your leave!"

I took a step forward, clutching Juliet's scroll. Where would I go? I had no money, no friends, no phone, no shoes. Four blocks away, eight dismembered heads sat on spikes.

"You said Thomas sent for you. Did he not?" Rabbie leaned against the doorframe, arms folded. Sounds of an argument rang from the street below, a crash and a woman's wail. I waited three beats before lying.

"Yes," I said. "Thomas sent for me."

Madam, I am here. What is your will?

"I knew it," said Rabbie. He let his arms fall to his side. A mistiness clouded his grey eyes, but only for a moment. He stepped forward, one hand extended, fingers long, white, and delicate. "Congratulations," he said, without sarcasm. "You have fallen into the greatest role for any young man in the history of theatre."

"Juliet?" I asked, a panicky whirl rising in my empty stomach, like a tornado of leaves in a vacant lot.

"Yes, Juliet." He strode to the cloth bag. "Here's Thomas's satchel," he said, tossing it to me. I caught it by the strap. "You can even have his bed so long as you don't fart in your sleep. Do you?"

"Um, no. I don't think so." I shoved the scroll into the bag and held it like a pocketbook. "But. Just for instance. What if I don't *want* to play Juliet?"

"Not a big enough role?" he joked. "I suppose you'd rather be the Apothecary. Well, sorry. That's my part. I have six whole lines at the end of the play." Rabbie smiled ruefully. More noises from the street below: a male singer accompanied by a stringed instrument; a street seller hawking the price of eggs; the plink and thunk of wooden wheels rolling on cobblestones. The world had fully woken up.

"Well, sure."

"Sure?" he asked, head tilted.

"Sure," I said.

"You keep using that word."

"Because it's a word."

"Do you mean 'cocksure'?" he asked.

"Uh. I don't think so," I flushed. "I just mean, yeah, sure, great. You play Juliet. I'll be the Apothemahoochy or whatever." I said this with no intention of playing anything anywhere, of course. Somehow or another I'd be gone by performance time. I just needed to find my stuff. My phone.

"Here. Take it." I flung him the bag.

"I can't play Juliet!" Rabbie looked abashed. He threw the satchel back to me.

"Why not?" I asked, flinging it back to him.

"Because," Rabbie sighed. "Master Burbage thinks I'm good for nothing other than cleaning props and, and—"

"Spear-carrying?"

"Carrying spears," Rabbie finished. He thumbed his nose, resigned. "Besides, despite what Thomas may have told you, he'll be back. I'm hard pressed to believe he'd walk away from his life's work, even with a new pair of boots."

"Wait, *what*?"

"His life's work. The same as mine," he said. "Do you know what that is? To know who you are? What you are meant to do? And in the course of that, find redemption in truth?"

"No, no, no… boots! You said 'BOOTS'!"

"I said 'boots,'" Rabbie repeated.

"Yes, boots! Were they *black* boots?"

"I'm discussing truth and redemption, and you want to talk about boots?"

"Yes!"

This pissant younker Thomas had my boots! I was cocksure of it.

"Perhaps we should get downstairs," said Rabbie. "You look that much peaked."

"Peaked?"

"Yes, Parrot."

"I have a headache." I dug the heel of my palms into my temple for a good rub, avoiding the sore spot where Thomas had slammed me with a steel toe. Feeling a tickle, I flicked my fingers. Another black thing sailed across the room. That made three bugs. Three bugs was a pattern. Screeching in a very non-boy way, I leapt onto Thomas's mattress and began rifling my fingers through my hair.

"If you don't like the creepers," said Rabbie, "the mattress is not the best place to escape them. Fleas won't kill you, though."

Fleas.

Flea bites.

A recollection surfaced from the depths of seventh grade History, the class that organized the Ren Faire. Wasn't that how the *bubonic plague* was spread? Through flea bites? Hundreds of thousands of people meeting their torturous ends through a contagion spread by fleas sucking the infected blood of rats and passing that onto humans? Only, no one knew that back then.

Back now.

I HAD THE PLAGUE!

This wasn't happening. *Not happening.* I was in a coma, critically injured from the lightning strike. Monica sat on one side of my hospital bed, Ms. Lanyer on the other, reciting snatches of half-remembered Shakespeare, like an incantation or prayer. I could feel their presence. I was dead, but not dead, like Juliet in her tomb.

I screwed my eyes shut.

Wake up!

I hazarded a peek.

Nope. I was still in the little room, with two flea-infested mattresses, a chamber pot that smelled like its previous contents, and a missing Boy Juliet.

"Sorry," I said to Rabbie, shaking off the willies. "I just feel like I'm in some sort of a play, you know, by Shakespeare..."

"Shakespeare?" he asked. "Who's Shakespeare?"

Chapter 18

I am none of his flirt-gills

"William Shakespeare," I repeated.

"Never heard of him," said Rabbie.

"The playwright. *Hamlet*. He wrote it."

"Not ringing a bell."

Was Ms. Lanyer right? Shakespeare was an imposter, a pen name for someone else? Ms. Lanyer's great-great-great-great-times-infinity grandmother? The world's greatest cover-up?

"But *Hamlet*?" I asked, not quite believing it.

"It's an old play," Rabbie said, as if that explained everything. "Soft. No, I think I've heard of him. Shaxper? Actor, right? Or used to be. Saw him play Old Adam in *As You Like It*. I think he's dead. He may have written a play or two. Or three."

"You don't *know*?" I asked.

"Playwrights," he shrugged. "Hard to keep them straight. What do they do but dress up old stories? Except Kit Marlowe. He could write a masterpiece about a bowl of porridge. Speaking of which, I think it time we broke our fast." He shoved his feet into a pair of leather slipper-shoes and threw the strap of Thomas's satchel over his shoulder.

"You mean breakfast?" I asked.

"You have the right of it, Parrot. Let's go."

***

The room downstairs was nearly full, men—and a couple of tough-nosed women—crammed on benches at the long wooden tables, cheeks ruddy and faces sweaty with the fug of bodies. Morning light streamed through small, square windows at the front of the parlor. Two serving girls rushed about the room, carrying trays with bowls and mugs. Rabbie led us to one of the last vacant places by the fire, heat radiating from an iron cauldron.

"That fire's pretty hot," I said.

"As fire normally is. You could remove your doublet," said Rabbie.

"My what-blet?" I asked, pulling the wool from my T-shirt. Steam rose from my still-damp sweater.

"You are wearing a multitudinous layer of clothes. If you are warm, it might be sensible to remove one."

"I have, um, allergies."

With my A-cups, I could pass as a boy, but not in a wet T-shirt.

"Aah," said Rabbie, scooting a hair back.

"I'm not *infectious*."

"I remember that much," replied Rabbie. "You said your name was Alex. I don't know anyone called 'Infectious.' Is that your stage name?"

Our table shifted, and suddenly a not-insubstantial-sized girl was in my lap. At least, I think it was a girl. I saw mainly a bonnet, with a riot of yellow curls that tickled my nose.

"Who's your friend, Rabbie?" she asked, eyeing me over her shoulder. "He's a comely Jack." She shifted her weight to one side, her soft rump straining the capacity of my right knee. "Not a whisker on him," she said, stroking my cheek. Her blue eyes were set just a tad bit close. She wrinkled an upturned nose, like a piglet scenting a truffle.

"Where's Thomas?" she asked, looking back at Rabbie.

"Gone," he replied.

"No great loss," she said, her babydoll lips in a pretty pout. "Too melancholy. His face was so tart, it curdled the cream. This one's a fine replacement," she ground herself further into my thigh, which was starting to lose circulation. I sat like a mannequin, limbs and face frozen. "Aren't you going to introduce us?" she asked Rabbie.

"This is Alex, Mary," he said.

"A merry Alex, then, is it? I could make you merry, lad." She lowered her eyes to her tightly-laced bodice, providing an ample view of the reason why *she* would never be mistaken for a boy. Unlike mine, her puberty had been successful. Or at least yielded tangible results.

"He's from the continent," said Rabbie, with a smile in my direction. "Doesn't speak much English."

"Da," I said.

"Oooh, even better," said Mary. She brushed her hand along my collar.

"Leave him be, Mary," said Rabbie.

"You wish to offer me better accommodation?" she asked, leaning across the table.

"Mary!" cried Mistress Taylor from the back of the room. "Stop your flirting and bring the boys their bowls!"

"Yes, Mistress!" Mary called. She skittered to the back bar, side-stepping the packed tables.

"I think she likes you," said Rabbie.

"Da," I repeated.

"Don't care for the serving wenches?"

"You could say that."

"I just did."

Mary returned with two steaming bowls and a crock of soft butter.

"What do you think, Rabbie?" Mary asked, eyeing me. "Is he not handsome?"

"Quite," Rabbie said, as I kicked him under the table.

"Well, Alex," she said. "My shift is over come eventide. Perhaps you'll see clear to walk me home. Rabbie here cannot be troubled."

"We are to meet Master Burbage," said Rabbie. "Alex must send his regrets."

"Alex can send me anything." Mary rested her tongue between her teeth. "Any. Thing."

"Mary!" cried Mistress Taylor.

"Anon!" Mary winked, sashaying back.

I took a cleansing breath and picked up my spoon. The greyish mass in the wooden bowl smelled edible enough, like honeyed oatmeal. Rabbie passed the butter, which actually wasn't butter, but a kind of thick yogurt. I scooped a small dollop, the sourness complementing the sweetness of the honey and the salted oats. Either I was famished, or this was the best gruel an orphan ever had.

Mary returned, mouthing a kiss in my direction as she placed two mugs of frothy amber liquid on the table. A beer? Really? For breakfast?

I'd tasted beer once. When I was five-years-old, I begged a sip off my mom's. It looked like a soda, and sodas were good, right? She put the bottle to my lips, a clink of baby teeth on brown glass. *"You didn't warn me,"* I whined, after I'd sprayed the kitchen linoleum. She wiped my face with a mildewed washcloth. *"Sometimes, Allie-gator, you have to learn for yourself."*

Beer and bay leaves. A bitter gall. The taste of poison in my mouth.

I pushed the drink away.

"You have no thirst?" asked Rabbie.

"Is there any water?"

"You mean from the river?"

Good point.

I stared at the frothing mug, swallowing dry sand. *I am not my mother. It may be morning, and that is definitely a beer, but I am not sitting on a fire escape with a twelve-pack and a boyfriend while my daughter watches cartoons in a dirty nightgown.*

The first, tentative sip went down easy, earthy-tasting, with a light and fizzy carbonation that invited chugging. Apparently, one of the side effects of being struck by lightning was a vicious thirst.

I contemplated the swirls of foam on the bottom of the mug.

"Have another?" Rabbie asked.

"No, one's my limit," I replied, thumping the tankard on the table. The pleasant warmth that filled my body gave way to another biological need. "Is there a bathroom around here?"

"A bathroom?" asked Rabbie. "There's a ewer upstairs if you wish to wash."

"Um..." Speech had become an in-body, out-of-body experience, empty word bubbles in a comic strip. I rocked my hip bones back and forth on the well-worn bench. Beer sloshed in my gut like an under-filled water balloon. "I have to pee," I said.

"You mean a privy? There's a jakes out back." Rabbie motioned to a rear exit.

"Thanks." I stood up, joints like Jell-O, a strange but not altogether disagreeable sensation. Down a short hall, fingertips tracing the scarred paneling, I passed a room to my right where two girls, faces sweaty, scrubbed dishes in a wooden tub. One pointed wordlessly to a back doorway.

The exit opened to a dirt yard. A flock of balding chickens greeted me with loud squawks, followed fast by a red-combed, kamikaze rooster, which flew at my face, talons first. Lacking cover, I kicked a herky-jerky dance, hands scissoring the air, embarrassing as a self-defense move, but surprisingly effective. The rooster screeched and flapped to the top of a small, foul-smelling shed.

"And stay up there, you ugly chicken!" I yelled.

BWAWK!

"I mean it. Don't make me make tenders out of you!"

BWAAAWWWWKKK.

"Ah, shut up!"

A man entered the yard from a side alleyway, balancing a barrel on his shoulder. "Good morrow to ye," he said. "We've a delivery of wine for Mistress Taylor. Do ye know whereabouts she is?"

"In the dining room, I think."

"Thanks be to you." He opened the rear door to the tavern, leaving me alone with the psycho rooster, pacing the roof of the outhouse like a battery soldier.

I twisted my legs. My bladder felt like it had gained another pound. Could beer spontaneously multiply its volume? The threat of another dive bomb, combined with the stench emanating from the shed, led me to ponder my options. The yard was small. Besides the outhouse, there was a wood-shingled coop and a fenced herb patch. No privacy. I peeked around the corner of the building, from where the delivery man had come. Boxes and barrels lined the deserted passage. With only a moment's hesitation, I scooted between two casks, undid my jeans and squatted, intensely relieved.

A minute or so later—allowing for drip time—I popped my head up. At the end of the alleyway, down the main drag, people went about their business, ignoring the side street.

"You!" said a voice.

I jumped. Rabbie was there, staring.

"Do you mind?" I asked, zipping.

"You—"

"What?" I asked, beginning to feel caught.

"You—you are—a girl," he spluttered, eyes round with incredulity.

"I never said I *wasn't*." I made to move past, not entirely sure where I was headed. Back to Mistress Taylor, to let her know I was an imposter? Somehow, I didn't think she'd continue feeding me, much less providing room and board. Flea infestations aside, it was better than sleeping in a mud puddle.

"You can't be a girl." Rabbie stopped me, an arm across my not-very-significant-chest.

"Okay, then, I'm not," I said, pushing his hand away. I put my other hand on my hip, figuring the best defense was aggressive indignance. Perhaps that would confuse him long enough for me to think.

"You are a girl," Rabbie repeated, as if to convince himself.

"*I know*, Sherlock."

"Shylock?"

"*Sherlock*. I'm familiar with my parts."

"You can't play Juliet if you're a girl. That's just indecent!"

I let that sink in. "You people are very weird, you know that?"

Rabbie jabbed his finger at me. "You don't know Thomas, do you? He never sent you!" he said triumphantly. "Who in heaven are you?"

"I'm ME! Okay?!" The words echoed in the close alleyway. I slapped his pointed finger. "I don't know who I am!"

Rabbie took a couple steps back.

"I'm not *crazy*," I said.

The problem with this pronouncement was, of course, that only crazy people felt the need to say they weren't crazy. Non-crazies just rested on the evidence.

Rabbie paced a half turn up the alley, looked both ways, then spoke out the side of his mouth. "What have you done?"

"What?" I asked. "I didn't *do* anything. I had to pee. I'm sorry I didn't use the outhouse. The crazy rooster tried to attack me."

"Not *that*," said Rabbie. "What are you running from? What have you done?"

"Nothing! I haven't d-done anything," I stammered. "Well, I didn't pay for the porridge. And, I- I probably shouldn't have drunk the beer. Not that I'm drunk. Well, maybe just a bit tipsy."

Rabbie put his nose next to mine. "No girl disguises herself as a boy unless she's in trouble. Where is your family? Do you not have one?"

"I—" The answer was too complicated. Did I have a family? Sure. Plenty. One bio mom. Thirteen foster mothers, countless foster grandparents, eight foster dads, twice as many brothers and sisters, some of whose names I could remember, others I could not. My first foster parents, Miss Lisa and Mr. Tim, had a nine-year-old daughter named Jade who put Cool Whip in my hair. Johnna, the fifty-year-old waitress, smelled of menthol cigarettes and fried eggs. Debbie and Rick, who took me to the San Francisco Museum of Modern Art. Renatta, who forced me to eat baloney. Foster siblings Robert and Brittney; Dana, Gemma, Jayden, Aiden, Ashley, Ashleigh, and Ashton; *ashes, ashes, we all fall down.*

The list went on and on, like names written on the inside cover of a yearbook, ghost signatures from people who passed in and out of my life.

And Monica, four hundred years in the future, sitting at a dial-up computer on a Formica table, sipping chamomile tea from a china cup. If I was *here*, and she was *there*, and time moved forward *there* as well as *here*, what must she be thinking? I'd vanished without a trace. Had she called the police? What would they do? I was a seventeen-year-old foster kid with no living relations, no friends. Who would look for me?

"No," I said truthfully. "I have no one."

Rabbie nodded.

"Look, I'm sorry I tricked you."

He brushed a bit of his sandy-colored hair behind an ear and shrugged. "I suspected."

"No, you didn't," I rolled my eyes. "I totally had you fooled."

"I was momentarily distracted by your continental accent. I thought all Russian boys were weak in the hams."

"Excuse me?" I checked my backside.

Rabbie cleared his throat. "Burbage, my employer, will *not* excuse you. That is the *point*. And if Burbage discovers you *lack a point*" —he nodded significantly to my crotch— "we'll both be on the streets." He sighed. "I think you'd better go."

The air in the alley seemed to solidify. For a moment, I thought time was messing with me again. Only instead of zooming backwards, I felt suspended, like last night in Monica's car. Wheels spinning, water rushing by. No traction. Nothing to hold onto.

Rabbie waited for me to go.

So I did.

After four steps on the packed dirt, I stopped. Rabbie was still watching.

I was angry, afraid, and, I don't know. "Betrayed" was the wrong word, but it came closest to describing what I felt. "You want to know why I'm here?" My voice shook. "You really want to know? I *met*

Thomas last night. Or rather, *he* met *me*. Your stupid friend, the *pissant younker*, STOLE MY BOOTS!"

"What?"

"Bashed me in the head, too." I lifted my bangs, revealing the raised sore spot on my temple.

"Thomas would not hurt a soul," Rabbie insisted.

"Kid about your age? Little smaller? Brown, shaggy hair? Pointy elbows?" I massaged my kidney.

"Aye, but..."

"Wearing mean-looking, black leather boots?"

"Aye," said Rabbie, looking worried.

I marched up to him. "Younker."

"I cannot believe he would do that."

I cocked my head. "Was he at the Globe Theatre last night?"

"We both were." Rabbie hesitated. His right hand drifted to his bruised eye. "I left. Came back to our room. Thomas returned in the middle of the night, wearing boots I'd never seen. He retrieved his things and left. I feigned sleep. Never said goodbye."

"I *need* my boots." And the rest of my stuff. "Your friend *stole* them from me."

Rabbie shrugged, defeated. "We will seek him then."

"Really?" I asked. I didn't think it would be that easy.

"I am sorry for what he did," said Rabbie. "That is not him. Believe me. He is my friend, and since the age of eight, the only real family I have known. We will find Thomas. We will find your boots."

The relief I felt was physical, to have Rabbie know the truth—or at least the partial truth—and not be abandoned. Nevertheless, doubt lingered. "How can you be certain?" I asked. "Either that we will find him, or that he's the boy you think he is?"

"There is fate, and there is faith. I put my hope in one, my trust in the other." Rabbie took a couple steps down the alley, then turned. *"The readiness is all."*

I paused. "Someone once said something very much like that to me."

"It's *Hamlet*."

"No," I smiled weakly. "Her name was Natalie." Last night. Good god, was it really just last night? Natalie Lanyer and I sat on her mother's concrete patio, the smoke from her clove cigarette diffusing the mist. On the other side of the kitchen glass, Ms. Lanyer and Monica washed the dishes, Natalie's mother and my "mother": one real, one play. Soap bubbles clung to the steamy window, insubstantial pockets of iridescence, air floating on air. Natalie put the cigarette to her lips. *There's faith, there's family, and there's something in between.*

I didn't know what Natalie meant. What Rabbie meant. What *Shakespeare* meant. About anything. Fate, faith, family. It was a logic puzzle with no solution. Family was origin. Fate was destiny. Did one determine the other? Star-crossed from the moment of birth? No, because faith was something different, a leap into the rushing water, even when there's nothing to hold onto.

But would the jump be enough to take me home?

Juliet never had a chance, the deck stacked against her, the dagger in her hand. What made me think my odds were any better?

"But I thought Thomas was already gone," I said hopelessly.

"*As that vast shore wash'd with the farthest sea.*" Rabbie leaned against one of the oak barrels that lined the alley.

"Huh?" My head felt hot, the pulse between my eyebrows twitchy. I understood the words that Rabbie said, the nouns, the verbs, the adjectives, but having to continually parse his meaning was beginning to feel like fire ants had invaded my brain.

"Romeo's line."

"Could you just speak English?!" I burst, kicking the oak barrel in frustration. This was not a good idea. First of all, oak barrels are hard. Second of all, a large cork dislodged, precipitating a gush of red wine. The acid smell of rotted grapes told me this was probably not the "good stuff," but Mistress Taylor, I imagined, would not be amused at losing sixty gallons of it.

"I'm sorry, I'm sorry." I hopped on my uninjured foot and scrambled for the cork in the wine-soaked dirt. Unfortunately the size of the barrel's hole seemed to have shrunk, as jamming the cork back in proved near-on impossible. Instead of a seal, I created a pressure nozzle. Red wine sprayed in all directions like an oscillating sprinkler.

"Give it to me!" Rabbie yelled, forcing the cork in with a kick of his own. Note to self: kick with *heel*, not *barefoot with toe*. We stood in a river of red, little drops raining from our hair and noses.

"Are you laughing at me?" asked Rabbie.

"No," I giggled.

"You look like a rum-soaked cherry." He licked a ruby bead off his thumb. "As I was saying—"

He paused.

"I'm not laughing," I insisted.

But by then, we both were. Rabbie laughed because I was laughing and I was laughing because he was laughing, and pretty soon the reason and the cause were one and the same, making as little sense as a word repeated over and over: laugh laugh laugh. It was just words, words, words, and words were nothing but air bubbles clinging to glass.

"The. Tide. Does. Not. Come. In. Till. Mid. Day," Rabbie breathed, eyes shining.

"I speak *English*." It was my best *Mean Girls* accent, hampered by the stitch in my side.

Rabbie hiccupped.

"Gesundheit." I pressed my lips to stifle further giggles. "So?"

"So, Parrot. We visit the docks."

"Well, then, what are we waiting for?"

"I gotta piss. Turn your back."

Chapter 19
God pardon sin!

Jumping muddy ruts and dodging wagons, drunks, and random farm animals, Rabbie and I made our way up the busy avenue towards London Bridge. We aimed to make it across and back before the 2 o'clock rehearsal at the Globe Theatre. Five hours to find Juliet. Thomas. Whatever. The kid who stole my boots.

"See the tall-masted ships?" Rabbie pointed to the wharves across the river. "Thomas's uncle is a galley cook on the *Marigold*. We go there first. If we can't find him, we'll have to think of something else."

I nodded, extricating myself from a rope held by a young girl leading a bleating goat. The population of the neighborhood seemed to have tripled in the hours since Mistress Taylor first led me to *The Shoulder of Mutton*.

Rabbie dodged a boy balancing two pails of water. "I do not know if Thomas is desperate enough to jump ship *onto* a ship, but if he means not to be found, he cannot stay in Southwark. Burbage knows everyone."

"What if we can't find him?" I asked. Pop-up stalls for vegetables, eggs, fish, and live chickens jutted in front of the taverns and brothels. The smell was yeasty, urine-y. Finding Thomas would be as easy as locating the proverbial needle in a haystack. A urine-soaked haystack. "I mean, there's like a billion people in this city." All of whom, apparently, forgot to bathe this morning.

"I don't know," said Rabbie.

"Well, you could play Juliet." I hopped over a rotten cabbage.

"Never," he said. "I already told you that."

"Don't you know the lines?"

"'Tis no matter." He patted his satchel with the scroll. "Players use cue-scripts."

A blast of steam from a blacksmith's forge hit me full in the face. A pair of teenage boys pushed and shoved until the blacksmith waved a red-hot hammer, causing them both to flee.

"But why couldn't you be Juliet?" I asked.

Rabbie stopped. "Listen close. The only reason I'm in the King's Men is because of Thomas." He looked down. "I'm not a true player," he confessed. "I am Thomas's *dresser*. I lace his corset, pin his wig, and play small parts when called upon. Burbage thinks I eat horse dung."

A heavily rouged woman whistled from a crooked doorway. There were a lot of half-dressed ladies in Southwark, too.

"Well, then, you'll have to prove Burbage wrong."

"I would never presume to do so. I know my place."

"But that's ridiculous."

"And Juliet is Thomas's part."

"Thomas is gone."

"Which is why we are going to find him. So you get back your boots, and Burbage forgets to have me whipped."

"Whipped? Like with a whip?"

"What else, Parrot, a lace sash?"

I blew air through my teeth. "Jesus, that's harsh," I said.

Rabbie stopped, jaw dropped.

"What?" I asked, looking behind me.

"You can't say that," he said, looking shocked.

"Jesus?" I asked.

"*Yes.*"

"What's wrong with 'Jesus'? It's not like I said the 'F' word."

"What's the 'F' word?"

"Forget it," I said.

"That's the 'F' word?"

"No. Jesus!"

"Stop saying that!" he hissed.

"Why?"

"It's heretical. Taking the Lord's name in vain." Rabbie shook his head. "A parrot, a bawcock, *and* a heathen," he huffed. "If we get out of this without our necks in a noose—"

"Hey, boys," catcalled the woman in the doorway. The red circles on her cheeks looked as though they'd been applied with a paintball gun. With her garish yellow wig and threadbare blue bodice, she was a study in primary colors. "Fancy a treat?" she asked, flashing a filthy ankle.

"Too early in the morning, Jenny," said Rabbie.

"Later, then, love." Her black toothy grin matched the inky birthmark on her wrinkled cleavage. Rabbie hooked my elbow and hurried us along.

"Hypocritical much?" I asked, when we were half a block away. A small crowd had gathered around a puppet show. Dusty children sat on the ground while two marionettes beat each other with sticks.

"Pardon?" asked Rabbie, who'd stopped to watch the puppets.

"You give *me* a hard time," I said. "But I'm not the one saying 'too early in the morning' to Jenny."

"I jest with her. There's no sin in that. There *is* sin in blasphemy." Rabbie clapped and tossed the puppeteers a penny. Church bells rang in the distance, a slow tolling of nine. We bent back towards London Bridge, the fetid smell of the river growing stronger with each mucky squish between my toes.

"Don't you believe in God?" Rabbie asked.

We passed three prostitutes on a balcony above a sign for *Hope Inn*. Underneath, a ragged woman cradled a grey-skinned baby. Everything happened for a reason, right? Children starved. Mothers died. *My* mother died. What was the point? That was the question. "I don't know," I said.

God was the father I never met. I'm sure He existed. Could He say the same about me?

"Things must be different where you come from," Rabbie sighed. "Just do not let anyone else hear you say such things. His Majesty is a mighty hunter of heretics."

"Heretics?"

"Yes, Parrot. Blasphemers and witches."

"Witches?" I envisioned the Wicked Witch of the West in green face paint, disappearing in a puff of red smoke. "You believe in witches? Like, seriously?"

"It does not matter what I believe, Parrot. Only what the King believes."

"What, like he's God or something?"

"You cannot say such things!"

"Well, next time I see the King, I'll keep that in mind. Remember, though," I trilled in my best Glinda voice, "*I'm a Good Witch, not a Bad Witch.*" I tapped his head with an imaginary wand.

The mother in the doorway lifted her eyes from the sunken cheeks of her child. She held out her palm. I put down my imaginary wand. I had no money, and Rabbie ignored her.

"I do not jest," Rabbie insisted, continuing down the street.

"Come on," I said, chasing after him, angry about the beggar woman. Rabbie could spare a penny for boxing marionettes, but not a starving baby? "When am I supposed to meet the King?"

"Perhaps tonight."

I tripped over my own toes. "Come again?" I was beginning to wonder about the hallucinatory effects of no sleep, a concussive head injury, and moderate alcohol intake. I wriggled a pinkie in my ear. "Did you say we were going to meet the King? Like, *the King*? A *King* King? Tonight?"

Rabbie halted again. "Burbage's players are the *King's Men.* What do you think that means? We perform for His Highness tonight at his palace in Whitehall—God willing—with a Juliet. We are to meet the others at the Globe Theatre in five hours' time to move the costumes and scenery."

"And if we don't find Juliet?"

"Then Thomas is ruined and so am I."

"Why would you be ruined?" I asked. "Thomas is the one who ran away."

"Because I am the reason Thomas is gone," burst Rabbie. He swallowed as if choking down a small ball bearing.

"You aren't responsible for him," I said.

"But I am. And if he is gone, if he is *truly* gone, then I have nothing. Burbage will toss me to the street. There is only one solution, to save you and to save me. It is madness, but you must take Thomas's place."

"What?" I stepped aside for a man pulling a woman from a nearby tavern, her chest brazenly bare. She yanked a stoneware bottle from the man's coat, stumbling after. "An hour ago, you said Burbage would kill me for impersonating a boy."

"No, just whip you. And only if he found out. As I said, I'm the dresser. I can help you."

"Are you kidding me?"

"Kidding?" asked Rabbie. "You mean young goats?"

"No!"

"Juliet is not a goat."

"Okay," I said, clapping my palms together. "Let's restart, shall we? I don't know what you think I can do, and why *you* can't do what you should *clearly* do, which is, HELLO, play Juliet instead of the... Apothemahootchy."

"Apothecary."

"Whatever. But I can't. I CAN'T. Okay?"

Ryan's face flashed in my memory, backlit by the stage lights, stars and planets in the blank void of space; his phosphorescent eyes casting a snake-charmer's spell; the smell of his cinnamon breath, rose petal lips; how Juliet's lines rose in my throat, words my own and not my own, but I knew who the fictional character was.

Me.

The fraud.

I was always playing a part: Foster Kid, New Girl, Responsible Student, Daughter of a Druggie. Pretty soon, I'd have no center, no core, nothing left but pretense.

I was done.

"Let's find Thomas," I said. "That's a good plan. A solid plan. But if we can't find Thomas, I can't take his place. You were right the first time. I can't be a girl pretending to be a boy pretending to be a girl. Do you know how ridiculous that sounds?"

"It sounds like a play."

"I CAN'T PERFORM FOR THE KING OF ENGLAND!" I bit my lips together. People were staring. Two merchants stopped their exchange. A beggar with a missing leg paused mid-limp. I bowed my head and backed away from a procession of metal-helmeted soldiers.

"Sorry," I whispered, when Rabbie caught up to me. "Jesus. Oh my god." I leaned against a brick building, folding my hands in a prayer against my forehead.

"You will do what you need to do to survive," Rabbie said. He pulled my hands from my face. "So will I. If surviving means putting on an act, then that is what you do. It is what we *all* must do." His eyes, grey like an overcast sky, held my own. The purple bruise could have been a shadow. His sandy hair brushed his cheekbones as he inclined his head. "Let us speak plainly. You are a girl. You have no resource. I could leave you to the mercies of the men who call on Jenny. Or I can help you, and by that, you will help me. I cannot say it plainer. Master Burbage despises me. He will not want me for his Juliet. If he finds Thomas has left, he will cast me out, in which instance, I shall be in no better straits than you. Thomas must come back. No doubt. He *will* come back. But till that time, you must be Thomas's surrogate, his cousin Alex. A player from the continent. Do you understand?"

I nodded, the muscles of my neck ignoring the wisdom of my higher faculties.

"*And...,*" Rabbie continued. "If I may offer a few more sage points of wisdom: When you come in the King's presence, you must refrain from all of the following." Rabbie enumerated on his fingers. "One, taking the Lord's name in vain. Two, declaring yourself as a witch. Three, questioning the legitimacy of His sovereign reign. And four, flaunting your femaleness in despite of all rule of law. You do any of the above, the King's Men will be finished, I will be left to starve with the scrapping apprentices, and, you, my friend, may end up on a pile of twigs with flames dancing round your ankles, burned alive as a witch. *Cox my passion,* am I clear?"

"Crystal," I breathed, feeling more than slightly giddy.

The air suddenly took on a whole new level of putrid. At first, I thought it was an olfactory manifestation of my terror, but no, this smell had legs. And arms. Lots of them. Greenish pustule-covered arms and legs connected to bodies dragged by a mule-drawn cart, wheels as high as my shoulder. A hairless old man drove the mule, lash slapping. The street crowds parted, silent as death.

"The Plague," said Rabbie.

I nodded, pressing hand to nose. I waited to speak until I was sure I could do so without vomiting.

The death cart turned the corner, but the sight of those limbs stayed in my mind's eye. The color of the corpses' skin looked like decayed asparagus, not even human. I'd never seen a dead body before, not even my mother's. Is that what happened when you died?

Think about something else.

Chapter 20
Poison hath residence and medicine power

"What the heck is an apothehootchy?"

"An apothecary makes potions," said Rabbie.

"Like a witch?" I asked. A woman with a basket of flowers shot a glance over her shoulder. We'd joined the jostle of humanity threading the needle of the first tower on London Bridge. The entrance loomed like a castle gate, decorated with pikes. Yep, they were still there. Like candles on a birthday cake, eight eyeless heads stared down, mouths in permanent "O's." *Welcome to London*, I thought. *Make a wish.*

"No," said Rabbie. "What is your obsession with witches? Apothecaries devise remedies. Healing draughts. There's one ahead."

At this point, I had myself together, my interior monologue looping a mantra of positive thoughts: Rabbie and I would find Thomas and all our problems would be solved; if we couldn't find Thomas, I'd…

I'd cross that bridge when we came to it.

This bridge was lined with shops, some buildings five stories high. We traveled down the center avenue, pressed by women in heavy skirts, men in capes, and small boys darting like minnows. Halfway across, Rabbie stopped at a vendor stand in the shade of a bookseller's awning. There, he purchased two savory pies, stuffed with roasted garlic and meaty mushrooms. I devoured the flaky pastry in three bites. "That was the most amazing thing I have ever eaten," I said, licking butter off my fingers.

"You think that is good, try a bite of this," said Rabbie, throwing another coin at the toothless, apple-cheeked vendor.

"What is it?" I asked, intrigued by what looked like a tiny calzone.

"Pigeon pasty."

"Oh, umm, no thanks. I'm a vegetarian," I said.

"I thought you were Russian."

"I don't eat meat."

"Pigeon's not meat. It's pigeon."

"I don't eat pigeon." Or rat either, no matter how flaky the crust.

"Suit yourself. There's the apothecary." Rabbie pointed to a sign swinging from an iron bracket. Carved and painted with a mortar and pestle, it read *Antonio's Apothecary and Teeth-Pulling.* "Do they not have apothecaries where you come from?"

"Uh, no. We have dentists." And people with a lot more teeth.

"So, 'dentist' is a word for 'apothecary'?"

"Maybe?"

We crossed to the beveled glass of the shop window.

"Shall we go in?" asked Rabbie.

"What about finding Thomas? Don't we need to hurry?"

"He cannot sail without the tide. It is not quite 10 o'clock. We can spare five minutes for your education. Plus, I would not mind revisiting the place. Perhaps I might find some detail that will help in the formation of my character."

"You said you had six lines. How much do you need to know? No offense."

"None taken. It is not the size of the part," said Rabbie, puffing his chest. "But the fullness with which it is inhabited."

"So says the Second Spear Carrier," I needled.

"So says the *best* Second Spear Carrier. I christened him Fernando Guttlesmouth. He was a tragic soul, really. His mother never loved him, he had to carry *very* big spears—"

"Overcompensating?"

"Quite," said Rabbie. "After you."

A bell above the door jingled our entrance to the shop. Floor to ceiling shelves lined the walls with bottles of every size and jewel tone.

I wandered, entranced. Most of the jars contained powders, some herbs, some liquids, some science experiments gone exponentially bad, organs in gelatinous goo. A large water-filled barrel sat on the floor in front of the counter, holding what appeared to be a live stingray, marked with five perfectly round blue spots. The flying saucer-shaped fish swam laps around my reflection.

"I would not venture too close," said a Spanish accent. A long-whiskered man emerged from a curtained back room. "That is a Torpedo Maculosa, an electricus from the Bay of Biscay. My new acquisition. Useful for gout or chronic headaches. It numbs the affected area."

"It bites?" I asked, instinctively drawing back.

"It *shocks*." He opened a jar on the counter and tossed a small, silvered fish into the barrel. The ray flattened against its prey, consuming it with two rippling shudders. "I am Signor Antonio," said the man, wiping his hands on his apron. "Are you in need of a poultice or charm? A tooth pulled?" His black, bushy eyebrows raised in question, like a pair of dueling caterpillars.

"Just looking," I said.

"My daughter can help you discover anything you require. Jessica!" A teenage girl pushed aside the curtain. Her caramel complexion was warmer than her father's mahogany. Long, dark hair hung in a thick braid. She tucked a dusting cloth into the side pocket of her skirt and smiled politely.

"I will be grinding herbs in the back, Jessica. Send for me if you have need." Signor Antonio nodded deferentially before retreating behind the curtain.

"What ails ye?" she asked. Her Spanish accent was less pronounced. "Or is it for a friend? We have all manner of cures. Bull's gall for styes, earwax for migraines, dragon blood for scabies, along with your everyday assortment of the finest herbs." She pointed to a row of ceramic jars behind the counter. "Calendula, burdock, dried garlic. Remedies for painful fluxes."

FINDING JULIET

"Painful fluxes?"

"Woman's monthly courses. Perhaps you have a *sister*," she stressed.

"You sell medicines, then?" I gulped.

"Herbals, potions, poultices, medicines." She waved a hand in the direction of a vial labeled, *Urine of Castrato*. I didn't want to know.

"What are those for?" I asked, pointing to a jar of live slugs. Two of them had poked tentacled heads over the rim. Jessica nudged them back into the jar, which she stoppered with a ventilated cork.

"Snail slime has marvelous restorative properties for burns and festering sores." Jessica eyed my mud-blackened feet. "Would you like one?" she asked.

"Maybe next time," I said. "Does it work?"

"Why, yes." She placed the slug jar next to the urine. A short-haired orange cat leapt onto the shop counter. Well, at least it wasn't black. If witches *did* exist, I bet they one-stop shopped here. "I sold three snails this morning. Poor lad. The shoemaker must not have fit his boots properly, though they were fine leather."

I looked at Rabbie. Could it be? "Thomas— "

"Did the boy have brown hair?" asked Rabbie.

"Were they *black* boots?" I added.

"Yes," said Jessica, stroking the cat, which rumbled a deep purr before rolling on its back. "He purchased the snails and a vial of deadly nightshade."

"What?" I asked.

"Belladonna," said Jessica, tickling the cat's white belly.

"Belladonna—deadly nightshade—is poison," said Rabbie, looking panicked.

"That which is poison in large quantities may be medicinable in small, Signor," said Jessica. "Belladonna can be quite useful in the aid of sleep." The cat dug its claws into Jessica's hand, but she didn't flinch.

"We need to go," I said, pulling on Rabbie's sleeve.

"Are you certain you are not in need of anything?" Jessica asked, inclining her chin. She had a mole on her neck the size and shape of a coffee bean.

"Aye, no. Thank you for your help," said Rabbie. We jingle-jangled out the door, back into the bright sunlight and the push of passersby on London Bridge.

"Deadly nightshade?" I asked. "Really?"

"It is probably for sleep. Why cure his feet only to take poison?"

"Maybe the poison is for someone else?"

"No," he said, more to convince himself than me. "I cannot believe it. But let us go posthaste."

***

Twenty minutes later, we crossed the threshold of London Bridge onto the cobblestoned streets of London city proper. Straight ahead, a sooty haze hung over the slanted roofs of skyscraping tenements, church spires lost in chimney smoke. We turned left and followed the river, where traces of the clear, blue sky remained.

Rabbie halted in front of a tavern called *The Gilded Peacock*, deftly side-stepping a 300-pound sailor. "I know those in here might know where the *Marigold* is docked. Will not take but a minute. Do you want to come in?" Rabbie asked. The door to the tavern swung open, releasing a wave of rough male voices and an aromatic mixture of beer and body odor.

"I'll wait," I said, pointing to a nearby pier, empty of ships.

Rabbie nodded, leaving me to the scavenging gulls. I moved a short distance through the lane of traffic, towards the wharf. Smells of dead fish and hints of sewage wafted from the gentle waves, broken by the occasional breeze. Across the river, the Globe Theatre resembled a miniature fort. A banner on the thatched roof waved tiny and white, like a flag of truce.

Surrender Dorothy.

The Wicked Witch of the West had scrawled the words in the sky, capital letters in black smoke, as Dorothy approached the gates of the Emerald City. Home to the Wizard of Oz, he was the all-powerful magician who everyone said would send her home. But, of course, he was an imposter, a pretender. Dorothy had the power all along. It was in her shoes, the ruby slippers that the Witch wanted so much.

I had to get home. But, how?

Follow the Yellow Brick Road and find the Wizard? Well, here in Oz, there was no Yellow Brick Road, no Wizard, only Thomas.

The Boy Juliet couldn't send me home, but perhaps he could give me the power to save myself. I put no stock in magic shoes. But, if he had my boots, he might have something else.

My phone.

The realization began as an earworm, niggling like the forgotten lyrics of my mother's favorite lullaby:

O my Darlin', O my Darlin',

O my Darlin' Clementine

I lost the rest of the words long ago. Buried them with my mother's voice. But the tune was there: sure and confounding as the blood beneath my skin, the blue ink scrawled along my wrist. I pressed my ring finger to the artery and felt the steady pulse, rhythmic proof I was alive. Just above, a fading tattoo, the ten digits of Ryan's cell phone number.

The area code was 613, the last thing I dialed before the lightning struck.

Only, I hadn't dialed 613. I dialed 1-613. 1613 on a cellular device that had the site of the Globe Theatre on its wallpaper screen—a picture taken by Ms. Lanyer in person, and therefore linked to a pinpointed position, the exact location a bolt of lightning "beamed" me, seemingly to the very year I dialed.

Was it really 1613? Was I four hundred years in the past?

Part of me didn't want to know. The very thought made me dizzy.

I looked up at the sky—no threats in black smoke, thank goodness—then down to the river. It was all so normal. That's what was so crazy. How did I get here? If it was the phone, then *how*? God?

Magic? Science? How on earth could I disappear from one time and place, and reappear in another? The human body doesn't *do* that. Flesh is solid. It can't break apart and re-form.

Rabbie stuck his head out the tavern door. He flashed a one-more-minute signal with a roasted turkey leg. Man, that boy could eat. His stomach defied the laws of physics.

The earworm exploded, which is a horrible metaphor for an epiphany.

Physics.

I hated Physics, but I loved Mr. Sparks. I remembered him jumping on a lab desk — he was always doing things like that to get our attention — exclaiming, "The human body is 99% empty space!"

The class laughed.

One boy slugged another in the arm. "Heh, heh, heh, feels pretty hard to me."

"That's what she said!"

Another shouted, "Veronica's head is 99% empty space!"

Mr. Sparks ignored Veronica's one-fingered salute, shuffling dangerously close to the beakers. "Each and every one of you is made of stardust." The class groaned, but Mr. Sparks continued. "Your atoms come from the beginning of the universe. But what are atoms? Protons, neutrons, and orbiting electrons, right? But those particles are less than 1% of your total mass. The other 99% is pure empty space."

If solidness was an illusion, why shouldn't it be possible to travel to another time, another dimension? Was it just dumb luck that the moment I dialed Ryan's number, lightning lit a path through the heavens?

If I was really hit by lightning, I should be French toast right now, not standing on the banks of the River Thames, centuries in the past.

Was it possible I was actually dead?

No, I wasn't dead. This wasn't heaven, and no anxiety dream had ever lasted this long. I must not have been directly struck by lightning. Perhaps it hit the phone. Maybe that's why I no longer had it. It was destroyed.

No. That would mean I was trapped here. I wouldn't accept it.

But was the phone really the key?

Ms. Lanyer said the cell hadn't worked since she went through the full-body scan at the airport, that the guy at the AT&T store worked some kind of "magic." Hyperbole, but *something* happened. What was a cell phone, anyways, but a radioactive transmitter? It sent signals across space. Could it send objects through time, too? No, not without some kind of amplifier—*what did Mr. Sparks call it?*—a particle accelerator that enveloped me from my head to my steel-toe boots.

A bolt of lightning.

My chest felt solid but empty, like the space between two electrons. *God, I want to go home.*

Rabbie came sprinting from the tavern, nearly knocking over a fish cart. He held out the gnawed turkey leg, offering me a bite. When I shook my head, he chucked the bone into the river. "The *Marigold* is half a league ahead, Parrot," he said, wiping his mouth. "It sets sail in two hours, but Thomas is not on board."

You are lost and gone forever,
Dreadful sorry, Clementine.

Chapter 21
Contempt and beggary hangs upon thy back

"So, we've lost Thomas?" I asked, trailing Rabbie up the riverside. "Then, where are we going?" We wound our way through fishing nets, rolling barrels, and throngs of hygienically-challenged seamen.

"The barkeep of the *Peacock* told me he's in the stocks. Detained by officers."

"You mean he's been arrested?" I grabbed Rabbie's arm, pulling him to a stop. "For what? Stealing?"

"I hope not. Thievery is a hanging offense."

"Hanging?"

"Yes, Parrot."

"You mean by his neck?" I swallowed tightly. "For stealing a pair of boots?"

"For less than that," said Rabbie. "If our Thomas is in the stocks, though, most like he was caught fighting or sleeping out of doors. Stealing is a graver crime. See that one?" Rabbie pointed a finger, slick with turkey grease, to a man roped to the wharf. The bald spots on his head blistered pink and white. Waves lapped at his midsection.

"Someone tied him there?"

"Well, he didn't do it to *himself*, Parrot. The constabulary will let him loose in a day or so. Not pleasant, to be sure, but better than losing a hand. The stocks are this way." He turned inland, where a ruined cathedral rose.

"To the church?" I asked.

"Yes. Saint Paul's," said Rabbie. "There's a stocks in the courtyard. Let's see if our Thomas is there."

The great building stretched two city blocks, fronted by an unkempt yard. Dozens of people milled in small groups. Despite the cathedral's crumbling stone walls, a hint of its former glory showed in the enormous stained-glass window above the entrance: ruby, emerald, and sapphire petals, arrayed in the pattern of a rose.

"What happened to the roof?" I asked. The central tower was oddly flat next to its neighboring points.

"A lightning strike hit the spire."

"Lightning, huh?" The memory of last night was still fresh in my fillings. Even now, I could taste the metallic spark of ozone.

"What year did that happen?" I asked.

"1550, 1560?"

"Was that a long time ago?" My fingertips tingled. My lips were numb.

"Well, sixty-odd years hence."

The wooziness spread, a sensation not unlike receiving an excess of laughing gas at the dentist. A dentist like Antonio the Apothecary and his jar of live slugs? I fought the rising giggle. No wonder no one had teeth in this place. All the dentists had fish hands. Tears streamed down my cheeks.

"Are you quite well?" Rabbie asked.

"Why?"

"Because you look a wee natural."

"I am not. Whatever that is."

"And you've gone the shade of a cod belly."

"I'm fine," I insisted. "Really. So, the year is now...?" I asked, wiping cold sweat from my brow.

"Perhaps we should sit," said Rabbie. Given that the nearby choices included a bench strewn with fish guts and a greasy barrel, I shook my head. Besides, I was close to the answer I'd been seeking all morning.

It is hard to hold your breath and speak, but not impossible. "1613?" I asked.

"Then you are not altogether addled in the brain," said Rabbie.

"Just a wee natural."

"Pardon?"

"Nothing. So, where are the stocks?"

There would be no further discussion about my brain, addled, scrambled, sunny-side up, or otherwise.

***

"Bombard cullion! Lousy beggar!"

A purple eggplant sailed past my ear. The bruised vegetable landed in the center of the courtyard, a few feet from a raised platform. On it sat an old man, perched like a doll on a shelf, feet locked in a vise. A group had gathered, hurling insults and refuse. A boy, about eight years old, broke through, pitching a rock at the podium. It glanced off the old man's forehead, leaving a smear of blood.

"That's the stocks?" I asked Rabbie.

"Yes, but that is not Thomas."

"I could have guessed. But where is Thomas?"

"Perhaps they set him loose for this man."

"What has he done, do you think?" The old man's clothes were threadbare, sticking to his body with grime and ancient sweat. The skin of his face stretched like a thin canvas over his skull.

"Belike he is a beggar."

"Begging is against the law?"

"It is without a license."

"How long does he have to stay there?" Another boy joined the second, armed with a fistful of pebbles. Plink, plink, plink, they rained at the old man's feet. The crowd applauded, like the audience at the puppet show.

"An afternoon. Or until someone commits a greater offense."

"And they're doing this *here*? Aren't religious people supposed to care for the poor? What kind of church is this?"

"St. Paul's belongs to the merchants now," said Rabbie. "It hasn't been a cathedral since the time of King Henry VIII."

"Can't you do anything?" I asked.

"Against the mob?" Rabbie replied.

FINDING JULIET

A white-haired preacher took the stage next to the stocks. "The sluggard does not plow after the autumn," he intoned, waving a Bible in the air. "So he begs during the harvest and has nothing!"

"Amen," chorused the crowd.

We had no food in the cupboards, even the Top Ramen gone. The night before, we ate spoonfuls of ketchup. Breakfast was cartoons and Kool-Aid.

"Come on, Allie-gator. Let's go to the restaurant."

Grace Memorial Church was a five-block walk from our apartment. I ran the first two blocks, my little-kid stride doing double-time with my mother's flip-flops, yellow rubber worn thin as cardboard. Round about block three, I scrabbled up her back, digging my fists in her neck.

"You're choking me, Allie-gator." I held my hands out wide, wings for an airplane. She sensed me falling and leaned as she galloped, my gravity secured to hers.

We reached Grace in time for the noon lunch, a plastic tray of warm spaghetti, crisp apple slices, cold milk, and a round butterscotch, wrapped like a present in bright orange cellophane. The grease of a thousand meals streaked the walls of the church basement, but it was warm and safe. We sat next to Walter-in-his-Army-jacket, who always gave me his candy.

"For the drunkard and the glutton shall come to poverty: and drowsiness shall clothe a man with rags," droned the preacher. The crowd shouted more insults. Another rock. Blood dripped down the ridge of the beggar's nose.

"We have to do something," I said.

"No, Parrot. We don't. Not unless you want to end up where *he* is."

I took a step forward. The beggar's hollow eye shot through me. He was Walter-in-his-Army-jacket, back bent over a trembling fork, while I sucked burnt sugar.

The preacher produced a switch, slashing it against the beggar's crusted feet. The old man screamed. The crowd laughed.

I ran.

I have never felt more ashamed in my life.

But I ran.

Chapter 22
A sail! a sail!

Rabbie found me at the river, where I caught my breath against a weather-beaten pier. I could no longer hear the beggar's screams, but the silence was cold comfort, evidence of my complicity. I ran away while another suffered. I was a coward. I could have stopped it, but I didn't. At some point, I needed to take charge. To *act*.

"It's none so bad," Rabbie said. "He'll not be permanently damaged. It could have been carting. Or the pillory. At least he'll leave with both his ears." He dug his pinkie nail between his teeth, freeing an invisible bit of food. The late morning sun peeked through wispy clouds, warming the winter-crisp air. Fragrant wood chips from a nearby vendor's stand mixed with smells of fresh fish, and the ever-present stink of the river.

"They'd cut off his *ears*?" I demanded.

"One or both. But it looks none so bad."

"What kind of a place cuts off a person's ear just because he's starving?" I asked.

"Not for starving. For *begging*," Rabbie explained patiently. "And they don't always cut off the ear, forbye, just nail it to a post."

Hands on my thighs, I bent my head to my knees and breathed in dirty denim.

"What is wrong with you?' asked Rabbie.

"Nothing," I said, straightening up. "Everything's great. Let's just lop off everyone's ears! How about whole heads? Oh, I forgot, *YOU ALREADY DO THAT!*" I yelled. Images flashed like picture reels: those death masks on London Bridge; the old man's toothless screams. "That guy in the stocks. The beggar. The starving man. How they treated him. That was *right*?"

"Right?"

"RIGHT!" I stomped, bare feet pounding hard earth. If I'd had my boots, the effect would have been much more satisfying. Rabbie leapt into my path.

"Why are you angry?" he asked, his voice calm.

"Why aren't *you*?"

"Y'are a strange one, Parrot."

I puffed air through my nose, like a bull deciding whether to charge.

"Now," he said. "If you are done shouting about things over which we have no control, perhaps we can do what we came for. Find Thomas." Rabbie grabbed hold of both my shoulders and pointed me upstream, where the *Marigold* was moored. "If he's been set loose from the stocks, perhaps he's aboard ship."

***

Close up, the *Marigold* dwarfed everything in its wake. Great white sails stretched seventy feet into the drifting clouds, bellying with the wind, listing masts weaving like drunken dancers. I imagined the great ship traversing the Atlantic, weathering thunderous storms, tossed on the open sea. My stomach lurched. How long would it take for the *Marigold* to cross the ocean? Two months, maybe three? Shorter than the four centuries needed to bring me home, but perhaps I could be there in a lightning bolt, if Thomas was aboard.

"Give uth a hand here, you two," lisped a sailor with a gold-hooped earring. The red stubble of his beard grew in unruly patches, like a poorly-watered lawn. He leaned his skinny frame into a sloshing keg, rolled halfway up the gangplank. "There'll be a tuppenth-worth for you," he smiled, his tongue peeping in the place where his two front teeth should have been.

"Come, Parrot," Rabbie said to me, jumping forward. We pushed our weight into the barrel, which rolled heavily up the incline, bumping over wooden slats. Once at the top, we crab-walked the keg to a man who lowered it into the ship's hold, a dark, cavernous area beneath the main deck. Sailors swarmed above and below, a colony of hairy ants moving in choreographed chaos.

Rabbie accepted a coin as payment before asking Stubble Beard where the ship was headed.

"Dover firtht, then Barbadoth, to the Indieth. Belike you've never thailed before? Captain prethed a lad thith morning. He may have room for two more." I picked a splinter out of my pinkie, wincing at the bubble of blood. "Or perhapth jutht one," the sailor said as I sucked my finger.

"No, thank you, though," said Rabbie. "We're employed with Master Burbage, of the King's Men," he added proudly.

"Players, then?" Stubble Beard asked, with newfound admiration. "I've theen a play or two. Fanthied me-thelf a player wonth upon a time." He struck a pose meant to signify an actor, arm outstretched. "*Wath thith the faithe that launched a thouthand thipth?*" he recited. "That Kit Marlowe, he wath my favorite. He could write playth, forbye."

"What about Shakespeare?" I asked.

"Thake your what?" He shot a phlegm-filled mass through the half-inch opening in his teeth. A ripple of nausea unsettled this morning's porridge and pastry.

"Never mind," I said.

"The boy you mentioned," said Rabbie, continuing on the previous train of thought. "The one the captain pressed into service this morning. Was he about my height? Dark hair? Face fair like a maid?"

"Like that one?" asked the sailor, pointing to me. I squared my shoulders and tried my best to look manly.

"Fairer," replied Rabbie, with an apologetic look in my direction.

"No offense taken," I said.

"*Ah, dear Juliet, why art thou yet so fair?*" quoted Stubble Beard.

"So you *have* heard of Shakespeare," I said.

"That's not Thakethpeare," said the sailor. "Thath *Romeo and Juliet*. Tragical tale. I could have made a fine player, I'll tell ye. I do not know if I could play a woman, though. Ith a hard thing to dithguise one'th thex."

I shrugged and brought my voice down another half octave. "I wouldn't know."

"Speaking of which," said Rabbie. "We are, in fact, after a runaway Juliet. A lad who is meant to play her. Might we see the boy who joined your crew today? Is he the nephew of the galley cook?"

"That I don't know, but you may thee below and have at it. Thath where the ladth are. Hurry, though. We thet thail thoon." A gust ripped through the ship's sails. "*Time and tide wait for no man.* Chauther. None tho great ath Marlowe, but, aye, I know me bookth." He trod down the plank, reciting to the wind.

"Let us go," said Rabbie. "We have twenty minutes, I think."

I followed him down a rope ladder into the bowels of the ship. A row of cannons lined the walls of the first level, the air charged with gunpowder and oiled metal. Rabbie and I sidled between men strapping the great guns, down another rope ladder to a cargo hold smelling of damp wood and dried animal skins. I bounced off a man who knocked me into another, like a pinball between Blutos.

"Watch yourself!"

Rabbie grabbed my arm. "The galley should be one more deck down."

"You've spent much time on ships?" I asked.

Rabbie lifted a trap door to a blast of heat.

"No," he said. "But I can smell food."

We hopped down the steps of a wooden ladder, the ship shuddering. Something had shifted, an anchor rising, another sail unfurled. Unless Rabbie and I wanted to end up in Barbados, we'd have to find Thomas soon.

"Hey! What are you lads doing here?" A red-faced man waved a giant spoon. Beads of sweat trailed from his temple to his grimy collar.

A kettle bubbled in a brick pit, next to pans lined with dozens of rectangular biscuits, the air thick and starchy. "You should be below decks with the others!"

"I'm sorry sir," said Rabbie. "We are looking for Thomas."

"Thomas who?" he spat.

"Your nephew?" Rabbie asked hopefully.

"I have thirteen nephews and none of them named Thomas." He scratched his backside with the spoon. "Well, one is named Tommy."

"Is Tommy aboard?" I asked.

"I should think not, being three-years-old."

"I thought you were someone else," said Rabbie. "I'm sorry."

"That's right. Everyone is *so* sorry I'm the new galley cook. If you ask me, the old one couldn't bake hardtack to save his life. Here, try that," he said, thrusting what looked like a prehistoric Pop Tart into each of our hands.

I took a small nibble. The biscuit was as hard as concrete and almost as tasty. "It's very good," I said. I swallowed, driving up the saliva to speak. "Can I save this for later?"

"Sure, take another." He handed me another couple of half-inch thick wafers. "The secret is in the bean flour. Don't need much salt. These beauties will last us all the way to the Indies."

"Thank you," said Rabbie, crunching his last bite.

"Of course, of course," said the cook. "And, say, you might check with the other lads. I heard they pressed a new one this morning. Might be your Tommy. And here, take another for your trouble."

"Thank you, sir," I said, following Rabbie to the only level we hadn't checked, three biscuits in my hand.

The lowest deck was narrower than all the others, walls slanting inwards, no portholes. Oil lamps swung from the rafters, throwing pools of light every thirty or so feet. Here, the ship seemed alive, moaning like the belly of a whale. "We're below the water, aren't we?" I asked, looking for cracks in the slats, telltale bits of condensation seeping through the boards.

"Yes. This way, Parrot."

We made our way through a passage lined with barrels stacked four high, roped with netting. Just ahead, two lanterns gleamed like eyes, illuminating a group of boys sitting in rows of flimsy hammocks stretched between posts. Two were arguing.

"THOMAS!" called Rabbie. "Are you back there?"

"Who wants to know?" An overgrown teenager in a pair of cutoff pants hopped from his berth and squared his shoulders.

"My name is Rabbie. I am looking for a lad pressed today. His name is Thomas."

"No one pressed except Fred the Farter," he thumbed.

"It's the *hard tack*!" yelled a pockmarked boy with bristly yellow hair. "The galley cook has done gone put bean flour in' em. 'Taint my fault!"

"Well, you're the only one speakin' out the wrong end, ain't ye? Fartin' Fred!"

"Say that one more time to my face!" Fred jumped to the floor, his acne flaring with volcanic peaks. The rest of the boys clambered for greater vantage, chanting, "Fart! Fart! Fart! Fart!" The scene was reminiscent of Peter Pan and his Lost Boys. These kids couldn't have been more than fourteen. Where were their parents?

"If the breaches fit, fart in them!" crowed the Head Lost Boy. The others howled.

I had to hand it to Fred. Outmatched by 50 pounds, he made up for it in bravery.

Shattering glass and the smell of oil burning followed a roar and a thud. Thirty seconds later, the fight, which had become a melee, was interrupted by a rush of feet. A massive forearm grabbed me about the waist, deflating my diaphragm. What happened next was a haze of noise and confusion, as my vision went spotty for the bouncing journey three stories up the hold, released above decks into a pile of adolescent limbs. I took a shallow breath of river air, and removed someone's elbow from my nose.

"Attention on deck!" shouted Pirate #1. He wasn't actually a pirate. I didn't see a peg-leg or a hook, but he had two gold teeth, a black beard, and a patch over his right eye. All that was missing was the *Arrrrrrrgghhh.*

I stood between Rabbie and Fred, knees knocking, still clutching my biscuits. The smell of passed gas wafted from my left. Fred shrugged and nodded to the dough congealing in my clammy hands.

"WHAT IS THE MEANING OF THIS?"

The group of sailors parted. A man in a three-cornered hat strode through the newly made column.

"Fighting in the bilges, Cap'n," said the Pirate. *Arrrrggghhhhh.*

The captain looked us up and down like a drill sergeant before a bunch of pathetic new recruits. "Right then, ten lashes each, and count yourselves on the side of fortune. Hurry and be about it. We sail with the tide."

Resigned, the Lost Boys stripped off their linen shirts, chests sunken, white and hairless. A six-foot-tall sailor with tattooed knuckles stepped forward and uncoiled a leather strap, smacking it against his palm. I gaped at Rabbie in horror. His own face had turned sickly pearl.

"May it please ye, Captain Sir," began Rabbie, his voice cracking. He cleared his throat and continued. "My fellow and I are not part of this crew. We came in search of a friend, and happened upon the fighting below decks."

The captain rotated his head. He aimed a steely eye at the gold-toothed pirate, then back at Rabbie. "Aye, then, what's this? You dare come aboard my ship a *stowaway*?" The captain stepped nose to nose with me. "You, too?"

"No, sir," I trembled. "We came in search of someone."

"WHO?"

FINDING JULIET

"A boy..."

"A regular orator we have here!" the captain announced to the amusement of his crew. My neck flamed. "What is the name of this mystery boy?"

"Juliet," I squeaked. "I mean, Thomas!"

"Keep your story straight, boy!" barked the captain.

"Please, sir. We just came aboard," I gestured with three damp biscuits.

"Ho, ho! And a THIEF!" he roared. "Stealing food from my ship! Call the constable! Have this one," the captain pointed to Rabbie, "put in the stocks for trespassing. And this one"—meaning me—"nailed to the pillory for thieving. OFF OF MY SHIP!" the captain bellowed.

The crew shuffled like a greasy pack of playing cards. Four hands lifted Rabbie and me down the gangplank, while a young sailor presumably ran for the law.

Ten minutes later, the constable appeared, looking bored and overdressed. Wearing a maroon cape with gold edging, a lace ruff, and a feathered hat, the mustachioed officer looked more likely to host *Fashion Police: Renaissance* than nail body parts to a post. He placed a casual hand on the hilt of his long-sword. I did what any sensible person confronted with an armed policeman would do: kept all smartass observations to myself.

"What's the to-do this time, fellows?" the officer asked our detainers. He swished his gold-lined cape over his shoulders. "Not another like the last one is it? The captain needs must find himself a steadier crew." Whistling slaps came from the direction of the *Marigold*, the Lost Boys receiving their lashes.

"Yes, sir," said a shirtless sailor. His hooked nose formed a near-perfect C. "Trespassing and thievery." He shoved Rabbie and me to the ground. I hit the cobblestones with a knee-crunching thud. Blinking away hard tears, my eyes refocused on the constable's boots, scuffed, steel-toed and bearing the Doc Martens logo.

"I beg pardon, sir," said Rabbie. "It was all my fault."

"Look!" I jerked my head significantly at the stolen boots.

"What's the matter with yon fellow?" asked the constable, twisting his mustache. "Is he a simpleton?"

Rabbie ignored my gaping. "Yes, sir. He was dropped as a babe. Hasn't been able to think proper since."

I clenched my teeth. "Rabbie, boots!" I rasped.

"Yes, Alex-Boots. That is our pet name for each other," Rabbie explained to the constable. He patted my head gently. "You need to go home, 'coz."

"Just a minute," said the constable, the dull thought visibly forming under his feathered hat. "I am in charge here. You've been caught trespassing and thieving. Those are mighty offenses." He pulled his sword an inch out of its metal sheath and let it fall with a sharp *SHINK*. He looked at me. "Are you or are you not a thief?"

Faced with the potential loss of a body part, thoughts of my hijacked boots disappeared into the soft blue sky, taking with them my ability to formulate an articulate defense. All I could muster was, "Uhhhhhhh," my head bobbing like an unbalanced seesaw.

"I see," said the constable to Rabbie. "He's not altogether *there* there."

"No sir. He's a natural idiot."

"I am not!"

"Constable," bowed the shirtless sailor. "Our ship is set to sail. The captain will be expecting us."

"Yes, yes," yawned the constable. "You are dismissed." Once the sailors had left, he turned to Rabbie. "Right, then," he said. "Have you any money? Anything of value?"

"A tuppence." Rabbie produced the coin given to us by Stubble Beard.

"A tuppence, hmm," said the constable, lip curling to match his mustache. "Not much. What about for your cousin? Captain wants him nailed to the pillory."

"But he's not in his right mind, sir," said Rabbie.

"I cannot pardon thievery. Even by a lackwit."

"The hardtack was given to us by the galley cook, sir. We did not steal anything."

"Says you. Not says the captain. I'll have your tuppence, but the idiot comes with me." He pulled me to my feet and shoved me forward. I focused on not having a full-on panic attack. *People got their ears pierced all the time. How bad could it be?* It was a dream. It was a dream. *There's no place like home. There's no place like home.*

"TWO CROWNS!" Rabbie cried. He took a couple gold coins out of a hidden pocket, and placed them in the constable's black-gloved hand. "Please, sir, it is all I have. Put me in the stocks. Let my cousin go free."

"Rabbie— " I said, muddled with tears.

"That's enough, 'coz!"

The constable examined the tuppence and two crowns with an approving sniff. "Well, then. Three hours in the stocks for you, son," he said to Rabbie, tossing the coins into a velvet drawstring bag. "And your cousin goes free. Make sure you don't cause any more trouble," the officer wagged at me. "Or next time I'll cut off that pretty little hand. Got it?"

I nodded, speechless.

"Thank you, sir," said Rabbie. "May I say a word to my cousin ere I go?"

"Be quick about it." The constable stepped to the side, jingling his purse.

"The load-out of sets and costumes starts in two hours," Rabbie whispered quickly. "Go to Master Burbage. Make my excuses, but do *not* let him know where I am. He'd not be over-fond of his player landing in the stocks."

"Rabbie. That mob— " I envisioned him surrounded by angry, jeering faces, hit by rocks or goodness knew what else. "I can't leave you!"

"*Go and be quick about it,*" Rabbie hissed. Then, for the benefit of the constable, he added, "Tell my mother I'll be home soon!"

"But Rabbie!"

"You owe this much to me!" He squeezed my arm, hard enough to bruise. There was fear in his expression, but something else, too. I understood then. I had to leave him to find Burbage, yes, but also to preserve his dignity. I could not add humiliation to injury.

"I will be fine," he said. "No one dies in the stocks."

I bit my lip and nodded. "I'll go."

"Good," he said, releasing my arm, the whisper of a smile back in his eyes. "And if you find Thomas, tell him I'll give him a knock to match the one he gave you."

"You mean the one he gave *you*," I said. Rabbie's lips thinned, a subtle admission that Thomas was responsible for the purple shadow beneath his eye. "Not if I give it first."

He took off the satchel with the scrolls and hung it around my neck. "Be Juliet."

The weight of what he was asking pressed my chest. "I don't know if I can do this, Rabbie."

"You can." He leaned closer. "Just don't squat when you pee."

"Come on, then," said the constable, placing a hand on Rabbie's shoulder. Three rings glinted with dime-sized gemstones. "Unless there are any more coins in your purse? No? Let's get it done, then."

"Where are you taking him?" I asked, as if I didn't already know.

"St. Paul's," the constable replied. "Lots of vegetable stands there, aye?" Rabbie winced as the officer laughed. "Tomatoes are in season."

Chapter 23
Chain me with roaring bears

Rabbie and the constable left, the latter striding shamelessly in my stolen boots, the former, head held high, refusing to look back. I stood in the middle of the riverside, paralyzed with guilt. Sailors and fishmongers eddied about me, a rock in the stream.

I couldn't change it, I told myself.

I couldn't stop the constable from putting Rabbie in the stocks. I couldn't stop the crowd from throwing things. I could only do what Rabbie asked, which was to cover for him with Burbage, and take Thomas's place as Juliet. I wasn't sure what I would do or say the moment I reached the theatre, but I *would* do something. If I could find Thomas in the interim, so much the better.

Pondering the whereabouts of the missing Boy Juliet occupied my brain during the miserable trek back over the river, the stone towers of London Bridge, turrets stretching skyward; street sellers of flowers and fresh-baked tarts, the scent of buttered pastry mixing with coal fires and the sour river. I ignored the old women, crones draped with shawls; the men in black robes, exchanging goods and money; the feral children and teenagers, pickpockets appearing like Wack-A-Moles behind the rich men's purses.

Was one of them Thomas? Would he have my phone? My backpack? In it were all my worldly possessions, my cherry Chapstick, a blue ballpoint, a bristled hairbrush, a pack of spearmint Trident, a pink canvas wallet with two ones, a five, two quarters, and two pennies.

I'd like to see Thomas try to pass off that five-dollar bill with the portrait of Abraham Lincoln. Was Lincoln even alive yet? *No, stupid.* Civil War. 1865. Over a century and a half in the future. Did America even exist now? Well, of course it existed. Exists. Just ask the Native Americans.

Indians. They wouldn't be called Native Americans now. Christopher Columbus thought he was sailing to India.

The Indies.

That's what the sailors on the *Marigold* called America, where the mysterious Thomas may or may not be headed.

Were there American colonies now?

My brain felt like spun sugar, all the random facts I'd memorized in History class one tacky mess: the Magna Carta, Manifest Destiny, Federalist Papers, Gutenberg Press, Bill of Rights, Mayflower Compact.

What happened when? I knew everything the day before the test, remembered a scattering of childhood rhymes, but what good did that do me now?

"*In fourteen hundred ninety-two, Columbus sailed the ocean blue,*" I recited. Luckily, the people on the bridge were too engaged in their own business to take note of a person talking to herself. "Good thing," I said.

"Who are you talking to, lad?"

Antonio's Apothecary and Teeth-Pulling was lit like a lantern from within. Jessica, the owner's daughter, stood on a wooden block, cleaning the store windows. "Did you change your mind about the slugs?" she asked.

"No, thank you." I hurried on. Between the jars of urine and barrels of electrified stingrays, the place gave me the creeps: a retail haunted house where Thomas made his mysterious purchases this morning. Where was he now?

To solve the mystery, I must be logical, think like a detective on *Law & Order*. As I crossed the bridge, I checked off facts silently in my mind, accompanied by the occasional musical sound effect of the TV show's gavel drop. *Dun-DUN.*

Sometime between last night and this morning, Thomas ran afoul of the law. The patrons in *The Gilded Peacock* said he'd been arrested, placed in the stocks. He wasn't in the stocks when Rabbie and I went to look for him, but this was probably because he bought his way out. Exhibit A: the constable's new boots.

So, where was Thomas now?

He wasn't on the *Marigold* with the other Lost Boys. Or if he was, he'd kept himself purposely well-hidden. This was a dead end. Either Thomas

1) never made it aboard ship

2) was kicked off shortly thereafter, or

3) managed to conceal himself in the darkness of the hold.

If it was #3, Thomas was now on his way to Barbados, with—thanks to me—a tube of Chapstick for the crackling sea wind.

So, putting aside Thomas's possible voyage to the other side of the planet (leaving me with no hope of returning to a place where the vast population did *not* smell like a combination of sewer rat and moist underarm hair), that left the only remaining two clues, if not to Thomas's whereabouts, then, *perhaps*, to his intentions.

Thomas purchased belladonna from Jessica. According to her, belladonna, a.k.a. "deadly nightshade," was poisonous in large quantities, a sleeping aid in small. Cool. Like Nyquil on steroids.

That left the final clue, and the sole bit of evidence I could consider fact. The previous night, while I lay passed out in a ditch, Thomas bashed me on the head and stole my stuff. This was before or after he punched Rabbie, his one-time close friend.

So.

Thomas was either—

1) a horrible bully *or* terribly misunderstood;

2) a stowaway on a ship *or* hiding out in the neighborhood;

3) a suicidal and/or homicidal teen, *or* a poor sleeper.

Frankly, the kid was a cipher. I wouldn't have been surprised to learn he was a figment of all our imaginations.

Dun-DUN.

Thirty minutes later, I reached the Globe Theatre, doors barred and deserted of people. I felt similarly bereft of ideas. What now?

I pondered returning to Mistress Taylor's to wait the hour or so before Burbage and company would arrive to move the sets and costumes to the King's palace, but I was done with sightseeing. My battered feet had settled into a convenient state of numbness, but my shins ached with the strain of walking without support, calf muscles tight with dehydration. I slid my back against the side of the Globe, and sat for the first time in what seemed like days. The roof of the theatre provided a welcome sliver of shade in the crystalline noonday sun. Stretching my legs in front of me, I pointed my toes and flexed my arches, wishing I had a Capri Sun or a Gatorade. A liquid that didn't have a thin coating of trough slime on it. Anything to make the inside of my mouth feel less like fuzzy sandpaper.

I let my eyes close. The light streaming through my eyelids cast a hazy burnt-orange glow. I could be on Mars, Jupiter, a red dwarf star, floating in the universe or back on Earth, the motion of the blue-green whirl pressing my body home.

I had no idea whether I dozed for ten seconds or ten minutes, but when I opened my eyes again, there was my dog companion from last night, this time sans decapitated rat segment, which upped his likeability quotient significantly.

Yellow Eyes.

His scraggly coat was patched and wiry, hanging in long grey and white wisps down his chin, like an untrimmed beard. I put his weight about 30 pounds, a medium-small dog, with legs too long for his body. Out of the pale starlight, he looked less ferociously coyote-like, more *Lady and the Tramp.*

"Here, boy," I called, snapping my fingers.

He wagged his skinny tail, a little metronome going triple time. He chewed something, a thin stream of saliva hanging from his mouth. "Whatcha got there?" I asked. He wagged towards me, motor butt rocking full power. "Something good?"

With a hack and a regurgitating cough, he flicked the stuck pieces onto the ground: a flash of green, a silvery foil. My breath caught in my throat.

No one chewed gum here. They didn't have enough teeth.

I inched my hand closer to the Trident wrapper, gingerly, as if the wad of dog drool were a detonation device. However, like many pets and small children, Yellow Eyes only wanted me to *see* what he had. He snatched the wrapper and bounded a few feet away. I stood up, suppressing the low growl in my throat. I was in no mood to play chase, but I didn't want to scare him.

"Here, boy," I said again, sweet as a packet of sugar.

The dog tucked tail and ran.

Game on.

Down a dirt road, past a building that looked like another theatre, Yellow Eyes jogged in and out of people, mules, and wagons, the Elizabethan equivalent of rush hour traffic. Any warm feelings I had towards the dog faded rapidly as he dashed through the legs of a vegetable seller, causing the fat man to overturn his cart, which apparently was *my fault* owing to the amount of indecipherable curses hurtled in my direction.

I waved an apology, but didn't stop to pick up the turnips. Yellow Eyes reached the end of the road and dove into a field of knee-high golden grass. I lost him for seconds at a time, while he bunny-hopped over mounds of earth. I followed less gracefully, nearly breaking an ankle in the crater-sized gopher holes. Midway through the field, a large insect whizzed by my ear.

"HEY, YOU! OUT OF THE WAY!"

As I was the only one on the field, I assumed the disembodied voice was speaking to me, although I couldn't tell from which direction it had come, or in what direction it wanted me to go. Looking left, all I saw were a bunch of hay bales painted with round circles rather like—

WHIZZZZZZ... THUMP!

TARGETS!

Yellow Eyes panted from the other side of the field, his head tilted as if to ask what I was doing, like he had no responsibility in the matter. To my right, a row of five archers were in various stages of cocking their arrows, not seeming to grasp the fact that my presence warranted special consideration. The good Samaritan (and least likely to shoot a shaft through my heart) continued waving me off, while the others aimed and fired.

WHIZZZZZZ... THUMP!

WHIZZZZZZ... THUMP!

WHIZZZZZZ... THUMP!

WHIZZZZZZ... THUMP!

I figured I had about ten seconds while they reloaded. Re-cocked. Whatever a person did with arrows to make them fly across a field and imbed themselves in hay or human flesh. I ducked, hoping the height differential was sufficient to avoid being pricked like a porcupine, but as the arrows whizzed by, I abandoned caution for speed. By the time I reached the other side, my heart was hammering as fast as the arrows, which continued to THUMP, THUMP, THUMP into the straw bales.

Past the threat of imminent death, I scanned for the gum-napper. I spied him in the next field, running between two rows of kennels. A dozen dogs strained against ropes wrapped around their necks, makeshift leads attached to pegs ground in the dirt. There were no doors, just individual stalls lined facing each other, ten to a side. The dogs snapped viciously, riled by Yellow Eyes zigzagging in their midst.

Frightened of the barking dogs, I took the long way around, skidding my heels in front of an enormous crowd. Hundreds, maybe a thousand, milled in front of a two-story building. Round like the other theatres, it, too, was sided with white weathered wood, roofed with thatch.

FINDING JULIET

The mood was festive, rowdy, loud enough to dampen the noise of the kennels. The barnyard smell mixed with the scent of roasted meats. Vendors held trays of nuts and bags of apples, hawking their wares like concessionaires at an NBA game, minus the team banners and foam hands. Men carried metal tankards, filling their drafts from sellers who sat atop kegs. Greeting each other with friendly and not-so-friendly jabs, they elbowed for position in front of two massive double doors, adding to the overall sense of Something About To Happen.

Yellow Eyes stood on the outskirts of the crowd, tongue lolling, ignoring and ignored by the crowd of semi-drunk and already-totally-drunk patrons. Sidestepping a bushel of chestnuts, I tiptoed to within three feet of the dog, close enough to see the shiny foil of the Trident wrapper still stuck to a gummy canine. I smiled, dove and missed, then lunged again, but the dog was already gone, leaving me with nothing but a handful of grey and white scruff. The last I saw before the double-doors opened was his wiry tail disappearing between the legs of a thousand people.

I followed as best I could, eyes trained a foot off the ground, knocked and bumped in the crush of bodies. Sandwiched between Smelly Hairy Man and his friend, Smellier Hairier Man, I began to reevaluate my course. I was never going to find the mangy dog in this chaos—a fine and reasonable conclusion, but one which came five seconds too late. Caught in the bottleneck of the double doors, there was no retreating: people ahead, people behind. I surfed the wave of sweat, noise, and feverish energy into the building, stuck like a bit of batter in a waffle iron, panicked, hot, and sticky.

I landed with a gasp into an open-air arena. Dust particles floated to the sunlit floor, a theatre-in-the-round circled by tiered benches behind a wood-paneled wall. In a section of the audience, four musicians in red-and-green tunics played fiddles, flutes, and small drums, a quick and lively "Renaissance-y" tune that added to the general festivity. Spectators stomped along with the percussion, shaking the rafters, raining more dust from the second-floor balcony.

I worked my way up the bleachers, looking for Yellow Eyes. No surprise, the dog had disappeared, vanished in the throng. I took a step down, thinking to fight my way out, look for the dog outside, when the musicians began a RAT-a-TAT drumbeat. It sounded like the beginning of a battle, matched by the audience's claps and footfalls. The bleachers shook. The walls shook. I half-expected the crowd to begin chanting *WE WILL... WE WILL... ROCK YOU!*

Then someone launched a firework.

Showers of sparks rained from the thatched roof. Apparently, this was intentional, for the audience roared, undisturbed by the fact that someone had set off a rocket in a building made of wood and straw.

Yep, this was my cue to leave.

Unfortunately, the exit was now blocked by a bear.

A real bear.

As if death by trampling, indoor missiles, and the impending collapse of the second-floor balcony were not enough, *the exit was now blocked by a bear.*

Of course it was.

Before this, the one and only time I'd seen a bear was on a field trip to the zoo. A round-bellied half-grown cub romped in a concrete grotto. Standing behind a Plexiglas wall, I could have been watching the animal on TV.

Here, there was no such separation: no moat, no spikes, just a fence of 2x4 planks that spectators reached across, patting the bear on its rump as it lumbered past. The handler, a small man with a tall hat, led the bear by an iron chain around its neck. He paraded the animal once around the arena before securing it to a thick wooden post. The great beast rolled its head from side to side as if scenting the rabid crowd, its eye sockets stitched together, scarred with light pink grooves.

The shackled bear was blind.

"That Harry Hunks is a mean fighter," said the man next to me, washing my face in beer breath. He grinned with a mouthful of yellow teeth, shades of pale daffodil to burnt saffron. Rank body odor combined with the funk of dental decay. "Always bet on him, lad, never the curs. You'll be left without a *penny* in your *pocket*," he said, spitting his *P's*. In the fold of his left nostril, a blueberry-sized wart sprouted three black hairs. He took a gulp from his mug, belched, then slapped me on the back. The blind bear roared in deep-throated surround-sound. "Tear 'em to shreds, Harry!"

Every part of me screamed this was hideous (whatever *this* was), but there was no leaving now. The standing-room only crowd had thickened in expectation of the main event, blocking the exit. Frenzied excitement rippled through the audience, palpable enough to raise the little hairs on my arms.

Two men, helmets strapped to their chins, entered the arena, brandishing stakes with sharpened metal tips. Were they going to fight the bear?

"Here they come!" Wart Nose cried, foaming at the mouth with anticipation.

At a signal, four dogs flew in from a side entrance, muscular, brown-and-white pit bulls, rough-coated, with massive haunches and muzzles like bricks, hell unleashed in a cyclone of hair, tails, and teeth.

The bear stood on its hind legs, head brushing the height of the second-floor balcony. The dogs darted in and out, haunches tight like wire coils, jaws snapping. Twisting to and fro, the bear lost its balance and landed hard, a front paw curled under its massive body.

Seizing the opportunity, the smallest of the pits scrambled up the bear's back—this to the enormous pleasure of the crowd, who signaled their approval by throwing apple cores and chicken bones—while the other three dogs rushed the tender parts of the bear's feet and face. The bear half-growled, half-screamed, blood spraying from nose and mouth.

"Give it to him, Harry!" shouted my neighbor, raining beer on my sweater. "You'll cost me fifteen shillings, you bugger!"

The smaller dog held on as his companions ripped bits of fur and flesh, consumed with the fury of bloodlust. The crowd went equally berserk, screaming at the dogs, cheering the bear, slapping each other with flat palms and calling for more beer, more wine, more wagers, bright pennies on the outcome.

It was awful.

It was loud.

It was sick.

But in the end, it wasn't much of a fight.

Ten minutes in, one dog lay bleeding from a belly gash, the large intestine bulging from its stomach like a water snake.

Another dog collapsed with its back broken, flipped against the barrier wall, spasms of shock shuddering from shoulder to tail.

The third dog retreated through the side entrance, whimpering and limping on three legs, sliced in the eye.

Throughout this, the small pit held on, maniacally gripping the bear's neck, the whites of its eyes visible in the bristle of fur. To the bear, the remaining dog seemed no more than a nuisance, a stray tick. He strode a victory lap around the post, flicked his ears and tipped back, crushing the dog's bones under its half-ton weight.

The audience cheered. The musicians played another jig, fiddles and flutes to accompany the scene of celebration. Some men collected coins. Others stormed out, throwing nuts, pushing their way through the crowd.

Me, I wanted to puke.

I sunk to the hard bench. The show was over. I felt nothing but disgust for my own species. If I ever made it back to my own time, I'd make a significant donation to the Humane Society. Maybe volunteer for PETA. Pass out pamphlets.

"Those poor dogs," I whispered, as a wet nose bumped my hand. It was Yellow Eyes, my beat-up backpack at his feet.

Chapter 24
That's the dog's name

My cell phone wasn't in the backpack.

I admit, a small part of me thought it might have been.

In stories, when everything looks its bleakest, somehow or another, something always comes along to save the day: a sword pulled from a hat, a blue fairy, a pair of sequined high heels. The movie soundtrack swells, and everyone lives happily ever after.

This would happen to me. I'd open my backpack, find my cell, and, poof, dial myself back to 2013. A triumphant ending, roll credits.

But this wasn't a story, and I couldn't cheat facts.

I'd been holding the phone in my hand when the lightning struck. What did I think? That it would have magically leapt into the zippered pocket of my backpack?

My cell was gone. It still felt like a sucker punch. If there was a soundtrack to this part of my movie, it would have been a sad trombone: *womp, womp.*

I took solace in the recovery of my other worldly possessions: my hairbrush; my cherry Chapstick; a blue ballpoint pen; my pink canvas wallet with seven dollars and fifty-two cents. I pulled the money out and counted it twice. *Hi, Abraham Lincoln. Nice meeting you here.*

Perhaps I could pass off the coins as a form of exotic currency. I tucked those into my front jeans pocket and shoved the dollars back into the wallet. A compartment behind my school ID contained my mother's 8th grade picture. I'd gone years without looking at it. Hesitating just a moment, I gingerly slid two fingers into the fold and pulled it out.

It was a standard school picture, a yearbook photo. She smiled for the camera, her shoulders a quarter turn angled, her natural brown hair in a simple, clean bob. Clear gloss on her lips, a dusting of freckles on pink cheeks, I saw my own face reflected in her golden-brown eyes, her angular bone structure.

I cradled her picture in the cup of my hand, fighting the urge to crush it between my fingers, to absorb the press of emulsion. Overexposed, bent-cornered, and wax-coated, the image of my mother was my only physical connection to reality, a duplicate of an illusion, the last remaining proof of where I came from, who I was.

I didn't have a picture of Monica. That was on my phone.

My phone.

My only chance of getting out of here.

Of going home.

Perhaps Monica found my phone next to the blackened oak. Would she think I was kidnapped? No. She'd think I'd run away. And she'd blame herself.

The thought left me feeling racked and raw, like a slashed tire. Between visions of Rabbie strapped to the stocks, the animal carnage I'd just witnessed, and the existential despair of finding all of my belongings except for the *one thing I needed*, I craved a dose of Monica's eternal optimism, culled from her stupid self-help books. *Chicken Soup for the Time-Traveling Teenage Soul*?

What did Monica say the night I disappeared?

Last night, I reminded myself, head spinning like a Tilt-a-Wheel. Last. Night.

Monica and I sat on opposite sides of her couch, a blue fabric ocean apart. Rain thundered on the eaves, wind howling in the flue, but the fire she built warmed the spaces between us.

Her and me.

Us and the elements.

The cold parts in the hidden places, marrow and bone, heart and ventricle.

FINDING JULIET

She folded her fingers in her lap like a little prayer, a way to hold on tight, which maybe was the same thing. She said that when she divorced, she felt helpless, alone. She read some advice that said the best way to move forward, to realize her goals, would be to write them down.

Yeah, like that would help.

The arena was all but empty, the victorious though maimed bear led away by the man in the tall hat, the dead dogs scraped off the floor, leaving blood-soaked patches of earth. No one remained except for the musicians packing up their instruments and a few drunk stragglers on the far side, tipped against each other. I uncapped the blue ballpoint pen, tiny teeth marks on the shiny plastic.

What were my goals?

To travel four hundred years back to the future? How about more long-term? To graduate and go to college? Oh, and not get pregnant at seventeen and become addicted to drugs? Where was I supposed to write this? And how could I put it in simple enough terms that I wouldn't need all the ink left in the pen?

First things first. One step in front of another.

I turned my mother's 8th grade portrait over and wrote, "I need my phone."

Okay, that was stupid.

I felt better, though, as if I'd entrusted something—the unknowable parts—to my mother's spirit. To God? That stupid country song came into my head again. The one playing in Monica's car the night she bought me Dippin' Dots. Maybe I didn't have to carry everything on my own shoulders.

I slipped the picture into its secret compartment, but I wavered on placing the wallet into my backpack, which, with its JANSPORT logo machine-stitched on slick canvas, was clearly not a 17th century artifact. I couldn't carry the backpack around. Too conspicuous. I tucked it under the stadium bench, and placed my wallet, pen, and brush into the satchel Rabbie had given me, the one with the cue-script for *Romeo and Juliet.* I applied three coats of Chapstick before tucking the tube into my jeans pocket.

Yellow Eyes thumped his tail, scattering nutshells. The smell of blood hung in the air. Iron and entrails. "Let's get out of here," I said. "You don't want to be next."

We strolled along the river, back towards the Globe. I felt fortified by a vague resolve I couldn't define, and the glorious feel of synthetic cherry on my lips. Yellow Eyes seemed equally heartened by my mood. Tired by the morning's chase, he settled into a happy trot, sticking firmly to my heels.

The dog needed a better name. Not only was "Yellow Eyes" stupid and clunky to say, his eyes weren't even yellow. They were amber, like my own. "Amber Eyes" was even dumber, though, like the title of a YA book.

What's in a name?

Juliet had said that. Or maybe it was Romeo. Thinking about Romeo brought back memories of Ryan, the kiss under the stage lights, the almost-kiss in my room, the misunderstanding with the police, his banishment, the crossed messages, my disappearance. It was only yesterday—yesterday!—but it felt like two lifetimes ago, a story about another girl, a sitcom, or a teen novel. *Amber Eyes.*

Shakespeare would've never written anything so sappy.

Shakespeare.

The Globe Theatre.

No longer deserted, the theatre was now a bustle of activity. In preparation for the evening's performance, men and teenage boys rushed about. They hauled fabric and boxes, musical instruments, and ringed curtains, loading these onto horse-driven wagons. Two men balanced on a flatbed, strapping set pieces with twine. Next to the double doors, a large man barked orders, while a woman with black curls hung on his arm. She was one of only two females. The other was a miniature, hunchbacked old lady, who stood to the side, picking a seam on an orange cape.

No one looked at me. While I mustered the courage to go up to the man—Master Burbage?—two barefoot boys exited the double doors. They half-carried, half-dragged what looked like a large coffin, bumping over the dirt.

A short, round man followed close behind, tapping the ground with his cane. His double-chin and doughy cheeks were framed by shoulder-length wispy blond hair. With his long, black coat and oversized white collar, he looked like a squat, fat pilgrim in a Thanksgiving pageant, minus the buckle hat.

"Careful, you dull asses. That's Juliet's bier!"

The boys lugged the sarcophagus onto the waiting wagon and scooted back into the theatre, avoiding swipes from the man's cane.

"You there! Apprentice!" He jabbed his cane in the direction of my chest.

"Me?"

"No, I was talking to Crab."

"Crab?"

"Yes, Crab. My dog."

"Your dog?"

I looked down. Of course. Yellow Eyes found me outside the theatre last night. He was here this afternoon. He must belong to the acting company. "*Crab*?" I asked, more to the dog than to the funny little man, although it was the funny little man who replied.

"Yes, and his mother before him."

"His mother?"

"Yes. Her name was Crab, too," the man said. "As was her father's. But bless him, he's no longer a dog."

"What is he then?" I asked, totally bewildered.

"A dead dog."

Crab nudged my hand. I gave him a little pat on his head. "I see."

"No, I don't think you do," the man replied. "For if you *did* see, you would see that Master Burbage sees *you*, and does not like what *he* sees."

As if on cue, the man standing with the black-haired lady moved towards us.

So, this was Burbage. Towering a foot over the man with the black coat, he wore a dirt-streaked shirt with an open collar, sleeves rolled to the elbow. The ensemble became more interesting from the waist down. His poufy green-and-yellow shorts were gathered mid-thigh, with an extra-large third poof in the center. It was very hard not to stare at this center poof, which was the size of a youth football and meant to suggest similarly sporting male vigor. Green tights completed the look.

Green. Tights.

"What's this, Armin?" Burbage demanded, a commanding tone that belied his poufy pants. No one would make fun of this dude, tutu or no. "Have you hired a new apprentice?" He inclined his large forehead. "What's your name, boy?"

"Alex," I replied.

There was a pause in which no one spoke.

"I was sent for," I said, filling the silence, which continued. "Um... I was looking after Yellow Eyes—I mean, Crab," I said, nodding towards the dog, who swiveled his muzzle to and fro, following the dialogue like a tennis match.

"Where's Thomas?" asked Burbage. "Where's my Juliet?" His voice was calm, but something in his tone suggested a pot set to simmer.

"Um," I said.

"And where's the other one?" he demanded, a bubble breaking the surface. "He should have been here a half-hour since to help with the costume load-out. What's his name, Armin, the dunderhead dresser who is to play the Apothecary?" This wasn't going to end well.

"Rabbie?" In my nervousness, it sounded more like a question.

"Here," said a breathless voice. Everyone turned to stare at my erstwhile roommate, who had miraculously materialized at my elbow. He winked at me under a fringe of dirty blond bangs. At least I think it was a wink. It may have been a nervous tick.

How? I mouthed.

He shrugged with an *ask-me-later* expression.

"You're late," pronounced Master Burbage.

"I am sorry, sir," said Rabbie, eyes on the ground. He didn't look any worse for wear. All limbs and appendages accounted for, no large fruit stains on his shirt.

"And where is young Thomas?" Burbage asked. Dried sweat made the theatre owner's reddish-brown curls stick to his temples, where a shiny blue vein popped a tributary.

"Thomas is gone," I said, trying to take some heat off Rabbie. Burbage, who'd apparently forgotten I existed, eyed me like a bug that needed squashing.

"BUT WE PERFORM TONIGHT!" he roared, rivaling the bear next door. Set a few rabid dogs on him, we could sell tickets. "GOD'S MY LIFE, FOR THE KING! WHAT'S THE MEANING OF THIS?!"

The other workers had (not so) mysteriously stopped coming out of the theatre. It was just me, Rabbie, Crab, the two ladies still lingering near the door—the curly black-haired one and the old seamstress—and the little Pilgrim, who seemed more amused than frightened at Burbage's outburst.

"I have three loads of sets to haul, two of costumes, one of properties, all to the river, set up in three hours' time for the evening performance at Whitehall to celebrate his Majesty's newly married daughter, the pride and joy of the kingdom." Burbage pounded his head with a meaty fist, then stepped close enough for me to appreciate the pores on his chin. "The King's Men are the first and only theatre company of London," he intoned. "We do not cancel performances. WHERE IS MY JULIET?!"

"Thomas's mother has taken ill, sir," said Rabbie bravely. "He begs your pardon. He will return as soon as possible. Alex is his cousin. He's a player from the continent. He stands surety for Thomas."

"Can you believe this, Armin?" asked Burbage. "Two piddling apprentices mean to tell me how to run my company!"

"No, sir," said Rabbie timidly. "I only mean to say, well, um, Alex can read."

"Can you, then, boy?' Burbage asked me. "And you think that's all there is to playing?"

"No, sir," replied Rabbie for me. "But he can act, too. Take out the scroll, Alex."

"The what?" I asked.

"God in heaven and all the saints," muttered Burbage.

"The *scroll*." Rabbie reached for the satchel draped around my shoulder. Picturing what he might do if he came up with my pink canvas wallet, I quickly tore the bag open and brought out the roll of parchment, the script with Juliet's lines. Rabbie took the scroll and advanced it to one of Juliet's longer speeches. "Read that," he said, thrusting it back into my hands.

"Can I just say something?" I asked the group.

"No," said Burbage and Rabbie together.

"But Rabbie knows the—*ow!*" I gasped as my friend dug his heel into my big toe.

"Read the lines," said Burbage. "I'd like to see what a player 'from the continent' can do. That is, if you are who this dolt says you are."

Rabbie looked at me with pleading eyes.

Resigned, I studied the script, hand-inked with a dripping quill. After a discreet clearing of my throat, I recited:

"Gallop apace, you fiery-footed steeds,
Towards Phoebus' lodging: such a wagoner
As Phaethon would whip you to the west,
And bring in cloudy night immediately."

I tried. I really did, for Rabbie's sake. However, the speech was not my finest. First of all, in Shakespeare's time, apparently all *"f's"* and "s's" look the same. Second of all, I'd like to see anyone correctly pronounce "Phaethon" on the first go.

A rumbling sound emanated from deep within Burbage. "I thought you said he could read."

"He can," insisted Rabbie, who eyed me as if I'd given a poor recitation on purpose. I shrugged my shoulders in apology.

"Enough!" hollered Burbage. "Out of my sight!"

"But sir!" Rabbie cried.

"You lie for your friend, and you mock me with this false player. Out!"

"Please sir," begged Rabbie, eyes glistening. "One more chance, please. Alex is a fine actor. He's just nervous. Pick it up here." He wound the scroll to a section a little further down, prompting me:

"O serpent heart, hid with a flowering face!
Did ever dragon keep so fair a cave?
Beautiful tyrant! fiend angelical!
Dove-feather'd raven! wolvish-ravening lamb!
Despised substance of divinest show!
Just opposite... to what thou... justly... seem'st..."

I'm sure Rabbie meant to only read a line or two, but halfway through the speech, the emotion of the moment overtook him. The words cascaded, crashing like a waterfall on Burbage's stony look, which remained impassive even as the verse slowed to a trickle.

Something had changed, though. It wasn't anything particular, just a softening of the air around us.

"What do you think, Armin?" Burbage asked, looking intently at Rabbie.

Armin pursed his lips. "I think we play for his Majesty in less than six hours. Put a dress on the boy, and let him stab himself."

Chapter 25
He fights as you sing prick-song

"You almost done, Juliet?" I asked Rabbie.

I sat on a crate on the other side of a green curtain, kicked out of the dressing room, or "tiring room," as Rabbie called it. He'd spent the past fifteen minutes behind the drape being stuffed into Juliet's under things by the seamstress.

"IS THAT EGGPLANT BEHIND YOUR EAR?" shouted Madge, the old lady seamstress. She stood four feet tall, with a small hump on her back, a curvature of the spine that made it look like she was carrying a sack of rice on her left shoulder. She was also nearly deaf. When Burbage told her Rabbie was taking over the role of Juliet, it took three minutes of over-enunciated directions and creative hand signaling to get her to understand that Thomas wasn't coming back, that, yes, the show was going on anyways, and, no, it was not me but Rabbie who was to assume the lead part.

"BUT THAT ONE LOOKS MORE LIKE A GIRL!" she cracked, pointing a gnarled finger in my direction. The dirt under my nails suddenly became very interesting. "RABBIE IS THE APOTHECARY!"

"TONIGHT, HE IS JULIET," said Burbage exasperatedly, miming two large breasts. "HIM," he said, waving a dismissive hand in my direction, "APOTHECARY." With no little reluctance, he'd offered me Rabbie's old part, after first confirming I could indeed read one short speech (with no "Phaetons" to trip my tongue). As Burbage strode back to his lady friend, he tossed one last bit of advice over his shoulder: "Don't botch it."

"DON'T WATCH IT?" Madge asked Rabbie and me as we stood outside the Globe's massive doors. The top of her head came just below my shoulder. "WHAT DON'T HE WANT ME TO WATCH?"

Rabbie and I shook our heads as if we didn't understand Burbage either.

"YOU THERE!" Madge called to the two barefoot boys I'd seen earlier. "FETCH ME THOSE COSTUMES! AND WATCH IT!" she warned, with a satisfied look in our direction. She set off around the building, her back bump bobbing. Rabbie and I and the boys followed her to a side entrance. Shelves of hats and wigs lined the small room. A beveled-glass mirror sat on a side table with a stool, next to two costumed mannequins. There, the boys deposited a trunk of skirts, dresses, and capes. Madge searched the bottom, hefting what appeared to be a burlap sack with sleeves. She shook it once before tossing it to me. "PUT THIS ON."

"Put it on over your clothes," said Rabbie. "Helps to avoid the rash."

"Thanks for the tip," I said.

"What 'tip'?" asked Rabbie.

"Never mind." I pulled the stale-smelling garment over my head. Madge was already at my feet, ripping a seam with her gums. Once the hem had been lengthened, she turned to Rabbie.

"ALL RIGHT, THEN. YOU! GET NAKED," she ordered. She turned to me. "WHERE D'YOU THINK YOU'RE GOING?"

"Just stepping outside," I said. Rabbie's face had gone the color of a ripe plum, and that was before he took off his clothes.

"I NEED YOU TO HELP LACE HIS CORSET," said Madge. "IF RABBIE'S NO LONGER THE DRESSER, IT'S YOUR JOB NOW." She yanked Rabbie's pants to his ankles.

I spun to face the two headless mannequins in the corner. On each hung an elaborate costume. On the female mannequin, a gaudy red dress was pinned, with bell sleeves and layers of skirt; on the male mannequin, a jacket of padded silver satin, with rows of glass rubies strung down the chest. "What are these costumes for?" I asked, lifting the silver sleeve. More glass rubies circled the cuff.

"FOUR COSTUMES? YOU ONLY HAVE THE ONE," said Madge.

"It's for a new play," said Rabbie, his voice strained. "We perform it in two days' time."

Not knowing in what state of undress I might find him, I kept facing the costumes. "That's a quick turn-around."

"Not at all. We perform most days of the week. Just not tomorrow. Need to move the properties back to the theatre. But the public—OOF—demands a show."

"Different plays each time?" I asked. No wonder the actors used scrolls.

"Except for the old favorites."

"Like *Romeo and Juliet*," I said.

"Just so."

"What's the name of the new play?" I asked, stepping behind the mannequin with the red dress, my chin peeping above the neckline.

"The play is called *All is True*."

"I've never heard of that one," I said.

"It's new. About King Henry VIII."

"Huh," I said, moving to a shelf crammed with wigs and hats. In the midst was a crown, beads and pearls glued to its points. A large cross ornamented the top, beneath a skullcap of purple satin. "Henry VIII. He was the one with the six wives, right?" I brushed my finger against one of the pearls, which looked real enough.

"Yes," Rabbie said. "A play unlike any other, a true spectacle."

"The costumes look amazing."

"Yes, but that is not all. At the end of the first act, we're firing a cannon!"

"A cannon? A real, live cannon?" What did these people have with lighting incendiary devices in crowded theatres? "Do you think that's safe?"

"GRAB HIS HANDS," said Madge.

I turned around to look at Rabbie.

I then attempted to look anywhere else.

It's not that he was naked. All the important parts were clothed, just in thigh-high stockings, mini-bloomers, and a full corset.

"Do not you laugh," begged Rabbie.

"I'm not."

Madge appeared behind his back, gripping two laces like a sled driver at the Iditarod. "HOLD HIM STEADY!"

I grasped him by the forearms as Madge put her hump into his buttocks, yanking inches off his waist.

"I can't breathe," Rabbie gasped.

"BUM ROLL!" Madge yelled, making me wonder if that was the name of the next undergarment—a croissant-shaped pillow she strapped over the corset—or instructions for action.

"You're laughing," said Rabbie.

"I'm not!"

Madge threw a petticoat over Rabbie's head. It floated like a parachute until it caught around his shoulders. Unable to move, he stood there puce-faced, like a sausage stretching its casing.

"Go away!" he hollered, when my eyes started streaming.

"I'm not laughing," I insisted, but I ducked outside the curtain. Crab sat beside the wooden crate, head cocked to the grunts coming from inside the dressing room. I let him lick my hand.

"Sorry, dog," I said. "I'm fresh out of Trident."

"SUCK IN YER AIR," cried Madge.

"It's sucked," breathed Rabbie.

"SUCK MORE!"

I smiled and sat on the crate. With a contented sigh, Crab settled at my feet. I opened my satchel, and took out the copy of my lines Burbage had tossed me, a single page, not enough to justify a scroll.

I didn't *want* to perform. The whole idea terrified me. But, Rabbie needed my help, and when a guy is willing to spend a couple hours in the stocks for you, you figure you owe him. Besides, it'd be kind of cool to visit a palace...

I could do it. My part was only a couple sentences. I practiced my lines: *"Such mortal drugs I have; but Mantua's law is death to any he that utters them."* Easy-peasy, lemon-squeezy. *"My poverty, not my will, consents."* Crab panted his approval. I recited the line again. *"My poverty, not my will, consents."*

"But not my will." said Rabbie from the other side of the curtain.

"That's what I said. *My poverty, not my will, consents.*"

"But! But! The line is '*My poverty,* BUT *not my will, consents.*"

"Didn't I say that?"

"No. You forgot the 'but.' *But not my will.*"

"My poverty, BUT *not my will, consents.*"

"No, No," he said. "Too much stress on the 'but.'"

"There's too much stress on *your* butt. Got the dress on yet?"

"How do women wear these things?" he grumbled.

"Don't ask me."

Undeterred by the drape between us, Rabbie continued coaching. "Don't put stress on the word 'but.' It's poetry. The rhythm of the line scans, *my POverTY, but NOT my WILL, conSENTS.*"

"Oh yeah, that sounds much better," I muttered.

"Well, don't say it like *that*. Say it more natural-like. *Speak the speech, I pray you, as I pronounced it to you, trippingly on the tongue.*"

"Are you quoting more Shakespeare at me?"

"You keep saying that. Who is this Shakespeare fellow of yours? OOF!"

"I KNEW A SHAXPER," shouted Madge. "HE WAS A PLAYER. NOT A VERY GOOD ONE EITHER."

Why did no one in this blessed place know who William Shakespeare was? Was I really in 17th century London? Or was this a dream wrought by Ms. Lanyer's wild conspiracy theories? Shakespeare was her great-great-times-a-million grandmother? Sure. And Homer of *The Illiad* was really a Simpson.

The curtain parted and out stepped Rabbie.

"Say something," he said.

"You look—"

"What?"

The dress was cream colored, with sage vines embroidered on the bodice, an intricate pattern repeated along the border of the skirt. A sheer neckline stretched to a delicate ruffle under his chin. The old seamstress stood on a wobbly stool and placed a waist-length wig on his head, brown curls ribboned with more sage and cream. Rabbie looked ready to cry, from embarrassment or joy. It was hard to tell which.

"I feel like a stuffed partridge," he said. His hands drifted self-consciously to the tiny female breasts with which he'd been provided, more womanly than my own.

"You look wonderful."

"No, I don't."

"Stop touching your boobs."

"I can't breathe."

"Say one of Juliet's lines."

"I don't remember any of them."

"Yes, you do. Let's go on the stage. You know you want to."

I grabbed Rabbie's hands and dragged him towards the center of the theatre, through a labyrinth lined with props, shelves of bottles, metal tankards, silk flowers, peacock feathers, flags, daggers and swords, candles, lanterns, and what looked like a real human skull. One curtain led to another, which opened onto the stage.

Rabbie and I stood for a moment on the threshold.

The theatre was magnificent. Three balconies of seating surrounded a raked dirt floor. The stage jutted into the center, so the audience could stand close to the actors. A wooden canopy stretched half the length of the platform, painted with constellations and shooting stars. Above that, the roof opened to the real sky, a brilliant blue.

I handed Rabbie his scroll and leaned against a red marble column.

"Romeo, Romeo," I prompted him. *"Wherefore art thou Romeo?"'*

Rabbie crossed to center stage and looked to the man-made heavens. His upper lip had a sheen of sweat. In a crystal voice, he recited from memory:

"Romeo, Romeo, wherefore art thou Romeo?
Deny thy father and refuse thy name,
Or if thou wilt not, be but sworn my love
And I'll no longer be a Capulet."

From the dirt pit below came a slow CLAP, CLAP, CLAP.

"Oh no," said Rabbie. "Eddie."

"Who?" I asked.

"Romeo."

A boy with white-blond hair stood with toes pointed perpendicularly, one hand on a bony hip. He wore a navy doublet, feathered cap, and light blue tights. "What are you doing?" he asked Rabbie.

"What does it look like, Eddie?"

"Edward."

"Since when do you go by Edward?"

"Since I'm to play for the King," he pronounced, chin jutting like an angry beak. He pranced up the stage steps. "Where's Thomas?"

"Gone," sighed Rabbie.

"Where?"

"I don't know."

"He was here yesternight. You were rehearsing with him," Eddie accused. What did you do?" His attempt to step nose-to-nose with Rabbie fell three inches short of the mark. "Does Master Burbage know?" Eddie asked, straightening his spine. It garnered him half an inch, tops.

"Of course he does," I broke in.

"And who are *you*?" he demanded.

"I'm the Apout—" What was I again? I looked at my script, but there were no names, just character abbreviations before each line.

"The what?" he asked.

"The Athop—"

"God's teeth, are you a simpleton?"

"The Apothecary," Rabbie finished for me.

"Maybe you two should practice," I suggested, aiming for a constructive end to the conversation.

"I know my part," said Eddie. "I don't need to rehearse, especially not with Thomas's *dresser*."

"What's that supposed to mean?" I asked, marching up to him. I had a good four inches on the twerp.

Eddie pointed to Rabbie. "It means he's no player. And he's too fat for that dress. He'll make a fool of both of us."

"You little jerk," I said.

"What did you call me?"

"Jerk."

"Not that."

"What, *little*?"

The punch came from nowhere. Eddie wasn't particularly strong, but his knuckles were bony, and he had the element of surprise. My vision went dark for a moment, broken by bright little swirlies that spun and floated, just like in the cartoons. Who knew that was a thing?

"No one calls me LITTLE!" Eddie cried, slamming me into a column.

Rabbie moved to defend me. Hampered by his corset and dress, he only landed a few blows. Still, the pushing and shoving was enough to send both Romeo and Juliet rolling off the stage and onto the dirt floor, tangled in Rabbie's layers of skirt. Crab, who'd followed the noise, happily barked at the show.

"Stop it, you two!" I cried, pulling on Rabbie's bum roll. Eddie grabbed my foot and yanked me into the fray. I'd just given Romeo a nice knee to the groin when a clearly identifiable voice boomed through the excellent acoustics of the theatre.

"ENOUGH!" bellowed Master Burbage, flanked by Madge and a half dozen members of the company, smirking at the sight of Eddie bent double over his ripped tights, and Rabbie in splits position with his petticoat over his head.

"Stand up, the lot of you." We did as he asked, some of us less gracefully than others. My toe caught on the hem of my cloak, so my straightening up turned to a forced bow. Eddie, recovering from my well-placed kick, stood curled at his midsection, one hand cupping the afflicted area. Rabbie flipped his skirt to the proper position, gathered himself onto his two feet, and assumed perfect posture, attempting as much dignity a boy can have in a ripped dress.

Burbage breathed in through his nose, out through his mouth, channeling inner reserves of peace. He spoke quietly, which was even scarier. "Give your costumes to Madge. She will clean and repair them. Load up at the docks," he exhaled a final time, then paused. "NOW!"

The onlookers scattered like a flock of pigeons upon a pistol shot. Burbage stomped back to the main entrance, conferring with Armin beneath the arches. Eddie gave Rabbie a look of pure murder, then followed Madge to the tiring room.

"I'm done for," said Rabbie, scratching at his lace collar. He now had a red welt to match the purple bruise under his eye.

"Madge can fix your dress," I reassured him. The rip looked worse than it was, torn along the seam. "A few stitches, dust off the skirt, and you'll look like Juliet again. Well, a Juliet who's been in a cage match," I added.

"A cage what?" he asked.

"A cage... never mind. Go on. Madge is waiting for you. Try not to hit any more actors, okay? Even if they deserve it."

Rabbie gave me a miserable look, then nodded. He turned and limped back to the dressing room, trailing a sage satin ribbon.

"You," I said to Crab, who was lying down, chewing on Rabbie's wig. "*Leave it.*" I grasped the long strands. Crab play-growled and shook his head back and forth, breaking the neck of the wig.

"Here, let me help you," said a woman. It was the lady from the front of the theatre, Burbage's companion, the one with the dark curls. Earlier, I'd seen her from a distance, and only from the side. Now she knelt before me.

"Ms. *Lanyer?*"

Chapter 26
Since this same wayward girl is so reclaim'd

The woman gripped my hand, nails pressing into my palm. "How do you know my name?" she whispered.

I didn't. That was the thing.

She wasn't actually Ms. Lanyer, my drama teacher from the 21st century. A second look told me that. There was a definite resemblance, but they weren't identical.

Her hair was the same mass of curls, streaks of silver mixed with black, only Ms. Lanyer's was shoulder-length, and this woman's hair reached nearly to the middle of her back. Her nose had a similar knife-edge quality, but instead of a down-turned nub, it pointed up, like she sniffed something suspicious.

It was her eyes. That's why I thought she was Ms. Lanyer. Her eyes were the same: dark brown rimmed with black, like two smoldering coals. They burned when they looked at me.

"Richard!" she called, not releasing her gaze or her grip. Where did she think I would go? Nowhere, in truth, but she was right to hold me. Her strange intensity triggered an instinct to bolt.

"What is it now, Emilia?" Burbage called from the entranceway. He spoke in a milder tone, tinged with impatience.

"Come *here*," she said.

He strode back, puffs of dust in his wake. "My dear," he said. "You realize, we're an hour behind schedule as 'tis. I cannot afford any more delays."

"You have one more delay," said Emilia, my drama teacher's doppelganger. "This boy cannot perform."

"I know he's a bad actor," Burbage said. *Gee, thanks.* "But he's the only lad I have."

"He's not a lad," said Emilia, letting go of my hand.

"Well, he's not a man."

"He's a *lass*."

Three.

Two.

One.

"ARMIN!" Burbage raged.

The little man waddled to Burbage's side. "Yes?" he asked, innocently.

"This boy is a girl."

"Well, so she is."

"Did you know?"

"Well, I suspected. Crab is partial to the female sex, ever since Maudlin gave him that bit o' sausage. Plus, the boy's got teats." He pointed his cane at my chest. "Not as big as Emilia's, I warrant you, but I see some double cherries."

I crossed my arms as my cheeks blazed.

"God's bodkins, why didn't you say anything?!"

"Because we're desperate, Richard, and if *you* didn't notice, I doubt the old King would, especially in that tarpaulin," Armin said, pointing to my sack-like costume. "I mean, the King's not in the tarpaulin, the boy is. Girl. But you'd hardly know it in the tarpaulin, would you? Just the place for ripening fruit," he leered. "Besides, the Apothecary's a throwaway part. Let him do it tonight. Tomorrow, when he's a girl, you can send her to the convent, where she'll pray for us sinners who put a girl onstage."

"I *cannot* put a girl onstage. The theatre is no place for a woman," said Burbage, with a cautionary glance at Emilia, who looked about to speak. "The King's Men will not risk its existence to a charge of lewdness. This... young personage... cannot play the part."

"Well, someone has to do it," said Armin.

"I agree. Madge must needs shorten the costume a good six inches for you." Burbage's look stifled any further argument. He ripped the cloak over my head and thrust it at Armin. "Now, get moving!"

"Come on, Crab," he said. "Give it up."

The dog dropped the wig into Armin's outstretched hand. Both headed backstage.

As they mounted the steps, Armin said to Crab, "*You* could play the Apothecary. With a hair more feeling."

Burbage, Emilia, and I stood in silence. Without the cloak, I felt a bit, well, uncovered.

"I'll hand it to you, lass," Burbage said at last. "You had me convinced. Perhaps y'are a player after all." He turned to Emilia. "Get rid of the girl. I'll deal with Rabbie on the morrow. He'll be scrubbing the stage until his voice drops."

"Yes, Richard," she said, offering her cheek for a kiss, which Burbage obliged before exiting the doors to the theatre.

The workers' hustle resumed, moving all the necessary parts to the palace for the performance tonight. I wouldn't get to see Rabbie make his debut. The thought left me sad. And more than a little fearful. My disguise was blown. I was discovered. Found out. Shortly to be homeless and penniless, competing for rat heads with Crab.

"Ms. Lanyer?" I asked, no longer trying to conceal my female voice.

"Yes," she said.

"You don't teach Drama, do you?"

"No, not exactly." She fingered a ring on her left hand, spinning the gold band.

"Am I in trouble?" I asked.

"No." She narrowed her eyes. "But you need to tell me what you're doing here."

"What do you mean?"

"Do not play coy with me."

"You know who I am?"

"I have seen you before."

"You have?"

"And I know your secret."

What? Where had she seen me? In a dream, a vision? What did she know? My heart thrummed in my throat. Was she a time traveler, too?

"What are you going to do with me?" I asked, scared to breathe the words.

"I'm taking you home."

***

Emilia meant *her* home. For a crazy moment, I thought she meant *my* home. But, of course, that was impossible.

Jefferson County wasn't my home, anyways. It was Monica's home. *Home, home on the range.*

The wooden wheels of Emilia's four-seat carriage bounced along the cobblestones. I sat across from her on a padded bench. The dusky rose cushions compensated for the lack of suspension, but only partly; it was hard to speak without stuttering.

"You were humming something," she said.

"Was I? S-s-sorry."

I wasn't delirious. Just a little out of sorts. Tired from chasing after dogs and missing boys. At least I was sitting. Bouncing. Traveling to whatever kingdom awaited me at the end of this particular Yellow Brick Road. Was Emilia the Wizard or the Wicked Witch? Would she help me find my way? Or was this actually all a dream?

The driver cracked his whip. Two black horses pulled the carriage along the river, the smell of sewage and day-old catch growing riper in the fading afternoon.

"You look a bit green," said Emilia.

"Wh-what?"

"Unwell."

Now that she mentioned it, riding backwards in a closed carriage did produce a kind of car sickness, especially when surrounded by the smell of dead fish.

Emilia patted the cushion next to her. "Come sit by me." She drew open the curtains of the carriage, which increased the smell, but added a welcome flow of air.

"Phillip!" Emilia called to the driver.

"Yes, mum?" he shouted back.

"Stop at *Antonio's*."

"Yes, mum!"

The horses turned left at London Bridge.

I'd set something in motion, not just the carriage. I'd recognized Emilia as Ms. Lanyer. She wasn't my drama teacher, but they had to be related. Same look. Same last name. Emilia must be her million-times-great grandmother. And, according to my drama teacher's wild conspiracy theories, the *real* William Shakespeare.

Could it be?

Nah.

Maybe?

Was this the reason I was here? Some cosmic reckoning on behalf of womankind? Shakespeare was *female*?

The evidence: no one in this time seemed to know who Shakespeare *was*, except for Madge the old seamstress, who called him "Shaxper," an actor, not a playwright. Burbage made a crack about the theatre being no place for a woman, a remark he addressed to Emilia, who seemed to have something to say on the matter. I hazarded a glance to my left. Emilia hadn't stopped studying my face.

Was the woman sitting next to me really Shakespeare, the most famous writer in the history of the world? A woman who knew I had secrets, perhaps a dangerous bit of knowledge about one of the greatest cover-ups of all time?

"Stop!"

FINDING JULIET

I jumped as Emilia yelled to her driver.

"Yes, mum!" he called.

We'd parked in front of *Antonio's Apothecary and Teeth-Pulling*, home of slugs and urine. A footman opened the carriage door.

"I won't be a moment," said Emilia. "You'll wait for me."

It was not a request.

The hum and drum of people continued outside the coach. Their strange accents, both like and unlike English, became an indecipherable white noise, punctuated by shouts: angry, commanding, jolly, inebriated.

So far, I hadn't seen anyone consume any liquid besides beer. Not coffee, not juice, certainly not water. Mainly beer. Beer was everywhere. In the pub, in the arena, in the streets. People's pores fairly glistened with the rank sweat of it.

No wonder Londoners were so noisy. They were all drunk. Drunk women snapped at their drunk children; drunk men yelled at other drunk men; drunk vendors advertised their stores of flowers and fruit to customers who were too drunk to care about peaches and peonies.

It'd be very easy to get lost in such a crowd of people. I jiggled my door handle, not thinking I would run—*not yet*—but wondering if I *could*. The handle clicked and the carriage door opened. I closed it gently. I could leave if I wanted to, but where would I go? What would I do? Join one of the toothless apple-sellers? The children who roamed the street?

From the window of the carriage, I saw a kid, no older than eight, huddled between two buildings. He was alone, hair matted, face dirty. Above him, a board was wedged, crudely diagonal, a roof pushed high enough for him to stand. At his feet, a balled blanket.

Strange how little things can wake memories. Time travel wrought by electrical connections, lightning bolts of the brain. Present sense to past experience. A smell. A taste. A blanket roll in an alley.

My mother called it camping. The pictures are fuzzy, edges blurred, only half-developed details come into focus. My yellow blanket pillow. The way I curled into her stomach, like the center of a shell.

We never slept downtown. Too many loud people. Too many bad smells. We'd ride the bus to the bay, where the sea lions lay on the piers, their black, oily skins smooth velvet in the moonlight. Sightseers ate churros and spoke in foreign tongues, Russian, Japanese, while gulls pecked the boardwalk for crumbs.

In the quiet time, we'd spoon under the docks, piers decked with barnacles and seaweed. Like mermaids washed on the tide, we'd wake with pinched necks, sore backs, limbs unused to land. Breakfast on tables with views of the water.

Bagels and cream cheese. Cinnamon rolls. Powdery, day-old french fries with sour ketchup, congealed like cold blood.

Tourists in San Francisco waste a lot of food.

"Sorry to keep you waiting," said Emilia, one hand helped by the footman, the other on the door to the carriage. She carried a black velvet pouch and two sachets full of lavender and dried lemon. "For the smell," she said, handing me one. I pressed it to my nose.

Outside, a wagon loaded with onions passed by. The driver goaded his mule through the crowds, not noticing as one of the wheels jumped a rock, and an onion rolled. Quick as a gull, the boy grabbed it, took a bite, skin and all.

The coach whip cracked, the carriage pushing its way through pedestrians and peddlers, no regard for who might be caught in its wheels.

On the far side of London Bridge, we landed hard on the banks of the city. I gazed down the waterway, where earlier Rabbie and I had searched for Thomas on the *Marigold*. The great ship had set sail. I could see the empty place on the harbor where its three-story masts had listed.

We didn't head along the river. Instead, the driver took us deep into the city. Businesses, pubs, and residences pressed haphazardly together, stacked like children's blocks, brown and black-and-white timbered. Woodsmoke and coal fires smogged the air. Refuse and excrement ran in rivulets down makeshift gutters, fed by emptying pots tossed out windows, and poured out doors. People clamored for space with horses and barrows, trudging through the sludgy bits between the rounded cobbles. Alleyways branched into darkness, like clogged arteries. The city was a beast, a throbbing organism, and we'd entered the heart of it.

Emilia closed the windows, then fastened the curtains, sealing us in semi-darkness. "Not much longer," she said. She pressed her sachet to her face with one hand, the other toying with the velvet pouch she'd gotten at the shop. I thought back to what Jessica, the owner's daughter, had said about Thomas, how he'd purchased belladonna, deadly nightshade.

What potion had Emilia bought? Medicine or poison?

And, was it meant for her or me?

Eventually, the noises outside the carriage became quieter, the ride smoother, the vestiges of air that found its way into the closed cabin cleaner, of earthy, fresh manure and grass. Emilia opened the windows once again. The vanishing light of early evening lengthened the shadows of the trees as the streets of London gave way to country manors, wide lawns and hedges, stone walls and iron gates.

A few cows grazed in the pastures, looking just like the ones from my own time. I thought of Presley and Joni, the cows from Mr. Albright's ranch, for whom Monica had kept a stash of hay, feeding creatures not her own.

I still didn't like cows, but, from a distance, I could appreciate their appeal: gentle giants content to stand on a hill and let the world pass by. It didn't matter if the year was 2013 or 1613. Cows didn't change. That, strangely, was a comfort.

We turned left at a gated drive, down a tree-lined path. A circular lawn fronted a red-stone mansion. Servants and groomsmen met the carriage, one to open the door, another to help Emilia to the graveled walk; two to unhitch the horses and lead them to a stable on the side of the yard. I crawled out Emilia's side, to the incredulous stares of the remaining servants. Emilia gave orders, then led me through the arched entrance.

A butler met us in the hall. He stood with ramrod posture as he listened to Emilia's instructions. "This is my new charge," she said. "She needs a bath and suitable attire. I will be in my closet, dressing for the evening. If Fordee arrives, let me know forthwith." Emilia turned to me. "Not to worry," she said, which had the opposite effect. "You are in good hands."

After a nod, Emilia departed to her private rooms. The butler stood a moment, taking in my appearance. He wore a long grey coat and a clown-size neck ruffle that could not conceal a tennis-ball-sized goiter. He swallowed once in resignation, his Adam's apple riding a tide of displeasure, then guided me up the central stairs, to a bedroom on the second floor.

"Wait here, please," he said, pointing to a spot of floor just inside the threshold. "Try not to touch anything."

I stared gaped-mouth at my new lodgings. There was a sitting area with a velvet chaise lounge and two stuffed chairs; a dressing table with a gilded mirror and marble vanity; a king-sized canopy bed, hung with curtains and stuffed with pillows. Leaded windows opened to a second-floor balcony overlooking a wide-open lawn hedged with fountains and flowers.

In the center of the room, a wooden tub lined with sheets stood before a crackling fireplace, where two copper kettles simmered. My bath. Better than a horse trough. I stepped onto the thick-piled carpet, a swirling pattern of roses and green vines. Behind me, a throat cleared.

"I didn't touch anything!" I squeaked.

A plump, grandmotherly lady stood in the door. With her white bun, light blue dress, and kind smile, she looked every inch Cinderella's fairy godmother.

I curled my toes in the roses.

"Well, bless your soul," she said.

Chapter 27
What, dress'd! and in your clothes!

"I'm Alice. That's Kitty," said the maid, motioning to a slim-faced girl who headed for the kettles in the fireplace. Both wore aprons and white lace caps pinned to their buns, Kitty's a mousy brown, Alice's pure snow. Kitty emptied the steaming water into the tub, then retreated out the door.

"Time for your bath. I'll take your—" Alice looked momentarily lost for words at the sight of my grey sweater and black jeans, which due to the events of the previous twenty-four hours, had begun to assume the same hue. "...whatever it is you be wearing."

"Now?" I asked, glancing around for a place to change.

"Yes." Alice looked at me expectantly.

I peeled off my sweater, t-shirt, and jeans, stunned by the fug of my own stink. (It's amazing what you can get used to.) Kitty returned with another two kettles, filling the tub three quarters full. She drew a glass vial from her apron pocket and poured five drops of jasmine-scented oil into the tub.

"A bit more, don't you think?" said Alice.

Kitty dumped the bottle.

Alice pinched my bra strap, snorting in surprise as the elastic snapped.

"What in all the devils and saints is this?"

"My bra." I unfastened the back hooks and held it to her with my other arm across my chest.

"Hmmm," she said, eyeing me with distrust. "You must be an outlander."

"You have no idea."

"Well, Kitty will see—it—laundered. Your smallclothes, too," she said, wrinkling her nose at my undies. "Tsk-tsk."

I bit my lip and stripped all the way, regretting my lack of a third hand.

"Any other necessaries?" asked Alice, unaware or uncaring of the fact that I was now completely nude. This was worse than gym class.

"No," I said.

Then it hit me.

I'd left Rabbie's satchel at the theatre. In it, my hairbrush, my pen, my wallet.

The picture of my mother.

Oh God.

It was gone, all of it.

"Don't cry, chuck," said Alice. "Just get in the tub. A nice bath solves everything."

***

Alice was right. The scalding water bit my feet and stung my blisters, but it was a delicious pain. The heat soothed the muscles of my calves and between my shoulder blades. I folded my knees to my chest, and rested my head, letting the curls of steam tickle my nose.

"Out you go," said Alice, interrupting my bliss.

"What?"

"Need to change the water." The bath had turned the color of my clothes, a dishwater grey. Alice pulled me from the tub, wrapped me in a clean sheet, and handed me a cup of broth. I stood facing the fire, feeling the liquid warm my belly, while she and Kitty began the laborious process of emptying and refilling the tub.

For round two, Alice went to work, scrubbing what hadn't come off in the first soak, the dirt behind my ears, in the creases of my knees. She held up one of my feet, bright orange polish on my toenails. "Where on earth did Mistress Emilia find you?" she asked.

"The theatre," I said.

"Hm. Should have known." She dried her hands on her apron, and held open a dressing gown. I stepped from the tub, wrinkled, raw, and smelling like jasmine. "Let's get you clad, chuck. Kitty is fetching you something proper. Here she is now."

The young maid lurched through the door, so laden with clothes that only her bonnet peeped over the pile. She staggered to the bed and dumped it all into a heap. "What do you think?" Kitty asked, holding up a skirt. "Blue and yellow?"

"No, brown and red," replied Alice. "'Twill go well with her coloring. Best find some pins, though," she said, smoothing my hair. "We'll need to tame the porpentine."

Like the bath, dressing me turned into a group project, only, unlike Cinderella, there were no helpful mice involved, no magic wand—just two slightly sadistic chambermaids.

First came a long-sleeved slip with a drawstring top, a 'chemise,' Kitty called it. Comfortable enough. Like a soft nightgown. "Do you have any underwear?" I asked, after pulling on some knee-height yellow hose. Kitty and Alice exchanged a look. "Nevermind," I said, shimmying down the chemise. I felt a little draft in the basement, but not bad.

Then came the corset.

When they whipped it around my waist, I felt something hard jab my rib, as if a small dagger had been sewn into the lining. That couldn't be right. "What is this *made* of?" I asked.

"Whalebone," said Alice, threading the laces.

'Whalebone? Like from whales?"

"No, from London."

"Can we skip it?"

"Skip where?" Kitty gripped my arms, while Alice did her best to suffocate me from the outside in, like a 17th century Heimlich maneuver.

"I can't breathe!"

"Are you currently speaking?" asked Alice.

"Yes!"

"Then you're breathing." I imagined my intestines reconfiguring themselves to their new locale, my lungs one solid organ, my liver settling somewhere around my left butt cheek. Earlier today, I laughed at Rabbie in his fitting. I shouldn't have done that.

Karma was a whalebone corset.

I looked down. "Oh, wow!" Breasts I didn't know I had popped like two Fuji apples. I'd gone up a size in fruit!

"She can still laugh," said Kitty. "I think we ought to go tighter."

"No," I gasped. "I'm good. Are we done yet?"

"Done? We've only just begun."

Next came a petticoat, a bum roll (like Rabbie's, a donut-shaped life preserver tied around the corset), a brown underskirt with red trim, a red overskirt with brown trim, a white blouse, and a brown vest embroidered with red grapes and butterflies. Lacing under. Lacing over. Lacing in the back. Lacing in the front, the ribbons double-knotted. Lastly, red satin slippers, a half-size too small. I closed my eyes. Clicked my heels three times.

No dice.

"Almost forgot," Kitty said.

"What's left?" I asked. Other than my face and hands, the only skin showing was the three inches from the base of my neck to my chin.

"Your bonnet!" She stood on a stool and pinned a lace cap to my head. "We wouldn't want you to go about all indecent-like, would we? Come take a look."

I crab-walked forty pounds of fabric to the gilded mirror above the vanity.

This wasn't a dress. It was an event.

I swished side-to-side, feeling the centrifugal force radiate from my heretofore non-existent hips. Baby got back, indeed. Hitting the second line of the chorus in my head, my J-Lo sized posterior unfortunately connected with a vase of periwinkle blossoms, toppling it.

"Ooops. I'm so sorry," I said. I bent over to help Kitty clean up the mess, but with my center of gravity altered, I tipped like a bell without its knocker, landing face down on the floor.

"Right, then," Alice said, taking charge. She motioned to Kitty, and with a huff and a grunt, they levered me upright.

"Take that to Cook," Alice instructed Kitty.

"Of course." Kitty gathered the remains of the vase before leaving the room.

"Never you worry, chuck," said Alice, picking chips of wet pottery out of my hair. "We'll have you fixed up in no time." Her gaze drifted to the circular water stain blossoming over my left breast. "Perhaps, though, you'll wish to stand before the fire a wee longer."

Chapter 28

Some consequence yet hanging in the stars

I stood beside Alice as she knocked on Emilia's door. The hallway was quiet, dim. I cracked my knuckles, waiting for her to answer. Despite Emilia's kindnesses—her bringing me home, the bath, the clothes—I felt more nervous meeting her now than when I'd first laid eyes on her, looking so much like my drama teacher. Was she the key to unraveling all the mysteries—about Thomas, about Shakespeare, about why I was here? What did she want from me? Why did she say she'd seen me before? Was this some sort of time-traveling paradox/alternate universe?

"Come in," said a smooth-coated voice, like a spoon dipped in honey.

At first, I didn't see her, lost in the breadth and furnishings of the room, twice the size of the one I'd just left. Beyond the picture windows, twilight had fallen, but candlelight gave the room a golden glow. Flames crackled from sconces and candlesticks, and one massive chandelier, three-tiered, hanging by a thick pewter chain. Wax dripped and settled in molten pools, hissing as it burned.

"Ms. Lanyer?"

"Call me Emilia, child." She rose from an armchair facing the window. Her blue gown shimmered like sapphire, her dark curls twisted into a mobius knot, a figure-eight that folded in upon itself, no beginning, no end. She kept her back to us. "That will be all, Alice."

The maid dipped a curtsy and left.

I tucked a stray bang behind my ear.

"Thank you for the clothes," I said. I glanced at my chest, the water stain still faintly visible, like a ring of Saturn. "And for the bath."

Emilia faced me. "What is your name?"

I shifted my weight in the too-tight slippers. My feet had begun to sweat, chafing in the yellow stockings. "I'm Alex."

"Alex?" She raised a crescent eyebrow.

"Alexandra."

Emilia crossed the room, circling me once. She smelled of her sachet, lavender and lemons, flowery and sharp.

"Alexandra," she repeated, as if she didn't quite believe me.

"Yes."

"And you know me?"

"I know someone who looks like you," I said.

"With my name?"

"Yes."

"That is a very interesting story, especially as I have no living female relations."

"It's true."

Emilia strode towards a wall-sized tapestry. The artist had woven a delicately embroidered scene of a unicorn, penned in a corral, a hunting party looking on. Despite their spears and dogs, the hunters did not look intent on harming the magical creature, just curious, like *Hey, Bob, what do we do now?* The unicorn seemed content to observe their confusion, lying bemused in a bed of flowers.

"That's beautiful," I said.

"It is," said Emilia. "Although I've always wondered why the unicorn allowed herself to be caught." She lifted the heavy cloth, then placed a hand on the wood paneling beneath it. A hinge clicked, and a section of wall opened inward. A current shivered up my petticoat. "There is someone who wishes to meet you," Emilia said. "Will you come?"

I contemplated my options. Once more, I found them lacking. As always, I could run, but where would I go? I could say no, but then I'd have no further information about why I was here. Emilia would lose interest in me, and I'd end up where I started, on the street with no money.

I followed Emilia into the corridor, a close and narrow passageway that opened to a small, windowless chamber. The sides didn't curve, but the panels formed a circular shape, much like the Globe Theatre. On every other panel hung a sconce, six candles in all, lighting a hexagonal table that dominated the room. An old man sat at one of six chairs, a roll of parchment before him.

"Good evening," he said. "I am Doctor Fordee."

I swallowed dryly, as if I'd just taken a bite of onion, skin and all.

"Please," he said, motioning to a chair. Doctor Fordee's head was perfectly hairless, the bones of his cranium visible beneath layers of age spots. His neck sagged, red and wrinkled, his eyes rheumy but alert, like an old vulture.

I maneuvered onto a velvet-cushion, not easy with a bumroll. Was this an interrogation? An exam? An arrest? If so, did I really need to put on a corset for questioning? Beneath the table, hidden from view, I grabbed fistfuls of the four layers of skirts I was wearing, the extra fabric buffering my courage. "Why am I here?" I asked.

"That is always the question, isn't it?" He unrolled the parchment, which appeared to contain a diagram, but of what? "You are in this room because Mistress Emilia wishes to know a bit more about you." With a skeletal finger, he tapped the paper.

Lines and geometric shapes crisscrossed three concentric circles. The symbols on the outer edges looked Greek, like fraternity letters, accompanied by drawings of beasts: a crawling scorpion, a charging bull, a horned goat rearing on hind legs.

The candles in the wall sconces shuddered, flickering shadows animating the symbols spinning in their spheres. I blinked to steady my vision.

The scorpion. The bull. The goat.

Scorpio. Taurus. Capricorn.

They were astrological signs.

"A horoscope?" I asked, more confused by the minute.

"Here is today's date," Doctor Fordee pointed to a line of dots—stars—branching to the right, a constellation like the Big Dipper. No, it was the Little Dipper. The Big Dipper was beneath it.

"Polaris," he said, a yellowed fingernail resting on the furthermost dot. "The Pole Star. The brightest one in the sky. It always points north. Useful to sailors in finding their way home, eh?"

Emilia sat down between us. She folded her hands on the map. "When were you born?"

"I, uh, huh," My head spun like a planet out of orbit. "Do you mean me?"

Doctor Fordee opened a drawer within the table, pulling out an ink jar, a white feathered quill and a knife.

"Yes. When were you born?" Emilia repeated. "What year?"

Doctor Fordee flicked the knife across the quill, sharpening it to a fine point.

It's funny how basic math skills can depart one's head while feeling in vague but impending danger. I raised my eyes, searching thought bubbles for the answer. Ooh, look. The ceiling had a painted zodiac, etched with metallic leaf, fish, scales, and golden arrows. Pretty.

Focus.

I was born in 1996. Four hundred years earlier would be...

"1596!" I cried. *Bingo!*

Doctor Fordee stared, quill suspended above the ink jar. A bead of indigo dripped onto the parchment. The birth of a new star.

He continued. "Your birth month and day?"

"May 29," I said quickly.

"Gemini," said Emilia. "Like me. Mutable."

"Mutable?"

"Changeable. You have multiple sides," Doctor Fordee explained. He dipped the quill, tapped it against the jar. "Do you believe in predestination?"

I said nothing.

He sketched a series of lines between the star-points on the parchment, like an elaborate dot-to-dot. When he finished, what would the picture reveal? A lighthouse? Strawberry Shortcake? A picture he already knew was there? Was that predestination?

Doctor Fordee stoppered the ink jar. He put it, along with the quill and knife, into the table drawer, seemingly satisfied by what he'd accomplished, but it was all Greek to me. Literally.

"You are not who you claim to be." He motioned to my boy's haircut, tamed into civility by a lace bonnet. Obviously, Emilia told him the unusual circumstances of our meeting.

I shifted in my seat. All the padding around my waist forced my back into an unnatural arch, like a question mark. Any attempt to shift myself into a different form of punctuation resulted in a stab of whalebone.

"What do you have to say for yourself?" he asked.

"I think there's been a mistake," I replied.

"No," said Emilia. "I do not think so." She exchanged a look with Doctor Fordee. He nodded his encouragement. "Alexandra. Do you believe in things unseen?"

"You mean astrology?" I asked.

I'd always thought horoscopes were stupid, pop culture mysticism, phony predictions that applied to half the population. Yet, this was something else. Maybe it was the room, maybe it was my altered state of being (hungry, tired, bewildered, corseted), but the star chart was something different, something tangible. A celestial map of my life. My atoms as old as the universe, and perhaps connected to it. All points led to Polaris, the north star, maybe my way home. Like time traveling, I didn't understand it, but that didn't mean it wasn't real.

I replied with the only fact I knew to be true. "I believe there are things that can't be explained."

Doctor Fordee lifted the corners of his lips into a shape approximating a smile. "Yes. Astrology, alchemy, demonology." He paused. "Witchcraft."

"Witchcraft?" I repeated.

"Witchcraft."

The corset left little room to breathe. "I... don't know what you're talking about," an unconvincing defense against a non-accusation.

"What do you know about Mistress Lanyer?" asked Doctor Fordee.

At first I thought he meant my drama teacher. Then, of course, I realized that was in another lifetime. I looked at Emilia, her face set in expectation. She'd brought me to this room, put me in front of Doctor Fordee, but her intentions didn't seem immediately malicious, more like the unicorn hunters in the tapestry, curious as to what she'd caught. Perhaps it was because she looked like someone I trusted, but I didn't fear her. Not exactly. This was my drama teacher's distant relative, a woman who might have authored the works of William Shakespeare under a false name. A dangerous offense. Any woman in that situation would have more to fear from *me*.

As for what I knew about her... I guessed she was Burbage's girlfriend. By all appearances, she was wealthy. She had an interest in the occult, in astrology and the supernatural, but perhaps no more than anyone else in this time period. She was beautiful, intelligent, crafty, and thorough, seeking the advice of an expert, quack though he might be.

I shrugged. "I don't know anything about Mistress Lanyer."

"You knew my name," insisted Emilia. "Today, at the theatre. How?"

"Lucky guess?" I offered.

"Some might think you were a witch," said Doctor Fordee.

"What?!"

"I do not traffic in evil," said the creepy old man. "But I acknowledge the holiness of those gifted by God. There is black magic, and there is white. Which do you practice?"

"I don't. I'm not a—"

"You have a witch's mark," Emilia said, almost apologetically.

'Where?" I asked.

"On your cheek." She pointed to the tear-drop indentation on my left eyelid, from my tumbledown crib escape at age three.

"That's a scar!"

"Perhaps," she acknowledged. "If Dr. Fordee pricks it with a pin will it hurt?"

"Umm, yes?" The edges of my bladder were beginning to feel loose. "I think if you stabbed anyone it would hurt."

"Not so," said Doctor Fordee. "Witches have places on their bodies where they cannot feel pain. It is one of the hallmarks."

"Doctor Fordee is an experienced pricker," said Emilia.

I bet he is.

"There are other methods of discovering the truth," he said. "Drowning."

"Wait, what?"

"Witches spurn baptism. Thus, water rejects them. If a witch is thrown into a body of water and floats, it is proof she is a witch."

"And if the woman sinks?" I asked.

"She is not a witch."

"But, but... she's drowned."

"Yes," said Emilia.

"So... you're either a witch or you're *dead*?" I asked.

"Sometimes the woman is rescued in time," said Doctor Fordee.

"But it should not come to that," assured Emilia.

"Well, that's comforting," I gulped. "Are there any less deadly witch tests? You know, like, multiple choice or something?"

"You mean transfiguration?" Emilia's eyes widened, like I was about to turn into a bat or something.

"What? No!"

"The devil hath power to assume a pleasing shape," said Doctor Fordee.

"I. Don't. Change. Shape."

"You came disguised," said Emilia.

She had me there.

"Yes, but, I mean—" How could I explain it? *Hi, I'm from the 21st century, where women wear jeans?* "I don't know what to say. I'm not a witch. I don't suppose you'd take my word for it?"

"I might," she said.

My lower lip trembled with relief.

"Yet," she added. Why did there have to be a yet? "There is your—mysterious—reflection."

"What reflection?" I asked. Fear and confusion warred inside me.

"Witches have no souls," said Doctor Fordee. "They cannot see themselves in glass, therefore there is nothing for a mirror to reflect. You understand?"

I shook my head, not understanding any of it.

"The soul holds a mirror up to nature," he continued. "What does it mean, though, when the mirror holds nature, but there is no soul?"

"What kind of riddle is this? I'm not a witch!" I exclaimed.

"Then what is this sorcery?" Emilia reached into a pocket of her gown, removed a glowing object. Gravity abandoned the room, leaving only painted constellations and dark matter.

The image was a face with an awkward smile, framed by a grey hoodie. Not just a face. *My* face.

Icons in the corner indicated no bars and half a battery life.

My cell phone.

Chapter 29
Alike betwitched by the charm of looks

MY PHONE!

My phone, my phone, my phone! They had my phone!

The electronic LCD burned obscenely bright, a radiant beacon in Emilia's hand. With the phone flipped open, the image on the inside screen showed me on my first day of school. My hair was covered by the hoodie, but it was clearly my face, a modern yellow school bus as a backdrop, and some wiseass kid giving me bunny ears. I felt a deep affection for that jerk.

I held out a tremulous hand. "May I see it?" I asked.

Emilia glanced at Doctor Fordee before passing me the phone. I advanced to the next picture—Monica, sitting in her Subaru, her Sacramento State sweatshirt unraveling at the sleeve, a shy smile. *Say 'fromage!'* "Cheese," I whispered.

Doctor Fordee grabbed the phone from my hands. "Please, what?"

"Nothing."

Think quickly.

The phone was clearly not of this time. If it was not of this time, it was magic. Dangerous magic. Witch's magic. Enough for the Pricker-in-Chief to toss me into the nearest lake. I should disavow it, recoil. But the stupid phone was my way home. I had no proof of this, only faith.

My salvation.

My damnation.

Doctor Fordee sneered as if he could read my thoughts.

"I have no idea what that is," I said, pretending aloofness. It was a good performance. "Where did you find it?"

"Outside the theatre this morning," said Emilia. "Next to the head of a rat, which Doctor Fordee believes may have been some witch's sacrifice. The image is you, is it not?"

"Um." I'd run out of lines.

She took the phone from Doctor Fordee. "Soft!" she cried, looking at the picture of Monica. "Who is *this*?"

"You were *here*," said Emilia, pointing to the screen. She turned the phone over, as if I'd escaped through the back. "And now you are gone. What does that mean?"

The good doctor was already peering over her shoulder. I could tell he had the old person's problem of not being able to see things at close range. He leaned back, tilting on the legs of his chair. "I believe we may be looking at the future." He squinted hard. "A form of crystal ball."

"The future," said Emilia, amazed. "Of course. When I found this— whatever this is—I did not know who the girl was. Then, *you* appeared. It foretold you coming! I do not mean to frighten you," she said to me. *Little bit late for that.* "But I must discover what this means. That is why I summoned Doctor Fordee. He is an expert on all things metaphysical, holy and unholy."

"Yes," he said. "I have been called before His Majesty sundry times to render judgment, and, if necessary, exorcise the devil."

I had a vision of a horned dude in red tights doing jumping jacks. Then, I realized 'exorcise' meant 'get rid of,' like in that old horror movie where a little girl's head spins around while spewing green projectile vomit. I shook my head side to side. Still attached. Not about to spin off. Although, puking wasn't out of the question.

Doctor Fordee rolled up the astrological chart. "We must determine whether you are the cause of this enchantment, or the effect. If you are innocent, you have nothing to fear."

Except torture and death.

He handed the parchment to Emilia, who placed it in a cabinet of carved oak, the panels inlaid with sunburst patterns of mother-of-pearl. She returned with a small dish, a candle lit from one of the sconces, and the black velvet drawstring pouch she'd purchased at *Antonio's*. My heart began to thrum, a steady motor rather than individual beats. I hoped whatever they had planned did not involve the extraction of any molars. Surely, that would be an in-house Antonio thing.

Doctor Fordee opened the pouch and removed a single leaf. Strange. What would they do with a plant? My mind flashed to Thomas, what *he* had purchased. Could that leaf be belladonna, deadly nightshade? Was this a witch test they'd failed to mention? I take poison, and if I die, I'm not really a witch?

Emilia placed the phone next to the dish, while Doctor Fordee mouthed a breathless incantation over the leaf. He handed it to Emilia. There was something familiar about its bony spine, the hint of eucalyptus.

"Is that a *bay leaf*?" I asked. I looked again, not quite believing, but, yes, it was the same herb Monica spooned from my stew at Ms. Lanyer's book club meeting. At the time, I'd thought it strange that anyone would put an inedible plant inside of a recipe. That was before I'd witnessed its usefulness in exorcism.

"Bay laurel," Emilia said. "Laurus nobilis. Charm against evil." She held the leaf by its stem and touched the tip to the flame. Dark smoke rose to her fingertips. The room took on the smell of burned lasagna.

Emilia placed the blackened stem on the dish. Her shoulders noticeably relaxed, as if she and Doctor Fordee had rid the room of boggarts instead of setting fire to a cooking herb.

"What is your name?" Emilia asked.

"I already told you."

"Who are you?" she asked.

"I'm *me*," I said, fumbling for the right answer. I wasn't a good liar. What did they want next? My mother's maiden name? Last known residence? I didn't know Monica's address. All of a sudden, this seemed significant. I closed my eyes and remembered a scorched oak before a short rise, a country lane bending to the right, but I didn't know the name of the road. I had never asked. Never looked.

Tears began to well, twin reflecting pools in which I saw no past, no future. How could I find my way home if I didn't know the name of the street? There was no way to look it up, no white pages, no Siri. It didn't exist. *I* didn't exist. I wasn't born yet. *If I wasn't born yet, how could I exist?*

Is this what they called a paradox?

"Why are you here?" asked Emilia.

I really had no clue.

"I'm... I'm..."

Frown lines appeared between her brows, furrowed deep. "Do you have a message for me?"

"Emilia," Doctor Fordee warned. "This is not the way to examine."

"What do you know of my future?" Emilia persisted. "I can see it in your eyes. You know something. If you have nothing to tell me, then this instrument is too dangerous. It must be destroyed." She picked up the phone, threatening to smash it on the table. Doctor Fordee gasped, but it was upon me Emilia trained her eyes.

If she shattered the cell, I'd better get used to corsets and chamber pots. AT&T stores wouldn't be around for another four centuries, no sales guys with viral infections pushing the next iPhone. No chance at returning home.

I didn't move, but Emilia read my expression: fear, acceptance, acquiescence—basically the desire to say anything, do anything, to prevent her from destroying the phone.

"This belongs to you," she said.

I nodded.

"Alexandra," she said.

I nodded again.

"Doctor Fordee, please forgive us. Alexandra and I are going to a play."

Chapter 30
I do remember well where I should be

Doctor Fordee looked like a chicken who'd laid an egg sideways.

"Emilia–" he began, his face turning pink, an under-blush to his age spots.

"Simon," she said. "There will be time enough for further study. Alexandra isn't going anywhere. She's agreed to be one of the first young ladies in my school."

I have?

"Emilia," said Doctor Fordee. "Not that foolishness again. What would your husband have said?"

"My husband is dead. I make my own decisions."

"You are as blasphemous as that device." He reached across Emilia, his arm in a half-embrace, but Emilia kept hold of the phone.

"Oh Simon," she said, putting a hand on his knee. "I will keep it safe till your next visit. Will you grant me another consult? Alone?"

A sheen of sweat glistened on Doctor Fordee's speckled head. "Of course, my dear. I will await your summons." He licked his withered lips and kissed Emilia's hand. "Enjoy the play."

The temperature of the room rose a good ten degrees in Doctor's Fordee's absence. Emilia took the phone and locked it in one of the table drawers. The key went in a pocket of her dress. "Alexandra." She offered me the hand that Doctor Fordee hadn't kissed. "Have you ever been to the palace?"

***

Emilia's driver helped me into her coach, and I braced my butt for the rocky ride. At least this time, I had padding. The carriage set off at a clip, the graveled drive turning onto the rutted road. Full dark had fallen. The coach lanterns swayed, as my head made occasional contact with the canopied roof.

Emilia called through the carriage window. "The Olive Garden, please."

We were going to Olive Garden? The Italian chain restaurant where Monica took me after back-to-school shopping? Had I finally cracked, or was this a rift in the space-time continuum? Would I see Ryan and Rabbie sitting in a booth, comparing acting notes and eating unlimited breadsticks?

Ooh, breadsticks!

The cup of broth from Alice and Kitty had been my only meal since morning. My mouth watered at the thought of those buttery mini-loaves, fresh from the oven, parmesan cheese and salt baked into the crust, warm marinara on the side.

When I imagined Ryan sitting at a table eating breadsticks, I felt overcome with longing. However, what I desired most was not the boy, but the breadsticks. The realization was as unsettling as the bumps beneath the carriage wheels.

I loved breadsticks more than Ryan.

And, I'd almost run away with him.

What was *that* about?

I was blinded by something, but it wasn't love. Ryan was good-looking, attractive, and—did I mention—gorgeous, but I didn't *know* him. Not really.

From a distance of twenty-four hours and four hundred years, it was clear.

What I loved most wasn't *him*, but the change he wrought in *me*. With him, I was a different person, someone new: impulsive, daring, willing to throw caution to the wind and rewrite my destiny.

Everything I was afraid to be.

But maybe it was me all along.

A love story starring myself?

And breadsticks. Definitely breadsticks.

"The Olive Garden, ladies," said the coachman.

Descending from the carriage, I saw no faux stone arch, no neon green sign. The "Olive Garden" was really the Olive Garden *Stairs*, a set of wooden steps to a torchlit dock on the River Thames. We'd be traveling to the evening's performance by "wherry," which, near as I could figure, was a sort of water taxi.

Boats bobbed on the river, waiting for passengers like cabs on a street corner. Emilia hailed a narrow raft with two oarsmen. I hiked my skirts and stepped onto the flat-bottomed boards, a difficult task when it's dark, the floor is moving, and you can't see your feet. The lead oarsman caught me by the bumroll and placed me on the center bench.

"Name's Jerry," he said, tipping a dirty grey cap. He wore short black pants, and a shirt that used to be white. A light breeze mixed his pungent body odor with that of the river. I scooted upwind. "Where to, mum?"

"The Palace at Whitehall," said Emilia as the second oarsman helped her onto the boat. He was a younger boy, maybe a teenager, with a bandaged hand.

"Woo-hoo, boys!" Jerry cried to the others waiting for fares. "We've got ourselves some royal guests!" He singled out a barrel-chested man in a small dingy. "Hey, Stew!"

Stew spat into the river, a thick, black glob.

"What's that ye say?"

"I'm takin' these comely maidens to see the King! How you like them beans?"

"Ah get on, with ye, ye dankish codpiece!" Stew waved his oar, precariously rocking his boat. "I'll take yer beef-witted, beetle-headed bladder and knock that smile off yer pate, ye yeasty, fat-kidneyed footlicker!"

"That Stew is a poet," Jerry said to us. "He just needs the inspiration."

"Less talk, more paddling," said Emilia.

"Yes, mum."

Stew continued to curse as Jerry pushed off from the pier. We passed other boats, big and small, from rafts with single oarsmen to covered barges. Oil lamps dotted the waterway like strings of Christmas lights. Lanterns swung from poles, rocking with the waves and the rowers' paddles, a double universe of stars reflected in the water, brighter than the first pinpoints in the soot-covered sky.

Distant calls surrounded us, from ferryman and foot traffic, but Jerry quieted to the silence of his rowing partner. I didn't say much, and neither did Emilia. I was still traumatized from the surprise interrogation with Doctor Fordee, lost in wonder at the discovery of my phone, locked away in Emilia's house. I didn't know why she'd decided to trust me—if, in fact, she really did, and this was not some elaborate trick. I was excited to visit the Palace, to watch Rabbie perform, but a sense of unease lingered.

"You look worried," said Emilia. "Are you thinking of your friend? Rabbie? The one who always plays the spear carrier? He will be fine as Juliet."

"I know that one!" interrupted Jerry. "That's a fine comedy, that is. Hey, mate!" he called to the other rower. "You seen that *Juliet and Romeo*? That's the one where the fairy falls in love with a donkey, isn't it? And there's those two sets of twins, but they keep getting mixed up. That's hilarious, that is. What's it called? *Juliet and Romeo?*"

"No," sighed the other oarsman.

"But, it's a comedy, right?"

"No."

"Oh," said Jerry. "That's right. I forgot. They drink poison and stab themselves, don't they? Not very funny. I was thinkin' of the other one. Where the girl pretends to be a boy. Rather inconceivable, if you ask me."

"Yes." Emilia shifted her gaze to me. "Rather inconceivable."

I swallowed. "Won't Burbage be angry that you brought me?" I remembered his volcanic-like expression when he learned I was a girl.

"Richard is all bluster, no bite. He's paid to be passionate."

"You're his girlfriend, right?"

"I am me," she smiled, using my words from earlier.

The oars slapped the water. I examined my fingernails. The bath had gotten most of them pearly clean, but traces of dirt remained, ground in by the journey. It would take days for the skin to slough, for the blisters on my toes to heal. *I am me,* I thought. Dirt, skin, and scars.

"I am a poet," said Emilia.

I didn't say anything.

She was a poet.

Shakespeare was a poet.

Could it be?

"You see something." Emilia reached across the bench. She pressed my hands in hers. "It's a vision, isn't it? Like in that—what did you call that thing?"

"Um, a phone."

"A phone?"

"Yes."

"Tell me. What do you see?"

How should I begin?

"You're trembling," said Emilia, my hands still clasped in hers.

There was no way into this pool without a deep dive.

"Have you heard of Shakespeare?" I asked.

"I've heard of Shake-spear," volunteered Jerry. "I think I seen him in the bear pits. A great big alligator. You seen him fight, Tommy?"

The other oarsmen shook his head, dark curls covering his eyes.

"Eh, what do you know?" said Jerry. "Tommy's new today. Don't talk much."

"A lovely quality," said Emilia.

Jerry dipped his oar.

"Do you write plays?" I asked Emilia.

She gazed blankly into the river. I felt more foolish by the second. It was all a hoax. There was no Shakespeare. He was just as much a mirage as Thomas.

Thomas.

Tommy.

Wait a second.

It couldn't be.

"I write *poetry*," said Emilia. "I assert the dignity and merit of all women."

"Uh-huh." I whipped my head around to the second oarsman. The right size and build, wiry frame, lean muscles pushing the tide. Tommy, *maybe* a.k.a. Thomas, wasn't wearing my boots, but then again, he wouldn't be if he'd bribed the constable with them. Last night, I saw him for only a moment, not enough to identify him, but there was something familiar in the wave of his hair, a suspiciousness in the way he hid his face.

One hand was bandaged. A split knuckle from punching Rabbie?

No. This was ridiculous, and far too much of a coincidence. Fate would not knock on my door this hard. Tommy was a common name, and there was no shortage of scrawny teenage boys in this city. This kid was just an oarsman. A teenage oarsman with a sneaky look and a bandaged fist, who started his job today.

It was him. It had to be.

Was he worried about being recognized? Surely, he didn't recognize *me*, not the way I looked now. The last time Thomas saw me, I was dressed as a boy, face down in the mud. No, Tommy was worried about someone else.

Emilia.

She would recognize him as the missing Juliet. She'd tell Burbage. He'd be whipped or worse.

Should I confront him? What good would that do? I had no proof. The boots were gone, and, besides, the reason I needed Thomas was because I thought he might have my phone. Emilia had my phone. I didn't need him anymore. Accusing him would only cause trouble for the both of us.

So much for finding Juliet.

Emilia released my hands. "And that is why I am opening a school."

I nodded, not having heard a word.

"I want a legacy as rich as a theatre." We drifted past the Globe, its three-story outline an ink blot against the sky. Torches lit the thoroughfare, casting shadows under the straw-thatched roof. "Generations of girls who will grow up knowing they have a story to tell."

Straw. Fire. Burn.

In my mind's eye, I saw it: the photograph in Ms. Lanyer's hallway, electric light reflected in the glass, behind that, her father amongst the ruins. He was an archeologist on the excavation of the Globe Theatre—this very site—destroyed by fire in 1613 during a performance of *Henry VIII*.

According to Rabbie, that performance was tomorrow.

Tomorrow, the Globe would burn.

Chapter 31

O, it presses to my memory

My first apocalyptic prophecy!

Hard to know what to do.

Was I paranoid? Imagining things? It had been a long day. Maybe a massive inferno wouldn't destroy the world's most famous theatre, along with, perhaps, the evidence of who Shakespeare actually was.

I mean, that's where it had to be, right? The evidence? The plays?

Natalie, my drama teacher's daughter, said no original manuscripts survived. They must have burned in the blaze. That didn't explain why no one here seemed to know who Shakespeare was. But, the plays existed, so someone must have written them. I didn't think it was Emilia. She was hiding something, but it wasn't that.

Should I warn her? How would that conversation go?

Me: I had a vision that tomorrow the Globe Theatre will be going up in flames.

Emilia: I was wrong. You are a witch. Time to burn you at the stake.

"Time to get off the boat," said Jerry. For a second, I thought he meant to chuck me in the water like one of Doctor Fordee's witch tests. When my heart rate slowed, I realized we'd arrived at a wide wharf, no witch-chucking involved.

How much witch could a witch-chuck chuck if a witch-chuck could chuck witch?

God, I needed a bagel or something.

A line of boats stretched the length of the dock. Servants in satin slippers skidded in dried bird poop, helping passengers to land. They wore white jackets with red buttons, short red pants, and white tights, like candy cane courtiers. One held our boat, while another offered a powdered hand. "Welcome ladies. The performance will begin in an hour's time."

"Give my regards to His Majesty," said Jerry, pushing off the pier. The boy Tommy looked back, only once.

Either I'd found Juliet, or not. Didn't matter. He was gone now.

We followed the flow of guests into a tunneled corridor, past a courtyard, through another building, to a wide lawn. Hedges carved into roundels surrounded a checkerboard labyrinth. Sculptures stood in the middle of each square, with columns of pale pink stone scattered throughout. We passed by a statue of a young girl, a butterfly in her hand. Gentle laughter and the sounds of a string quartet floated in the air.

"My father was a court musician," said Emilia, nodding to the violins and cello. "I spent my childhood playing here, in the Privy Garden."

"Really?"

"Yes. You are from the continent?"

I nodded. I didn't say *which* continent.

"That explains your accent. My father was from Venice. He played the virginals."

"I'm sorry, what?"

"What do they call it where you're from? The harpsichord, maybe?"

"Oh." I didn't know what a harpsichord was, but it sounded better than the other thing.

"A cousin on my mother's side was a court composer. Queen Elizabeth loved music. Every night there'd be concerts or masques. Once, the players let me be a fairy in *A Midsummer Night's Dream*. Peaseblossom. I had purple-blue wings, and I rode on Puck's shoulder. Afterwards, Her Majesty presented me with a violet marchpane."

"Marchpane?"

"A flower of spun sugar. My father said it was too pretty to eat, so I kept it on my windowsill. It melted with the morning sun."

We reached the inside of one labyrinth, where a statue of an angel held a spear. Or perhaps it was a weathered cross. "You are an orphan?" asked Emilia.

"Yes," I said.

"My father died when I was seven. He left a dowry of one hundred pounds. For my future husband, of course, not for me. My mother and I were penniless." She gazed up at the angel, her face just as serenely emotionless as the one made of stone. "I fostered with the Countess of Kent. She did not have to take me in, but she did. She gave me an education. She taught me Latin. More importantly, she taught me I was worthy. My book of poetry is dedicated to her, and to all women, free from the subjugation of men."

"Whoa."

"Yes," she said, in private acknowledgment. "Free from woe, from patriarchal enslavement; free to determine our own destinies."

She sounded like her descendant Natalie, smoking a clove cigarette outside her mother's kitchen window, railing about the systemic oppression of women. I could picture this 17th century woman at home in a Berkeley cafe, sipping a soy latté with my foster moms, Debbie and Rick.

"You must think me heretical," said Emilia.

"No," I shook my head.

"Then you are heretical, too." She reached into a hidden pocket of her dress and placed my phone in my hand. I felt the warmth of the battery like it was a living thing.

The battery!

I flipped it open, blinked my eyes against the glare. The battery was down another quarter. I jammed my thumb into the power button, extinguishing the light.

"I thought you locked it away," I said.

"I did," she smiled. "Then I unlocked it."

"But... Doctor Fordee—"

"Is a lecherous old man. I am sorry I frightened you. I was afraid myself. For a moment, I saw all in jeopardy. Will you forgive me?"

I nodded, too overcome to speak. I tucked the phone into my cleavage. Its compact size slipped neatly into the only space left to me by my corset. Having it there acted as a pacemaker to my heart. I had my lifeline. Now I only needed an electrical current. How hard could that be to find in the 17th century?

Inhale. Exhale. One thing at a time.

"Come," Emilia said, slipping an arm through mine. "The play will not begin for another two hours. Despite what the courtier said, royalty moves according to its own whims."

We reversed course, unwinding our path through the labyrinth. More guests filled the grounds, gentlemen in high boots and ladies with lace fans, a pageant of grace and sophistication. Every few feet another torch lit the grounds as clear as midday.

"There is the bowling green," said Emilia, pointing to an expanse of lawn. Nine pins sat in a grid in the center, with balls scattered throughout. They were smaller than normal bowling balls, wooden and misshapen. Two men in powdered wigs took turns throwing a flat-sided ball, which rolled like a drunk hedgehog.

"The Banqueting House is where the play will be. You can see it just beyond the garden." She pointed to a three story building of white and rose marble, rising in the distance. The palace wasn't really a castle, but a complex of buildings, each one grander than the last, surrounded by more gardens and greenery. The London streets, with their muddy cobbles and noxious smells, felt worlds away.

"And there's the old orchard," Emilia said. "Just over there." Rows of leafy trees stood like watchful soldiers at the western edge of the grounds. We cut left and right though the waist-high mazes, breathing in the scent of lemons and fresh grass. Servants strolled with silver trays and goblets of wine, dark ruby in crystal. Others carried bite-sized hors d'oeuvres. Emilia took a dish of what appeared to be white gelatin.

"Lamprey?" she asked.

"Umm..."

"Jellied eel."

"No, thank you," I shook my head. "I'm not hungry."

"Apricot tart, miss?" offered another servant.

I grabbed two.

"I'm not mush of an eel purshon," I explained, spraying apricot tart crumbs. The jamminess made my tongue stick to the roof of my mouth.

Emilia arched an eyebrow.

"My fashurr—father—died in a tragic eel accident."

"Really?"

"No, eely." After a count of three, we both burst out laughing. The servant with the apricot tarts looked at me as if *I* were a drunk hedgehog. I shoved the other tart in my mouth and handed my plate to the next servant, who swapped it for a deviled-egg creation, the yolk neon orange and light as foam.

"What on earth is that?" I asked, wiping my lip of paprika and cream.

"A goose egg?"

"Goose? Really? No, *that*," I said pointing.

In the center of the garden was a ten-foot construction of stone, brass, and wood. Glass spheres jutted from five tiers of iron branches, looking like a fountain of globes. A servant stood guard, keeping a close eye on the party guests who stopped to marvel.

"The King's Sun Dial," replied Emilia. "Marvelous, is it not?" She motioned to one of the middle tiers, portraits of the King and Queen painted on glass. "His Majesty is learned in many arts. Astronomy, geology, theology. The Sun Dial not only displays the hour of the day, but our place in the universe." Emilia took two crystal goblets of wine from a passing servant. "Come, there's a lovely spot over here." She led us down a side path, under a willow tree. Its long branches parted like curtains, revealing a stone bench.

"You asked me if I knew a Shakespeare," she said, handing me a glass. I took a small sip. The wine tasted syrupy sweet, like something you'd pour over ice cream. Between that, the tasty hors d'oeuvres, the magical garden, and having my phone back, I felt a contentedness where the wine settled, spreading like apricot jam.

"There was an actor by that name," said Emilia.

"Who?" I asked, taking another sip.

"Shakespeare."

"Oh yeah."

"He was handsome and clever. He retired to the country two years ago."

"Did he write the plays?" I asked.

"Which plays?"

"*Romeo and Juliet. A Midsummer Night's Dream. Hamlet.*"

"Ah, *Hamlet*," said Emilia. "I always loved Ophelia. Hated when she drowned."

"Who drowned?" Doctor Fordee's witch trials were still fresh in my mind.

"Ophelia," Emilia said patiently. "In the play, she drowns."

"Oh," I said.

I'd never actually read *Hamlet*. I knew that it had something to do with a guy holding a skull, and the whole '*To be or not to be*' speech was pretty famous, but I didn't actually know the story.

"Was she a witch?" I asked.

"No," said Emilia, looking amused. "She was a girl."

I took another sip of wine.

"Do you really believe in witches?" I asked.

"I believe in things unseen." Emilia smoothed her skirt. In the torchlight, the blue satin turned a glimmering indigo. "Ophelia was not a witch. She was lost."

I bit my lip, tasting sweetness. "How did she get home?"

A cell phone? A bolt of lightning?

"Not that sort of lost," Emilia explained. "She was alone."

"Oh."

The willow exploded as a woman in yellow burst through the branches. She rounded the trunk, chased by a man in a silver wig, ponytail askew. He grabbed his companion about the waist and began nibbling her neck. Emilia cleared her throat.

"Sorry!" the woman called, red-faced and giggling, as the man yanked her back through the branches.

Emilia shook her head. "I always wanted a happier ending for her."

"Who?"

"Ophelia." Emilia circled the edge of her glass with an index finger. The crystal gave a low hum. "My daughter's name was Odillya." The branches of the willow billowed, but no one burst through. It was just the wind.

"You have a daughter?" I asked.

"Had." A sad smile played on Emilia's face. "Odillya died two months before her first birthday. She would have been fifteen this year, six years younger than her brother, who is off at university. Although he brings me great joy, I cannot help but see the missing shadow of his sister." She stared at the remnants of wine in her glass, ruby liquid, like heart's blood. "I remember her plump little fists. The way she smelled of porridge and peaches. Her hair was spun gold, just like her father's." A black curl escaped Emilia's twisted knot, dangling like a broken spring. "You'd never have known she was mine."

I heard the string quartet, low and slow, the moan of the cello. Above that, the guests chattering like birds and squirrels, indistinct and oblivious. The distant calls of the river boatmen. People, instruments, places, things, cushioned by a cocoon of air, sacred space defined by the distance between two people.

Emilia set down her goblet. "Why did you ask me if I knew Shakespeare?"

"I don't know. I don't think it's important."

"You must have, if you saw it in a vision."

"It wasn't a vision exactly." More like a conversation four hundred years in the future. "I don't know what it was."

"You lie."

I looked at her. "No one here knows who Shakespeare was."

"I do. He was an actor."

"But who wrote the plays? Who wrote *Hamlet*?"

"We all did."

"We?" I didn't understand anything.

"It's an old story," replied Emilia.

"I know, but— "

"The stories have been with us for hundreds of years. Before there was Hamlet, there was a Scandinavian poem about a hero named Amleth."

"And it's the same story?" I asked. "Shakespeare just ripped it off?"

"No one tore anything."

"The play *Hamlet*. Is it the same as the poem?"

"I do not know."

"You don't know?"

"No. The poem does not exist."

My head felt primed to explode. "But—if it's gone, if it doesn't exist—how do you know it was there in the first place?" I didn't know why I was so upset, but something about this point felt key. "How does anyone *remember*?" Tears cooled my cheeks as I steadied my breath.

Emilia cocked her head.

"I remember my daughter."

I sat still as a garden statue, a butterfly in my hand.

"Words are not legacies," she said. "People are. My father was wrong about the marchpane. Some things don't keep."

Chapter 32
My naked weapon is out

The sound of a trumpet signaled that it was time to head towards the performance in the Banqueting House. We joined the procession of guests moving through the central walkway. At the edge of the Privy Garden, where the path turned to pebbles, Emilia broke from the crowd and steered us towards the rear of the palace, where wagons from this afternoon circled like a traveling caravan.

"We have time yet," she said. "Let us give our good wishes to the players."

I dug my slippered heels into the smooth gravel, recalling Burbage's temper. I wasn't sure he'd forgiven me for impersonating a boy. "Maybe I should wait out here."

"Richard will not even recognize you," she said, reading my thoughts. "Men often do not see what is in front of them."

A servant opened the door to the player's changing room. Lanterns illuminated a controlled chaos of fabric and noise. Stepping over the threshold was like entering a sultan's tent of color, with players in fantastically striped costumes, practicing their lines and warming up their voices. A trio of musicians tuned guitar-like instruments, while Crab sat in a corner, chewing something blue.

"GET THAT GIRL OUT OF HERE!"

"Now, Richard," said Emilia.

"Now, *Emilia*." Burbage's cheeks were scarlet beneath his rouge, his hair slicked back, and his costume half on.

The top half.

Emilia stepped between me and a vision I'd likely never forget, one with hair in regions I didn't know it could sprout.

I turned and walked in the opposite direction, smack into Rabbie, who blinked his eyes in recognition, then disbelief.

"Parrot!" he cried. "You're dressed like a girl!"

"So are you!" His Juliet costume had been mended, the cream and sage satin cleaned, his wig re-curled. His black eye had been erased by powder, lined in black, his lips a soft pink. I knew he'd make a prettier girl than me.

"You look so different," he said.

"You already knew I wasn't a boy," I whispered. I looked over my shoulder to Emilia mollifying Burbage, who was bent over pulling up his stockings. I quickly turned back to Rabbie, shaking my head like an Etch-a-Sketch, trying to erase the picture. Seriously, Crab had less fur.

"I know," he said. He took in my russet skirt with the delicately embroidered grape vines and butterflies. "But you are beautiful."

Heat rose from my collar bone up my neck, the only part of me not covered in linen and lace. Rabbie wasn't flirting, though. He said it as a statement of fact, the way one would describe a painting or a sunrise. Somehow, that made me blush harder.

"Well, *you* look amazing," I pronounced.

"I look like you."

It was true. The length of his wig was longer than my hair, but the color was similar to my own, brown with auburn highlights. His eyes were a smoky grey instead of brown, but they were almond-shaped, same as mine. In our dresses and shoes, we were the same height, with the same slim build. We weren't identical, but we could have been sisters.

Well, except for the fact that he was a boy, and I was born 400 years in the future.

Except for that.

"Why, who do we have here?" Armin, dressed in the musty black robe, appeared beside Rabbie. "Ah! It's you! The girl-boy!" He took my hand in his chalky old palm, gave it a moist kiss, then leaned in conspiratorially. *"Alas the day, what shall I do with my doublet and hose?"*

"Um..."

"I must thank you for your lack of male parts. I had forgotten what a delightful role the Apothecary is. For instance, I'm the one who gives *him* the poison." He nodded to Eddie, Rabbie's Romeo, puckering his lips to rival any Kardashian selfie. He stood on his tiptoes, feathering the plume in his cap. Perhaps he thought it would make him look taller.

"SUCH MORTAL DRUGS I HAVE, BUT MANTUA'S LAW IS DEATH TO ANY HE THAT UTTERS THEM!" Armin thundered. "I like that line."

"Where is my shoe? Has anyone seen my shoe?" Eddie asked. He squatted beneath his dressing table in an attempt to keep his tights clean. "I cannot find my shoe. Who took my shoe?"

"Is it blue?" asked Armin.

"Yes," said Eddie.

"Is it covered with dog spittle?'

"CRAB!" yelled Eddie. The dog dropped the slipper and ducked behind a curtain.

"Don't you worry, young Master Romeo. Crab has few teeth." Armin picked up the ball of wet satin and tossed it to Eddie. "'Tis a good dog," he whispered to me and Rabbie, then turned away, bellowing. "MY POVERTY, BUT NOT MY WILL CONSENTS!"

"He's good," I said.

"Who, Eddie?"

"Armin."

"Well, he's loud," said Rabbie. "And funny."

"That, too."

"He plays most of our comic roles."

"I guessed."

"What?" Rabbie seemed distracted.

"Armin. He seems like a funny actor."

"Eddie is loud, too," said Rabbie. "And good. He's not the most agreeable chap." We looked over to see Eddie pounding his wet slipper on his chair. "But he *is* ... good. He is a good Romeo. He's been playing Romeo for over a year now. He's played at court before." Rabbie took a shuddering breath.

"You will be fine," I said.

"I know."

"You will be great."

"I— what?"

"Are you nervous?" I asked.

"Nervous?"

"Yes, nervous," I said gently.

"No. I have been performing all my life. This is what I have prepared for."

"But it's okay to be nervous. That's natural."

"I'm not nervous. I think I am more just—"

"Excited?"

"Yes. Filled with excitement."

"I'm so happy for you," I said, squeezing his hand. His fingers felt like ice. "You really did it. You are about to achieve your life's dream. That's amazing!"

Rabbie's lips formed themselves into a thin smile.

"And you're playing Juliet without any rehearsal at all!" I continued. "Performing in front of the King and Queen and, like, hundreds of guests. There's a huge line of them waiting to come in—"

"I think I'm going to puke."

I dropped his hand. "Did you just say, 'puke'? Wow, I didn't even know that was a word back then. Back now. Never mind."

"What?" He held both hands to the sides of his corset, breathing shallowly.

"Puke."

"Stop saying that," he said.

"What, 'puke'?"

"O heavens," he said, running to the door.

"Nice," deadpanned Eddie. He pulled his dog-slobbered shoe over a stockinged foot. "Anyone have a candied mint?"

I twiddled my fingers, waiting for Rabbie to finish retching. I thought about going outside and offering to hold his wig back, but decided that might make it worse. No one else in the room seemed to think an actor vomiting was cause for concern. Burbage was now dressed (thank goodness), having a discreet conversation with Emilia while finishing his makeup.

"Who are *you*?" The actor was another teenage boy, rail thin, wearing a striped green velvet jacket and yellow tights. A shock of orange hair set off his blue eyes.

"Alex," I said.

"Alex?"

"Alexandra." When he didn't respond, I continued awkwardly, "I'm with Mistress Emilia. And Rabbie." The latter could be heard dry heaving just outside the door, but the boy ignored it.

"Any friend of Rabbie's is a friend of mine." He plucked my hand— the one Armin hadn't slobbered on—from my side and gave it a nice dry kiss. "Have you seen *Romeo and Juliet* before?"

"I've seen the movie—uh... I mean, yes."

"What is a *moo-vee*?"

"It's... uh... a type of play."

"Oh. Hm. I play Benvolio. Romeo's best friend. He's a tragic figure, really."

"I know." I laughed, remembering the guy from Ms. Lanyer's Drama class who said they should change the name of *Romeo and Juliet* to *Benvolio Superstar*.

"Did I say something comic?"

"No, sorry."

"Benvolio is not Romeo, not by any measure. But in a way, he suffers a fate worse than his friend. After all, who lives to tell the story? In the final scene, Romeo just has to lie there, dead. That's easy. Benvolio must placate the Prince, console the families, and live with the guilt of what he could not do. His final soliloquy is heartrending."

"Um, yeah. He's great."

What was that guy's name? The one in Ms. Lanyer's Drama class? He wore super cool tie-dyed high tops, and a T-shirt that read *National Sarcasm Society: Like We Need Your Support*. Not drop-dead gorgeous like Ryan, but cute in an oversized teddy bear kind of way, with a rash of pimples on his cheeks and a quirky, self-deprecating sense of humor. I liked him.

Jeremy! That was his name!

"So, you *have* seen the play."

I shrugged, non-committal.

"I'm Angus." He kissed my hand again. "Perhaps I will see you after the *moo-vee*," he said as he sauntered away.

Apparently, I had a date with a dude in yellow tights. And his name was Angus.

Rabbie returned, wobbly-kneed. His face matched the green satin trim on his dress. "I'm sorry," he said.

Madge, the crook-backed deaf seamstress, handed him a handkerchief. "DON'T YOU WORRY DEARIE. EVERYONE PUKES BEFORE THEIR FIRST ROYAL PERFORMANCE."

"*I* didn't," said Eddie, flipping his plume.

"NO, THAT'S RIGHT. YOU ONLY PISSED YOURSELF."

Eddie turned to his mirror, redder than a rooster. "I spilled some water," he mumbled.

A man in a black frock coat emerged from one of the backstage curtains. His round head was covered with white fuzz, like an under-ripe peach. A pair of floating spectacles balanced on his nose. A bushy white mustache sprouted above his upper lip. He looked like the Monopoly Man, minus the top hat, double the monocle.

"Master of Ceremonies," Burbage called. "How long till curtain time?"

"His Majesty is detained in private audience. The performance will begin when he arrives at the Banqueting House."

"Yes," said Burbage, maintaining his politeness. "But when should that be?"

"Why, whenever that is."

Burbage grumbled but said nothing. Rabbie's complexion paled to curdled milk.

The Master of Ceremonies looked in my direction. "I need the young woman to come with me." The business of the backstage halted as everyone turned to stare.

"Me?" I asked.

"I do not see any other young women here," he said, a wax smile on his face. "Begging your pardon, Mistress Lanyer."

Emilia stood. "You need my ward? To go where?"

"If you were to have been told the information, I would have offered it," the little man said.

"This better not have anything to do with this afternoon," Burbage said to Emilia. He addressed the Master of Ceremonies. "We are obedient servants to His Majesty, the King. We do not permit women on the stage."

"Of course you do not," said the Monopoly Man, bobbing his round head. "That would be obscene. Your theatre company would be *ruined*." He trilled his r's, enjoying the sound.

"Then why—" Emilia began.

"Enough questions. Players, make you ready." The Master of Ceremonies held open a side curtain for me. "Miss?"

I stepped through, my stomach as fluttery as if I were the one going onstage. I turned back to Rabbie. "Break a leg, friend."

Rabbie looked down, horrified.

I laughed. "That's just what we say where I come from."

"Y'are a strange one, Parrot."

"And you are...Juliet."

Chapter 33
Short Interlude: a Play within a Play

The Monopoly Man took me to jail. I did not pass go. I did not collect $200.

Everything began nicely, like a five-act comedy that turns sour at the climax, when the characters drink poison and stab themselves.

Act One

Setting: a royal garden. A girl, the protagonist and heroine of the play, shares a touching moment—and a delicious deviled egg— with a mother figure, who reassures her that life is wonderful and precious. Musicians play. The air is fragrant with fruit trees and possibility. Lanterns light the way to a magical palace. The girl sees players set to perform one of the greatest works in all of mankind. She meets her friend and encourages him to achieve his life's ambition and live happily ever after.

Act Two

Setting: a series of hallways much like the squares on a Monopoly board. Blue, orange, red, green rooms, each one grander than the last. Priceless paintings and statues. Hustle and bustle. Servants carry chairs and tables, platters of exotic food, goblets of wine, sights, sounds, and color everywhere: velvet pillows and peacock feathers; candles and crystal; silver and fine china. Round and round they go, where they stop, nobody knows. The girl is lost, disoriented, out of place. A thimble on a game board. "Where are we going?" the girl asks. "To the King," says the Master of Ceremonies.

FINDING JULIET

Ten-Minute Intermission

(The audience returns from going to pee. The girl finds she needs to do so, too, but is stuck waiting for the King of England, which makes her have to pee more. The corset is not helping. Curtain rises.)

Act Three

Setting: the King's Private Chamber. Stage right, an arched stone doorway with a chiseled lion holding a crown. In the center, a raised dais with an ornate chair, carved and cushioned. On one side of the wall, a fireplace with antique-work and golden roundels. On the other, a fountain set into the wall, decorated with crystals and pearls. The floor is laid with black, red, and white tiles. The girl stands on a black circle within a white square, as the King enters with his retinue. He sits, center stage. The Master of Ceremonies (M.C.) nudges the girl, who curtseys. Owing to a full bladder and a forty-pound dress, she is less than successful in the attempt.

King: What are you doing?

Girl: Bowing?

M.C.: Say "Your Grace" to His Majesty.

Girl: Your grace to his majesty.

An old man steps from behind the King's entourage. His bald head is marked with age spots, his expression terrifying as he points a bony finger towards the girl. She recognizes him as the Evil Doctor Fordee from the Prologue.

Doctor: She mocks you, Sire.

King: Do you mock me, girl?

Girl: No!

Doctor: She lies. I charted her stars. She aligns with Gemini, two-faced and duplicitous. Mistress Lanyer caught her intriguing herself with the King's Men, your players, set to perform tonight. She came disguised as a boy in order that she might come near to Your Grace to work her dark magic. I have seen it myself: a glowing orb of malevolence that shows things not as they are, but as what they will be.

She is the Devil's handmaiden, come to cast ruin upon your daughter's marriage. There can be no other reason for her appearance tonight.

King: Is this true?

Doctor: Upon my life, it is.

King: What do you have to say for yourself?

Girl: Is there a bathroom nearby?

Doctor: You see, Your Grace. She evades.

Girl: No, I just really have to go.

King: You will go nowhere until you answer these charges. This evening's gathering is to celebrate the union of my daughter and her husband, the continuation of the royal line in health and perpetuity. Have you come to curse it?

Girl: No, of course not.

Doctor Fordee: She would not admit it, Sire.

Girl: Because I haven't!

M.C.: Actually, she has.

Girl: What are you talking about?

M.C.: I heard you.

Girl: What?!

M.C.: You cursed that boy.

Girl: What boy?

M.C.: The one playing Juliet.

Girl: How did I curse him?

M.C.: You told him to break a leg.

Girl: That's not a curse!

King: What is it then?

Girl: An expression!

Doctor: A curse.

Girl: AAARRRRGGGHHHHHH!!!!!!

Doctor: Your Grace, the fiend has overtaken her spirit. She is possessed by the Devil!

Girl: I am not! What kind of a crackpot are you?!

FINDING JULIET

Just then, a sound emanates from the young girl's chest, unearthly and strange, almost like... mooing? The King and all his court have never heard anything like it, either from man or beast. Panic ensues.

Doctor: GUARDS! SEIZE THE WITCH!

Act Four

Setting: Newgate Prison.

Act Five

Setting: My deathbed. No spoilers.

Chapter 34
Shut up in prison, kept without my food

The straw that covered the floor smelled like urine. The cell was windowless, the walls made of large stone bricks. I was brought to a common area with about a dozen women and half as many children and young teenagers, all huddled amongst themselves. Besides two small windows at ceiling height, the only light came from beyond the bars of the steel door, where torches threw flickering, striped shadows. In one corner, a baby cried. In another, a woman squatted, going number two in the rushes. I wasn't dead, but imprisonment in a dark, dank, and reeking cell wasn't much of a step upwards.

And all because my boobs started mooing.

When the alarm on the cell phone went off, it was like time froze. I stood there, in front of the King, taking a ridiculously long time to process what was happening. By the time I realized I hadn't turned off the phone as I thought (the power button had always been sticky), it was too late to look around like, *Hey, did you hear that? How odd...*, not with a distinct vibration coming from my chest, or the fact that every time I opened my mouth to explain why I wasn't the devil's servant, the call of a horned beast emanated from my being.

So I ran.

That was the wrong decision.

By the time the King's guards caught me, the alarm had stopped sounding.

Good news: I wasn't strip-searched for a strange 21st century artifact that would have explained why I wasn't possessed.

Bad news: everyone thought I was possessed.

The King couldn't ruin his big night with hundreds of guests waiting, so the order was given to remove me to a place where I could be held—then presumably tried and executed—for infiltrating the King's court by means of witchcraft.

And I didn't even get to see the play!

"Whatcha in for, love?" asked a rasping voice.

I squinted, focusing in the gloom. The warden said this area was for women and children only, but the person who spoke was wearing men's clothes, an oversize coat and baggy pants. There was a scraping sound and flash of flame, then a fragrant puff of tobacco. The man held a curved pipe between the gaps in his teeth, contorting his smile into a grimace. As fire flared in the bowl, his eyes lit red.

I backed a step away, my slipper coming down on something soft. My squeak was louder than the rat's. The man clamped a hand around my wrist. I opened my mouth to scream, but he held tight. "Don't slip in the muck."

And then I realized.

"You're a woman," I said.

"Aye," she said. "And you're stepping in shyte."

It was true. The squishiness extended beyond the rat. "Oh god."

"He's not here, lass," the woman puffed. Chin-length hair hung greasily in her face. "And if He were, I don't think He'd care overmuch. That's what we all are. A bit o' turd in God's toes."

I stared, visualizing the metaphor while standing ankle-deep in its literal application.

"Name's Mary, though most people call me Moll. Moll Cutpurse. Ever heard of me?"

I shook my head.

"Really? Dekker wrote a play about me. *The Roaring Girl*. You never heard it?"

"No, I'm sorry."

"Eh. Was a good piece of work, but that boy what played me was awful. Too girly. What they think? All ladies walk about with turtledoves stuffed up their arses? That every time we fart, a bird takes flight? That's why I convinced 'em I had to play meself. Was a great success, too. I'm surprised ye never heard of me. Everyone knows old Moll Cutpurse."

"But... I thought women couldn't be on the stage."

"Rules is meant to be broken, love. Who else is gonna play me if not me? I'm not saying I didn't get in trouble for't, but some things is worth the trouble." She slapped herself on the cheek. "Damn fleas. Wish we was in Bridewill. Now that's a nice prison for you. Not so much lice, and you get a bit of gristle in your stew. They ain't even given us our supper yet. Bridewell is where we need to be."

"Uh huh." It may have been my imagination, but I could swear I felt the pitter patter of tiny feet up my tights. I was afraid to move, though, wondering if the next squashy bit might be worse than the one I was already standing in.

"You got a fancy look about you," Moll said. "Not like these slatterns and scroungers." She hooked a thumb towards the huddled groups, looking like extras from *A Christmas Carol*. "Bunch of wretchedness they are."

"Why are there children in here?" I asked.

"Beggin. Stealin. No families."

"They're orphans?"

"Some."

"Isn't there some other place for them?" I counted two babies on their mothers' breasts, a toddler throwing straw, two young boys playing a violent game of thumb war, plus a couple of older kids of indeterminate age sleeping against the wall.

Orphans and single mothers.

I thought of a tenement in San Francisco. The smell of Kool-Aid, stale beer, and piss in the stairwell. Of nights when the heat was off, and blankets couldn't keep the cold from my bones.

I thought of a country road with rolling hills and old oaks. A freshly painted bedroom with walls the color of sunshine. Monica *tap-tap, tap-tap-tapping* on the door, asking if I wanted spaghetti or grilled cheese.

The longing felt like hunger.

"You never said what you was in for," said Moll, sucking on her pipe.

"The King," I muttered.

"The what?"

"The King. He thinks I'm a witch."

The whispering from the other women in the cell took on a more animated quality. There was a subtle shift in atmosphere, as if I'd released a noxious gas. I assumed Moll, too, would shrink from me in horror, but she just laughed, a rich barking noise followed by a hock of phlegm. "Oh, they all do, sweeting. Can't say nothing against us 'cept we're all witches."

"Are they going to... burn me?"

"Eh. Probably not. If they burned every woman they thought was a witch, there'd be no more left to warm their beds."

"But they might?"

She paused to cough for a racking minute, then continued. "Mayhaps. But what you going to do? Worry about something that ain't happened yet? When they light the fires, that's when you start worrying, I say. And remember," she leaned close, a whisper in my ear. *"It is a heretic that makes the fire. Not she who burns within."*

The creaking moan of the steel door followed the rattle of keys. Torchlight lit a path into the jail cell. "Mary Frith!" bellowed the jailer.

"That's my cue," said Moll.

"Bail's been paid. You're free to go."

"Awe, Dekky came through. Best of luck to you, girl. You never did say what your name was."

"Alex."

"That's a boy's name." She looked thoughtful. "I like it. Luck to you, Alex."

"You, too."

"Oh, Moll Cutpurse makes her own luck." She scratched under her arm. I fought the urge to do likewise. "Mark me. Sometimes you're the flea, sometimes the rat. Fortune is a wheel. What goes down, must come up. The trick is to stay on for the ride. Ain't that right, Tommy?" She called to a boy in the corner. "Yesternight, he was Juliet. Can you believe that? Today, he's—well, looky there, Jailer—today he's getting murdered in a cell!"

Chapter 35
Like a poor prisoner in his twisted gyves

I'd never punched anyone before.

I'd punched a pillow, sure. The satisfaction of pummeling a bag of polyester/cotton-fill was second-to-none, but I'd never actually hit a person.

At the group home I couldn't go a day without one of my bunkmates kicking a hole in the wall, punching a tree, or bashing another kid over the head. I'd never stopped to wonder if any of it hurt.

I mean, of course, the person being hit would get hurt. That was the point.

I never thought about the person doing the hitting.

Or fully appreciated the fact that the human face is full of bones.

Life Lesson #206 (the number of bones in a person's body): Bones hitting other bones hurts both sets of bones, especially when the little bones in a person's fist hit the big bones in a person's face.

After punching Thomas in the jaw, I spent the next five minutes cradling my hand like it was a broken-winged bird.

"What'd you do that for?" Thomas demanded. He'd responded to my sucker punch by elbowing me into the one patch of stone floor not covered by filthy straw. Luckily my bum roll absorbed the shock.

Instantly regretting starting a fight I had no desire or ability to finish, I looked around for back-up. Moll and the prison guard were gone, the show over. The other inmates might as well have had their eyes closed, fingers in their ears, see no evil, hear no evil. If Thomas wanted to retaliate, he wouldn't have interference.

"You robbed me," I said, sucking on a knuckle. The iron taste of blood filled my mouth. "I think I broke my thumb."

"No, you didn't." He raked his bandaged hand through a mess of matted dark hair. Since I'd last seen him rowing the boat across the Thames, his appearance had taken a turn for the worse. His shirt was ripped, his pants smeared with some unknown substance, hopefully dirt. He reeked of the funk of the prison cell, but I imagined I was also no longer a bed of essential oils.

And my hand hurt. Really bad.

"How do you know it's not broken?" I asked.

"Let me see." He squatted next to me.

I flinched, my elbow smacking his chin.

"Would you stop hitting me? I am not going to hurt you. Let me see your thumb."

I offered my hand, curled like a conch shell.

"Can you open and close your fingers?" he asked. "Like this."

"I think so."

Gingerly, I did. My knuckles felt on fire, but they moved.

"It'll be swollen for a day or two," he said. "But you don't need a barber."

"A barber? You mean someone who cuts hair?"

"And sets bones."

"Really?"

"They also perform enemas."

"Yeah, I don't think it's broken," I said, flexing through the pain. As an afterthought, I asked, "Are *you* okay?"

"Pardon?"

"I'm sorry I hurt you."

He waved me off. "You didn't."

"Oh," I said, feeling a bit disappointed about the first and last fistfight of my life. Kind of anticlimactic. "Well, then. I'm still sorry I hit you."

"Why *did* you hit me?"

"You stole my shoes."

He glanced down at my slippered feet. "You're wearing shoes."

"And you hit me in the head," I said.

"You hit *me* in the head."

"Because you hit me first!" Last night felt like a dream, but I remembered everything: Thomas pressing me into the mud, wrenching off my boots, then slamming my head with a steel toe. I wanted to punch him again, but my hand hurt too much.

"I do not know who you are," he said. "I have never seen you before in my life." His eyes widened. "Unless... soft, you were the girl in the boat with Mistress Emilia! Going to see Rabbie in the play before the King. What are you doing here?"

"Oh, I just thought I'd pop in for a spot of tea," I said in my best British accent, not deranged at all. "Stop changing the subject! Last night, the night before this night, right? This last, past night, did you or did you not steal a pair of boots?"

He shifted his gaze to the other prisoners. "I found a pair of boots."

"On a person. You found a pair of boots on a person."

"On a person," he admitted, looking embarrassed. "A drunk wastrel."

"That was ME! And I wasn't drunk, I was sleeping, and I don't even know what a wastrel is!"

"Lower your voice. It means a lown."

"What?" I asked, not lowering my voice.

"A Meazel. A bombard. A cony-catcher."

"Not helping. You took my boots."

"I thought you were dead."

"You said you thought I was *drunk*." *Law & Order* had nothing on me.

"Firstly," said Thomas. "I thought you were dead."

"And secondly you tried to KILL ME!" *Dun-DUN.*

"I panicked," he said. "The punishment for stealing is losing a *hand*."

"What's the punishment for murder?"

He looked me dead in the eyes.

"Don't have anything to say?" I asked, still breathing hard. Everything was coming to a head. No pun intended. I wasn't even sure if I was angry at Thomas, or if he was just a convenient receptacle for all the pent up emotions of the past twenty-four hours.

Thomas stood. He shook his head, then crossed to a patch of light beneath one of the two windows. High above, the opening was about a foot square, too small and high up to figure as a means of escape. No moon shone, but the window let in a hint of air, a bit of nighttime glow. For a moment, the cell was quiet as an empty church.

I moved behind him, just outside the light.

"I made a mistake," he said at last. "It was all a mistake." He kicked the straw with his bare foot. "I beg you to forgive my most grievous transgression."

I sighed, remembering how Ryan and Rabbie couldn't seem to hold a conversation without quoting random lines. "Is that from one of your plays?"

"No! I am making amends."

"For your 'most grievous transgression'? Really? Who wrote that?"

"Me! But I did not write it, I am saying it. To you. I should not have hit you. I should not have taken your boots." He rubbed his face. Despite his protestations that I hadn't hurt him, there was a mark on his left cheek.

"I accept your apology." I held out my hand for him to shake. The left one.

"Good."

A moment passed.

"I'm sorry, too," I said.

"No, you are not. I deserved it," he said, releasing my hand. He turned and slid his back against the wall

"You're right," I said, sitting down next to him.

"Last night... I was not myself."

Rabbie had said the same thing earlier this morning. I could see them as friends. They were about the same age, the same build, one fair, the other dark. Two sides to the same coin. "I was running away," he said. "But I had no money, no resource, no place to go, not in London. I thought to sell the boots to book passage on a ship."

"To America?" I asked, thinking of the search for Thomas through the bowels of *The Marigold* ... the Lost Boys, Fartin' Fred, and the captain who threw Rabbie and me to the constable for trespassing. Rabbie spent time in the stocks for that, humiliated and alone, sacrificing himself to protect me. All to find the boy now sitting in a jail cell. Next to me, also sitting in a jail cell.

This had not been a very good day for any of us.

"Why would I go to America?" asked Thomas. "There is nothing across the ocean but empty wilderness." He shrugged his shoulders, not knowing that wilderness would one day be populated by millions of people, miles of mini-marts, Starbucks, and Jefferson Snips. Destynee, the purple-haired barber who neither set bones nor performed enemas. "My mother died when I was born," he said. "But I thought I might seek her family on the continent. I cannot stay here."

"Why?" I asked. "Why leave?"

"I cannot speak of it."

"Is it Rabbie?"

"Who are you?" he demanded. "How do you know Rabbie?"

"He's my friend."

"I am Rabbie's only friend," he pronounced, subtext: *Duh.*

I didn't like his tone. "Not anymore."

"Did he tell you what happened?"

"Yes," I lied.

Rabbie never revealed the reason for their fight, why he woke up with a black eye and a missing roommate, but I was beginning to suspect it wasn't any ordinary argument.

"You hit him," I pronounced, pointing to Thomas's bandaged hand. He winced. "It hurts, doesn't it?"

"I think it's broken."

"Send for a barber?"

"Not in here. They'd sooner cut it off."

"Oh," I said, and was quiet for another moment. "He forgives you, you know."

Thomas looked away. "I do not believe that."

"OH CRAP!" I yelled.

A keening shriek pierced the stone walls, ricocheting from the corner where the baby had just awoken, bouncing off the mortar. I clapped my hand over my mouth, but the damage was done. The mother jiggled furiously, shooting metaphorical daggers in my direction. My popularity with the prison set had reached an all-time low. I didn't care.

"Ohcrapohcrapohcrapohcrapohcrapohcrapohcrap," I mouthed.

"Are you really a witch?" asked Thomas.

"What? No," I said.

"I overheard you with Moll."

"Crapcrapcrapcrapcrapcrapcrap."

"Is that an incantation?"

"NO!"

"It sounds like an incantation."

I grabbed Thomas's arm. "I need you to turn your back and cover me."

"Cover you with what?"

"Yourself. Just sit in front of me and look over there," I said, pointing to where the women were taking turns passing the baby around like a squalling hot potato. The lethargy of the room had morphed to red-alert. Not the ideal circumstances to do what needed to be done, but I didn't know how much time I had before everything was lost, including me.

"Why?" Thomas asked.

"Please," I begged. "You owe me."

"Just so. But if you turn me into a newt— "

"*I'm not a witch!* Just do it!"

With Thomas blocking the sight of me from the others, I reached down my dress for the phone, which seemed to have slipped to my navel.

"Why are you grunting?" asked Thomas.

"*Shhhhhhh...urgh...*got it. Don't turn around," I hissed. The phone was still on. Between the chase with the King's guards, the locked carriage ride with my escort, and the prison check-in, I hadn't had a chance to turn it off. The unearthly light flooded my face as I flipped it open, saw the inside wallpaper of the archeological remains of the Old Globe Theatre, and mashed my thumb into the stupid freaking power button.

"*Stay OFF,*" I ordered the phone.

"I am not on you," said Thomas.

"OW! My thumb, my thumb..."

"What did you do to your thumb?"

"I hit you in the face with it. Turn around, or I'll do it again."

I tucked the phone back down the front of my dress, where hopefully it would no longer ring, vibrate, or moo. Maybe forever. Before I flipped it shut, the low battery warning popped up. Whatever I was going to do with the phone, I'd only get one shot. Maybe not even that.

"I'm done," I said.

Thomas turned around with a look that said, *Are you insane?*

Before I could reply with a look that said, *Long story,* the door to the cell clanged open. The jailer reached into a pail and tossed hunks of bread to the ground. The women and children ran to the circle of light, Thomas with them. He returned with half a stale baguette. "Dinner is late tonight." He broke off a chunk. "For you."

The bread was hard as a piece of driftwood, covered with bits of filthy straw.

"No thank you," I said, handing it back, but Thomas wouldn't take it.

"Eat it," he said. "You need your strength."

I wasn't hungry. Even if I hadn't spent the evening eating party hors d'oeuvres, even if I *could* manage to put food into the tangle of knots that was now my stomach, I had no desire to put the nasty crust in my mouth.

But I accepted the bread for what it was. A gift.

I bit off half the crust, offering a silent prayer against food borne illnesses.

"I think I broke a tooth," I said.

"Your tooth. Your thumb. Is there anything you have not broken in the past ten minutes?"

"Ha, ha."

"Hold the bread in your mouth," said Thomas. "Your spit will soften it."

"Yum."

We chewed awhile in silence.

"Rabbie is my friend," said Thomas, finishing his loaf. "He is like my brother. Yet he never told me of you. Why? Who are you?"

I shrugged, pointing to my mouth, not having reached the point where I could swallow. The bread was softening, but it was still like driftwood. Soggy driftwood.

"Keep chewing," he said.

The other prisoners were settling in for the night. The baby had stopped crying, gumming a bit of crust like a teething biscuit. His mother sang softly,

Golden slumbers kiss your eyes,
Smiles awake you when you rise;
Sleep, pretty baby, do not cry,
I will sing a lullaby.
Cares you know not, therefore sleep
While over you a watch I'll keep

Sleep pretty darling, do not cry
And I will sing a lullaby.

"I suppose it does not matter who you are," said Thomas. "If Rabbie told you, he must trust you." Thomas spoke hesitatingly, but the dark and the quiet gave him courage to continue. "It was the play, you see. Rabbie always helped me with my lines. That is all it was. But it was a mistake."

I knew it. I knew everything.

"You love him," I said.

"I cannot stay here."

"He loves you."

"You must not say such things. We were rehearsing."

"And you punched him in the eye."

"It was the play!" Thomas moved to stand, but I grabbed him with my good hand.

"That's why you ran away," I said.

"I cannot stay here. I cannot play this part."

"So you ran."

"I had nowhere to go. After I took your boots, I crossed the bridge, waited in an alley for the sun to rise, so I might find a ship, a captain who would take the boots as currency. The constable woke me in a doorway, threw me in the stocks for vagrancy. I bought my freedom with the boots."

"How did you end up rowing that boat?"

"I was hungry. I had no money. I thought I might work for a fortnight, buy my way in as a cabin boy on one of the ships. My mother's family is from Prussia. Your accent is strange. Is that where you are from?"

"No." I paused a half second. "I'm from America."

"How... how marvelous! You have been on a great journey, then?"

"Yes."

"Where is your family? Your parents?"

"They're dead." Actually, they weren't alive yet, but why quibble?

"And Mistress Emilia has taken you in?"

"Yes."

"You are fortunate. Perhaps she will offer surety for you. No one will come for me. No one even knows I am here."

"Why *are* you here?" I asked. "How did you end up in jail?"

"I heard you on the boat. You and Mistress Emilia. Rabbie was to play Juliet for the King! I could not believe it. I wanted to see him do it. I thought I might be able to steal in through the rear of the Banqueting House, catch a glimpse from backstage. I should have realized what lunacy it was. A palace guard caught me in the Privy Garden. I dared not explain I was one of the King's Men. Prison is better than Burbage's wrath."

"I agree."

"You know him, too?"

"He was going to make me play Rabbie's old part."

"The Apothecary?"

"That's it. I can never remember how to say that word."

"But you are a girl!"

"I know. Burbage was not too happy about that either."

"I still do not understand how you know Rabbie."

A loud clanging came from beyond the jail cell. "Who do you want again?" called the warden.

"The girl."

"We have lots of girls. Come here and pick her yourself."

A grandmotherly face appeared in the barred window of the cell door. I recognized the round, white bun and the blue servant's dress underneath a grey shawl. "That's her," the maidservant said, pointing to me in the gloom.

Alice. My Fairy Godmother.

"Come on out now, chuck," said the warden. "You have important friends."

I stood, my heart billowing with relief. Then I looked at Thomas.

"I can't leave you here," I said.

"Never you worry. I'll be out soon."

"What will you do?"

"All will be well."

I stood for a moment longer. "But Rabbie?"

Thomas's eyes met mine. "Go."

I crossed to the open door, my fellow prisoners eyeing me with muted jealousy. Something was wrong. Thomas hadn't told me everything. "One moment, please," I said to Alice. She clutched her shawl, her nose set in a permanent wrinkle.

I rushed back to Thomas.

"Give it to me," I said.

"Pardon?"

"Don't give me that. *Give it to me.*"

"I don't know — "

"Give me the belladonna."

"What?"

I kneeled. "The deadly nightshade," I said. "Give it to me."

"How did you —?"

"You don't want to do this."

"How do you know?" he burst.

I threw my arms around him. Sobs racked his body. "Because if you wanted to kill yourself, you would have done it by now. Because Rabbie loves you, and if you die, it would kill him." I pressed my forehead to his. "Because this is not a play. You are not Juliet. She never got a choice," I said. *"You do.* Look at me."

He did. The pale light made him almost transparent. A ghost of infinite space. "I'm afraid," he whispered.

"I know."

He pressed the small, black vial into my damaged hand.

Chapter 36
Such mortal drugs I have

Cathedral bells rang midnight as we journeyed through the darkened streets of London. The carriage wheels turned, bumping and jostling over the ruts, but the coach didn't turn into a pumpkin, and the horses stayed horses. On Alice's advice, I'd left both slippers behind, kicking them into the weeds, but no prince would find them. I was rescued, but based on Alice's forbidding expression, this wasn't the end of my fairy tale. I couldn't muster the energy to care. I stretched my stockinged feet, leaned my head against the wood paneling of the coach, and let the cobbles lull me into an uneasy doze.

"Huh! What?" I asked, wiping a line of drool from my chin.

"We're here," said Alice, as a footman opened the door to the carriage. Another stood guard at the entranceway to Emilia's house, but he wasn't dressed in the servants' garb of blue and grey. Instead, he wore a red overcoat trimmed with gold, kilted by a black belt. At his waist hung a sword, decorative, but—no doubt—pointy.

"Who is that?" I asked.

"King's Guard," hushed Alice. "Come along and keep quiet. The Mistress is in enough straits as 'tis."

The household was dark and quiet as I limped up the stairs. The guard followed, trailing the edge of my shadow in the torchlight.

"Where *is* Mistress Emilia?" I whispered to Alice. My redeemer must have bribed someone to release me—at least temporarily— but what kind of influence would she have with the King?

"She is in her chambers."

"Oh. I wanted to thank her for rescuing— "

"She is with Doctor Fordee," Alice said.

"Oh."

"Now hush."

Alice opened the door to my room, leaving the King's Guard to stand sentry in the hall. I stepped past the threshold into the center, feeling like the ballerina in Monica's music box, immobile, trapped, waiting for gears to turn.

"You'll be needing another wash," Alice said, picking up a porcelain pitcher. The stand-alone tub was gone, but she'd prepared a shallow basin and towel. "I'll fetch us some water, then we'll have you out of those clothes." She left to the clanging of keys and the slide of a bolt.

House arrest.

With an armed guard.

It was still better than that awful prison. A shiver scuttled up my spine like the soft rustle of rats in the straw, searching for crumbs the children had missed. When I left Thomas, he'd been huddled on the floor, his face in his hands.

He'll be all right, I told myself.

I saw my reflection in the panes of glass overlooking the garden, a girl in a dirty dress standing in a sumptuous room, the four-poster bed, the dark green carpet with yellow roses, the fire blazing in the hearth. A new vase of blue periwinkle was back on the dressing table, replacing the one I'd knocked over. Everything set to rights except me.

I pulled my phone and the vial of deadly nightshade from the front of my dress. I crossed to the window, undid the latch, and chucked the bottle into the night. No matter what happened, I would not be drinking poison.

That left me with the phone. Where to hide it?

The dressing table didn't have a drawer, or the fainting couch any removable cushions. There wasn't a closet. That left the bed. I slid the phone under the mattress and skidded back to my original place, just as Alice returned. She held the porcelain pitcher in one arm, juggling my old clothes under the other.

"You look flushed," Alice said, setting the pitcher on the table. "Is the fire too warm?"

"No. It's perfect. Thank you."

"I've given these a wash," she said, placing my jeans and sweater on the couch. "Such peculiar dress." She held up my bra, eyeing it with renewed suspicion, as if it were proof of my waywardness. The events of the evening had definitely cooled her attitude towards me. "What did you call this?"

"A bra."

"A bra?"

"Um. Yes, a bra," I replied, feeling as if I'd just confessed to truancy and underage drinking. Oh wait. That was the other timeline. In this one, it was witchcraft and attempted regicide. And wearing a bra.

"For your bosoms?"

"*Yes.*"

"Hm. Peculiar." She placed the offending underwear under my folded sweater.

"Is Emilia—?"

"As I said. The *Mistress* is indisposed. You will not be seeing her tonight. Tomorrow morning, you are to be brought before the King's examiners. The Mistress was able to secure your release by promise of surety. You must be a person of great worth." Alice's look suggested she thought otherwise.

I nodded, my throat too constricted to reply.

I could be back in prison by tomorrow afternoon.

Or worse.

"'Tis a shame," said Alice.

"Yes. I don't know what—"

"You've ruined such a beautiful dress. Off with it now."

Was it me, or did I spend half my life today getting dressed and undressed? I supposed this was what people did without internet.

FINDING JULIET

First came the laced vest, then the blouse, the overskirt, the underskirt, the petticoat, the padded bumroll, the filthy stockings, until I was down to the slip-like chemise and bodice. The whalebone corset had molded itself to my body like an exoskeleton. When Alice pulled the last tie, I felt like a mollusk that had lost its protective shell.

Alice sat me in a cushioned chair, handed me a washcloth dampened with rose water. She combed my hair with a drop of scented oil, while I scrubbed my face and neck. The chemise stuck to my skin in tracks of dried sweat. I peeled the linen from my stomach and wiped my chest and underarms. With a clean, wet cloth, I turned to my feet, dabbing the weeping blisters. I tore off a blackened toenail. It should have hurt, but I felt nothing. Mollusk-life had its upside.

Alice replaced my chemise with a fresh dressing gown. The pale satin felt like the whisper of a cloud, and I drifted shapelessly to bed, almost forgetting I was under armed guard.

After pulling up my blanket, Alice produced a miniature glass of dark purple wine. From where, I didn't know. This place was magical like that: doors opening to hidden rooms; lost items mysteriously finding their way home.

Like a missing boy, a backpack, a cell phone.

My cell phone.

What was I going to do? The battery life was almost gone. Even if I didn't turn it on, eventually the power would drain. I needed an energy source, some way to simulate lightning, to "beam" myself home. But where, in the 17th century, was I going to find electricity?

Electricity...

Oh my goodness.

Alice handed me the crystal goblet, a finger-full of wine.

I knew where to find electricity!

All I had to do was (1) escape a locked room, (2) make it past the King's Guard, and (3) travel to the place where enchantment lived.

Easy peasy lemon squeezy.

"Drink," said Alice. I tilted the glass. Let the liquid run down my throat. It tasted of sour berries, a bitterness on the back of my tongue. "What was that?" I choked. "What did you give me?" I asked twice, once to each of the Alices that swam double-vision before my eyes.

"Belladonna." Alice pushed me into the pillow. "A draught to help you sleep."

Chapter 37
The Balcony Scene

The key turns the bolt slides I am alone. My deathbed.

I'm not dead.

Poisoned.

Not dead.

Must not sleep.

Sleepy sleepy good night sleep tight don't let the bedbugs bite.

I stand. The floor does not feel like a floor. It feels like a ship. Ankles don't work. Nightgown off. Bra shirt sweater on. Underwear on. One foot through pants leg. Fall down. Get up. Other foot through pants leg. Train going through the tunnel. Choo choo. Pull up pants.

How do zippers work?

Right.

Heart races. Head pounds. Mouth dry.

Too tired. Go to bed.

Ha! I remember.

The bed is alive. Blanket lips, pillow eyes, my hand in its jaws. I reach into the gullet. Pull my phone past its teeth.

Phone goes back into back pocket.

That's where phones go.

Open the windows. Step onto the balcony. Wrought iron, a trellis of winter roses for Presley. Where's Monica? Home. Climb onto the railing. Look down.

That's a long way down, Romeo.

Click heels.

Jump.

Chapter 38
That kind of fruit as maids call medlars

I woke up under a tree.

For a moment, I thought it was the other tree, the one where the lightning struck, next to the country road with a double yellow line running all the way to Monica's house.

The next moment, I knew the truth, blinding as the sun hovering in the sky, shooting laser bolts through my corneas. What time was it? Noon? No, later than that. Mid-afternoon. I'd slept over a dozen hours.

That was some high-powered Nyquil.

Everything hurt: my hand, my back, my ankle. My head felt encased in cotton, my mouth as if I'd chewed sawdust.

But I was alive.

Alive and free.

Somehow in the night, I'd stumbled into a wooded area bordered by a thicket of blackberry briars. Surrounding that were acres of wild grasslands and fields fronting country estates. If I crawled through the brush, I could just make out Emilia's gated drive.

Right across the road. Too close. I needed to get going before anyone spotted me.

And I had a plan.

I stood, testing my ankle. The fall from the balcony had been broken by a mature rose bush, leaving me with a limp and a collection of thorns. Tiny daggers, but none of them fatal. I plucked them out, one-by-one, beads of blood competing with blackberry juice. Checking to make sure I still had my phone in my back pocket, I edged along the woods towards an overgrown orchard.

Spongy leaves and rotting fruit squished between my toes. I tripped over rows of roots, suddenly overcome with a hunger that left me lightheaded and clammy. An aftereffect of the belladonna? Among the branches, I found a mid-day meal of bitter apples, pears ripe-to-bursting, and walnuts, which, although a welcome source of protein, became a test of my problem-solving abilities.

After numerous unsuccessful attempts to crack the stone-like shells, including stomping on them with my bare foot—not a good idea, BTW—I grabbed a rock from the crumbling wall bordering the orchard and commenced pounding them into shell-nutmeat dust. I'd popped the first bite into my mouth just as Emilia's carriage came thundering down the dirt road. I slammed myself to the ground, face-deep in a mound of mushy pears.

Watched her speed away.

Emilia was kind to me. Compassionate. She met with Doctor Fordee in the middle of the night, and I didn't think they were reading astrological charts.

Why had she helped me?

Even as the question formed in my mind, I knew the answer. Everything Emilia did was in honor of her daughter. She'd never recovered from her baby's death, yet the loss had inspired her to make the world a better place for all women. In the garden last night, she'd said, *Words are not legacies, people are.* That's why she wanted to build a school. All the girls she helped *were* her daughters. Including me.

I felt the walnut pieces lodge in my throat.

I deceived her. I ran away, leaving her to answer for my supposed crimes. Would the King blame her for my escape? Would she be tossed in prison as an accomplice?

What could I do? I couldn't tell her the truth. I couldn't face the King.

Would the support of Doctor Fordee be enough? After all, if she'd been with him all night, he could vouch for her innocence. I shuddered at the thought of her with that predatory old man, but his testimony could prove key to her exoneration.

I peeked over the orchard wall. The carriage was gone, the dust clouds settled.

She'll be fine, I told myself. *Like Thomas. He'll be fine, too.*

But the truth was, I didn't know.

Was this what I had to do to survive? Abandon people?

No. That wasn't it either.

Like it or not, there were some things I couldn't control.

I felt bad for Thomas, but I couldn't help him any more than I already had.

As for Emilia... She'd endured widowhood and the death of a child. She defied expectations for what a woman, wife, and mother could be. Beloved by powerful men, she was England's first published female poet, dedicated to the uplift of all women.

She'd survive my betrayal.

I wiped the rotting fruit off my face and turned toward home.

***

The rest of the journey was pleasantly uneventful. No one beat me or robbed me. No one accused me of being a witch, threw me in jail, or fed me poison.

Good times.

Just past the orchard, a stream meandered through a ravine, clean and cold. Kneeling, I cupped the icy water in my hands, then dunked my whole face, gulping till my brain froze. A shadow blocked the sunlight. I looked up to see a tan and white cow chewing her cud. Her eyes were placidly curious, like a neighborhood lady coming to welcome a new, strangely dressed cow to the block.

"Moo," I said.

"MOOOOOOOOOOO." The cow dipped her head for a drink, her purple tongue lazily slurping the stream. She lumbered back to where five or six other cows stood on a grassy knoll under a wide branched tree. Above, puffy white clouds floated in a turquoise sky.

I love the country.

"Boy!" shouted a voice from the road.

I looked for a place to hide, then decided that, having already been seen, hiding would be futile. As casually as I could, I walked the fifty feet to the road, where an old man sat on a cart driven by a mule. The wagon tilted haphazardly, a load of melons threatening to spill. A wheel had come off its axle, landing in one of the ruts that pockmarked the road.

"Can you help me lift while I reattach it?" he asked, jumping off his seat bench. For an old man, he was awfully spry. He looked a bit like Monica's neighbor, Mr. Albright, his face lined and weathered, but with kinder eyes and fewer teeth. He wore a woven straw hat, calf-length pants, and no shoes. Bracing himself under the wagon bed, he beckoned me to squat next to him.

"Put your hands on your knees. That's it," he said, releasing a couple hundred pounds onto my back. I felt like the painting of Atlas on the side of the Globe Theatre, saving, if not the world, at least twenty ripe melons.

I held steady as he fetched the wheel, slid it back onto the axle. He fastened a bolt through the center of the spokes, then gave the wheel a spin. "You can come out from under there now," he said, brushing his hands against his shirt.

"Oh. Right."

I released the weight of the wagon and squirmed into the open, rubbing my shoulder.

"I give you much thanks," said the old farmer. "Would you like a cantaloupe?"

He held up an extra-large melon.

"No, thank you," I said, my belly full of fruit.

"Casaba?"

"No."

"I have big casabas."

"I see that," I laughed. "But no, thank you."

"Suit yourself," he said, hopping back onto the wagon bench. His mule had found a patch of dandelions in the road and was happily munching. The old man picked up the reins. "Where are you going to, lad?"

"I'm sorry?"

"Where might you be headed?"

"Oh. Um. London Bridge. Antonio's—"

"*Antonio's Apothecary and Teeth-Pulling.* Haven't had much use for the place, meself," he said with a gummy grin. "Well, hop on. Just don't bruise my casabas."

Chapter 39
Too like the lightning, which doth cease to be

I spent the journey to London riding backwards, with melons for armrests. Slowly, country fields and open skies gave way to clouds of soot, city streets crowded with people. Washerwomen scrubbed linens in barreled tubs boiling over open flames. Fish-sellers tossed their end-of-the-day catch to waiting customers. Dirt-covered children dashed into alleyways. Butchers slaughtered pigs in makeshift stalls. Everywhere I looked was a new play: of brawling boys, calling women, soldiers, merchants, mounted men, milkmen, yeomen, young girls peeking behind shutters, a teeming tapestry of life.

And it hit me. *Everyone* had a story.

Despite the improbable nature of my given circumstances, I, myself, was not that unique. I was one of a crowd. Insignificant in the great, grand scheme of existence.

A strange comfort. Like melons for armrests.

I remembered my first night at Monica's. After she went to bed, I turned off my bedroom light, and opened the window. Having grown up in the city, I wasn't prepared for a night sky without light pollution.

The moon shone like a silver sun. Above that, a rush of stars scarred the sky, a thousand-million pinpoints of light, light-years away. The Milky Way wasn't just a candy bar.

I had never felt more insignificant.

More at peace.

The group home didn't matter. Neither did the cows, my hair, or even *me*. Everything was compost for the worms.

Only the stars mattered.

And home.

"Might be faster for you to walk," said the melon farmer.

"What?"

Traffic had come to a standstill at London Bridge. I stood in the wagon, shielding my eyes. The sun hovered halfway to the horizon, burnishing the iron river with streaks of gold.

"Clear out! Let us through!" A battalion of officers on horseback pushed against the crowd.

My heart leapt to my throat as I recognized their uniforms — the same as those the armed guards wore last night.

They caught me! A fugitive from the King's justice, I'd be put back in prison, but this time with no one to rescue me. I jumped from the wagon, wondering if I could outrun a horse.

"The Globe!" a woman called. "It's on fire!"

"Make way! Make way!" the officers shouted, cracking their whips for emphasis.

They aren't *after me!* They were firefighters; their horses pulled water cannons and wagons loaded with pick axes and buckets. I jumped out of the way of a ladder truck, called my thanks to the old farmer, and followed the crowd to the river.

Across the Thames, a plume of smoke curled like an angry thundercloud. Flames licked the skeletal remains of whitewashed beams where the theatre used to be.

With everything that had happened — the play, Emilia, the King, Thomas — I'd forgotten about the Globe. My memory jumped to the picture in the wooden frame hanging in Ms. Lanyer's hallway, a Polaroid of my drama teacher's father kneeling in a dirt pit, an archeologist at the excavation of the old theatre. And now, here I was, witness to the destruction: the stage, the canopy of stars, the costumes, painted marble, props, and glass jewels.

The plays.

No.

The plays weren't gone. They were handed down, in memory and actors' scrolls. But what about the manuscripts? Natalie said none survived. Did they burn along with the timber, columns, and—

My mother's 8th grade picture.

It was in the satchel I'd left at the theatre, distracted by Rabbie's fitting, my impending debut, the vein popping on Burbage's forehead.

I closed my eyes, clicking through memories like a cardboard reel in a red plastic viewfinder, trying to find her face.

The yellow hair turned to straw.

Click.

Bloodshot eyes.

Click.

Twig-like arms. Stained sheets. Unicorn shadows on a water-stained wall.

Click. Click. Click.

I'd lost her, my mother as a girl, the girl I never knew—the one that was *me*, before she became *her*. The girl with flyaway hair and freckles on her nose, a blank page of possibilities before her.

"How did it happen?" asked the man next to me.

"I don't know," I replied.

***

Spectators lined the wharf, the crowd now a party on the docks. Sellers came round, hawking oysters, sausages, and meat pies. Gulls screeched, diving for scraps. A bucket brigade formed on the opposite bank, hauling water to the ruins, but the Globe was gone.

The man next to me explained to anyone who would listen, "The roof caught fire during the performance. They fired a cannon into the thatch."

"Well, that doesn't seem like a good idea, now does it?"

I felt in my back pocket for my phone and headed to London Bridge.

Traffic was light now that the firefighters had gone. I passed under the tower entrance, pausing at the sight of the heads on spikes. I was no longer afraid to look. Eight skulls grinned, skin picked to the bone. They could have been anyone.

My jaw moved in silent prayer, but the only words I could think of were the lyrics to the country song playing in Monica's Subaru on the night she bought me Dippin' Dots. I hummed it all the way to the shop. The sign was no longer hanging above the entrance, but splintered on the doorstep, as if someone had taken one of the fireman's pickaxes and split it for kindling. The interior was dark, the front window cracked into a spiderweb of broken glass.

"I'd stay away if I was you," said an ancient woman in a black shawl, a basket of apples on her arm. "Bunch of heretics, they was. Seemed like such good Christians, too." She nodded solemnly, then held up a shiny red fruit. "Would you like an apple?"

"No, thank you."

"Apricock?"

"Excuse me?"

"Tuppence for two."

"I don't have any money."

"Well, get on with you then." She wagged a finger as she hobbled away.

I jiggled the shop door handle. It was locked, but the latch was broken. As the door swung open, the bell above gave a merry jingle, a counterpoint to the smell of ammonia that hung in the air, antiseptic and harsh. I tiptoed through the broken glass, shards of blue and green, towards shelves of shattered jars. An escaped slug crawled across the counter.

Had they destroyed it?

No. Thank God.

I took out my phone, pressed the power button. The battery was almost dead. Not much time.

Time.

Wait a minute.

The time.

The time on the phone read 10:46pm. That was the time in the *other time*, just before the lightning struck. Had the jolt of electricity fried the clock function? That didn't make sense, not if everything else was working. I stared at the phone for a minute. Then another. The time didn't change. It was frozen at the exact moment I left. Would I return, no time having passed?

Don't get ahead of yourself.

I had no idea if my plan would work. It grew in absurdity by the unchanging minute. At least I didn't have to explain myself to the owner of the shop, an assumption quickly dispelled by a voice hissing from the back corner, *"What do you want?"*

"Aiiieeeee!" I yelped, jumping like a cartoon character with its feet on fire.

"AAAAHHH!"

"AAAIIIEEEEEEEEEEEEEEEEEE!!!!"

I screamed until the unknown figure body-slammed me into the barrel next to the counter. Water sloshed and a hand pressed against my mouth.

"Will you be quiet?!" Before I lost my bladder, I recognized the owner's daughter, Jessica, a wild look in her eyes.

"Murmurvingmose."

She removed her hand. *"What are you saying?"*

"I said, 'You're covering my nose.'"

"Oh." She stepped back. "Sorry." Her long dark braid had come undone, her blouse untucked. She wiped her hands on her skirt before wringing them into a knot.

"That's okay," I said. "I'm sorry, I—"

Jessica paced to the front door, distracted.

I checked my phone. The battery was desperately low, but I hesitated to turn it off. Turning it back on again might drain even more power.

"You were here yesterday," Jessica said from the broken window. "Why have you come back?" She turned to me, registering the glowing phone. "What is that in your hand?"

I snapped the phone shut. "It's. Uh." I picked a sliver of broken glass from my heel. "Ouch. It's. Um." Oh, heck with it. "It's my phone. I'm from the future. I need to electrocute myself with your stingray to send myself back home."

"The Torpedo Maculosa?" Jessica crossed to the barrel. It stood whole, just a few splinters of wood floating alongside the pancake-shaped stingray swimming circles in the inky water. It was unlike any creature I'd ever seen before, a flying saucer from the Jurassic period, a thing wholly out of time and space. How appropriate.

"Oh," Jessica said, dismissing me, my phone, and the Torpedo Maculosa with a single syllable. She drifted back to her hiding place behind the counter.

This was not the reaction I anticipated.

"I said I need to electrocute myself to travel to the future."

"I heard you."

"You believe me?"

"Why not?" She sat on the floor. "I can't find my cat. I think he ran away."

"What happened here?"

She looked about the shop, before so tidy, now looking like a miniature tornado had spun and laid waste, splitting shelves and spilling bottles. Disbelief clouded her eyes. She spoke with the detachment of denial. "I was at the bookseller, fetching a tract for my father. Do you read?"

I nodded.

"Have you heard of *Sidereus Nuncius*?"

"No."

"What about Galileo?"

"He was an astronomer, right?"

"Was?"

"I mean *is*. It's *is*, right?" Galileo was alive right now? "That's cool."

"What does the temperature have to do with anything?"

"Nothing. I just mean, that's neat."

"You mean cleanly?"

"No!"

Why were words so hard?

"Please," I said, attempting a patient tone. "Continue with your story."

And make it snappy. I have a fish to catch.

"Galileo has seen beyond the spheres into heaven itself. He has a telescope. *Sidereus Nuncius* means *Starry Messenger*. In it, Galileo sketches the moon, not once, not twice, but from seventy different viewpoints, all as if he had trod the very ground himself. It's a whole other planet!"

"Well, technically, it's a moon."

"Pardon?"

"The moon is a moon. Not a planet. Never mind."

"What are you saying?"

"What are *you* saying?" I asked. This conversation was a lovely digression, but I figured I had about five more minutes before—

"They arrested my father."

The only sound came from the ray in the barrel, orbiting in its own wake.

I remembered her father, a trim little man with a white mustache and bushy eyebrows. He reminded me a bit of Gepetto from *Pinocchio*, a busy tinkerer of herbs instead of toys. Between him, Alice a.k.a. Cinderella's Fairy Godmother, and the ancient old woman outside who looked like the evil crone from *Snow White*, I was beginning to think I wasn't trapped in 17th century England, but a Disney nightmare. Maybe I really was imagining all of this.

"They arrested my father," Jessica repeated. "I returned to the shop just as they were dragging him out. At first, I thought it was because of the tract."

"Galileo's book?"

"Yes."

"But why?"

"Galileo believes the earth revolves around the sun. This is heresy to the church. My father was reluctant to let me buy the book, but he knew how important it was, how magnificent. It contains the secrets of the universe! The *galaxías kýklos!*

"The whatty-what?"

"*Galaxías kýklos.* It means "milky circle" in Greek. In Latin, this translates to *via lactea,* a pathway borne of mother's milk, infinite light. What looks like a cloud in the sky is a band of stars too numerous to count. Galileo has seen it. He describes it all in his book. Can you fathom what this means?"

"And the book is why your father was arrested?"

"I tore it apart," she said, as if afraid to answer. "I stood on the outskirts of the crowd as officers pounded my father with clubs, ripping the stars out of their constellations. I scattered the remnants to the wind, but it was meaningless. No one even saw the book."

"Then why was he arrested?"

Jessica ignored the question, lost in unseen agony. "He raged for everyone to hear, *My daughter betrayed me!*" She clawed at her temples, everything coming undone. "I am a coward. I am a wretch. I destroyed the moon."

"You turned him in?" I asked.

"No! He forswore me to protect me!"

"I don't understand. What did he do?"

Jessica wailed. "He murdered babies! He drank their blood!"

"Really?" I backed into the Torpedo Maculosa.

"No, you lack-wit!"

"Why did you say that, then?"

She took a breath. "Because my father is Jewish."

I didn't understand. "So?"

Jessica looked at me as if for the first time, her hair a dark halo around her head. She wiped her nose with the back of her hand. "You really are from the future, aren't you?"

I shrugged. "Yeah."

She smoothed her skirt and studied the back curtain to the shop, not seeing the brown drape, but a far off time, a far off place. "My father brought us here from Spain, to escape the Inquisition. I was three. My mother died in a cargo hold. I do not remember my homeland. *England* is my homeland. We were good Christians," she insisted, fingering the gold cross around her neck. "We played our parts well. No one knew. I thought no one knew." She took a shaky breath and stood, reaching for a broom that leaned against the back shelf.

"What are you doing?" I asked.

"Sweeping," she said, but she remained still, broken ceramic at her feet. The broom handle was a staff, holding her upright.

"Maybe you should sit."

"My father gave his life for mine."

"He's not dead yet."

"He will be. The officers accused him of poisoning a gentlewoman. He is an apothecary and a Jew. He has no defense. They will execute him for the entertainment of the masses. The only reason I am not to be hanged beside him is that he publicly proclaimed his guilt, naming me as his accuser. I should die, but it would kill him a second time. I pay his debt by living. I have to go on." She swept debris into a pile, then started another pile. She paused a moment. "May I ask you something?"

I nodded.

"How do *you* go on? How does it work?"

She was asking *me* for advice? This girl who had seen her father beaten, arrested, and dragged off to be hanged? Who was now alone in the world, with no friends, little prospects, on an island of distrust?

"How to go on?"

She nodded.

"That's the question, huh?"

I thought of my journey over the past twenty-four hours. Before that, the nine years since my mother's death. After that, the thirteen foster homes ending with Monica. It seemed like a math problem, but with no answer.

"I think you take it one day at a time," I said.

"I do not understand."

"You live. One day at a time."

"I *know* that," Jessica said. "How do you go on to the *future*? How does *that* work?" She pointed to my phone. "What does it do?"

My face flushed. "Oh, right. You use it to call someone."

"I can already call someone. I just lean out the door."

"You can call someone far away."

"How far?"

"If you want, on the other side of the world."

"On the moon?"

"No. I think the astronauts use a satellite."

Jessica shook her head. "Astronauts?"

"Long story. To call someone, I press these buttons." I flipped open the phone. Jessica gasped as the numbers illuminated. "Oops," I said, "I need to change something." I pressed a few more buttons, switching the wallpaper screen from the site of the Globe Theatre to my lopsided selfie standing in front of the old oak.

"It's magic!" she cried.

"No, not really," I said. "It's. Uh. Kind of like a telescope." I checked the battery. *Yikes.* "I don't have much time."

Jessica crossed to the barrel. "What do you need to do?"

"I don't know." I peered into the swirling water. With its perfectly round spots, the ray seemed to have five eyes, all of them looking at me. I held my phone in one hand, hovered the other over the barrel. The ray's skin was smooth and iridescent as an oil slick. Its torso rippled with the current, tiny tremors whipping its tail. "Just touch it, I guess? Would that be enough to shock me?"

"Oh yes. My fingers glanced its belly once while feeding it a herring. I thought my heart had stopped."

My self-electrocution idea suddenly didn't seem so hot.

Not to mention, would it even work? A minute from now, would I still be here, passed out on the ground, a bit of static electricity lighting my hair, a dead phone in my hand? Could this thing actually kill me? And what about Jessica?

"Why do you hesitate?" she asked.

"I don't want to abandon you."

"You're not. I'm strong. And this is where I need to be. Where do *you* belong?"

"Home," I said. I dialed 2-0-1-3, the year I left. The screen pinpointed my destination. Polaris. To go home, I just needed to head toward myself.

I lowered my hand an inch above the water.

"Good fortune," said Jessica.

I swallowed. "If this doesn't work, I'll help you clean up."

"Thank you," she smiled. "*Wait a moment!*"

My breath hiccupped.

"Sorry," she apologized. "But, before you go, may I ask you one more thing?"

I nodded, my hand trembling as if I'd already been electrocuted.

"Will it get better?"

"Better?" I asked. After her previous question, I wasn't sure how to answer. "For you? Honestly, I don't know."

"My people," she whispered. A single tear rolled down her cheek, the first one I'd seen her shed. It hung suspended on her chin, before gravity took it to earth. "Will it get better for them?"

I knew my history. World War Two. Millions of Jews murdered: mothers, fathers, little children, endless suffering. I knew my own time, bigotry and hate, but also love and hope, where freedom of religion was enshrined into law.

That was progress, right? A time in which you could not only draw the moon, but take a picture from its surface, an image of the world, blue and green shards surrounded by infinite light.

"First, it will get worse," I said. "Then, it will get better."

She nodded. "Then I will have faith."

I plunged my hand into the water.

Part 3: 2013

Chapter 40
I do remember well where I should be

Everything was soft.

I had never felt such softness in my life.

Pale light lent an ethereal glow, a golden white fading to silver-grey. I was floating in a cloud, weightless and secure. If this was heaven, I wouldn't mind being dead.

Tap-tap, tap-tap-tap.

The cloud was knocking.

Tap-tap, tap-tap-tap.

Why was the cloud knocking?

"Can I come in?"

Monica?

Was she dead, too?

"Alex?" Her voice was muffled, like she was wrapped in a blanket. Or maybe I was the one wrapped in a blanket.

The light became brighter as my foster mom pulled the comforter from my head.

"I thought you smothered yourself." She brushed a sweaty lock of hair from my brow, then drew back her hand, embarrassed by the familiar touch. "You were so cold last night, I broke out the down quilt."

"Oh."

The clock on the bedside table blinked red, 9:16 a.m. I pushed the comforter to my waist. "What am I wearing?" The cotton nightgown had ruffled sleeves and pearled buttons up the front, like something out of a Renaissance romance. I had never worn anything so *girly* in all my life.

"It's mine," she said, blushing. "I hope you don't mind. You were so filthy and wet, and—well—kind of out of it. We needed to get you washed up and dressed in something easy."

"We?"

"Pippa and I. Me and Pippa. I mean, your teacher, Ms. Lanyer. We were both so worried when we found you at the old oak."

At the old oak.

A shelter of broken limbs in a thunderstorm.

Sinking to the ground in despair, clawing the mud.

Lightning.

Then nothingness.

I fingered the pearl button at my neck. "You—bathed me? You and Ms. Lanyer?"

"Oh, no! You took a shower. By yourself. Stayed in there for a long time. I almost thought you had fallen asleep. I handed you a towel and the nightgown, and helped you to bed. You don't remember *any* of this?"

"No. I think the lightning fried my brain."

"Lightning? You were hit by *lightning?*"

"No." I shook my head. "Maybe? I don't know. Definitely not. I'd be dead if I'd been struck by lightning, right?"

"Oh, my goodness." Monica looked increasingly panicky. "We should get you to the doctor. Maybe the ER. Do you have a fever?" She reached for my forehead, but I waved her hand away.

"Why would I have a fever?"

"Well, you were out in that nasty storm."

"For about fifteen minutes." I flung the comforter the rest of the way off and swung my feet to the floor. Gripping the wrought iron bedpost, I levered myself to a standing position. The ground tilted, but I kept my balance.

"Are you okay?" asked Monica.

My head felt stuffed with cotton balls, all sensory input delayed. Something was missing, but I wasn't sure what. I fought the sensation of disembodiment, of watching myself have this particular conversation as if I were in the audience at my own play.

"I'm fine," I said, surprised at the strength of my own voice.

"You sure?"

Orange toenails glimmered when I wiggled my toes. "I'm just a little tired."

"I'm sorry I woke you. Pippa—I mean, Ms. Lanyer—is here. She came by to check on you." Monica crossed to the window, drew open the lace curtains, revealing a gleaming view.

I gasped. "It's all white."

Everything outside the window was white. Everything. The world was breathtakingly devoid of color. Bleached white sky, white clouds, white hills, white trees.

Was this *actually* heaven? *What was going on?*

"Why is everything so *white?*" I demanded.

"Are you okay?" Monica asked again. "You're really pale."

"Am I dead?"

"Let me get a thermometer." Monica dashed out the door.

I gathered the comforter around my shoulders and crept toward the window, terribly afraid that the world outside had been erased.

My breath fogged the glass. More white. I brushed my hand against the pane, leaving a cold, wet streak. Through it, clarity.

"Snow," I marveled.

"I could only find the dog thermometer," Monica said as she came back into the bedroom. "Believe me, you don't want to put *that* in your mouth. I'm so stupid. I should have bought a first aid kit before I brought you home. I don't even have Band-Aids. I mean, I have gauze, but that's for the dogs, too, when Clyde can't stop licking the fatty tumor on his tail. I promise, though, we'll pick up a thermometer and Band-Aids tomorrow on our way home from the court appointment."

"I don't need any—"

"Sorry, not tomorrow. Monday. We'll explain everything to the judge. The whole thing is so stupid. I'm stupid. I'm so sorry for what I said last night. I just don't know how to do this very well, because I've never been a mom, and I know I'm not *your* mom, but I'm willing to try to be a female support system if you'll give me a second chance, if you think you might still want to stay here—"

"It snowed."

"Yes. Last night." She stepped beside me. The eyes behind her wire-rimmed glasses regarded me like a curious owl. "Haven't you seen snow before?"

"No." The landscape had changed into something unrecognizable and pure. Crystalline. "I didn't know it would be so white."

"We can go outside in a minute. Do you mind saying hello to Ms. Lanyer, first, though? She's waiting in the kitchen. She was really worried about you last night."

"Sure."

Monica retrieved my grey hoodie from the closet. "Here. You must be cold. I haven't made a fire yet."

I dropped the comforter and pulled the sweatshirt over the frilly nightgown. Monica's Golden Retrievers, Bonnie and Clyde, met us halfway down the hallway, their wet paws leaving slippery tracks on the wooden floor. They bumped my bare legs with icy noses.

"What are you doing, dogs?" asked Monica. "Go on, get outside!" She ushered them back through the sliding glass door, hooking the latch. The two of them stood like furry beggars on the old blue towel meant to catch their mud and drips, then one or both heard a noise, and they were off.

Ms. Lanyer sat at the kitchen table, her hands wrapped around a steaming mug of coffee. "How are you feeling?" she asked.

"Fine."

Monica poured herself a cup of coffee from the pot. The mug had a picture of a Golden Retriever with a Santa Hat.

"What does it say on your cup?" I asked.

"Oh," she said. "*Fleas Navidog*. I figure if it's December, I can break out the Christmas mugs." She added sugar and stirred, having what appeared to be a telepathic conversation with Ms. Lanyer, who kept flicking her eyes in my direction.

"It's funny," I said.

"What?" asked Monica, a little too quickly.

"Your mug," I said. "*Fleas Navidog*. It took me a second to get it."

"It *is* pretty funny. I got it last year, at the library Christmas party. It was meant to be a gag gift, but I loved it."

I nodded.

"Would you like some coffee?" Monica asked. "I suppose you're old enough, right? A little coffee never hurt anyone. Just don't drink those energy things. They're really bad for you. Or I suppose you could drink them if you want to. After all, you'll be eighteen in less than six months. May 29th, right?"

"What?"

"Your birthday. It is May 29th, isn't it?" She set down her mug and gave me an anguished look. "Did I get it wrong? I'm so sorry. First I forget Thanksgiving, and now this."

I hadn't celebrated my birthday in ten years. Maybe more.

My own mother would forget.

"My birthday *is* May 29th."

"Oh, good," she said. "We'll have a blowout bash before you graduate. Or maybe take a trip somewhere, if that's more your speed. Yosemite is beautiful in the spring. Or maybe we could drive north to, like, Salem or Portland. Do you prefer the city or the country?"

"I don't know. I've never been anywhere."

"Well, we have plenty of time to decide." Monica opened a cabinet for a mug. "Um, do you take milk or sugar in your coffee?"

"Do you still have cocoa?"

My foster mother bit her lip and nodded. "I sure do. Let me make you a cup. Go ahead and sit down. You still look a little, um—not quite…here." She took the milk from the fridge and poured it into a saucepan on the stove. The gas ring clicked, then kicked to life in a fiery blaze that Monica adjusted to low. "This will just take a couple minutes," she said. "Don't want to scorch the milk."

I sat next to Ms. Lanyer at the kitchen table.

"Will I see you in class on Monday?" my drama teacher asked.

"I don't know," I said, remembering how Ryan had kissed me under the stage lights, the pull towards something that made as much sense to me as gravity. Couldn't see it. Couldn't define it. Couldn't be sure it was real, even as it pressed me into myself.

Did I love Ryan?

I didn't know.

But he was gone now.

I looked at my wrist. The shower from last night erased all but three numbers. Ryan must be in Los Angeles by now. Would I follow him? I brushed a finger against my wrist, over the arterial ridge that led to the heart.

613.

Must dial the 1 first. 1-613.

What?

What was my brain trying to tell me?

"Are you okay?" asked Ms. Lanyer.

I shivered. "Just cold."

Monica set the hot chocolate in front of me. It was in another holiday mug, this one featuring a picture of a gingerbread man missing a leg. The caption read, *Bite Me.*

"Another gag gift?" I asked.

"No," said Monica, topping the cocoa with a cone of whipped cream. "That one I bought myself. Pippa, I have a book for you. Let me go get it."

"Oh, I almost forgot," said Ms. Lanyer. "The reason I drove over here last night." She pulled a burgundy purse from the back of her chair.

"Oh, yeah." Despite the warmth of the cocoa, a cold shiver coursed up my spine, memories flashing like headlights on a dark country road, blinding against the night. The past was coming back to me. "You brought me my phone. Why did you do that?"

"My father said you needed it."

"But why?"

Her father was an old man, his face sunken by stroke. I'd exchanged maybe two sentences with him at the book club party, before his retreat upstairs. I remembered the picture of him in Ms. Lanyer's hallway. He was an archeologist at the site of the Old Globe Theatre from 17th century London....

I'd been *there. Woke up there this morning. But I* hadn't. *I was* here. *Wasn't I?*

The shiver expanded from my spine to my fingertips like the epicenter of an earthquake. My mug rattled as I set it on the table. Melted whipped cream ran over the side, frosting the painted gingerbread man.

What was wrong *with me?*

And why did an old man feel the need to urgently deliver my phone?

"I don't understand it either," said Ms. Lanyer. Tears glistened her eyes. "I find it easier sometimes to just humor him."

"Here you go," said Monica as she came back into the kitchen. She handed Ms. Lanyer a brick of a book. "This should keep you busy over winter break. If you like it, we can suggest it for the next book club choice."

"It's from the same author?"

"Yep."

"Awesome! I love a series. The heroine has a choice to make, doesn't she?" Ms. Lanyer checked her watch. "Oops, I'm out of time. Dad's physical therapy appointment is in half an hour."

As she stood, she reached into her purse and handed me an envelope, a word on the back scrawled in shaky blue ink. "Here, Alex. Dad wanted me to give you this. It's addressed to 'Prudence.' I reminded him your name is Alex, but he wouldn't listen. Parents. Can't teach them anything. Right, Monica?"

My foster mom rolled her eyes. "I'll walk you to your car, Pippa."

They stepped out the front door.

I sat for a moment, looking at the scribbled name on the envelope, then drew my thumb under the flap. Inside, a line of cursive shuddered like jagged streaks of lightning.

Turn back, dull earth, and find thy centre out.

The photograph in the envelope should have been tucked inside my wallet, a keepsake I couldn't bear to look at: my mother's 8th grade picture. I hadn't seen it in years.

I loved it and I hated it.

I wanted to press the photo to my chest, then tear it into a thousand pieces.

Because it represented all my mother could have been.

Who she was before she lost herself.

The picture was not as I remembered, though. Faded to ghostlike transparency, the edges charred by fire, it looked as if it had weathered centuries. I turned the picture over, revealing my own halting handwriting.

I need my phone.

I held the picture to my heart and stepped to the sliding glass door. Outside, Bonnie and Clyde wrestled, creating runnels of slushy mud. Beyond that, only white.

Clean and crisp, like a blank page.

Acknowledgments

First and foremost, thank you to Cris Flint, for being the coauthor of our life story, and the guardian of my solitude. You are the best husband and dad a man can be.

Thank you to my son Bud, for reading the parts I thought were funny, and then actually laughing. You are and always will be my patronus.

Thank you to Editor and Publisher Extraordinaire M.R. Street for believing in my book enough to give this first-time novelist a chance. I am so grateful for your patience and support in guiding me through this process. Thank you to Elizabeth Babski, for creating the beautiful cover, making the visual representation of *Finding Juliet* a truly collaborative effort.

Thank you to Jess Moore, who is the only person besides MR Street to have read a full version of *Finding Juliet* before publication, generously critiquing drafts for eleven years. I still remember standing in my yard, our two toddler boys climbing the play structure that had not yet fallen apart, telling you that I'd started to write a book. Our boys are now teenagers, and along the way, you've become an author, too! Thank you for helping me "kill my darlings" and pointing out my unconscious predilection for naming side characters Jessica. I'm sure it was just a coincidence. PS - "I hate cows" is still a good opening line.

Thank you to the readers of my early chapters, the wonderful writers Leslie C. and Kathy Boyd Fellure. Your detailed feedback, useful suggestions, and kind encouragement helped motivate me to keep going.

Thank you to Linda Hein and the amazing independent bookstore, Hein & Company: first, for providing the venue in which the first drafts of my early chapters were read (on the "streets" of Baker Street West), to supporting me in my novel's West Coast debut - a true full-circle moment.

Thank you to Kori Tearpak and April Quist Maroot for helping me understand a little more of what it would be like to be a foster kid - Kori, from the perspective of the legal system, and April, from your life's mission of giving teenage girls a safe place to call home. Thank you both for all that you do to make the world a better place for the most vulnerable among us.

Thank you to my Book Club Ladies for picking *those* books. We all need a tribe, and I'm so happy to be part of yours. BTW–I'm pretty sure Emilia has your hair, Sinead.

Finding Juliet was originally supposed to be a love story, and it is, sort of. It's a story about loving yourself. Undoubtedly, this is made easier by being surrounded by people who love and support you in turn.

Unlike Alex, I've been blessed with an abundance of father figures who have reinforced some of life's most important values, including hard work, independence, faithfulness, and generosity: my dad Dr. Bruce Levinton, my stepfather Ian Croxall, and my father-in-law Dr. Austin Flint. Thank you for all you have done to shape me into the person I am today.

Finally, as *Finding Juliet* is chiefly concerned with mothers and daughters, I'd like to end where I began, and close with the heart.

Thank you to my mother, Emily Croxall (Mommo), for inspiring me with your resilience, humor, and passion, and for teaching me that there is no higher power than unconditional love.

To my mother-in-law Bea Flint, thank you for being a second mom to me for almost 30 years, for your steadfast example of kindness and grace. I want to be you when I grow up.

Lastly, to my daughter, Charlotte Alexandra. I began this book before you were born, but it was always meant for you. A time-traveling paradox… but not really. You are as brilliant as the stars from which you were made. No beginning, no end, just love.

About the Author

Dale Lisa Flint is a mom, wife, teacher, academic, actor, director, playwright, voracious reader, amateur painter, enthusiastic hiker, and keeper of the family zoo (bearded dragon, snake, snails, fish, canary, cat, and dogs). Her life has been a series of plot twists, from meeting world leaders as a child ambassador for peace, to performing in over a hundred stage productions, including iconic Shakespearean roles (Juliet, Titania, Portia). She loves waterfall hikes, perfectly ripe mangos, and strong female protagonists. *Finding Juliet* is her first novel.

Dale Lisa Flint Photo © Eryn Brown

Other Books for Young Readers from Turtle Cove Press

The Dragon Box
Rhett DeVane

Nobody Kills Uncle Buster
and Gets Away with It
Susan Koehler
(Children's Book of the Year,
Royal Palm Literary Awards)

Queen of the Clouds: Joan Merriam
Smith and Jerrie Mock's Epic Quest
to Become the First Woman to Fly
Solo Around the World,
Taylor C. Phillips
(Two gold medals, Florida Authors
& Publishers Association [FAPA])

Dahlia in Bloom
Susan Koehler
(Starred Review, Kirkus Reviews)

Charlie's Song
Susan Koehler

So Many Animals!
A Child's Book of Poetry
(Anthology)
(2nd place, Mom's Choice Awards)

The Claddagh Book 1: The Loyalty
of the Leprechauns
M.R. Street

Surf Dude: The Dog of
Ochlockonee Bay
Zelle Andrews
(Gold Medal, FAPA)

Blue Rock Rescue
M.R. Street
(Gold Medal, Royal Palm
Literary Awards)

The Werewolf's Daughter
M.R. Street
(Gold Medal, FAPA)

The Hunter's Moon
M.R. Street

Betsy and Bernie: Eco-Guardians
Abby Hugill

The Health Is Power League in Attack
of Zombacon
M.R. Street
(2 Silver Medals, FAPA)

https://www.turtlecovepress.com

www.ingramcontent.com/pod-product-compliance
Lightning Source LLC
Chambersburg PA
CBHW051101030726
47504CB00006B/1728